J. J. DIBENEDETTO

Ten Years

and Then...

ISBN:
Kindle: 979-8-9997996-0-9
Paperback: 979-8-9997996-1-6
Hardcover: 979-8-9997996-2-3

Any references to historical events, real people, or real places are used factiously. Names, characters and places are products of the author's imagination.

Cover design by:
Book design by: Caerus Kourt (bookery.design)

Printed by: Amazon
First printing:

Writing Dreams
Abilene, Texas
www.jjdibenedetto.com

Also from J.J. DiBenedetto

The Dream Doctor Mysteries
Ten book cozy mystery series

The Jane Barnaby Adventures
Three book thriller series

Standalone Novels
Mr. Smith and the Roach
The Queen of Emerald Falls
Ten Years and Then...

Sweet Romance Novellas
Finding Dori
A Reel Christmas in Romance
Twice Blessed

All available in ePub, Paperback and Audiobook formats at:

www.amazon.com
and
www.jjdibenedetto.com

Part 1

Fall 1988

Chapter 1

Nora—August 25, 1988

Nora Langley hopped off the bus, just barely keeping on her feet. She hoped that wasn't a bad omen; falling on her face before she even set foot on campus would have been a crummy way to start a whole new life.

Maybe she should look at it the other way: it was a good omen that she almost—but didn't—fall. Keeping her balance despite being weighed down and in unfamiliar territory might be a metaphor for...

No. She muttered to herself, "Stop overthinking everything!"

It didn't mean anything. There were no omens, good or bad. Just a new world, new people, new places, maybe a new her, too, if she could manage it.

The first thing was to find her dorm and drop off the fifty pounds—well, it felt that heavy, anyway—of stuff she'd brought from home. She headed away from the bus stop, scrunching up her nose to keep out the fumes, and walked straight through the main gates of the campus.

She stopped on the far side of the gates for a moment, taking everything in. Between memories of her visit here last fall, and the campus map she'd stared at for a good hour on the train from Providence to Albany, she knew where she was supposed to go. Morris Hall, her home for the next year, wasn't quite visible from here, but it ought to be right behind the red brick tower in the distance that had to be Carlisle Library, just off the main quad.

It took a half hour to make it there; she stopped every twenty or thirty feet to absorb a new view. She imagined herself on every bench she walked by, every window she looked in. Nora felt like she'd lived her whole first semester by the time she walked into the lobby of Morris Hall.

It was barely controlled chaos; an older woman, maybe in her mid-twenties, sat behind a little table stacked with papers and yellow envelopes, calling out to anyone who would listen. She had to be the dorm director, but nobody was listening to her. Before Nora herself could go over to her and—she assumed—sign for her room keys, she felt a tug on her arm. She turned to see a freckled, redheaded girl a couple of inches shorter than her.

"Nora? Nora Langley?"

This had to be her roommate. After Nora had been accepted, and her father had paid the tuition deposit, she'd been promised a letter with information about her roommate. She hadn't ever received it, but this girl clearly had.

"That's me. My letter must have gotten lost in the mail, sorry."

The girl laughed. "Nothing's perfect, right? I'm Kim. Kim Hartman. So we're up on the third floor, let's get out of the way here before we get run over." Nora allowed Kim to take her hand and lead her up the stairs.

♡ ♥ ♡

Daniel—August 27

Daniel Keller couldn't believe his luck.

He'd walked into West Hall, checked in with the RA, Monica Shields. Her boyfriend had been the RA back in Morris Hall last year so he'd seen her around. She had given him the news that his roommate wasn't coming to school this fall. "He transferred to Cornell," Monica said. "And they're not replacing him, so it looks like you've got a single room at least for this semester."

It hadn't been so bad having a roommate last year. Phil Jensen had been reasonably clean, generally polite, never once kicked him out of the room because he wanted to bring a girl over—it hadn't been a possibility for either of them, sadly—and he'd even taught Daniel how to play *Battletech*, which had been very cool of him.

But without a roommate, there'd be no snoring. No having to go through the phone bill line by line to divide up the long distance charges. No horrible smells from the weird tofu cookies Phil's mother insisted on sending to him every couple of weeks. Daniel wouldn't miss any of those things.

And if—unlikely as it seemed, and unlikely was probably a generous assessment—there ever was a situation where he wanted to bring a girl up to the room, he wouldn't have to worry about anyone being there.

All in all, it was a promising start to his sophomore year.

Nora—August 28

This wasn't how things were supposed to go. She shouldn't be tiptoeing into her room at three o'clock in the morning, hoping she wouldn't wake her roommate up. First because it would be rude, but more importantly because if Kim woke up, she'd see that Nora's makeup was smudged beyond recognition, and her clothes were a rumpled mess.

She'd know exactly what Nora had been up to. She'd decide that Nora was still the girl she didn't want to be anymore. The Nora she'd hoped she could leave behind and start a whole new life here.

It was one time, right? Peter, their freshman orientation leader, had invited everyone in their group—Nora and eleven other freshmen from Morris Hall—to a party in his off-campus apartment. Kim had been one of them, but she'd begged off. Only three other people besides Nora had shown up: Eileen Marshall from California, and Rick and Dan, roommates whose last names she'd failed to catch.

Nora had been the last to leave, and she should have known better. She should have gone with Rick and Dan when they left around one o'clock. They hadn't asked her to come with them, but they wouldn't have had a problem with her walking home with them. It had been stupid to stay. She'd known what would happen once she was alone with him, and of course it had. He'd refilled her drink, and his hand was on her knee, and she hadn't said anything about it, let alone done anything to let him know she wasn't interested.

She put the key in the lock gently, turned the doorknob ever so slowly, pushed it open an inch at a time, and went inside one hesitant step at a time. Kim didn't seem to stir, and Nora made it over to her bed, undressed as quickly and quietly as she could, and got under the covers.

And that's when she saw Kim's eyes blink open, and even in the dark she could see the disapproving frown on her roommate's face. The same frown she'd seen in her own mirror too often back in Providence.

She didn't want to see that frown anymore. But the only person who could make it go away was the girl she didn't know how to be.

Daniel, August 31

All summer, Daniel had told himself he wouldn't get down over being single. He wouldn't think—obsess, really—about being lonely. He wouldn't be jealous when he saw friends and classmates pairing off and going on dates, laughing together, smiling together, going back to an empty dorm room together.

His resolve lasted three days, until he saw Phil Jensen and Jeannette Morgan walking out of Phil's room down the hall at eight o'clock in the morning. Together. Holding hands.

It wasn't that he had a crush on Jeannette or anything. Sure, she was pretty, nearly as tall as he was, with long dark hair maybe half a shade lighter than his own. But he'd never given her much thought one way or the other. It was more that Phil had somehow made a connection with her three days into the semester.

Phil, who, objectively, didn't dress any better than Daniel, didn't look any more handsome than Daniel, and absolutely wasn't any less of a geek than Daniel was.

It was one thing seeing preppy guys with money and charisma to spare having luck with girls. It stung to see someone who was just like him having that same luck. Why Phil and not him?

He had to stop thinking that way. Aside from the fact that it made him seem desperate, it was just crappy in general. Phil deserved good things as much as anyone else, even if he did snore and receive regular shipments of foul-smelling baked goods.

Fine, he'd lapsed into crappy thinking. But he could change that, couldn't he? Next time he saw Phil alone, he'd say something like "I saw you with Jeannette. Good for you!" and he'd try to actually mean it. Or maybe just saying it was enough to start with. If he said the right things often enough, maybe his thoughts would change too, and he wouldn't have to try and mean what he said—he just naturally would.

Nora, September 4

It was another late night, another attempt at tiptoeing into her dorm room without waking Kim up. But this time, Nora wondered if she should. Because this time nothing happened.

She left before it could happen.

Before, the girl she didn't want to be anymore would just go along with whatever a blond-haired junior with no roommate and too much confidence wanted to do.

She didn't owe Kim any explanations. She didn't owe anything to anyone, except herself.

That was it, right there. That was the secret, wasn't it? That was the thing that she needed to remember. It didn't matter what anybody else thought of her. It didn't make a difference if they were disappointed in her, or if they judged her, or if they called her names or any of it.

It only mattered if she was disappointed in herself. Tonight, she wasn't. And that felt fantastic.

Daniel, September 5

Once the semester officially started, it got easier for Daniel to keep his promise to think better—less jealous—thoughts. All of his classes were interesting, especially Introduction to Operating Systems with his advisor, Professor Maddox.

He'd managed to impress the man three times just in the first week. After the third time, Professor Maddox asked him to come to his office.

"Mr. Keller," he'd said, peering at Daniel through his unfashionable—even Daniel could see they were terrible—bifocal glasses. "You know I advise a dozen students, so I apologize for not always giving each of you as much attention as you deserve. It's clear that I've been remiss with you in particular."

Daniel wasn't sure what that meant. "Sir?"

"I was just looking over your transcript, and I spoke to several of your teachers from last year. You are a talented young man. If I'd paid attention sooner, I would have offered you a position over the summer in the lab downstairs. What's done is done, but I can correct my oversight moving forward."

Wait—was this a job offer?

"Thank you, sir. I think."

His advisor smiled; well, as much as Daniel had ever seen the man smile, anyway. "Thanks would be appropriate. I'd like to offer you a position as a lab assistant for this semester. It would be unpaid for now, but assuming you continue your excellent work, I think we could pay you something in the spring semester."

It was all Daniel could do to keep from shouting in triumph. They didn't have to pay him—just working in the lab would be more than enough. He'd learn a ton, and he could put it on his resume, too.

"Yes, sir. I accept! And thank you."

He might not have a girlfriend, or much of a social life. But he had an advisor—a respected expert in the field—who wanted to hire him. He had a head start on the future he came to college to try and build. That was more than good enough.

It was pretty darn great, actually.

Chapter 2

SEPTEMBER AND OCTOBER—ALBION COLLEGE

Nora—September 10

Nora shuffled the pages of her Introduction to Modern Journalism assignment. Page one had to be in there somewhere.

"Here, look at mine," Tammy said, seeing her frustration. Tammy Webber was a junior, and she'd taken pity on Nora when everyone else in the class had partnered up on this assignment. "And can you remind me why we're even doing this in the first place?"

"Personalized news is the future of journalism. Isn't that how Professor Williams said it? Although I'm not quite sold yet." A blank screen with a blinking blue cursor didn't really seem like a promising future. That wasn't what she was supposed to be seeing, according to the instructions on page one. "I don't expect HAL or anything, but a basic welcome screen or something would be nice."

Tammy stared blankly at her. "Who's Hal?"

Everyone knew that, even if they'd never seen the movie. Or not, apparently. "HAL-9000? From the movie? *2001: A Space Odyssey?* He's the evil computer who takes over the ship and kills everybody."

Tammy shrugged. "I'll take your word for that. But I see what you mean. The instructions definitely say we should see a menu."

From somewhere behind her, Nora heard an exasperated groan. "I told Bob ten times to restart CompuServe." Then there was a laugh, and the voice was louder. A male voice—a student, definitely. "OK. Sorry. Somebody didn't do what they were supposed to do. But it's easy to fix. Just type CSlaunch and hit enter. CS in capitals, launch in small letters, and you should be all set." A pause, then it—he—spoke again. "And by the way, HAL was not evil. He's just misunderstood."

Nora did as she was told, and after a moment of whirring and beeping, the CompuServe logo appeared on her screen, followed by an instruction menu. She turned around to thank her mysterious helper, but he must have left—there was nobody else in the computer lab but her and Tammy.

Daniel, September 23

There were four professors standing over Daniel, one of them—Professor Feinberg—was the chair of the Journalism department. Under normal circumstances, he'd have felt intimidated, even more so because he was on their turf, in their department office.

But not today. He'd volunteered to come over, when his advisor had asked if anyone was willing to go and demonstrate to them what their brand new Macintosh could do. It might be their office, but right now, it was his turf.

Even better, he was getting his hands on not just a Mac, but a Macintosh SE, with a twenty megabyte hard drive. What would you even do with that much storage? It was unimaginable.

Professor Feinberg spoke up. "You really like this—this thing?" The man wore a bow tie, and looked like he belonged in an old movie—the crusty editor who bossed around the plucky young heroic reporters, maybe.

"I love it, Professor. And you will, too, once you see it in action. It's going to change everything."

There were disbelieving grunts from the other professors, and Professor Feinberg simply said, "Convince me, young man."

Daniel pointed to the screen. "See that icon? PageMaker. Desktop publishing. Watch this." He clicked it, waited for the program to start, and then opened up one of the tutorial examples. "This is just a sample document, so you can learn how the software works. You see?" He scooted back a little to let them see better. "Looks like the front page of a newspaper, right? Headline, big photo, articles. But say you want that picture smaller, and the article on the left to be two columns instead of one." A few clicks, a couple of keystrokes and it was done.

"Just like that?" He glanced up at Professor Feinberg, who looked stunned. "That would take half an hour to do by hand!"

"Exactly," Daniel said. "And that's just scratching the surface of what you can do with this. Want to see more?"

They did, and they were suitably amazed. Just as he was about to step aside and let Professor Feinberg try it out, a voice—a girl's voice—spoke out somewhere behind him.

"Did you see that? That was really cool!"

He froze. He knew that voice. He'd heard it—her—although he couldn't think where. But when he turned around to see its owner, she was gone.

♡ 🖤 ♡

Nora, September 25

In three weeks using CompuServe, Nora hadn't learned much about the future of journalism. But she had lost several thousand fake dollars at online blackjack, confirmed her incompetence at Wheel of Fortune and been hit on in a chat room by someone who claimed to be a millionaire from Argentina but who she was pretty sure was really a junior high school boy from Iowa.

She was about to call it an afternoon when she heard that voice again; the same guy who'd helped her get started her first day here in the lab. And the same one who'd dazzled Professor Feinberg with the magic of desktop publishing. He was in the other room of the lab, where the computers were all set up for word processing.

"OK, so if that happens again, do what I showed you." There was a pause. "Yeah, exactly like that. But also remember to save every few minutes. I lost a fifteen page paper last year because I didn't do that."

Nora sighed. That was something that would happen to her. The only reason it hadn't yet was that she hadn't written a paper on the computer yet.

Ten minutes later, Nora was still listening to him—whoever he was—helping a girl who was not the world's quickest learner. Although maybe that wasn't fair. If her anonymous helper hadn't told her what to do three weeks ago, she might still be staring at a blinking blue cursor herself. Maybe she should walk right over there and thank him. That wouldn't be weird at all, right? Just good manners. But then, why were her palms suddenly feeling sweaty?

Sweaty hands or not, she was about to stand up and do exactly that when there was a sudden, horrible sound—a grinding, wheezing, metallic sound, and then the guy's voice yelled in frustration. "God, Bob! I told you not to mess with the laser printer!"

So much for good timing. Definitely not the moment for an introduction.

Daniel, September 27

Daniel crouched down to get a closer look at the bottom shelf. Every good find he'd made at Turn the Page—a used bookshop right off campus, just down the street from the Green Lantern Café—had come from the bottom shelf.

He guessed that most people simply didn't look there, so anything really good got overlooked. It wasn't surprising; kneeling on the concrete floor was painful, and they didn't sweep or dust nearly often enough. But sometimes it was worth it. Like now—a copy of *The Hobbit* in perfect condition. He'd read it before, of course, but his copy at home had disappeared, probably borrowed and then lost by his sister.

He was about to stand up and bring his prize to the register when he heard a voice. *Her* voice.

She was just on the other side of the aisle. She was talking to someone. A friend, maybe? Her roommate? "Yeah, it's trash. But it's fun trash. Please buy it? Or I'll even buy it for you. I want someone to talk about it with, okay?"

On the other side of the Fantasy/Science Fiction shelf was Romance. Daniel could name a few of the biggest romance authors because both his sister and mother read them, but he'd never actually looked at any of the books himself.

The girl continued badgering her companion. And then she started reading aloud. It was definitely trash, and he wasn't sure he'd call it fun, except that it was because of how she was reading it. She was even doing character voices. He balled his hands into fists to try and keep himself from laughing. It was very difficult; this girl was hilarious.

She stopped after five minutes, halfway through a love scene— just before things got R-rated, he assumed—and her friend, or whoever she was, finally gave in. "Fine, Nora! I'll read it! But you have to promise to let me pick something halfway decent for you to read in return."

Nora!

He finally had a name to match the voice, and the laugh. And now he knew she wasn't merely funny. She was beyond funny. Hilarious didn't even really cover it.

He didn't know what she looked like, but after everything he'd heard from her, that almost didn't matter.

But what could he do with her name, and everything else he knew about her? He already knew she was a Journalism major, and most likely a freshman. That meant she'd have most of her classes in Addison Hall, and—unless she was local to Albany— she'd live in the freshman dorm, Morris Hall. It wouldn't be difficult to meet her, knowing all that. But what would he do if he did? What would he say?

He wished there was a book somewhere on the dozens of shelves in this store that could tell him that.

Nora, September 29

"We already handed in the assignment. Why do you need to keep going over to the computer lab?" Until Tammy asked the question, Nora hadn't consciously realized what she was doing. Or, more to the point, why she was doing it.

"I want to try out Word Perfect. See if it's easier to use than my old typewriter."

It didn't sound believable to her own ears, and Tammy's expression said very clearly that she didn't buy it any more than Nora herself did. But, equally clearly, her classmate couldn't think of any ulterior motive Nora might have to visit the computer lab. She just shrugged and said, "Have fun. I'll see you in class tomorrow," and headed for Whitman and, Nora assumed, an early lunch.

Nora made her way to Ellis Hall, shivering a bit at the unseasonable cold. It wasn't even October yet—she shouldn't need a jacket this soon. She jogged the last hundred feet or so, panting as she entered the building.

She actually did have a paper to work on, and she could try out Word Perfect, but now that she was here, she could admit to herself the real reason she wanted to go to the computer lab. *He* might be there. And maybe, just maybe, she'd see him today. Or—miracle of miracles—actually talk to him face to face.

She didn't appear to be in luck; the computer lab was completely empty, both the main room with the CompuServe terminals, and the smaller room where the computers dedicated to word processing were set up. Well, at least she could start on her paper for 20th Century American Literature.

A half hour later, Nora had—she hoped—figured out enough about Word Perfect to get started writing. Once she got going, it was—much to her surprise—a lot easier than working on her typewriter. She quickly got into a rhythm, and got nearly two pages done before she was distracted by voices from the main room of the lab. Both male, but neither one of them was *him*.

An older man, probably a professor, was looking for someone. "I thought Mr. Keller would be here."

He was answered by a younger man, definitely a student. "He's usually here early, Professor Maddox. I'm not sure where he is."

"I thought he'd want to help take this machine apart. Well, it's his loss."

Mr. Keller? Could that be him?

Nora didn't have to wonder long. She heard footsteps, and then a voice—her voice—speaking through ragged breaths. "Sorry I'm late, Professor. My RA was having a minor crisis with her computer. I ran all the way over from West Hall as soon as I got her sorted out."

The younger man said, "Good timing, Daniel. Professor Maddox was about to open up the PC here, he didn't want you to miss out."

"I can speak for myself, Mr. Thompson," the professor said. "But he is correct. I'm glad you made it, Mr. Keller."

Daniel Keller.

That was a good, solid name. For a good, solid guy. A guy who helped his RA, then sprinted across campus so he wouldn't disappoint his professor. And whose professor thought enough about him to be disappointed by his absence.

She knew something else, too. He lived in West Hall, so he had to be a sophomore, at least. Probably not a senior, though. It was hard to be sure just from a voice, but she didn't think he sounded old enough for that.

So: smart. Responsible. Helpful. Friendly. Respected. Sophomore or junior.

Not bad for less than a minute of overheard conversation, plus where he lived. All that, *and* she'd knocked out two pages about The Great Gatsby and the Tragedy of the American Dream. Nora considered that a very successful outing.

Should she push her luck and try to actually speak to Daniel?

It wasn't to be. When she poked her head out the door of the word processing room and into the main computer lab, all she could see was the backs of two young men, both bent over the innards of a computer. Which one was Daniel? The dark-haired one in what might be a polo shirt, or the redhead in a ratty T-shirt?

She didn't wait around to find out; she'd learned enough for one afternoon.

Next time, though.

Next time, she'd catch him alone.

Or maybe the time after that. It had to happen sooner or later, didn't it?

Daniel, October 13

He hadn't seen—well, overheard, anyway—Nora in two weeks. The last time he'd been in the same room with her had been at the used bookshop. Daniel had been back three times since then. He told himself it was in hopes of another lucky find like the mint-condition copy of *The Hobbit*, but he wasn't very convincing, even to himself.

Regardless, she hadn't been there on any of his visits. Nor had she returned to the computer lab.

Or maybe she had. He had no idea what she looked like, only how she sounded. He could've walked past her a dozen times these last two weeks and never known it. Knowing his luck with girls, it wouldn't surprise him. It felt like exactly the kind of cruel joke the dating gods would play—dangle the possibility of a smart, funny, wonderful girl just out of reach and out of sight.

And if he ever did see her? That might be the cruelest joke of all. It would be like the Looney Tunes cartoon where the Coyote finally catches the Road Runner, except the Road Runner was fifty feet tall and the final shot was the Coyote holding up a sign reading "Now what do I do?"

Daniel shook his head and turned back to his cheeseburger. He didn't like eating alone precisely because it usually led to thoughts like that. Not even a piece of cherry pie with whipped cream could lift his mood.

Maybe he could train himself to think more positively? The brain was sort of like a computer, wasn't it? And after all, that's what he was majoring in. If he started giving himself instructions to focus only on good, uplifting, encouraging thoughts, that's what he'd get. His cousin Bianca told him the same thing nearly every week—without the computer analogy, which she would mock relentlessly.

There! He saw his face reflected in the window. Smiling. It was already working. So what else could he be positive about?

The cheeseburger was really excellent. The Green Lantern Café always did a good job, but whoever was on the grill today had nailed it. Yesterday, Professor Maddox had praised him in front of the whole class—that had felt fantastic. And hadn't he beaten Bob and Phil in that brutal game of *Battletech* yesterday that went until nearly midnight?

There were plenty of good things in his life. It was just a matter of reminding himself.

His reminders were interrupted suddenly by a voice.

"I'll pay, Kim. You sat here for an hour reading over ten pages of nonsense about *The Great Gatsby*, it's the least I can do."

Definitely her voice. *Nora.*

He sat up straight, searching for where it had come from. There was only one booth it could be, right by the front door.

Two girls sat there. One was a redhead, dressed in a school sweatshirt and jeans. The other—it was hard to tell from across the café—maybe had dark blonde hair, and she was a little taller than her friend. She was wearing a frilly orange blouse and a skirt. Both of them were smiling.

Both of them were pretty.

But the blonde girl was more than that. Even from twenty or thirty feet away, her smile was entrancing. That was the only word that came to mind. And her eyes, blue or green, it was impossible to tell from here, but either way, they *sparkled*.

"Thanks, Nora. But you have to let me pay next time, deal?" It was the redhead.

Nora was the blonde. The girl who was as beautiful as she was funny. The girl who was smart and read out loud in the middle of the bookstore. The girl who even knew who HAL-9000 was.

Now he knew.

Now he'd seen her.

And now he had to do something about it.

Nora, an hour later

Nora hadn't been paying attention to the time at lunch with Kim, and she'd run all the way from the Green Lantern Café back to campus and Addison Hall to try to make it to her two-thirty class on time. Well, jogged. Mostly jogged.

Half jogged, half walked—either way, it hadn't mattered, because when she got to Addison Hall and dragged herself up the stairs to the third floor, there was a sign taped to the door of Room 307. Professor Madison was sick, and class was cancelled today.

That left her afternoon free. Really free, since Kim hadn't found anything in her Gatsby paper that she needed to edit, and she had no other assignments that were due this week, or even next week.

She didn't know what to do with herself. There wasn't much to do on a Thursday afternoon, really. She wasn't hungry. She didn't feel like going shopping anywhere—not that she had a lot of extra money to spend anyway. And she definitely didn't want to go back to her room.

Indecision, and a perfect October afternoon, made the choice for her. She sat herself down on the steps in front of Addison Hall, enjoying the cool-but-not-cold breeze and doodling in a notebook.

She was engrossed, filling several pages, not paying the slightest attention to her fellow students walking past her, chattering about this or that. Not until she heard a gasp, followed by her name.

"Nora?"

She looked up from the notebook to see a dark-haired boy wearing a Yankees T-shirt standing at the bottom of the steps. He had the prettiest blue-gray eyes, and a voice that she recognized. *His* voice

"Hi," she said, her breath catching. "Daniel?"

His jaw dropped. Nora didn't think that actually happened in real life.

"You know who I am?" He was almost smiling, almost laughing. And it only hit her now that he somehow knew who she was, too.

"I think we both know who each other is. I'm not sure how, but there it is." It was obvious, wasn't it? Just like she'd been overhearing him in different places the past few weeks, he'd been overhearing her. "God, we're both so dense, huh? You've been in all the same rooms I have, of course you know me. If I could hear you, obviously you could hear me, too."

He looked—she couldn't describe it. She saw embarrassment, frustration, relief and joy all together on his face, as though there was an argument going on inside his head about how he should be reacting right now.

"Would you believe that never occurred to me?"

Yes, she would. "Well, I didn't think of it until right now, either, and we've been just missing each other for more than a month, so, yeah."

Daniel, a moment later

When he saw her sitting on the steps—all by herself, there couldn't possibly be a better time to introduce himself and actually talk to her—he hadn't managed anything beyond blurting out her name.

Maybe the positive thinking really did work. Maybe it had even convinced the dating gods to look kindly on him. How else to explain that she knew his name, knew who he was, and that she seemed genuinely glad to see him in person?

"It is kind of wild," he said. And then he went on, not sure where the words were coming from. "I probably shouldn't tell you this, but a couple of weeks ago, I was one shelf over at Turn the Page and I heard you and your friend, and you were doing all the voices from that terrible book." He shouldn't have said that. It made him sound like a weirdo. Or maybe even a stalker.

But all she focused on was one word. "It was *not* terrible!"

"I heard you," Daniel said. "You yourself said it was trash. But I'd listen to you read it out loud anyway. You're funny—no. You're the funniest girl I've ever met." He shouldn't have said that, either. But, again, she wasn't reacting as though he'd just made an idiot of himself.

"You're just saying that. That's a cheesy pick-up line, you don't mean that." Except her tone didn't match her words. Like she believed him, but she was having to convince herself of it. Bianca did that sometimes. On the very rare occasions she let her guard down, his sister Lisa did, too.

"It's true. And not just because you do great character voices. I was in the next room when you were talking with that brown haired girl, I guess she's in one of your classes, when you were playing around on CompuServe. You were hilarious. And sometimes when you were by yourself—you know you talk to yourself, right?"

She was staring at him now, hard. He still couldn't say for sure whether her eyes were greenish-blue or blueish-green. Either way, she was looking for something from him, and then—whatever it was, she found it.

"I guess I do, don't I? I—like I said, I didn't think about you hearing me. I was concentrating on you. The way you're always helping people out in the computer lab, and how you always know what you're doing. Or how you rendered Professor Steinberg speechless when you showed PageMaker to him. Everybody was talking about it. And on top of that, you're pretty funny too."

Now he was staring into her eyes, looking for proof that she meant what she was saying. He couldn't define what he saw, or explain it, but he believed her. She really did mean it, all of it.

"Wow. That's ... I ... okay, I'm just going to say it, before I lose my nerve." Yet another thing he shouldn't have said. But maybe she was the one girl in a thousand, or a million, who could hear what he meant instead of the awkward words that came out. She hadn't laughed at him, or gotten up and run away yet. "Would you— would you want to go out? Dinner, maybe? Tomorrow night?"

She smiled. It was the sweetest, most open and welcoming smile he'd ever seen. "Yeah. I'd love that."

"Really?" He wanted to kick himself. But she was still smiling that same smile. She really was that one in a thousand, or million, girl, wasn't she?

"Yeah, really. Seven o'clock, does that work? You can pick me up outside Morris Hall." She stood up, reached over, patted his arm. "And thank you. For saying I'm funny. That—it means more than you know."

Chapter 3

FIRST DATE, PART I—ALBION COLLEGE

Nora, October 14

Nora kept replaying his words in her head, oblivious to everything else. She barely even realized she was back in her room until Kim's voice cut through her thoughts.

"Hey, Nora!"

It took her a moment to focus on her roommate. "Oh. Hi, Kim. I guess I'm a little distracted."

That earned her a sharp laugh. "A little? I was about to throw something at you to get your attention."

She didn't quite blush. "Okay, a lot distracted." Nora hesitated, not sure why. There was no reason not to tell Kim, was there? It was just a date. "I just got asked out," she said.

Her roommate started to roll her eyes, then she really looked at Nora. "Like, a date-date? Not just a 'let's hang out and see what happens,' kind of thing?"

Nora knew exactly what her roommate meant but was too polite to say more bluntly, and she let it pass. "Yeah. He was— remember I told you about the guy who started giving me unsolicited tech support a few weeks ago? That's him. I never saw him, we just shouted at each other across the room. But I guess he saw me."

Except he said he hadn't seen her—only heard her. Just her voice and her laugh and how she talked when she thought nobody was really listening.

And she believed him.

"That's cute," Kim said. "Like a secret admirer, kind of. Right?"

It was kind of like that. "He said I was funny." Nora took a breath before going on. "Actually, he said I was the funniest person he ever heard." As she said it out loud, she realized she didn't just believe him. She knew it. Absolute certainty. She'd stake her life on it, that he meant it, even if she couldn't say why.

"Wow. That's cool, I'm happy for you."

Nora almost answered that she was happy for herself, too, but that would have been too much. Even if it was true. She couldn't say the other thing, either. That this was the first time anybody ever acted interested in her because of anything other than the version of herself she usually put on for guys. The one that said without need of words that it wouldn't take too much convincing to get her up to their room or into the back seat of their car, and she wouldn't be too demanding once she got there and she certainly wouldn't be too clingy afterwards. That Nora was nowhere to be found when she was talking to Daniel. He'd never seen that girl—and maybe nobody else would ever have to see her again.

No, that was putting far too much weight on one conversation, one boy, one date, assuming he even showed up.

Except, maybe it wasn't after all. Even if tomorrow night was a washout, if she was totally wrong about him, he had seen through to who she wanted to believe she really was. And if one person saw it, then other people would see it, too.

Kim was staring at her again; how long had she been debating herself? "Thanks. I really—I've got a good feeling about this."

Daniel, later that day

Daniel had been replaying the conversation in his head over and over. She'd actually said yes! She hadn't laughed at him when he told her the truth—even though it had been her laughter that made him notice her in the first place. Her laughing at him wouldn't even have been the worst thing. She could have really meant it when she'd asked him if it was just a cheap pickup line. She could have lumped him in with the jerks who didn't notice anything but what was on the surface and didn't want anything but a hot night or two with her before they moved on to the next girl.

Bianca had met a guy who turned out to be one of those, and Daniel had listened to her for three hours afterwards. Remembering it now, a year and a half later, he could still feel his anger rising at the guy who'd dared to treat his Bee that way.

No, that was then, and what was important now was that Nora didn't do that. She listened to him, heard him. Believed him. Wanted to see him. And he wanted to shout about it.

Nobody on the third floor needed to hear it, though. But there was someone he could tell, and the phone was in his hand—and ringing—before he even realized he'd picked it up.

"Who is it—Danny, is that you?"

"Yeah, Bee. I … I wanted to—no, I had to tell you."

There was a giggle on the line. "You don't sound upset, so I'm guessing this is a good thing you have to tell me?"

The best thing. Hopefully. "Yeah. I—well, I asked her out. And she said yes. So we're ... we're going out tomorrow night."

Now it was a laugh, the kindly laugh that always made him smile. "That's usually how it works if you ask somebody out, Danny. But back up. I don't know who 'her' is. You've been holding out on me."

"No, I only found out her name yesterday. Nora. She's Nora."

Another laugh. "OK, she's got a name. That's progress."

He didn't mind her teasing; honestly, she was the only person he didn't mind it from. "She's a freshman, I saw her—no, I heard her. Overheard her first. She was in the computer lab, we have some terminals set up for CompuServe, and I guess she was using them for a class assignment, and I was across the room and I'd hear her talking with her friends. Or classmates. Whoever. And she was just—she was really funny. And she just sounded like, well, kind of like you." That wasn't right. "No. Not like you, but like she's somebody I could talk to all day long and never want to be anywhere else—how it's always been with us."

Now she sighed. "Are you telling me I spoiled you for all the girls on campus there?"

"Don't say it like that! That makes it sound weird."

More laughter. "I know what you meant, Danny. Wanting somebody you can imagine talking to all day long, that's a good thing. And if this girl—"

"Nora."

"If Nora's one of those people, then I'm happy for you. Just promise me, you won't do that thing you do, where you get caught up in your own head and get all nervous and she never sees the real you."

If anyone else had said that, Daniel would have hung up the phone, and then probably cursed at it once he was sure the line was disconnected. "Yeah. I'll—I'll do my best, Bee. I really don't want to mess this up. She's—like I said, I liked her before I even saw her, and when I did see her ... God, she's beautiful. And I don't think—I swear to you, I mean it—I don't think it would have mattered what she looked like. But she really is beautiful, on top of everything else."

There was silence for a few seconds. "I believe you, Danny. I hope it goes great tomorrow night, and I want to hear all about it afterwards. Deal?"

"Deal."

Nora, October 15

This was ridiculous. She'd been in the cosmetics aisle of the drugstore for half an hour now. Nora had never spent even half this much time trying to pick out the perfect shade of lipstick before, not even for her senior prom. On the other hand, it wasn't like Robbie Fairbanks and his powder-blue tuxedo had deserved that level of effort anyway.

Hopefully Daniel would be worth it.

And there it was—she'd found it. Berry Kiss. A deep red with just the tiniest hint of something she couldn't quite name. It was perfect. And even if Daniel didn't notice—and to be fair to him, those subtle details were lost on most guys—she'd know it was perfect. And that was good enough.

Now to go back to her room and figure out what to wear. *That* detail certainly wouldn't be lost on him.

Daniel, the same time

Daniel's body was sitting in his usual seat in Room 220 of Ellis Hall, just like every Monday, Wednesday and Friday at two o'clock. But his mind was elsewhere, in a booth at the Green Lantern Café, sitting across from *her*.

He tried to focus on Dr. Maddox's lecture about Virtual Memory, but it just wasn't happening. Every few minutes, he managed to pull his attention back to class, only to look down at his notebook and see random words—"page fault" and "clock override" and so forth—scribbled there in handwriting that barely resembled his own.

He'd already imagined what she'd be wearing a dozen times—a dress, a blouse and a skirt, maybe a T-shirt and jeans? And he'd played over what she might say and do when he met her outside her dorm—a friendly hello, a hug, a kiss on the cheek or maybe a clever joke?

"Mr. Keller?" His professor's voice cut through his musings. "Would you care to contribute to the discussion?"

What exactly *was* the discussion? He glanced down again at his notebook and found no help there. For an instant he wondered if he could fake it, but you had to have at least some idea what you were faking. "I'm sorry, sir. I—I guess I'm a little distracted today."

Dr. Maddox squinted at him through his awful plastic glasses. "Clearly. But I suppose you get points for honesty, if nothing else." He gave Daniel a momentary half smile. "Do try to keep up, Mr. Keller. I'd hate to see one of my better students blow the midterm."

"Yes, sir." Easier said than done; he was already imagining telling Nora about this tonight, hearing her laughter, not at him but with him. And then telling her that she was the reason he'd been called out in class. Would she laugh at that, too? Be touched? Or some other reaction he couldn't even guess at?

He couldn't wait to find out.

Nora, about 6:30 p.m.

"You've got to be kidding me. You were standing in that exact spot when I left for dinner."

Nora turned away from her closet to see Kim aggressively rolling her eyes. She hadn't even heard her roommate open the door. "I think I was about six inches to the right when you left," she answered.

"Very funny. But what gives?" Now Kim was looking at her more seriously. "It's just a date, right? You're kind of obsessing here."

It wasn't just a date, no matter how Nora tried to convince herself otherwise. Yesterday, she'd told herself that even if tonight was a total washout, what Daniel had said when he'd asked her out was enough all by itself.

She wanted to believe it, but one conversation couldn't erase everything she'd thought about herself since she was fourteen. On the other hand, maybe one really fantastic date that reinforced what he'd said could help her start to write a new chapter. In permanent ink.

"I guess I am," she said after a while. "So can you help me decide what to wear, since I'm not having any luck figuring it out for myself?"

Kim put an arm around her and with her free hand started shoving hangers aside. She didn't speak for a couple of minutes, except for the occasional "hm" and "uh, maybe" and, once or twice, "ugh!" Then, "There. That's it! It's perfect."

Kim's hand was on a pale blue floral-print dress. Her aunt Rachel had bought it for her Christmas before last, and it had sat untouched since then in her closet, first at home and now here at school. Nora couldn't honestly recall packing it—but, hadn't Rachel helped her pack for college?

She pulled the dress out, held it up against herself. Kim nodded. "It really brings out your eyes."

"But does it fit? I've had it for almost two years and I never wore it."

Kim took a step back, eyed her up and down. "Looks like it should. You haven't put on the freshman fifteen, so I don't see why it wouldn't. I'm very jealous about that, by the way, but we can talk about that another day."

"Only one way to find out." A minute later, she had it on, and it did fit. Better than just about anything else in her closet, truth be told. How had Rachel managed that?

It didn't matter. What mattered was that Kim was right, it was perfect for tonight. It was cute without being too much—exactly what a girl who Daniel had noticed for being funny rather than for how she looked would wear on a date. At least, she hoped so; she'd only been that girl for a little more than twenty-four hours.

"It definitely fits," Kim confirmed. "Now twirl for me," Nora did, and Kim grinned at her and clapped. "And it does totally bring out your eyes. He's going to love it. Now let's get your makeup on and get you out the door already."

Daniel, the same time

Before he walked out of the stairwell and onto the second floor of the dorm, Daniel was already rethinking this. Did he really need to iron his shirt? Nobody noticed little things like that, right?

Of course they did. Maybe not doing the little things like that was why he hadn't had a proper girlfriend since 1986. Probably not the only reason, but definitely one of them.

He was at the door to Room 218 without even realizing it. Even though it was ajar, he knocked anyway, and a voice answered, but not the one he was hoping for. This was Jeanette Fitzgerald's room, and while there had to be a dozen people in the dorm who owned an iron, Jeanette was the only one who he knew for sure had one.

"Come in." It was Anjali's voice. He'd forgotten that she was roommates with Jeanette. "Daniel? What are you doing down here?" She didn't sound unwelcoming, just confused. She sat on the bed, looking up at him with those soft brown eyes, pushing dark hair away from her face.

"I was hoping your roommate was here. I need to borrow her iron." It was only now that he realized he was carrying his shirt. He couldn't help laughing at himself when he saw her noticing it. "I guess I'm a little distracted today."

"What, are you getting ready for a hot date or something?" Anjali's tone wasn't quite teasing, but almost.

The answer came out before he knew what he was saying. "Yeah. And I really want everything to be just right." Normally, he never would have admitted that, and if by some miracle he had, he'd be blushing almost into the infrared.

But not tonight. And Anjali noticed.

"Good for you," she said, staring up at him appraisingly now. He couldn't recall her—or any of the girls in the dorm, for that matter—ever looking at him quite that way before. "Jeannette isn't here, but her iron is. I'm assuming you know how to use one?" His hesitation was all the answer she needed. "Never mind. Give me the shirt, I'll do it for you. Wouldn't want you burning it."

It only took her a couple of minutes to iron it. It did look much better now. "Thanks." He laughed. "It's kind of weird, you're the last girl I kissed, and you're helping me get ready for a date." He hadn't expected to say that, either. But why not? Why shouldn't he be confident enough to joke around? Nora saw—well, whatever she'd seen in him, why shouldn't he believe she was right to see it?

For her part, Anjali was surprised as well, and then sad, maybe? But only for an instant, and then she laughed herself. "You probably shouldn't mention that tonight. Your date might not appreciate it."

For the third time in five minutes, Daniel surprised himself. "Actually, I think she'll think it's hilarious. I'm definitely telling her."

Now Anjali was staring hard at him, and he could almost read her thoughts. Last Christmas, under the mistletoe, she'd kissed him and then touched his cheek, called him sweet and then hadn't looked at him again the rest of the school year. She was seeing a different version of him now—the Daniel that Nora had seen yesterday. Maybe she was even wondering if that person had been there last Christmas and she'd just missed it.

"Hey, good luck tonight," she said. "I hope you have a great time. And, Daniel?" She handed back the shirt, patting his hand as she did. "She's lucky. Remember that, okay?"

"I'll try," he answered. "Thank you, Anjali. I really appreciate it." He hoped she understood that he meant not just the ironing but her words. Her smile—equal parts hopeful and wistful—said that she understood him perfectly.

Nora, 6:55 p.m.

In the end, Kim had to just about push her out the door. "Your hair is fine, your makeup is fine, the dress is fine, now go already," she'd said, and then locked the door the moment Nora stepped into the hallway. She was halfway to the elevator when Kim opened the door again to shout, "And have a good time! Dates are supposed to be fun!"

It was good advice. If Daniel really meant what he'd said, and if her initial read on him was correct, there wasn't anything to be nervous about, was there? There was no reason not to enjoy a nice meal with a cute guy and maybe afterwards a romantic evening walk on a moonlit October night, right? The quad got pretty dark, you could see plenty of stars. It would be lovely.

Even better, when she got outside, the weather was perfect. There was a slight chill, just enough to really feel it, but not enough to be uncomfortable. She couldn't have asked for better circumstances.

She checked her watch—the gold one her father had given her for her fourteenth birthday. The one she hadn't worn since her high school graduation and only then because she knew he'd ask about it if she didn't. But it just seemed right to wear it tonight, and she couldn't even say why.

6:58 p.m. Would he be right on time? She didn't have any idea—how could she have any real sense of his personality from a five minute conversation? But he was a CompSci major, and she assumed that made him the sort of person who would always know exactly what time it was, and always be punctual.

She saw something—someone—coming up the walk, just passing under the light post at the edge of the main quad, and felt her heartbeat speed up suddenly. Was that him now?

Daniel, 7:00 p.m.

At first, he didn't see her. When he was almost to the western edge of the main quad, close enough to see Morris Hall clearly,

Daniel looked up to the fifth floor. Three windows over from the left, that had been his room last year. The lights were out; whichever freshmen lived there now were out. For a moment, he wondered what they were doing. Were they at a movie? Having a meal somewhere off campus? Home for the weekend?

Then another question came to him. Did they know Nora? Pass by her in the lobby? Chat with her in the crummy, fire-trap kitchen on the first floor? Kill a spider in the laundry room while she was standing on top of the dryer and shrieking her head off the way he'd done last January for Collette Daniels?

He looked back down to ground level, and all those questions disappeared, because there she was. His pace quickened, and he tried to absorb every detail he could make out from a hundred feet away. She was wearing a dress, down to just below her knees. It was blue.

At maybe sixty feet, he could see that it was light blue, and that there was something on her head—in her hair. A flower, maybe?

At thirty feet, he could tell that it was definitely a flower, and he could see the delicate pattern of flowers—roses, he thought, but he wouldn't swear to it—woven into her dress. Was woven the right word?

Did that even remotely matter? No, because all that mattered was, at about ten feet away he could see her smile, and those wide open, shining eyes, and there wasn't anything else in the world that he cared about.

Nora, a few seconds later

It was him. He met her eyes, trying desperately not to seem like he was trying too hard. Nora had seen that same look staring back at her in the mirror often enough that she couldn't mistake it for anything else.

"Hi," she said.

Her voice seemed to jog something loose for him; his whole face relaxed, and he blinked a couple of times. "Hi. You look—wow, you're beautiful. That dress—your eyes." He took a breath, blinked again. "I mean, the color is just perfect, it sets off your eyes."

She laughed. "Yeah, my roommate said the same thing. Guess she was right." She reached out, took his hand in hers. "You ready?" Nora gave his hand a little squeeze, and she saw a shudder go up his arm.

"Definitely," he answered. He kept his voice level in spite of the nerves he was clearly holding in check only with a ton of effort, and she couldn't help but be touched. And impressed despite herself. "Is the Green Lantern still okay?"

"It's perfect. Let's go!" And she started off, leading him back towards the main quad. He followed along, squeezing her hand in return. It felt—she wasn't even sure what the word was. Nice was woefully inadequate. Maybe she didn't need the word, just the feeling. Maybe that was enough.

Daniel

They walked and chatted, and Daniel was thrilled just to be holding her hand as they made their way to dinner.

He couldn't explain why that was such a big deal; he was nineteen years old, not an eighth grader discovering girls for the first time. He'd had a girlfriend before and they'd done—well, not that much, to be honest, but certainly a lot more than hand-holding. It shouldn't have felt as important as it did.

He needed to stop overthinking and overanalyzing and over-whatevering, and just enjoy the moment. This funny, beautiful girl wanted to be with him here and now. She wanted to feel his touch, and hear what he had to say, and he had to trust it. Bianca had said the same thing, and she'd never steered him wrong.

Nora stopped suddenly, turned to stare at him. "Who's Bianca?"

"What?" Had he said that out loud? He blushed, feeling the heat in his face and in his heart. "Oh, God. I can't believe I—I'm sorry."

She was smiling now, a gentle smile, but it didn't quite go all the way to her eyes. "Sorry that you're two-timing me?"

"Bianca's my cousin. Well, we call each other that, I'm not sure if we're actually blood-related or not, but she's family. I told her about you, and she told me not to,"—he tried to recall her exact words—"get all caught up in my own head and not let you see the real me." Now he laughed; what else was there to do? "I guess getting caught up in my head *is* the real me."

"You tell your maybe-not-actually-a-cousin about all your dates?" Now her smile did reach her eyes, and she was patting his arm.

"Well, you're the first actual date I've had since I started here last year, so, yeah." Why had he told her that? He knew the answer instantly; because he wanted her to know him, even if it was embarrassing. Because that smile and that look in her eyes said that she wanted to know him. "We've always told each other everything, since we were little. She's the best. There's nobody in the world I trust more than her, and I'm pretty sure she'd say the same about me."

They were walking again; he hadn't even noticed until they'd passed through the main campus gate. "She was right to tell you not to be nervous. I'm glad I'm here with you." He also hadn't noticed the way she'd not only taken his hand again, but laced her fingers with his. He wasn't noticing a lot of things, but he heard her words, and he believed them.

Nora

"You know, your shirt really picks up your eyes, too." Nora had only just noticed that. And that the shirt was freshly ironed. She ran her free hand down Daniel's sleeve. "And I didn't figure you for having an iron in your room." Maybe that wasn't fair; what did she actually know about him, really? "Sorry, I shouldn't have said that. I was just—well, you're a CompSci major, and I guess I was stereotyping."

He laughed. "No need to apologize. It's a stereotype for a reason. And you were right. I had to go down to the girls' floor to find somebody who actually had an iron." He went silent for a moment, and Nora saw something—indecision, maybe—in his eyes. But it passed as quickly as it appeared, and he took a deep breath. "Time to see if I was right about you."

What did that mean? Nora had no idea what was coming next.

"I'm not sure if it's a coincidence or an omen or what. But the girl I borrowed the iron from—well, not borrowed, she did the ironing, as long as I'm being honest. Anyway, Anjali, she's the last girl I kissed."

That was too absurd. She couldn't help herself; she broke out into a fit of giggles, and she didn't stop until she was out of breath. "That's—you're making that up, you have to be," she finally said, once she got control of herself.

He laughed in return. "I told her! She said I shouldn't say any-thing, and I told her you'd think it was hilarious. And I was right!" He really was cute when he laughed. Adorable. And something more—he didn't care that he looked silly. Or sounded ridiculous. Or maybe he just trusted her that much already to be ridiculous with her, when he probably wasn't with anyone else, except the maybe-not-a-cousin he'd told her about.

It took them both a couple of minutes to settle down, and as they started walking again—her still holding his hand—she asked, "So is there a story as to why she's the last girl you kissed?" Maybe it wasn't fair to pry, but he'd been the one to bring it up, and Nora was genuinely curious.

"Last and only, at least here. It was one kiss at the Christmas party last year." He proceeded to tell her about it: a cup of punch, a moment under the mistletoe, a soft kiss that promised nothing more and then the kindest rejection she'd ever heard of.

"That's sad. And sweet, I guess. But you know what I think most of all?"

Daniel didn't.

"I think it's her loss. And good luck for me." Then she stopped, turned to face him, leaned up and kissed him—just for an instant, the slightest, quickest touch of lips. "There, now she's not the last girl you kissed anymore. Isn't that better?"

He didn't say anything, but the smile on his face was answer enough.

Daniel

How could the slightest brush of her lips against his, for a fraction of a second, change his whole world? Daniel didn't know.

He also didn't know how Nora looked like she was glowing, under the neon light of the green lantern sign that gave the café its name, when that same light made almost everybody look pale and sickly. He wondered if she thought he was glowing, too.

He shook his head with what he knew was an idiotic grin on his face.

"What's going on in there?" She actually tapped a finger on his forehead. Who did that? Nora Langley, apparently. And he didn't mind one bit.

"Just getting all in my head again. I was thinking how pretty you look in this light, and how usually it makes everyone look all washed out and terrible, and then I was wondering how I looked to you under it." Now he felt himself blushing. "I know I shouldn't have said any of that, probably."

She shook her head. Her hair fell to the side so nicely when she did that. "You definitely should have said it. I want to know you. Isn't that the whole point of tonight?" She took both of his hands in hers, squeezed. "And just so you know, you do look very pretty under this light, too. But I think you'll look even better inside. And I'll be a lot warmer." Then there was a rumbling, gurgling sort of sound, and for a moment Daniel felt his face go violently red, until he realized it hadn't come from him. Nora must have realized it at the same time, but she wasn't blushing at all. "I guess I'm pretty hungry, too." She pushed the door to the Green Lantern Café open. "Shall we?"

Chapter 4

Nora

Daniel was obviously a regular here. He didn't wait for anyone to come to the hostess stand, he just smiled at the closest waitress, nodded his head towards the back corner of the café and took Nora's hand and led her towards an empty booth. He didn't even give the waitress a chance to confirm it was okay.

"I've been here at least once a week since freshman orientation last year. They ought to put a little plaque with my name on this booth," he said, standing back and waiting for her to sit first. She slid in, and she noticed that the table wasn't quite even with the seats and he'd given her the side with a little extra room.

So now she knew something important about him: he paid attention to small details. And a second thing, too: he didn't make a show about it, he just did it as a matter of course and didn't expect any thanks.

"I've only been a couple of times," she said. "But they do make a great cheeseburger. And an even better chocolate shake." Which she ordered when the waitress came over five minutes later. She'd given it some thought earlier, what to order. What would Daniel think if she ordered a salad? Would she spill all over her dress if she got soup and a grilled cheese? But he'd been so open, so honest on the walk over here, that she'd decided to stop overthinking and worrying, and just get exactly what she wanted.

As for him, there didn't appear to be any thought or deliberation at all. The waitress—Belinda, because of course he called her by name—started his order for him, a patty melt and a Coke. "And I'll tell Freddy to make sure it's medium-rare," and he just nodded his thanks.

"You weren't joking," she told him. "It's kind of cool to have a regular order. Like in those old movies, you walk in and they've already got your drink lined up. By the way, do you have a regular drink? Besides Coke, I mean."

"Nope," he said, frowning slightly. "But I can tell you what I don't like. Anything that gets mixed in a five gallon bucket, for starters."

She'd been to more than her share of house parties where she'd been served out of a bucket, or, on one particularly nasty evening, a plastic trash can. "I know what you mean. You can probably use that stuff to strip paint. But," she went on, thinking back to the summer and a night at her Aunt Rachel's apartment. "I'll never say no to a really good margarita."

"I'll have to remember that in a year and a half." Daniel looked down as he said it, and it took her a moment to realize why. Did he think they'd be together then? Was he afraid she'd think he was making long term plans in the middle of a first date? She wouldn't have given his words a second thought if he hadn't acted like he'd said something wrong.

She reached across the table, took his hand, gave him her best smile.

"Or you could just get yourself a decent fake ID, and then you could buy me a margarita anytime you wanted."

Daniel

She'd joked about him getting a fake ID, and then showed him hers, which he had to admit was pretty good. It would have fooled him, anyway. And then, while they waited for their food, the conversation had just dried up. They had been talking like real people, joking around, saying things that actually meant something. He'd been more open with her than he'd ever been on a date, or really with anyone anytime, besides Bianca.

And now they were exchanging boring details about classes and assignments and whatever else they'd been saying the last ten minutes. Not even any good stories about classes, like the way he'd zoned out this afternoon. Just stupid things that you'd tell a distant relative at Thanksgiving to fill time while you were waiting for the gravy to come back around the table.

It was weird that the service was so slow tonight. Maybe that was it, maybe she was just hungry and it was throwing her off, or his nerves were catching up to him, or—it didn't matter why.

This was *stupid*, this was not how tonight was supposed to go, not how it had been going. And not how it was going to go from here, if he could help it. "Nora, what's going on? What are we doing?"

Her water glass was halfway to her lips, his words stopped her as though her system crashed. She blinked, blinked again, like she was trying to reboot herself. "What do you mean?"

"I mean, we were really talking, and now we're not. Both of us, and—I don't know what happened, but I liked how it was going." He reached over and took her hand, looking down at it, willing her to understand what he was saying. She looked down, too, both of them staring at their hands. "I mean, I got called out in class today for daydreaming about you, so I really want things to go right, you know?"

She looked back up at the same instant he did, and their eyes met, and he felt—he didn't know how to describe it. It was something like the way Bianca would look at him, but more. So much more.

"You were daydreaming about me? Tell me about it." She was grinning, but then her expression changed, becoming somehow both softer and more serious at the same time. "Please tell me?"

Without realizing it had happened, both of his hands were on the table now, holding both of hers. "I was trying to picture what you'd wear, what you'd say when I met you, what I'd say and would you think it was funny, just—everything about tonight. It's all I've been thinking about."

Nora

She wanted to lean across the table and kiss him. Just like Molly Ringwald at the end of "Sixteen Candles." She would have done it, if the waitress hadn't picked that exact moment to bring their food.

It was fine. There'd be other opportunities before the evening was over, and anyway, a kiss over a cheeseburger wasn't as romantic as one over a birthday cake, right? "I've been kind of obsessing about it, too," she said. "About you." Maybe she couldn't kiss him right now, but she could still make sure he knew how she felt. "Because of what you said yesterday. How you liked me just from hearing me, before you saw me. You—you have no idea how that made me feel."

His eyes hadn't left hers the whole time. "Please tell me?"

"It made me feel like even before you saw me, you saw who I—who I want to be. Who I hope I really am. Not the girl—oh, God, you told me stuff that had to be really hard to say, I can do it too." She owed it to him, after the way he'd said things that he had to be afraid she'd think were stupid, or worse. "Not the girl who wouldn't put up a fight and wouldn't make any trouble afterwards. I don't like her. I don't want to be her anymore. And after what you said, I thought—I hoped—maybe I wouldn't have to be."

He didn't say anything for a while, but he didn't look away, and he didn't look disappointed, or freaked out. If anything, he looked angry, but—and she couldn't say why she thought so—it wasn't at her.

"I hate that you ever felt that way." He finally looked down, stared at his cheeseburger for a moment, then back up at her again. "Bee—Bianca—met a guy, this was last winter, and after she told me about it—he treated her like—like how you said you felt, like that kind of girl. And we talked for, I don't know, two hours, and afterwards I wanted to get in Dad's car and drive down to Philadelphia and find that guy and beat the crap out of him, for treating her that way."

Nora hadn't expected that. Not any of it. She wasn't sure what she expected, she only knew she had to be as honest as he had been to her, and in return she'd gotten—God, if this was who Daniel really was, maybe—maybe she did deserve him, after all. Maybe she always had.

"Really?"

He gave her a sad little smile. "I'm still kind of ashamed I didn't do it. But Dad would have killed me for taking the car, and the guy—Bee never said what he looked like, he might have been six foot four and built like a tank for all I know, on top of being four or five years older than me." He reached out, took her hand. It was warm and strong and she felt better—and maybe safer—than she could ever remember feeling. "You shouldn't ever have felt like you had to be that girl. But I think it's because so many guys—that's what they're looking for, I guess. It sucks, and they suck, but—I guess there are an awful lot of them, so probably, you just—what were you supposed to do? But that's not who you are. I can see it. I hope you see it too."

She couldn't help herself. This time, she did lean across the table, cheeseburger and all, and she kissed him.

Daniel

Daniel was shocked when he looked up at the clock over the bar. It was nearly ten o'clock. Had they really been sitting here, talking and laughing, for almost three hours?

Nora followed his gaze, and she must have been thinking the same thing. "Wow. I had no idea we've been hogging this table all night. We probably ought to let them have it back."

He didn't really want to. He'd be happy to sit here with her until the café closed, but she was probably right. He stood up first, offered her his hand, and as he did so, the jukebox came to life. The first notes of the song instantly sent him back two years, to a night in June of 1986, and to the parking lot of the movie theater on Central Avenue. She noticed his reaction—of course she did.

"What, you didn't like *Top Gun*? Or is it just Berlin you don't like?"

He couldn't tell her what memory *Take My Breath Away* brought back. There was honest, and then there was *honest*. And didn't they say, talking about past relationships was the kiss of death on a date?

"I loved the movie," he said as he led her out of the café. "Just a bad memory with the song, that's all." It wasn't really bad, exactly.

Complicated was probably more accurate. Too complicated to tell Nora about, at least on the first date.

She squeezed his hand. "Embarrassing bad, or painful bad?" she asked, but there was no teasing in her voice, or her eyes.

"More like I never figured out what to think about it."

She nodded, and gave him the softest, sweetest smile. "I understand." She probably would, too. "If you ever do want to talk about it, I'm here. Or not. No pressure, I promise."

Maybe if there was a third or fourth date. Maybe after they—if they ever—maybe then. Then it wouldn't be weird or awkward. And maybe if that did happen, it wouldn't be a complicated memory anymore, anyway.

Nora

Nora had a decent idea about Daniel's bad memory. *Top Gun* came out in 1986, in the summer if she remembered right. He was a year ahead of her, so it would have been the summer before his senior year of high school. So, a summer romance, probably his first. He'd mentioned he'd gone to an all-boys high school, so when else would he have been able to meet girls but during the summer?

First love, first breakup, first broken heart.

Maybe not just first, but also *only*? He'd already told her he didn't date anybody his freshman year here at Albion, it wasn't a stretch to assume that there wasn't anyone his senior year at an all-boys school, either.

Of course he wouldn't want to talk about something like that on a first date.

"Thanks," he said. "That—it means a lot to me that you—I don't even know how to say it. That you want to listen."

With every word, he was proving that what he'd said yesterday was true, and that what she thought—hoped—about him was true, too. "I want to know you. You deserve to be known. Because you're pretty great."

He didn't have any words, but a moment later his arm was around her, pulling her close, and that was a better answer than anything he might have said. They walked in silence, with him glancing over at her every so often, with an expression she could only describe as blissful. And then, right in the middle of the main quad, he stopped.

"Look up, over a little to the left." He pointed. "That's Androm-eda." Now he took her hand, held it up. "There, see that smudge there, that's the galaxy of Andromeda, but the constellation is there. See the star just to the left, and then go up, you see?"

He was full of surprises. He hadn't said anything about being a stargazer. "How do you know that?"

"Our neighbor had a telescope, a really nice one, up on his roof. He'd let me look in it sometimes. I don't remember all that much, but I do know some of the constellations. That's Cassi-opeia, above Andromeda, and then Perseus to the left of that." He laughed. "Perseus and Andromeda go together. I mean, they were together. He—he saved her, they were going to sacrifice her, let some huge sea monster eat her, but he saved her, and then he killed the Gorgon, and then they flew off together."

That all sounded vaguely familiar to Nora. "That's from a movie, isn't it?"

"*Clash of the Titans*. I loved that movie when it came out. I think I might be misremembering some of the details—I was, like, eleven or twelve when I saw it—but I know they ended up together. So it's romantic. Like tonight." He looked away when he said that, as if he thought she wouldn't see him blushing.

She pulled herself closer to him, started walking again. "I agree. Tonight is pretty romantic. But if it's all the same to you, maybe we can skip the sea monsters."

"I think we're safe from them. We're, what, a couple of hundred miles from the coast? But I'd fight one for you, if they made it here."

He probably would, too. But that wasn't the most important thing he'd said. It was that last word.

Here.

Because right now, here was right outside West Hall. His dorm. And she'd been the one to lead him here; it was her feet they'd both been following.

"How—this is my dorm. How'd we get here?"

She took both his hands in hers. "I guess I didn't want our night to end just yet. And it's starting to get a little chilly out."

She could stand the cold, if he wanted to sit on a bench out here and talk for another hour. Or three or four. She could see the indecision—and maybe fear?—in his eyes as he thought her words over. Then he blinked, and the indecision was replaced with clarity.

"I don't want it to end, either. I—I'm having a great time."

"I'm glad. I am, too." She felt her own moment of indecision, but it was gone as quickly as it came. "So are you going to invite me up to your room?"

He'd fumbled with the key to the front door of the dorm, nearly tripped on the first step of the staircase, and it took him three tries to unlock his room. Daniel appreciated that Nora had very pointedly not noticed any of that.

He pushed open the door, and ushered her into his room. The first time he'd ever had a girl in his room, here or ever. There was no point hoping she wouldn't know that, his nerves made it obvious. But maybe it didn't matter. She'd said it herself—she said yes tonight because he wasn't like the jerks who had a different girl in their room every other night. Because *he* was different.

So what was there to be afraid of?

Nothing, but that's why they called them "irrational fears."

Whatever showed on his face, she didn't seem to notice. She was too busy looking around his room, running a hand along his bookshelf, picking up the occasional book to look more closely at it.

"You keep things pretty tidy, don't you? I bet it's always like this. You didn't clean up just in case we came back here tonight."

He felt himself going beet red. "I—I didn't think, I didn't expect..."

She put down his copy of *The Hobbit* and put a hand on his arm. "You didn't? Really?"

He hadn't. Until he'd heard that song back at the café, he hadn't thought about anything more than dinner and talking. And even then, he didn't picture anything more happening—if it did at all—tonight. "Honestly, no. All I wanted was to not mess up tonight. And—and it's been amazing. I don't want to mess it up now."

She sat on his bed, patted the space next to her. This was so far beyond anything he could have hoped—or even imagined. It took him a minute to get up the courage to sit down with her. "You didn't mess up. And you're not going to now." She grabbed his shoulders, turned him to face her. She was only a couple of inches away from him. "I'm here because I want to be, because I want to be with you. Because you're the amazing one. And I'm not going anywhere."

She leaned in, and the inches became millimeters, and then he bridged that last tiny distance, his lips on hers, her arms around him, his hands cupping her face.

After a moment, she pulled away, but her arms were still around him, holding him close. He could almost feel her heart beating. He wondered if she could feel his, feel how it was racing. "I—I know what you said. I don't want you to go. I just ...I don't want ...if we—if this ...I want it to be..."

Words failed him, but she understood all the same. She caressed his cheek, then leaned in and kissed him again, deeper this time, and he responded. He wasn't sure how long it was before they both took a breath.

"Can I ask you something?" He nodded; he still didn't have any words. "Is this your first time?"

He probably should have had some reaction, he didn't even know what it ought to be. All he did was nod again.

"Okay."

"Okay?" He surprised himself that he could even manage that word.

"Better than okay. It's a lot better. It's a gift that you told me. And that you're trusting me with tonight." They kissed a third time, and now, finally, he found his voice.

"I do trust you, Nora. There's nowhere I'd rather be than here with you." And this time, he was the one who kissed her, and pulled her close, and didn't let go.

Nora, just after midnight

It had been halting and awkward. But that didn't matter. What mattered to Nora was the way he didn't look away from her the whole time. And what she saw in his eyes, the way he trusted her, and, more, the way he was *present*, in the moment with her, as nervous as she knew he was.

And he still was present, an hour later. He held her close, as they lay together under the blankets. She'd never been cared for like this afterward, and she told him that.

"Really? Why ... I don't get it. Why wouldn't—what's wrong with your old boyfriends?"

They mostly weren't boyfriends, for one thing, but that was something she could tell him another time. "I think it's more what's right with you."

He didn't respond for a little while. "I—I like this. This is—who wouldn't want to be with you, after ... well, after?" Then he fell silent again, and there was a faraway look in his eyes.

"Hey, Daniel? Where'd you go?"

He blinked, and focused on her again, but he took his time answering, and she knew he was trying to think of the right way to say whatever was in his mind. "It's what I was thinking about back at the café, when *Take My Breath Away* came on the jukebox."

"She was your high school girlfriend?"

He nodded. "Peggy. We dated for, like, eight months or so. She was a senior at St. Barnabas, it was our sister school. When we needed girls for a play, or when we had a dance, that's where they came from." She'd wondered how that worked when he'd told her about his all-boys school. "Anyway, she was always at my bus stop in the morning and we got off the bus in the afternoon, and I guess she was flirting with me for a while and I didn't realize. Bee said that's what she was doing, then the day she got her class ring, she was so excited, she showed it to me on the bus, and we just walked together when we got off. We ended up at her house, and she invited me in, and her parents weren't there."

"And you had your first kiss." Nora could picture exactly how it had gone.

"They say you're not supposed to talk about old relationships on a date."

"They say a lot of things, whoever they are." She kissed him, slow and long, and when they broke apart, she caressed his cheek and said, "But I really want to hear it, if you want to tell me."

"I guess you really do." He wasn't quite blushing. "Okay. You're right, she kissed me, and we—we ended up making out until right before her parents came home. And I guess after that—we never really said anything, either one of us, we just started spending more time together. It was probably two months before she called me her boyfriend in front of anybody."

"I wouldn't have waited that long. I would've wanted everyone to know you were mine." She surprised herself as much as him with that.

"I think I'd like being yours," he answered, and she thought she heard a hint of teasing there. That was almost better than his words, that he felt comfortable enough to joke around with her. "But let me—let me finish, I really want you to know. We dated, and it was—it was nice. She was nice. She asked me to her prom, and then she graduated, and it was, I guess the middle of June. We went to see *Top Gun*, she drove—I had my license but Dad didn't want me driving at night, so we were in her dad's car, and when the movie was over, we went back out to the parking lot."

Now she knew exactly what the bad memory was, but she let him tell it.

"We got in the car, and she locked it, but she didn't put the key in the ignition. She—we were making out, and then she—she touched me, she ... anyway, she wanted to—right there in the car."

Nora knew precisely how and where he'd been touched. This might as well have been one of her own memories, except from the reverse perspective. The girl she didn't want to be anymore would have been touching Daniel like that. The girl she hoped she was stayed quiet and still, because she knew he needed her to hear him. So she just stared into his pretty—*so pretty*—eyes, and listened.

"I mean, we were way far away in the corner of the lot, and pretty far from the streetlights, it was like she knew, like she planned exactly where to park."

"But you—you weren't ready?" She wished she'd been brave enough or strong enough to say she wasn't ready, in a parking lot the summer after freshman year of high school.

"I felt like—it just wasn't right. I liked her, but I didn't—this will sound ridiculous, but it's true. I didn't really know her. I know you better after a few hours, I mean who you really are, better than I knew her after eight months. It just—I didn't want to do it just to check off a box, or just because I was too horny. And for sure I didn't want to do it in the backseat of a 1974 Buick Skylark."

She couldn't help laughing, and at the same time feeling a sympathetic twinge of pain. "Believe me, you did her a favor. There's nothing sexy about a seatbelt buckle grinding into your back."

"Swear to God, I thought of that—it looked like it would be really uncomfortable for her. And probably me, too." He went silent again, then pulled her up against him. "But why I wanted to tell you is, I'm really glad I didn't that night. I'm glad I waited. I'm glad it happened with someone as amazing as you." He was holding her eyes as he said it, not blinking, not moving a muscle, just telling the absolute truth.

For once, she couldn't think of anything to say or do. She just let him hold her, and replayed his words over and over, really believing them, and how amazing was that?

Chapter 5

THE NEXT DAY—ALBION COLLEGE

Daniel, October 16, around eight o'clock in the morning

Daniel stirred awake, sunlight streaming in from the gaps in the curtains. It was very bright, more than usual—he supposed because it was later than he usually woke up. He felt so peaceful, so much better rested than he could ever recall feeling.

The reason why was staring at him, a teasing, perfect smile on her face.

"Good morning, sleepyhead," she said.

"Good morning, yourself." How could it not be good, after last night? It had been—he didn't have the words for it. She'd led him back to his dorm, invited herself up to his room, and she'd made love to him. She hadn't even said a word about his inexperience.

And then, after he'd told her about Peggy, they'd done it a second time, and he thought—hoped—it had been better for her. If her smile now was any indication, it must have been. When—if—no, *definitely* when it happened again, he would make sure it was better for her. He'd opened his heart to her, surely he could talk honestly about how things were when they were intimate.

"Tell me the truth," she said. "When you fell asleep, did you have a moment where you wondered if the universe was playing a joke on you, and you'd wake up alone and it was all just a dream or something? Because I did." She pulled herself close to him, kissed him.

"No." As much as he could get lost in his head, there was none of that once they got back to his room. "Because the last thing I remember feeling before I fell asleep was you holding me."

She kissed him again. "That's really sweet. Everything was sweet. Especially waking up with you here." Now she pushed herself away. "But—I hate it, but I have to get back to my room. I call my Dad every Saturday morning. Just to check in, you know?" Daniel understood perfectly. "And he's got caller ID—he paid extra to get it—otherwise I'd just call from your room." He liked that she just assumed he wouldn't care about the long-distance charges; she was absolutely right about that.

"I'll walk you back, if you want."

"I want. I really want."

Nora, an hour later

They were only a few steps outside his dorm, Daniel holding her hand as they walked, and a dark haired Indian girl waved to him, then stopped and did a double-take.

He waved back. "Hi, Anjali."

The girl with the iron. The last girl he kissed. The girl who—lucky for Nora—had been too blind or too dumb to see what was right in front of her.

Nora couldn't help herself. "Thanks for helping him with the ironing yesterday. He was so handsome in that shirt. I'm Nora, by the way. Nice to meet you!"

Poor Anjali didn't know what to say. She finally settled for, "Nice to meet you, too," in a small voice, and she headed into West Hall without another word.

Daniel didn't move for a moment or two; had she gone too far?

"I guess I did say it last night. That I wouldn't mind being yours. And you know what? I don't. Not one bit."

She hadn't gone too far. Maybe she *couldn't* go too far with him. And wasn't that good to know?

Daniel, a moment later

He hadn't thought about last night becoming public knowledge. But now it was—Anjali would surely tell her roommate, and it would go on from there. He had no illusions that he was especially popular, but the novelty of it would guarantee that there was talk. Quiet, nervous Daniel Keller spending the night with a girl and not even trying to hide it would surely be good for at least a couple of days of gossip in West Hall.

"It's funny," he told Nora as they made their way across the main quad, "I think before yesterday I would have freaked out if I thought anybody was talking about me. But Anjali's going to spread it around that she saw me walking you home, and it doesn't bother me one bit."

She squeezed his hand. "Well, you said you wouldn't mind being mine. Everybody knowing it is part of the deal."

"Good. It'll be really nice to hear people saying how lucky I am." He stopped, right there in the middle of the quad, and kissed her. "Because I am. And I don't—I hope—I don't think it should be a one-time thing. I really want to see you again." He kissed her again, and she kissed him back, and they stood there in each other's arms for what seemed like minutes before they broke apart. "And not just for—well, not just for that. I told Bee that you seemed like somebody I could just talk to all day long and never want to be anywhere else. And now I know I was right."

She seemed surprised—shocked, even. "You said that?"

He took her hands in his. "It's true."

"I—I don't know what to say to that." She still looked nervous, but she was holding his eyes. "I can't believe you—anybody— thinks that."

"Well, I do. And you should believe it, because it's true." How could she not know it herself? Maybe for the same reason he could never see what she said she saw in him. Maybe it took someone else to make you see what was in the mirror all along. "So, what do you think? Do you want to see me again?" He was pushing a little bit, but it felt like this was the moment to do it. "Dinner. Or a movie. Or just sitting out here on a bench and talking for three hours. It doesn't matter, as long as we're together, right?"

Nora closed her eyes for a long moment, and he could feel her hands shaking. Maybe he had pushed too hard.

She took a deep breath, steadied herself, and answered, "Yes. Definitely yes." He let out the breath he hadn't realized he was holding. She pulled her hands away from him, fished around in her purse. "Of course. Pen but no paper. Wouldn't happen to you—if you carried a purse, you'd have a little notebook in there just in case." She reached back and grabbed his left hand, writing on his palm. "Never mind, that works. My phone number. Don't forget to write it in a notebook when you get back to your room. Not that you would forget. You probably never forget important stuff."

He kissed her one more time, and put an arm around her and walked her the rest of the way back to Morris Hall. "I definitely won't ever forget anything about last night. Or anything about you, Nora Langley."

There was one last kiss, at least for the moment. Then she opened the door and started to walk inside, but she poked her head back out. "Call me later today. Maybe we can just talk for three hours." She blew him a kiss, and disappeared inside.

He stood there for a couple of minutes, staring at his palm, memorizing her number, just in case anything happened to it on the way back to West Hall.

Nora, ten minutes later

Nora unlocked her door, half-wondering if Kim would be there, and what she'd say if she was. This wasn't the first time she'd spent the night elsewhere, and while Kim had never said anything about it before, her body language had been somewhat less than warm. Nora didn't know if she wanted to—or even could—put into words how different last night was from all those other nights.

But she didn't have to; Kim was nowhere to be found. So she did the only thing she could. She threw herself face down on her bed and squealed in delight, at how wonderful last night had been, at how it had made her feel.

When was the last time she'd had reason to squeal? She had to think hard before it came to her—the fall of her freshman year of high school. The phone call when she got home, telling her she'd won the last spot on the girls' volleyball team over horrible Brenda Makepeace.

Even thinking of that day four years ago felt like a bad omen. Things had fallen apart almost immediately; she'd lasted less than a week on the team. Brenda's friends had tormented her, Coach Benson had been a tyrant and nobody had believed her when she said she'd pulled her calf muscle even though they could all see she couldn't walk more than a few steps without stumbling. So the night before the first game of the season, she'd snuck out of her house to a party she hadn't been invited to, gotten drunk for the first time, and showed up at the gym hungover the next morning.

Definitely a bad omen.

Except it wasn't. Daniel would believe her if she told him she pulled a muscle, and he wasn't a tyrant. He definitely wouldn't torment her, so, really, she was being silly to even think about it.

He had been so sweet—so much more than sweet. He hadn't known what he was doing when they were together in bed—not at all. But, unlike anyone else she'd ever been with, he knew it, and did his best to learn as he went. He'd paid attention to her every word, every reaction and tried his best to respond accordingly. And it *had* been better—still awkward, but definitely better—the second time.

Far more important, though, was everything outside of the act itself. The way he'd held her, the way he'd talked to her, the way he'd made her feel safer, and more cared for, than anyone she'd ever known.

She wanted to tell someone. Had to. But it wouldn't be during the weekly call with her father, that was obvious. Even if she felt like she could talk to him about anything really important—and when was the last time she'd felt that?—this wasn't a subject any daughter ever talked about with a father.

Her mother was, if anything, worse. The last time she'd talked about a boy with her was in sophomore year of high school, and that had been a debacle, to put it mildly.

No, she wouldn't be telling either of her parents about last night, or about Daniel at all. If she had any say in the matter, the next time Nora mentioned a boy to them would be when it was time to send out wedding invitations. And maybe not even then.

She could call Aunt Rachel. She'd listen. And she'd be thrilled to hear good news about a date from Nora. It was early, not even nine o'clock yet. But this was worth waking Rachel up for.

It took six rings for Rachel to pick up, and her voice was groggy when she greeted Nora. Nora ignored that. "Rachel, I—I had the most amazing night. It was—don't laugh, please don't laugh—it was magical. He was so sweet. I've never had someone act like that with me."

"Good morning to you, too, Nora." Nora could hear the smile in her voice despite the sarcasm.

"I'm sorry. I know I woke you up. But I had to tell you. I mean, I can't just keep this to myself. I want to go up on the roof and shout about it."

Now Rachel laughed. "I think I'm getting the idea. How about you start at the beginning?"

So she did. She told Rachel about hearing Daniel without seeing him in Professor Feinberg's desktop publishing lab, and joking with him still without seeing him in Ellis Hall, and him asking her out, and—almost—every detail of last night and this morning.

"Writing your number on his hand was a nice touch. He won't forget that." There was a pause. "I assume you don't want him to forget. You're planning on seeing him again?"

"Yes!" She kept her voice barely below a shout. She wasn't sure how she managed it.

"You deserve somebody great. I'm so happy for you that last night was special." There was a pause. What was Rachel hesitating about? She'd just said she was happy for her, but she didn't sound happy. "You sound—I'm sorry, I shouldn't say it."

What the heck did that mean? "Rachel, whatever you're thinking, tell me! You've always told me the truth, even if you didn't think I wanted to hear it."

But what could be wrong with anything about last night? What problem could Rachel possibly be seeing with it?

"I'm probably wrong, so don't pay any attention to this. But you sound a lot like your father did when he met Karen. I was little, six or seven, but I remember it clearly, because I'd never seen him that happy before."

"What? You're comparing—you're saying—Dad and Mom?"

Obviously Rachel was wrong. Like she'd just said, she was only a little kid. On the other hand, Nora knew that her father had still been living at home right up until he'd married her mother, so Rachel would have seen him every day of her whole life, and even a little kid can tell when her big brother is happy or sad.

"He said she was magical, that she was the most wonderful girl he'd ever met. He sounded just like you did a minute ago."

Rachel didn't need to say anything more; Nora knew the rest of the story. Her mother was pregnant four months later, they'd gotten married two months after that, the fights began shortly after she herself was born, and there wasn't a week that went by without a screaming match that shook the paper-thin walls, from Nora's earliest memories to the vicious divorce eleven years later.

That's what her aunt took away from Nora sharing the best night she could remember ever having? Her room felt darker, colder, as though the sky had suddenly clouded over. Maybe it was just in her head. Or her heart.

Nora must have told it wrong, or left out some important detail so Rachel didn't understand. Or maybe Rachel was jealous—she was still single, wasn't she? Never had a serious boyfriend as far as Nora knew. Maybe she'd never had a properly magical night of her own and she couldn't stand to hear about one from her niece.

Or maybe there was some other reason, but Nora didn't care to know what it might be. "I've got to run, I think I hear my roommate," she said in a flat, careless tone. "And I've got to call my father anyway. I'll talk to you next week." And she hung up before Rachel could say anything more.

Daniel, the same time

Daniel walked back to West Hall, to find three of his dorm-mates sitting in the lobby. Fred Phillips, four doors down from him, greeted him with, "I heard someone got lucky last night."

Jeannette Morgan, sitting across from him on the ratty old sofa, glared at him. "God, what are you, a caveman? And you wonder why you're always alone and bored on Friday nights."

Daniel paused. Before yesterday, he'd probably have run up the stairs taking them three at a time, to get away from this conversation. Not today. "You're half right, Fred." Fred and Jeannette and Bill Thompson, upstairs from him and two doors over, all stared at him in surprise. "I am lucky. I met somebody amazing, and she acted like she saw me the way I really, really hope I actually am." It felt good to say it. It felt even better to want to say it. "Oh, and, Jeannette, I guess I owe you thanks for borrowing your iron. She definitely noticed the effort."

"You sound like a Hallmark card, Keller. I never thought I'd see you go all sappy," Fred said. Daniel figured he was mostly joking. But Jeannette threw a cushion at him anyway.

"It's not sappy, it's acting like an adult, Fred. Maybe you could learn from it." Then she turned to Daniel. "You're welcome, by the way. I'm glad it was for a good cause."

He grinned at her, and headed upstairs. He couldn't deny that it was good for his ego, but there was a thin line between confidence and arrogance and he didn't want to cross it. Not now.

Not with *her*. Besides, there was only one person he wanted to talk to right now.

When he unlocked his room, the phone was ringing, and it was just that person on the other end of the line. "Daniel? I hope I'm not interrupting anything. But I'm sure you have enough sense not to answer the phone if there was anything to interrupt. Please tell me I'm right."

"Good morning to you, too, Bee." He laughed. "I actually just this second came back from walking her home."

He heard the sound of clapping on the line. "Very gallant! I'm impressed. My little Daniel, all grown up and acting like a gentleman, who would ever have thought?"

"You thought. You kept telling me, and—well, you were right." She had told him, over and over. "It was—God, it was amazing. She was amazing. She was so ... I don't even know. So—everything."

"I want to know," Bianca said. "Tell me everything. Well, almost everything. Keep it PG, if you don't mind. And don't roll your eyes at me!" She knew him too well. "I know you haven't forgiven me for going on and on about Paolo that one time, but in my defense I was very drunk and he was very handsome." She'd shown him a Polaroid of Paolo at Thanksgiving a couple of months after her trip to Italy, and he couldn't really argue.

"Strictly PG, I promise." He proceeded to recap the night and the morning for her, omitting the most physical details, but not skipping the part about how little he'd known, and how sweet she'd been about it.

"That girl..."

"Nora."

"Nora really must have been something. I'm so thrilled for you. You deserve this, Danny." There was a lengthy pause. He couldn't guess what she was hesitating to say. "Just—trust me, you know I've been there. Take it one step at a time. One date at a time. Don't get ahead of yourself. You know we both do that. Enjoy every minute with her, and if it's going to be more, then it will be, but let that happen in its own time. Remember how I scared Alex off?" That had been a year ago, last October. He'd missed the dorm Halloween party talking to Bee for probably three hours. "Don't do that. Please, just enjoy this and let the future take care of itself. Promise me, Danny."

He hadn't been thinking ahead—not yet, anyway. But he had to be honest with himself, those thoughts would have started bubbling up by this afternoon. "I promise, Bee. But you might have to remind me every so often."

"You know I will, Danny. Now go get yourself some breakfast. Love you!"

Nora, a half hour later

What the hell was wrong with Rachel?

No. What was wrong with *her*? Why had she snapped at someone who had never been anything but good to her, never lied to her? Someone who was the closest thing to a confidant she'd ever had.

It wasn't as though Rachel had said anything she didn't know, even if she'd never really given it much thought. Why would she have? Nobody sat there and dwelled on what their parents were like when they were dating, right? That was weird.

Rachel had even told her on occasion that she had her father's temperament—and temper. Always when she'd needed to hear it, too. Without her aunt's words, she probably would have gotten herself expelled from high school half a dozen times.

Or worse than expelled. Rachel had talked her down the last week of sophomore year, after she'd learned that Eileen Renfro was the one who'd broken into her locker and stolen the locket Bill Jenkins had given her. She had been so angry—even now, more than two years later, she could feel her heartbeat spiking just thinking about Eileen—and Rachel had kept her from doing something she would have regretted.

Most of the time, it was wonderful to have someone who knew you that well, and would be honest with you no matter what. Every once in a while, though, it really sucked.

Rachel meant well, and she was much too perceptive. But that didn't mean she was infallible.

Yes, Nora shared some traits with her father.

Yes, she wore her heart on her sleeve.

Yes, she sometimes—often—acted before she thought.

But she wasn't her father's clone. She was herself. And just because her father blew up his marriage—with plenty of help from her mother—that didn't mean that she was doomed to follow in his footsteps.

She'd call Rachel back later and apologize for being so rude and horrible, and that would be the end of it. She wouldn't plead her case, because there was nothing to plead, was there? Rachel had made an observation, and it was wrong, and in time she'd see that. What else needed to be said?

Now, though, it was almost ten o'clock and her father was probably wondering what was up with her.

Sure enough, the phone rang just as she put a hand on it to pick it up and call him. "Morning, Pumpkin."

Nora didn't really like his nickname for her. It had barely been cute when she was in kindergarten. But she always smiled at it anyway. At least he was trying. That counted for something. "Hi, Dad. Sorry I didn't call you, I overslept this morning."

He laughed, more than her words deserved. That was something else that hadn't ever really been cute. "Working too hard?"

For an instant, she debated actually telling him about Daniel, about—with a *lot* of editing—last night. She didn't like how little her father really knew her. Maybe it was on her to bridge the gap and tell him something real. Something that for once he'd actually understand since he'd lived it himself, too.

Then she ran quickly through the many, many ways that conversation could—probably would—go horribly wrong and leave her feeling guilty or angry or depressed or flat-out hopeless. Or most likely all of them at once.

"Well, I am." It was even true. She'd worked far harder this semester than she ever had in high school. And—to her surprise—she'd enjoyed the work.

"But I had dinner with a friend last night, and we stayed up late talking. You know how that is." That was also, technically, true, despite being completely dishonest.

She had become very skilled at that sort of lying truth-telling with her parents. And all her high school teachers and classmates. And her roommate here, too.

And she hated that about herself.

She swore then, even as she kept on lying to her father with misdirected truths, that she would never, ever, *ever* do that with Daniel.

Chapter 6

HALLOWEEN—ALBION COLLEGE

Nora, October 31

Nora had a very clear vision of how this outfit was supposed to look. The idea was something like Sandy at the end of "Grease" with a little more skin. Something that would make Daniel completely lose his mind.

Not that he didn't already, every time she came back to his room with him after a date, but tonight she wanted to really up her game. Halloween was her favorite holiday, she loved getting into a costume, and she'd never had a boyfriend who was worth getting dressed up for.

Unfortunately, her closet wasn't cooperating with her. She'd thought she had everything she needed to make the outfit work, but—well, this is what she got for assuming. The girl looking back at her in the mirror wasn't Sandy at the end of "Grease."

Maybe Sandy at the beginning of "Grease" trying to go all sexy without the help of the Pink Ladies.

No, it wasn't even *that* good. Olivia Newton-John on her worst day wouldn't be caught dead wearing what Nora had on now.

But there was nothing for it. She didn't have any other costume ideas, and it was too late to shop for anything. Not that she knew where to go even if she did have more time.

So, that was that. She'd just have to go over to Daniel exactly as she was, and hope for the best.

Daniel, ten minutes later

Daniel wasn't wearing a Halloween costume. He wouldn't have known where to start; there was nothing he owned that could even remotely be turned into one.

He hadn't dressed up for Halloween since fifth grade, and only then because he'd have been the only one in his class without a costume if he hadn't. He had given it some thought last year, for the dorm party, but he couldn't stop thinking about how ridiculous he'd feel. Then he'd berated himself because it was ridiculous to feel ridiculous when everyone would be in costume, and even if anyone did laugh at him, being laughed at was hardly the end of the world. And then he'd missed the party anyway, consoling his cousin on the phone for three hours.

It didn't bother him when Nora laughed at him, but it was *different* when she did it. Because she never meant it hurtfully. And because—although he hadn't yet, and couldn't picture any occasion where he might—he knew he could laugh at her, too.

He should have planned ahead, come up with a costume and dressed up for her. She deserved it. She deserved anything and everything he could think of. But it was too late now, so all he could do was do his best to make sure she had a great time, whatever it was that she had planned.

He wondered what exactly she did have planned. There was a party here at West Hall. He assumed there'd be a party at Morris Hall. There was a big bonfire out in the parking lot off of the main quad. She might want to go to any of those, or there might be something else she'd heard about. Whatever it was, he'd be happy to be there with her next to him.

At eight-thirty, there was a knock at his door. "It's open, come in!" There she was. Nora.

His Nora, and wasn't it amazing that he could say that?

His Nora, and—what on Earth was she wearing?

He could see what she was trying for. God, it was unbelievable that this beautiful girl would want to dress up in a sexy outfit for him. But he was biting his lip to keep from laughing. The leather jacket smelled exactly like his father's old high school letterman jacket when Dad took it out of storage last year. The miniskirt was too tight, and in all the wrong ways. The black leggings were torn, and he'd bet everything he owned that had happened when she put them on tonight. And her makeup was running, probably from her tearing up on the way over. With her own laughter, he was sure.

Put it all together, and his girlfriend—*was* she his girlfriend? He hadn't called her that yet, but they'd been dating for two weeks, they'd slept together on two different occasions, why shouldn't he call her that? She'd want him to, probably.

His girlfriend looked like—oh, God, he knew exactly who she looked like. The image and the name came to Daniel's mind, and he wished more than anything in the world that he could forget both right now, because it was an image and a name he never wanted to associate with Nora.

♡ ♥ ♡

Nora, that exact same moment

Nora figured he'd probably laugh. She'd laughed herself on the way over here. She did look ridiculous, there was no way to sugarcoat it. She had hoped that, maybe, he would be so over-come by the effort she'd made that he would overlook ... well, everything.

But if he'd showed up at her door in some ridiculous attempt at a hot beefcake guy? She'd be rolling on the floor in laughter herself.

So she could accept his laughter—and he *was* trying to hold it in. She appreciated that. It was the face he was making now—something like a frown, but more serious. A lot more serious. Darker, even. She hadn't expected that. And it hurt to see it on her boyfriend's face—*was* he her boyfriend? She hadn't called him that, not even to herself, but he was, wasn't he?

Suddenly she wasn't sure. She didn't want somebody who could look at her like that, when she'd gone to all this trouble and embarrassed herself just to give him a fun surprise.

She stepped into his room and pulled the door shut behind her. If they were going to have their first fight, or maybe their last one, she at least owed it to him not to do it with the door open for everyone else on the floor to hear it.

Her anger must have been showing, because his frown—or whatever it was—disappeared, and he ran to her. Hugged her, and—against her better judgment—she let him. "I—I know I look silly. But I didn't think you'd hate it." She tried to keep her voice level, and almost succeeded.

"I don't! I ... it's—I love that you wanted ... I just—it just reminded me..." He pulled back from her, took her hands, squeezed them hard. She could hear him trying to calm his breathing. "Let me try again. I really do love that you got dressed up for me. And it's great, you look—you look incredible." Well, incredible—not credible—not to be believed, that was an accurate word for sure. "But seeing it all together, it made me think of someone. And please don't ask me who."

What the hell did that mean? "I thought we had—well, I thought we were working on something real. Where we actually talk to each other, and we don't lie to each other. I really liked that, Daniel."

It came out a little sharper than she meant, although she had meant it to be kind of sharp. He definitely heard it, and she could see the conflict behind his eyes. She had no idea what the conflict was, though.

"It's not a secret or anything. It's just—I don't want to say it out loud. You'd probably laugh about it but I just—I can't say it."

Nora wasn't angry anymore; she was totally confused. She had no idea what Daniel was talking about; she couldn't even think of a question to ask to try and make sense of his words. "Hey. It's okay. I know it's only been two weeks. Well, more like six if you count all the times we kept missing each other. But we've both told each other some really personal things. Really hard things. You can tell me anything. I hope you know that."

"I know. But I just told you. It's not you I don't want to tell."

He'd said that twice now, and it was just as incomprehensible the second time. "I don't understand." He didn't answer for a moment. She let him hold her hands, gave his a squeeze, kept looking into his pretty eyes, and finally, he let go of what he was holding in.

"Because If I say out loud that looking at you right now reminds me of my sister and her jackass of a boyfriend, I'll always have that picture of her in my head when I'm with you." He looked away from her, glancing back towards his bed for a moment, then he turned to her again. "How can I ever *be with you* the way I want to be—the way you deserve—if I'm thinking about that?"

Daniel, one moment later

He was being irrational. Ridiculous. Crazy. Pick any word out of the thesaurus—not that he owned one, but Nora probably did—and it would fit.

The problem was, just because something was irrational didn't mean you could just switch it off like a computer and it would be gone when you rebooted yourself.

Besides, now that he'd said it, he needed to tell the story, so Nora would understand. And, despite his ridiculousness, she wanted to hear it. She was sitting on his bed, gesturing for him to join her.

"It can't be that bad," she said.

And it wasn't, except in his mind. "I know. I just need to get my head straight. You'll understand when you hear the story. So this was two years ago, a couple of weeks before Christmas. Lisa—my sister, obviously—she wanted to do something really big for her boyfriend. He was home from college, and his birthday was right around then, and she got the idea..."

He'd always assumed it was her idea, but now that he thought about it, he wondered if someone else had put the idea in her head.

"Daniel?"

"Sorry, I was just thinking about it. So Lisa—if you think I get lost in my own head, I've got nothing on her. I don't think it was her idea. I think somebody put her up to it."

"To what?" Her arm was around him. Whatever anger she'd been feeling towards him was definitely gone now. "She decided to surprise him. Like I said, she wanted to go really big, and make a show of it. You know how in the movies, you see somebody jump out of one of those huge birthday cakes?"

She snorted. "No way!" Daniel couldn't laugh with her. Even two years later, it hurt thinking about how Lisa had felt.

"Yes way," he said after a moment. "I don't know where she found a giant cake—I have no idea what you'd even look for in the Yellow Pages for that. But she found it. And she dressed up for him—I can't even describe it. Like a Victoria's Secret kind of thing. All red and lacy and—you can imagine." She nodded. "God forgive me for saying this, and if you ever meet her you cannot breathe a word, but she—she's not built right for that, if you know what I mean." She pulled herself a little closer to him. He wondered if she'd focused on the part about meeting Lisa. Was she picturing some big meet-the-family moment? Did she think he was?

"I get it. I feel bad for her already." She leaned over, kissed him, much too quickly. "And I'd love to meet her someday—but I promise I won't say a word about how much you obviously care about her."

Nora, a few seconds later

Everything about Daniel's weird reaction to her outfit made sense now. She shouldn't have jumped to the wrong conclusion the way she had. Yes, they were still getting to know each other, but nothing he'd done or said from the first moment they'd properly met justified her making a negative assumption. He'd more than earned a hell of a lot of benefit of the doubt.

"So—everything I'm telling you I heard afterwards. I was friends—well, sort of friends, you know what I mean—with Jack's little brother."

"Jack was the boyfriend?"

Real anger flashed in Daniel's eyes; this was the first time she'd seen that. "Ex-boyfriend, thank God. Anyway, his brother told me all about it the next day, and he showed me a Polaroid of Lisa coming out of the cake. Her outfit, well, I already said. But she'd been sitting inside the cake for an hour, and I guess it got really warm inside, so her makeup was totally ruined, I mean, in the picture it looked like bad clown makeup. And her outfit, it kind of—she was crouched down inside the cake, and it—it moved around on her. Please don't ask me to describe it."

Nora didn't need to. She had a vivid mental picture and it needed no further details. "That's horrible. The poor girl."

"Yeah. So she jumped out, in front of Jack and all his friends and his little brother and God knows who else, and they all laughed at her." He looked like he was in physical pain just talking about it two years after the fact, and it hadn't even happened to him. All she could think to do was hug him. It took a couple of minutes for him to gather the strength to finish the story.

"She came home, and Dad asked her—I don't even know what he said. She shook her head, and she said—I won't ever forget this—'Eff off, Dad. You and every other crappy man in the whole world!' Except she didn't say eff."

Nora couldn't blame her. She would have said something similar in Lisa's place. She also couldn't help smiling at how adorable it was that even two years later and a hundred miles away, Daniel couldn't bring himself to repeat a curse to his father. "Wow."

"He could see how upset she was, he didn't even get angry at her. And I found out what happened from Jack's brother the next morning. I didn't tell my parents anything except that she had a really bad night with her boyfriend and they needed to give her as much space as she needed." He took a deep breath. "I did, too. She didn't come out of her room except to go to the bathroom for three days. So I brought up her meals on a tray and left it outside her bedroom door. And I put my Discman on the tray, because she'd broken hers, so she could listen to Bon Jovi over and over until she was ready to come out."

He would have been just seventeen. And he did all that for a sister he didn't even really get along with.

"My outfit made you think of all that?"

Now, finally, he laughed. "I think it was the way your makeup ran. It brought that whole thing back. I mean, you look nothing like her." He got up, went over to his desk, grabbed his wallet. "Here," he said, opening it up to reveal a family photo. "See?"

He was right; she looked nothing at all like his sister. He'd also been right that his sister, cute as she was, was not quite built to wear anything from Victoria's Secret. "I take back what I said before about not telling her how much you care about her. She already knows, Daniel. She's very lucky to have you. And, you know what else?"

He met her eyes, and his smile told her that he did know what else. Which meant she didn't need to say it, she could just kiss him instead. Kiss him properly. So she did.

Daniel, three a.m.

It was almost three o'clock in the morning. All they'd done, all night, was talk.

Well, they'd made out for a few minutes here and there. And they'd danced through all of *Slippery When Wet*. Right there in the middle of his room, with the CD playing on his little boombox. Truthfully, it was mainly Nora who danced, while he mostly shuffled his feet around and waved his arms in a sad attempt at rhythm.

At least they'd been able to slow-dance to *I'd Die For You*. That had been pretty wonderful.

But she was yawning now, and that got him yawning. They were back on his bed, just sitting, just together. Nora really was the girl he'd told Bianca he was hoping for, someone he could just talk to all day long—or all night—and never want to be anyplace else.

"You know something?" She took his hands in hers. "This is the first time I've been up to your room and we haven't..."

He hadn't even thought about that tonight. They'd been too busy telling embarrassing stories, looking out the window and making fun of their classmates' Halloween costumes, dancing badly to Bon Jovi and just learning more about each other.

"Don't get me wrong," he said. "I—of course I want to, but tonight was pretty great just as it was."

She was still holding his hands. "I feel the same way. I'm really glad I came over tonight. It was special. You're special, Daniel."

"So are you, Nora." She was so much more than special. He wished he knew a word that would describe it, but maybe there *wasn't* a word big enough for her. All he could do was kiss her, and then walk her home.

Who would have thought that tonight would have started out with his girlfriend showing up in the most ridiculous outfit imaginable, progress to him telling a horrible story about his sister, and end without either one of them taking a single item of clothing off and somehow it would be the best night of his life?

Chapter 7

THE LAST WEEK OF FALL SEMESTER—ALBION COLLEGE

Daniel, December 15

Daniel glanced at the calendar as if it might say something different this time. But of course it didn't. Today was still December 15th. Still only five days until he headed home for Christmas break.

Only five days to find the perfect Christmas gift for Nora.

This was why he always tried to do important things well ahead of time. But he'd had two final papers to write, four final exams to study for and a special project to work on for Professor Maddox. And on top of all that, he'd spent two nights helping Anjali and Jeanette cram for their Physics final after they'd come down to the lobby and begged for someone to save them.

On one hand, eight tedious hours over two nights felt kind of like overpayment for the five minutes Anjali had spent ironing his shirt before his first date with Nora. On the other hand, maybe that had been the detail that made everything work, and that made it priceless; eight boring hours with occasional teasing thrown in was an insignificant price to pay.

Either way, those two nights were gone now, and he still had no idea what to buy Nora. Especially with only $20 to spend.

He did have the emergency credit card his father had given him right before he got on the train to come to Albion last year. But how would he explain charging a gift for her, when he hadn't even told his parents he had a girlfriend?

Could he *make* something? Probably not. The last handmade gift he'd given anyone was a bracelet he'd made for his mother in summer camp after third grade. It had been pathetic, even by the low standards of camp crafts produced by eight year olds. The only reason Mom hadn't thrown it away the minute his back was turned, was that Mom never threw anything away, ever.

Except—maybe there was something he could make for her. There, taped up by the window, was the picture strip from the photo booth at the mall. They'd gone right before Thanksgiving, wandered around the mall for three hours, split a Cinnabon, and before the day was over, Nora had insisted on doing the photo booth.

Four shots. She was making devil horns behind his head in the top one. They were kissing in the second one, which didn't look nearly as romantic in a 1.5 inch by 1.5 inch photo as it had felt inside the booth. They were both making silly faces in the fourth one.

But the third one—he remembered that moment. They'd just kissed, and she had pulled away a little from him, and he was staring into her eyes, and she into his, and neither one of them had even noticed the flash going off.

That was the one. He could do something with that. An hour with PageMaker on the Mac over in Addison Hall, and he could blow up that tiny photo and make it into something beautiful. More beautiful. And a nice frame to put it in wouldn't cost much.

If he knew Nora at all—and he really hoped he did—she'd absolutely love it.

♡ ♥ ♡

Nora, exactly the same time

"I've never bought a gift for a boyfriend before. I have no idea what to get him." There had never been an occasion to buy a gift for a guy before. At two months today, her relationship with Daniel was already the longest she'd ever had.

"Calm down, Nora," Rachel said. Her aunt said that a lot. To be fair, Nora gave her a lot of reasons to say it. "I think he'll love whatever you get him, just because it's you giving it to him."

That was probably true. "Yeah. You're right. But it's the first gift I'll be giving him. And he's only had one other girlfriend, and I don't think she ever bought him any gifts, so it'll be the first gift he ever gets from a girl. It can't just be whatever I can find for under $10 at the mall."

She thought she heard Rachel laugh, but maybe it was just noise on the phone line. "So that's your budget? $10?"

That was actually pushing her budget. "Pretty much. What can I get for $10 that'll be special?" Before Rachel could respond, Nora's eye caught on the photo strip pinned to her corkboard. "Never mind. I think I know what to do. And it'll blow some crappy little $10 souvenir from the mall out of the water."

She definitely heard Rachel laugh at that. "I'm almost afraid to ask."

"I'm going to make something for him. Something personal." She talked out the idea with her aunt, and she could picture it taking shape. "It'll be perfect. I just need some art supplies— never mind, I know where to get those, too. I better get started while it's all fresh in my mind. Thanks, Rachel! Love you!"

Before any of the details could fade, Nora sketched it all out in a notebook. It really would be perfect—if Lacey Fitzpatrick down the hall had everything she needed. Lacey was an art major, surely she'd have a full set of colored pencils, and watercolor paints, and art glue, and glitter, and—well, she just had to have everything Nora needed, that's all there was to it.

Daniel, December 17

It ended up taking three hours in PageMaker for Daniel to get the photo perfect. And the assistance of a woman named Kat Miller, who was a professional photojournalist teaching a high-level photography course this semester.

She came into the office, saw what he was doing and asked a lot of questions—really good ones—about the software. Then she'd pointed out that his photo would look very different printed out on the laser printer than it did on the screen; that hadn't even occurred to him. She helped him adjust the hue and saturation of the photo so it would really pop on paper.

"She's a lucky girl. Tell her I said so," she told Daniel when they were finished, and he saw how the enhanced, enlarged photo really *did* pop when it came off the printer.

"Actually, I think I'm the lucky one." The words came out almost automatically.

Kat picked up the photo and studied it thoughtfully. "Maybe you both are."

Nora, December 18

It was almost finished. Nora had used every single thing she'd borrowed from Lacey to create a miniature scrapbook of her and Daniel's relationship—six 5.5 by 8.5 cardstock pages.

On the cover, on top of swirly pastels in watercolor, was the title:

Daniel and Nora: a story in four photos and way too many doodles

She'd drawn a cheeseburger and milkshake, or at least that's what they were meant to be; and the neon sign of the Green Lantern Café, which was more clear, probably thanks to all the straight lines involved.

Inside, the first page had the photo of them kissing, surrounded by little hearts in several colors; a barely-recognizable drawing of a computer monitor; and the front door of Morris Hall. Well, a door, anyway, if you looked close enough and you were feeling generous.

The next page featured the photo of them both making silly faces. She'd decorated that page with an attempt at illustrating her Halloween costume; more hearts; and a very sad effort at drawing one of the little miniature figures from the Battleheads game, or whatever it was called. Daniel had tried to explain it to her, and she was very proud that she'd managed to last five whole minutes before her eyes had glazed over.

The page after that had the photo of her making devil horns behind his head. She'd added quotes around that—the funniest things Daniel had said to her so far. Pride of place went to his review of the trashy romance novel he'd heard her reading from at Turn the Page. "This is the dumbest thing I've ever read, and I've read *Battlefield Earth*, so that should tell you something."

The next to last page held the best of the photos, the one where they were just staring into each other's eyes as though nothing else existed in the world but each other. That's how it felt in the moment. If she was being honest, that's how it felt almost all the time with Daniel.

There were more hearts on that page, in every available color; and the best drawing she'd managed—the two of them, holding hands and smiling like the two happiest people on Earth.

On the last page, she'd used the watercolors again, pastels again. And she'd written, in big letters:

I've never said this before except to blood relatives. And I haven't said it to many of them. But I'm saying it now, and I mean it with all my heart: I love you, Daniel Keller

She added a few more hearts to the last page, then something she hoped he'd recognize as a Christmas wreath.

Perfect. Absolutely perfect.

Daniel, December 19

Between cramming for his last exam, and Nora having three papers to finish, they hadn't had the chance to exchange Christmas gifts, or even more than a few words.

Come to think of it, they hadn't talked about gifts; he didn't know if there was going to be an exchange at all. But it didn't matter. It wasn't important whether or not she'd bought anything for him. It would be enough for her to open his gift, to see how he truly felt about her.

They only had a couple of hours now. "I'm sorry, Daniel," she said when she arrived at the Green Lantern Café and slid into the booth across from him. "I can't stay past ten o'clock. I haven't even started packing, and my train leaves at seven in the morning tomorrow, so I have to be out the door by six."

He wanted to make a joke about leaving things to the last minute, but it wouldn't be funny now. Besides, who was he to talk? He'd put off studying for his Introduction to Operating Systems final until the night before, and he'd be lucky if he managed a C on it.

"I get it," he said. "I'm just glad we have this much time. I—I got something for you. Our family, we always wait until Christmas morning to open all the gifts, but—I guess it's selfish, I want to see you open it."

He handed over the gift. He'd had to buy a whole roll of wrapping paper, and it had felt silly to do that for one present, but if you were going to do something important, it was worth doing it the right way. He'd also spent an hour in the little gift shop next to the used bookshop going back and forth over which frame was the perfect one for the photo.

"That's so sweet," Nora said. He only noticed now that there was a gift-wrapped package stuffed into the top of her purse. So there would be an exchange after all.

"Before you open it, I just have to say something." He hadn't planned on saying it, the words just spilled out, and he couldn't stop. Didn't want to. He needed her to know, even if she probably already did know. "I—I don't know if this is the right time, or the right place, but I have to tell you. I don't want to not see you for three weeks and not say it." She reached a hand across the table, took his. He was right; she already knew what he was going to say. "I love you, Nora. I mean, you probably already knew it. But—there it is. I love you."

She grinned at him. "I know." It took him a heartbeat, maybe two, to comprehend what she'd said, and why. And then he burst into giggles and so did she.

♡ ♥ ♡

Nora, one moment later

Once she'd stopped laughing and came over to Daniel's side of the booth to kiss him—because there was no other response to his words—there was a tiny part of Nora's mind that was disappointed.

She'd wanted to say it first.

Technically, sort of, she had, with his gift. But he hadn't seen it. If you told a tree in the forest you loved it, and there wasn't anyone else around to hear, did it really happen?

But that was ridiculous. Her boyfriend, who was amazing, told her he loved her. There shouldn't be even the tiniest part of her feeling disappointed. Besides, she could tell him right now.

"I know you wanted me to open my gift first, but I think you should open yours." She handed it over, and he took it. He very carefully pried up one edge of the wrapping paper, then slowly pulled it up. She hadn't guessed that he was one of *those* people. Well, nobody was perfect.

It took him a minute to completely unwrap the scrapbook. When he did, his face lit up. "Nora, this is—God, this is so cool!"

"Open it up! Read it!"

He did, and his expression went from joy to—shock, maybe? "You're kidding," he said. "I don't believe it. How could you ... how could we...?" His voice caught before he could finish whatever he was trying to say.

This was not the reaction she'd been expecting. Not remotely. Not after all the work—and love—she'd poured into it. Whatever she was feeling—disappointment? Hurt? Something she didn't even have a name for—must have shown on her face. He reached over, cupped her face in his hands, and there was a pleading look in his eyes. "Nora. Your gift ... it was ... never mind, I don't even know the words. Just, please. Open my gift now, and you'll understand. I promise."

Unlike Daniel, she tore into his wrapping, and—she couldn't believe what she was seeing. How could he—how could they—it was unbelievable. Of course he was stunned when he opened the scrapbook and saw the photo. It *was* unbelievable.

If she'd opened his gift first, she'd have reacted exactly the same.

The same idea. The same photo. Of course it was the same—what else could either of them have done?

"It's the *Gift of the Magi!*" She kissed him again—like before, there was really no other response—and he kissed her back, and they went on doing that for what seemed like a very long time.

Daniel, nearly midnight

They were back outside Morris Hall. It was freezing tonight, but Daniel didn't feel it at all, and he was pretty sure Nora didn't, either. They'd taken forty minutes to make the ten minute walk from the café. Every few steps, one or the other of them had stopped to point out Christmas lights, or a particularly bright star or something else that wasn't actually worth stopping for except that it provided an opportunity for another embrace, another kiss.

"I wish this night didn't have to end," she told him. She'd said almost the same thing after their first date, except there was no last minute packing or early morning train the next day.

Something about that night came back to him. A taste. Why was he thinking of raspberries now?

He leaned close, kissed her again, and he knew. "Your lipstick. That's the same one you wore the first night."

"Oh, my God! It took two months and you finally noticed!" But there was no exasperation in her voice, or her face. Nothing there but joy—and love. "I remember thinking you might not notice even though I spent half an hour in the makeup aisle picking it out just for you, because guys never notice that kind of thing."

"In my defense, there was a lot going on that night. And honestly, there are so many amazing things about you, your lipstick is pretty far down the list."

Now she kissed him, and he kissed her back, and they held each other so close he could feel her heartbeat even through her coat and his.

He didn't want to let her go. Forget even going back to his room; it would be enough to just stay out here with her, kissing her until dawn. Or until they both got frostbite, but even that would be worth it for more time with her.

But there wasn't any choice. They had to be adults about this. It was only three weeks. Well, actually, twenty-three days.

It would be the longest twenty-three days of his life, waiting to see Nora again. To see his girlfriend again. To see the girl—*the woman*—he loved again.

"Daniel, how are we going to manage this? I know it's ridiculous, but I don't want to wait three weeks to see you again. That feels like forever."

Of course she was thinking exactly the same thing he was.

"We can talk on the phone, at least. That's better than nothing." Except, he didn't have her home number in Providence, and she didn't have his in the Bronx.

"Wow, I'm really thick. Give me a pen," he said, and when she dug one out of her purse and handed it to him, he carefully pulled the soft leather glove off her left hand and wrote the number down on her palm.

She tried to hold back laughter. "Aren't you going to tell me to write it in a notebook as soon as I get back to my room?"

He took off his own glove, held his left palm out to her. "Do I need to?"

She wrote her home number down. "No. I don't think either of us need to be told."

He embraced her again, awkwardly with only his right arm, and she did the same. He could only imagine how ridiculous they must look, each holding up their left hand in the air as they kissed one final time before she finally pulled away and headed into the warmth of Morris Hall.

Daniel didn't care if he looked ridiculous. He only cared that in twenty-three days he'd see the woman he loved again.

Part 2

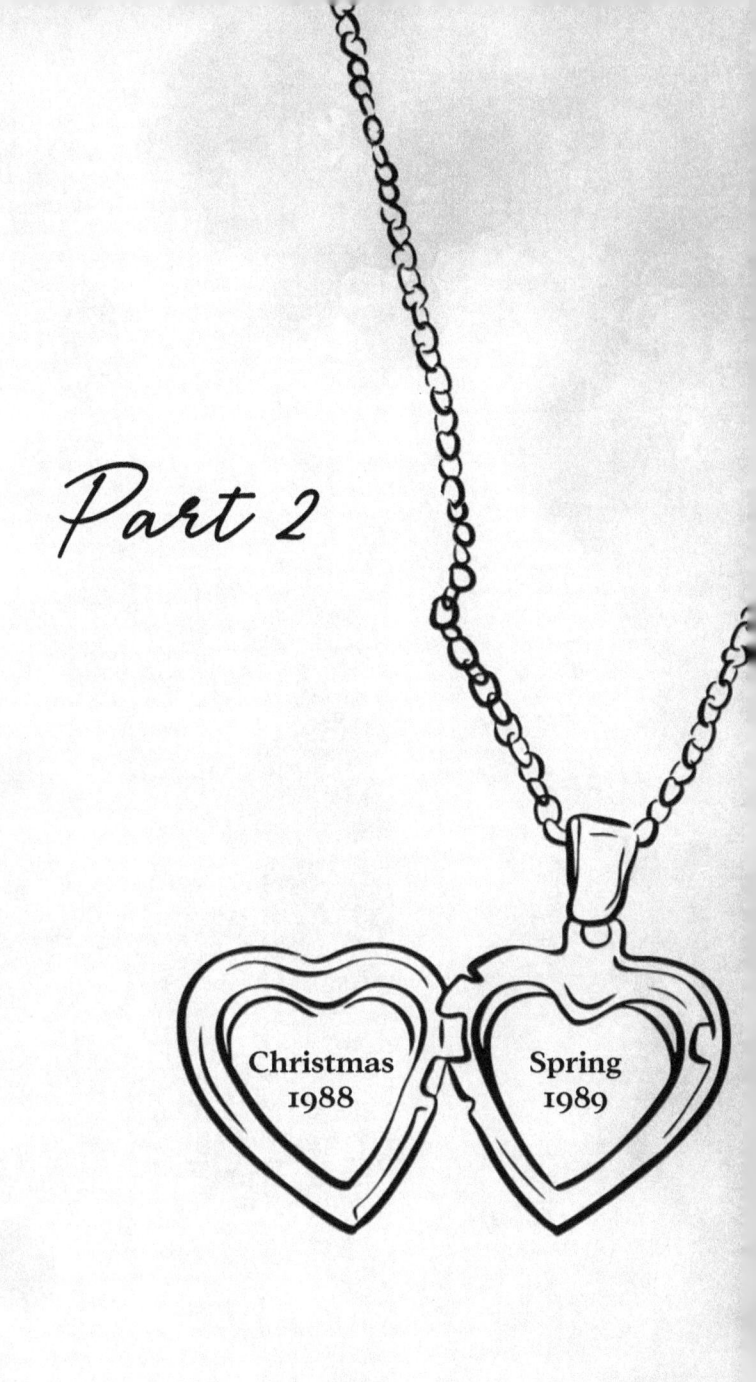

Chapter 8

Nora, December 20th

Nora wondered when her grades would arrive. Her advisor said they wouldn't even be mailed out until after Christmas, but Daniel said his had arrived the same day he got home last year.

She felt good about how she did. She was pretty sure she managed at least a B in even her shakiest class, 20th Century American Lit. Her father—who was paying her tuition—would be satisfied.

How would Daniel grade her, if he had to hand out marks for her performance as a girlfriend? What would his criteria be? Nora tried to picture the report card he'd give her:

Affection: A+
An A+ was very fair. He'd probably grade her even higher on this if there was something above an A+.

Sense of Humor: A–

Nora considered herself very funny, and Daniel always genuinely laughed at her jokes. But on occasion she laughed when maybe it wasn't totally appropriate, and even if Daniel wouldn't count that against her, she had to be honest with herself.

Good Table Manners: B

Daniel never mentioned the Milkshake Incident after it happened (and pretended he hadn't even noticed it in the moment), but if she were him, she'd definitely mark herself down a grade for it.

Intimacy: A+++

Daniel would be grading on a curve here, since he had no basis for comparison, but he had never been less than—well, completely satisfied, to put it as delicately as possible.

Supportiveness: A

He'd probably grade her at A+ for this, but there hadn't really been any occasion where he had truly needed help, so she had to mark herself down just slightly.

Overall, she was—all modesty aside—an A+ girlfriend.

Except—there was one area where she needed some serious remedial work. There were a couple of times when she'd nearly—and, in hindsight, completely irrationally—lost her temper at him. Nora had no illusions that things would be perfect forever with no arguments or difficulties. But at Halloween, and then again last night when they exchanged gifts, she—oh, God.

It only now hit her what she'd done.

She'd done that thing her mother did. The thing she absolutely hated, and one of the (many) things that had driven her parents to divorce. Her mother had a habit of deciding ahead of time exactly what the other person's reaction should be to whatever she was saying or doing, and if the other person didn't respond precisely as Karen Langley thought they should, she'd get nasty almost instantly. Cruel. Hateful, even.

And that's what Nora herself had started to do, when Daniel saw her ridiculous Halloween outfit and instead of laughing or smiling, he'd been reminded of his sister. And again last night, when he'd responded with disbelief at the way they'd used the same photo to make their gifts for each other.

Nora had felt the immediate disappointment—and more— when she didn't get the instant response she expected, just like her mother. And her temper had flared, just like her father.

She'd calmed down right away, and Daniel hadn't said a word— maybe he hadn't even really noticed—but it had happened.

What would happen the next time, if she didn't catch herself, and Daniel did pick up on her sudden anger, and she said something horrible? One wrong word at the wrong moment could undo weeks or months of good things.

There was a reason her mother, in addition to the divorce, didn't have many friends and had strained relationships with a lot of the family.

Even if Daniel wouldn't give her a bad grade in Temper, she had to be honest and mark herself with a big fat D and a "needs improvement."

Daniel, around the same time

Daniel had a companion for the train ride from Grand Central Station home. His neighbor across the street, Jane Barnaby, was a year ahead of him, and attending college in Cleveland. He'd asked what she was doing in Grand Central—he'd have thought she would be flying from Cleveland.

"I actually got home yesterday. I just had lunch with my best friend and her mom downtown."

Jane was pretty, smart, and funny, and Daniel had always assigned her to the category of "Girls I have no possible chance with, so maybe I can talk with them without thinking about if they'd ever go out with me." For the most part, that never really worked the way he'd hoped.

But now, Jane was in a new category: "Girls who aren't Nora." And it was surprisingly easy to talk to her for the forty minutes on the train and the ten minute walk from the Wakefield Metro North station to his house.

She noticed, too. "You seem different, Daniel. You look—I'm not sure, I can't put a finger on it. But I can see it. Whatever it is, maybe you can tell my brother about it, because he needs it for sure."

Jane had a twin brother who was painfully shy—more than Daniel had ever been, which was saying a lot. Daniel answered without really meaning to; the words spilled out. "He just needs to have an amazing girl fall in love with him, that's my secret." Then he cringed; that sounded obnoxious, and also totally unhelpful. "Sorry. I shouldn't have said that."

She clapped him on the shoulder. "Why not? You're a great guy. You deserve it. And,"—she stared critically at him—"that's exactly the difference. I'm happy for you. And for her, too."

Daniel felt a sudden urge to show Jane the scrapbook. He couldn't say why, except that he wanted to share it with *someone*, and there wasn't anyone else. He wasn't going to show it to his parents. Or, God forbid, Lisa. He'd let Bianca see it, except she wasn't going to be here for Christmas.

Why not show it to Jane? "Can I show you something? I feel like I'm going to burst if I don't talk about it with somebody." She nodded, and he pulled it out of his backpack, handed it gingerly to her.

"Wow," she said, after she'd looked through it. "I've never felt—there's nobody I'd do something like this for. This girl is a keeper, Daniel."

He smiled the rest of the ride home, and the walk from the station, and into his house. Nobody seemed to be home, even though his father's car was parked in the driveway. He made enough of a racket between dragging his suitcase inside and the front door slamming shut—Dad still hadn't fixed it—that anyone anywhere in the house should have heard him, so where was everyone?

He went into the kitchen to fix himself a snack, and he was still smiling when he came back out with a peanut butter sandwich.

There his parents were, and they weren't smiling. His father had a slip of paper in his hand, and he waved it at Daniel. "What happened, son? These are not the grades we expect from you." Daniel felt the smile disappear off his face at his father's words.

Nora, an hour later

Nora walked out of the station and into the biting wind, looking for her father. She couldn't see the silver Honda anywhere. He had his faults—quite a few—but lateness was not one of them. She couldn't ever recall a time when he was supposed to be somewhere for her and he wasn't there.

"Hey, Pumpkin!" Apparently he was here. But where? His car was nowhere to be found.

"Over here! Follow my voice!" It was difficult to tell exactly where it was coming from between the wind and the sounds of the traffic. But then she thought—yes, there! She saw him at last, leaning out the window of—what the hell was he driving?

It was red. Bright, candy-apple red. And it was a sports car. A convertible; she could see the soft fabric roof as she walked over.

"What do you think, Pumpkin?"

What Nora wanted to say was, "You could just have printed 'I'm having a mid-life crisis' on a T-shirt and saved a lot of money." She almost did say it, but she was caught short by the sight of someone in the passenger seat. A woman. A very blonde woman. A very blonde woman who looked far too young to be with her father.

"Looks great, Dad!" She tried her best to sound enthusiastic, but it was difficult. The blonde couldn't be more than thirty years old, and probably closer to twenty-five. She was smiling brightly at Nora. "Hi," she said to—she assumed—her father's new girlfriend.

"Hi, Nora! I'm Joelle. Your father's told me so much about you, but it's so cool to finally meet you in person!" She got out of the car, and somehow folded herself into the back seat without even reclining the front seat. If nothing else, she was definitely flexible. "You get up front with your father, I know he's been missing you."

Joelle. What kind of a name was that? Was she even really blonde? What was she doing with her father? Why would she want to date someone who had a kid nearly as old as her?

"Thanks, I appreciate it."

Nora obediently climbed into the passenger seat and they were off. Her father asked her two or three questions about school, and then the conversation turned to Joelle, and what college had been like for her, and Nora barely got another word the whole drive. She hadn't exactly been looking forward to a long, awkward conversation with her father—but that would've been way better than listening to him fawn over a woman who was, like, ten minutes older than her.

Twenty-two days. Twenty-two days and she'd be with Daniel again, and they could laugh about this. As long as she didn't reach for the steering wheel to drive them into traffic just so her father would shut up about his new barely-legal girlfriend. She could tolerate this for a few more minutes. Couldn't she?

Daniel, around the same time

"I'm not saying these marks are terrible, Daniel. Just that we know you can do better." His father had been going on for almost ten minutes now.

"I understand, Dad. I just—I guess I was a little distracted over finals week. I'll do better next term." He hadn't mentioned Nora. He hadn't had the chance to mention much of anything.

"I know you will, son. I just,"—his father put an arm around his mom—"we just want you to get ahead in life. We saved up—I'm not saying this to make you feel bad—we saved for years so you and your sister could get a good education. So you'd have a better start in life than we did."

He knew all that. And he *did* appreciate it. More than his parents knew, probably. And if that was true, it was on him for not making sure they knew. Then again, big emotional declarations were not a regular feature in the Keller household.

"I know, Dad. You and Mom have done everything for me. Maybe I don't tell you enough, but I'm really grateful for it. And I won't waste it." He tried to put everything he felt for his parents into that, and it seemed to work.

His father clapped him on the shoulder, smiling. "That's all we ask, son. Now why don't you go upstairs, get unpacked, and we'll all go out to dinner. Okay?"

Dinner probably meant Dad's favorite Italian place over on Lincoln Avenue. Maybe over greasy pizza and a family-size bowl full of mussels, he'd find the nerve to tell them he had a girlfriend.

Maybe.

Nora, a few minutes later

Nora's father and Joelle took her to her favorite pizza place for lunch. Well, it *had* been her favorite pizza place when she was a kid. She hadn't been there since her thirteenth birthday party, but at least Dad remembered she'd liked it once upon a time. That counted for something, she supposed.

She spent the first few minutes suppressing every snarky remark and cynical comment that came to mind about her father dating Joelle. It wasn't her fault, and she seemed like a genuinely nice person.

Nora's mind was so busy controlling her sarcasm that her self-control slipped in another way. When her father asked if any of the boys at college had caught her eye, she didn't even realize she'd said Daniel's name out loud until Joelle suddenly perked up.

"Who's Daniel?" Joelle asked, all wide-eyed curiosity.

She heard herself talking in a faraway voice. "He's the best. He's so sweet, and he's smart, and he thinks I'm funny, and he has the *prettiest* eyes." As she spoke, Nora felt her hand rummaging through her backpack—why had she even brought it into the restaurant?—to pull out his Christmas gift. "See what I mean?"

Joelle took the photo frame out of her hands and examined it critically "He really does have pretty eyes, you're right. And who took the picture? It looks almost professional."

"It was from one of those photo booths, you know, with the little tiny strip of pictures?" Joelle nodded. Her father just sat there, an unreadable expression on his face. "And Daniel took that little tiny picture, and he used the computer to do his magic. He enlarged it and cleaned it up and—I don't even know what else he did. He made it perfect."

"I think he's a keeper, Nora," Joelle said, handing the photo to Nora's father. "See, Richard? See how she's looking at him? That's exactly the way you look at me sometimes. Like father, like daughter. Isn't that cool?"

Nora did not think that was cool.

What she did think was that the queasy sensation she was feeling had nothing to do with the four pieces of pizza in her stomach.

Daniel, bedtime

Daniel didn't tell his parents about Nora at dinner. He'd just about worked up the nerve to talk about her on the drive over to the restaurant. But then Lisa showed up right after they were seated, and that was that.

His sister talked almost nonstop through the entire meal, and dessert. He heard more than he ever wanted to know about her new job, and how annoying her boss was ("She has a voice like Minnie Mouse! How can she not hear herself?"), and the poor hygiene habits of the weird girl she was sharing an apartment with ("She clips her nails in the tub and leaves them there! Who does that?") and every other absurdly detailed aspect of her life.

He supposed he should be grateful to her for taking the spotlight away from him for the evening. But at the same time he was curious why Lisa was so talkative. She'd never been like this before. He remembered countless family dinners where his parents had to pry the tiniest nuggets of information out of her as if she was a mussel that refused to open up.

Daniel wondered if having a weird, unclean roommate had made Lisa appreciate her family more. If she couldn't talk at home, and she couldn't talk to new coworkers she didn't trust yet, well, everything she was feeling had to come out *somewhere*. Maybe—he wasn't making any promises, not even in his own head—he'd try to talk to her over the break. Really talk to her, like siblings ought to be able to do.

Maybe he should have done that a long time ago.

By the time they got home, it was almost ten o'clock, and he yawned theatrically once they were back in the house. "Go, I bet you can't wait to sleep in your own bed again," his mother said. "But you're not off the hook, Daniel. I know you must have had some fun in between all your classes, and I want to hear all about it tomorrow."

Fine. Tomorrow he'd tell them about Nora. Maybe.

In the meantime, Mom was right. He couldn't wait to sleep in a proper queen bed, with super-comfortable sheets, and his 1986 Super Bowl Champions pennant on the wall.

And one thing that was new. Nora's scrapbook under his pillow, so she'd be with him when he fell asleep, and with him when he woke up in the morning.

♡ ♥ ♡

Nora, a couple of hours earlier

Her father dropped Nora off at his apartment. "You probably need a nap. Go get yourself settled in, and I'll take Joelle home and then you can tell me all about school when I get back," he said.

"Okay, Dad," she said, trying to put a bit of enthusiasm into her voice. She didn't really succeed. Maybe she'd be lucky and he'd take his time with his new girlfriend, and by the time he returned, she actually would be sleeping.

Before that, though, she felt like she needed to call her mother. They hadn't made any firm arrangements for Christmas break. Karen Langley did not like to plan anything in advance. "Not even for me," Nora muttered to herself as she dialed the phone. It took her mother eight rings to pick up.

"Nora?"

"Hi, Mom. I'm home—uh—back in Providence."

"I assume Richard picked you up. Did you see his new toy?"

Nora didn't know if her mother was referring to the Corvette, or Joelle. She didn't want to know.

She couldn't think of any safe way to answer the question, so she just ignored it. "Dad did pick me up, and he took me out for pizza. But maybe we can have dinner tonight?" Nora forced as much good cheer as possible into the question. She hated how things were with her mother, and Mom wasn't going to change, so it was up to Nora to try and build some kind of bridge.

"Let me think," her mother said, and Nora sighed. It would be easier to build a bridge if her mother wasn't a moving target. "I'm having dinner with Jean-Paul." She waited, presumably for some protest from Nora, but Nora knew better than that. "He's a charter boat captain. You'll like him. He's a lovely man. I met him on that brunch cruise back in October. Let me call him and see what he thinks, and I'll call you back."

Her father introducing her to a new girlfriend was quite enough for one day. Nora couldn't deal with meeting her mother's new boyfriend, too. "No, Mom. It's fine. Maybe tomorrow night? You can call and let me know." The bridge she wanted to build was already burning, and she hadn't even laid down the first—whatever the hell it was that you used to build a bridge.

So she just hung up.

Daniel, December 21

Daniel had forgotten how nice it was to shower in a normal bathroom, where there weren't eight stalls and guys coming in and out all the time. He took his time, enjoying the peace and quiet, dried himself off, put on his bathrobe and walked back to his bedroom.

His mother was sitting on his bed. She had the scrapbook in her hands.

"Mom? What are you doing?" The words came out before he could catch them. At least they didn't sound too panicked, or accusatory.

"I was just getting your laundry together and straightening up your bed, and—it was right there." He couldn't tell what she was thinking; her expression was somehow pleased, sad, and hurt all at the same time. He wasn't sure if she knew herself, and she took a moment to gather her thoughts before she spoke again. "I wish you felt like you could tell us about this girl." She needed another moment before she could continue. "Nora. You're supposed to—Daniel, when you feel something this strongly, you shouldn't keep it inside. I can see from the pictures that you love her. And if she made this, she loves you, too."

"I'm sorry, Mom." He felt—could you be both relieved and more worried than ever, at the same time? "I—I don't even know why I didn't tell you about her. I guess I was afraid of what you'd say. What you'd think. I know how hard you worked so I could go to college, I didn't want you to think I wasn't taking it seriously, that I was just there having a good time."

Now she just looked hurt. "That's your father, Daniel. I would never say that. I wouldn't think it. The only thing I care about is that she treats you right. You're a good boy." She took a breath, then another. "A good *man*. And you deserve a girl—no, a woman. It's hard to say that. You'll understand one day. You deserve a woman who loves you with all her heart." Now she stood and walked over to him, hugged him. "I know after that girl from St. Barnabas, you've been so lonely. I know how much you hurt. I hated that for you."

He never talked about any of that to his parents, or his sister. And Bianca wouldn't have told them; she'd never betray his confidence like that. But he'd never needed to say it, had he? It was all right there, plain as day to anybody with a pair of eyes. Of course his mother would have known how he felt.

"I'm so sorry, Mom. I—I didn't think you saw all that. But that was pretty stupid, wasn't it?"

Now, finally, she laughed. "Daniel Joseph Keller, you really can be dense sometimes. But like I said, you'll understand when you have children of your own. You never stop hurting for them, or wishing you could fix everything with a Band-Aid and a choc- olate Frosty like I did when you were small."

Out of nowhere, the thought came to him: if he and Nora ever had a baby, what would he look like? Which one of them would she take after? What would they do when that hypothetical child got hurt?

His mother patted his head. "When your time comes, whenever that is, you'll know what to do. That's something I can promise you." How had she known what he was thinking?

Because she was his mother, and she always knew. Maybe he should have trusted that more.

Nora, the same time

"Nora? Are you home from school?"

After the conversation with her mother, Nora considered opening up her father's liquor cabinet with the key he thought was cleverly hidden, and drinking enough vodka to forget all about her parents' love lives.

She'd thought better of it, though. Once the hangover passed, Joelle and Jean-Paul would still be there, plus Dad would be livid. So she called Aunt Rachel instead.

"I wish I wasn't. Did you know Dad has a new girlfriend? And she's barely out of high school?"

Rachel didn't quite laugh. "Yeah. She's a year younger than me. That was a surprise. But I'll tell you something, I think she really cares about him."

"Maybe." Nora didn't want to admit it, but she had gotten that same feeling from Joelle. She still didn't want to be a party to it. "And my mother's got somebody, too. I just—I can't do this, Rachel. Can I come down and spend Christmas with you?"

There was no hesitation at all. "Of course, honey. Except—it won't be with me. I've got to fly out tomorrow night. There's a crisis in the London office, and apparently only I can handle it."

Well, that sucked. Still—all alone in Rachel's apartment in Manhattan, or a third wheel with both of her parents and their new partners?

Wait—Manhattan was part of New York City. And so was the Bronx.

Where Daniel's house was.

"Can I come anyway? I don't mind staying by myself."

Now there was hesitation. "I don't think you ever told me where your boyfriend lives, Nora."

She'd blurted it out too fast. Of course Rachel guessed what she was thinking. "He's in the Bronx."

"Nora Kathleen Langley, you have to promise me. On your honor. If I let you stay in my apartment, that boy doesn't stay over."

"Daniel."

"Daniel doesn't stay over. Do you promise?"

Nora thought about crossing her fingers. Or just saying whatever Rachel wanted to hear and ignoring it when the moment came. But she couldn't. Even if Rachel wouldn't find out, she couldn't lie to her like that. Anyway, it would be enough to see Daniel without having him up to the apartment. It would be more than enough.

"I promise, Rachel. Thank you so much!"

Chapter 9

Daniel, December 21, early afternoon

Daniel was sitting in his bedroom, thinking about everything his mother had said, for—God, was it really two hours?

It wasn't just Mom's words that were going round and round in his mind. There was also the sudden, crazy idea that had popped into his head while they were talking—a baby? With Nora? Where had something like that come from? Neither he nor Nora had said a word about the future. He was only nineteen, she was just eighteen, he wouldn't even graduate for two and a half years!

It was because Mom had gotten him so emotional, and she was talking about parenthood and stuff. That made sense. It wasn't even his own thought, really. He could just forget it, he never needed to think about it again. Nice and easy.

It probably wasn't going to be nice and easy when he went downstairs, though. His mother would have told his father about Nora. Obviously she would have. And Dad would have something to say about it, especially with his grades. Which weren't even that bad. Yes, it was mostly B's with only one A, rather than mostly A's with a couple of B's as it had been last year. But that was still solid, he only needed to maintain a 3.0 GPA to keep his partial scholarship and he was well above that.

However much he didn't want to be lectured, he had to go downstairs sooner or later. He might as well get it over with. And, anyway, his stomach was rumbling, and the kitchen was downstairs, too.

He took a deep breath, headed out of his bedroom, down the stairs and into the living room and, sure enough, Dad was sitting in his recliner with a very stern expression.

"I guess we know why your grades slipped, don't we?" His father had never been one for small talk. At least you never had to doubt where you stood with him.

"It's not like that, Dad." Except, obviously, it was. His father wasn't stupid, and Daniel had learned as a young boy that excuses didn't impress him. "Okay—I've been spending a lot of time with Nora. I didn't study as much as I could have before finals."

His father nodded, but his frown didn't ease up at all. "You're nineteen years old, Daniel. You're not a high school boy with his first crush. You're smarter than that. You should be able to get your schoolwork done without letting this girl get in the way."

"Her name is Nora, Dad. And she's never in the way. She's—I love her, Dad. And she loves me."

He knew as he was saying the words they were only going to make this worse. "Daniel! You're there to get an education, to get your degree, to be able to get a good job so you don't have to fight for every inch of life the way me and your mother had to. We're not paying all that money for you to play house with some little—"

"Shut up, Dad!" Daniel hadn't really understood the expression "seeing red" until this moment. He'd never said anything like that to his father before, never heard the raw anger in his voice that he said it with. "Don't you call her—I don't even care what you were going to say. You don't know her! You don't know how amazing she is! You don't know how she looks at me, how she sees past how nervous and uptight and whatever the hell else I am, and she loves me anyway! How she didn't even care that I ..."

His voice trailed off; even having lost nearly all control of his emotions, he knew enough not to finish that sentence.

His father wasn't frowning anymore. He looked shellshocked, but that probably wouldn't last long. Thankfully, his mother picked this moment to come running in from the kitchen, and she stood behind Dad, talking to him in a soft voice; Daniel's heart was pounding too loudly for him to hear what she was saying.

And then the phone rang, and Daniel was both thrilled and terrified that it might be Nora calling.

Nora, at the same time

Rachel had gone well above the call of duty. She'd cashed in frequent flyer miles to pay for Nora to fly to New York. She'd arranged a car to pick Nora up from LaGuardia. And she'd even called Nora's father and made it sound like the out-of-the-blue trip was her idea, while omitting entirely the little detail that she wouldn't be there and Nora would be all alone in Manhattan.

And now, here she was, in Rachel's gorgeous two bedroom apartment overlooking Central Park. It had never before occurred to her to wonder how on earth her aunt could afford this place. But a semester of being—sort of, anyway—on her own and having to watch her budget carefully had opened her eyes to a few of the realities of adult life.

She could ask Rachel about that some other time. Right now, something far more urgent took priority. She didn't even bother to put her suitcase away before she picked up the phone to call her boyfriend.

It only rang once. "Daniel?"

A woman answered. Her voice sounded older—it had to be his mother. "He's right here, I'll put him on."

A moment later, she heard him. His voice was shaky, what was going on in his house? "Hello?" Maybe he was just nervous about talking to her in front of his mother. That made sense. Especially if he hadn't told them yet that he had a girlfriend. But surely he had, by now. Right? Or—did he not want to talk to her for some reason of his own?

"It's me!" She couldn't hold her excitement in. "And, guess what? I'm in Manhattan! We can get together!" They were only twelve miles apart—she'd measured it on a map.

"Really?" He was still—what? Nervous? Upset? Had he told his parents, and they had a problem with her? Well, not with her specifically, but with the idea of Daniel having a girlfriend at all. Then she heard him breathe deeply, and she could picture exactly how he looked. His eyes always got all serious when he was gathering up his courage to do or say something really hard. "Do you want to come over and meet my parents today?"

She could hear a low, angry voice that she couldn't quite make out—his father? And then Daniel talking back to him, which she heard perfectly clearly. "You can see for yourself I'm not wasting my time or throwing away my future, okay? I never ask for anything, but I'm asking for this. I want you to meet her so you'll love her as much as I do." There was more low talking, both his father and his mother, and then he was talking into the phone again. "I know it's short notice, but I really want you to meet them, if it's okay with you."

It wasn't really okay. She wanted to see him, more than anything. And she did want to meet his parents. But not under duress—was that even the right word? Whatever the word was, it didn't change the feeling.

If she said no, though, that would be worse. Then in addition to whatever his parents thought about her already, she'd be flaky and unsupportive of their son. *And* she'd be leaving Daniel to face all that disapproval on his own.

On the train home, she'd graded herself with an A for being supportive to Daniel, even though he'd never needed her to support him. Well, here was her chance to earn that A.

"I would love to meet them. Just tell me how to get there."

Daniel, two hours later

Daniel thought about driving over to the Metro North station, to spare Nora the ten minute walk back to his house. But he wanted that walk and that ten minutes to warn her about his parents—well, his father mostly.

Except she had to already know. She must have heard him yelling at his parents, and even if she didn't catch every word, it was hardly difficult to figure out what was going on.

He only had to wait a couple of minutes for the train to arrive, and—down at the end of the platform, stepping out of the last car, there she was. She wore her heavy blue winter coat, the one she said she rarely wore because "I can barely move my arms in it, like the little brother in 'A Christmas Story.'"

He ran to her, threw his arms around her and kissed her, right there on the platform, in front of—well, nobody, she was the only one who'd gotten off the train. But he would have kissed her in front of everyone on the train, or 56,000 people in Yankee Stadium. He didn't let her go until she pulled back to gasp for air.

"Wow," she said, still catching her breath, but smiling brightly—the smile that was just for him. "I missed you too, Daniel. Even if it's only been two days." He led her back to the stairs up to the street, and gently pushed her ahead of him. "What, you're not going to hold my hand?"

He laughed. "My father told me once, a gentleman always walks behind a woman going up stairs like these."

"Why?" He could picture her eyes rolling as she asked the question.

"So you'll feel me behind you, to help support you. And so if you fall anyway, you'll land on me instead of the concrete."

She burst into giggles. "You're kidding."

He had to laugh, too. "No. That's what he said."

"Well, it is kind of chivalrous," she said once they got up to street level. "Gruesome, but chivalrous." Then he did take her hand. "Speaking of gruesome, what exactly am I walking into?"

He told her, leaving nothing out except for his momentary insane thought about babies. As he said it, he had to admit that everything would have gone better if he'd told his parents about Nora before he got home.

Or well before that.

Maybe not after the first date, but definitely after the second. Not telling them made it seem like he knew she was hurting his grades and he was lying to them by omission.

She hesitated for a moment when he finished. Then she asked, very quietly, "*Did* I distract you? Did you get worse grades because of me?"

No! Absolutely not.

Probably not.

"Well, I guess if I'd had another few hours to study for my Discrete Mathematics final, I might have gotten an A instead of a B."

She was silent for a couple of minutes. "But you made my gift instead."

"That was more important."

She stopped right in the middle of the sidewalk. "You really mean that, don't you?"

"Yeah. Of course." He willed her to believe it, but that wasn't necessary. She didn't just believe it—she *knew* it. "But maybe let's not tell my father about that."

Nora, fifteen minutes later

Nora's first impression of Daniel's house was that it felt comfortable. Like it was a good place—a *safe* place—for a kid to grow up in.

She'd never lived anywhere that felt that way. Even staying with Rachel never felt that way, because she knew it was always temporary and before long she'd have to go back to her parents and their endless sniping at each other.

Her first impression of his parents was less comforting. Daniel was holding her hand when they walked in the front door, and she saw the flash of—suspicion? Anger?—on his father's face, gone as quickly as it appeared, replaced by a smile that barely made it halfway to his eyes. And then Daniel's mother ran over to her and hugged her, which was definitely better than suspicion or anger, but not what she'd been expecting, either.

"Nora, it's so nice to meet you. Here, take off your coat, come into the living room. Tony will get the fire going, that'll warm you right up." His mother gave her an approving nod when she saw what Nora was wearing: a dark blue blouse and a skirt down nearly to her ankles, both borrowed from Rachel's closet. Neither was really her style, and the blouse was half a size too big, but she'd been right that demure was totally the way to go.

She proceeded into the living room, where there indeed was a fireplace, with family photos atop the mantel. While Daniel's father worked on getting the fire started, Nora peered at the photos.

There was a black and white picture, faded with age. A wedding photo, probably of Daniel's grandparents, but she couldn't guess whether they were maternal or paternal. Next to it was another wedding photo—his parents. She leaned in to examine it more closely. A thought came immediately into her head, and she squashed it just as quickly: *Wow, you used to be hot, Mr. Keller!*

Maybe she'd tell Daniel about that later. Or maybe she'd take that particular thought to her grave. But there was no denying the fact that his father had been very handsome.

The photo was sad, though, the more she looked at it. His parents weren't really looking at each other, and neither of them looked as happy as people were supposed to at their wedding.

And then there was a photo of Daniel, probably four or five years old, with a little girl who looked to be seven or eight. She had to be his sister. They were splashing around together in a swimming pool.

"Yeah," Daniel said, when he saw what she was looking at. "Cute picture, right? Nobody took a picture of her holding me underwater five minutes later." But he said it with a laugh, and she heard the warmth there, too. She already knew how much he cared about his sister, even if he'd never admit it directly. His story about her back on Halloween said everything that needed to be said.

"That was fifteen years ago, Daniel," his mother said. "I think you can let it go already." She was laughing, too. Even his father chuckled.

"There!" The fireplace was crackling with a small, but growing fire. Nora clapped in approval.

"Nice job! We had a fireplace in the apartment we lived in when I was in grade school, but my dad could never get it going." She turned to Daniel, lowering her voice to a whisper, "I learned every curse word there is by the time I was seven, from him yelling at that stupid fireplace."

"Tell my Dad what you just said," Daniel said out loud. "It'll make him feel better."

Nora had no idea what that could mean, but she did as her boyfriend asked, and—Daniel was right—his father shook his head and grinned. "This one here," he reached over and ruffled Daniel's hair, "learned them all from me and my neighbor across the street watching the Giants. We thought they couldn't hear us—Daniel and his kids—until Mrs. Parlato down the street heard the three of them cursing up a storm walking to school one morning and she ran over here to complain. I never saw an old woman run that fast in my life. And I couldn't even punish Daniel, because he didn't have any idea what any of the words meant."

That was too cute. Nora could picture little first grade Daniel saying the foulest language to his little friends with a big smile on his face.

"Dad! She's never going to let me live that down now."

"You're the one who made me tell her the story," his father said. And just like that, she felt her shoulders relax, her breath come more easily. All the tension she'd been feeling drained right out of the room.

Daniel, two hours later

It had gone better than Daniel had dared hope. Nora had been a little uncomfortable at first, but she relaxed when Dad told the story about inadvertently teaching him how to curse. Everything had been easier after that. And both his parents seemed to really like her.

How could they not? What was there not to like?

His mother even invited her to Christmas dinner on Saturday. "It'll be a full house," she'd said. "Lisa's coming with her roommate, and my sister, and Tony's brother and his wife and the Barnabys across the street. Everyone'll be too busy arguing over whose gravy is best to interrogate you like we did tonight. So you can just come and enjoy yourself, Nora."

Nora had gratefully accepted.

After dessert and coffee, Daniel drove Nora back to the train station. The only thing she'd asked him on the way there was, "You invite your neighbors to Christmas dinner?"

He sighed. "Mrs. Barnaby died a couple of years ago. Right before Jane and George—they're the ones Dad taught to curse along with me—right before they went away to college. She was in a wreck. It was a drunk driver."

Even now, two years later, he shuddered. It could have been his Mom, or Dad or his sister. Or him. It was just dumb luck that it had been Mrs. Barnaby at the wrong intersection that morning.

"That's horrible," Nora whispered. He felt her arm slipping around him as he pulled into the parking lot.

"Yeah. The whole street looks after them now. Somebody invites them for every holiday. Everybody knows everybody around here. We all look out for each other, you know?"

Nora made a quiet, pained sound he hadn't heard from her before. Then, after a moment, "I wish I knew that. Is that how you learned—I don't know, how to be how you are? How to care about me?"

He pulled into a parking space, turned off the car, and leaned over to hug her. "Maybe," he said. "But I think even if I grew up somewhere else, I would have known how to care about you. I look at you, and there's nothing I want to do except make you happy."

She kissed him, and he kissed her back, and in moments the windows began to fog. If she touched him now—really *touched* him—they'd end up in the backseat, uncomfortable seatbelt buckle or not.

But she didn't. Her willpower held. So did his.

"Daniel, I wish ..."

"So do I."

Thank God it was freezing out. It was a good distraction from what they both wanted so desperately.

He walked her down the stairs, this time in front of her. "Same logic, right?" she teased. "I fall, you cushion my landing?"

"Something like that,"

They didn't talk for a while after that. They just stood there on the platform, wrapped in each other's arms, until the train arrived.

"I'll call you when I get back to Rachel's apartment," she said. "Just so you know I'm safe. And—let's do something tomorrow. You're the native New Yorker, your call."

She stepped inside the train, blew him a kiss before the doors shut and he jogged down the platform, waving at her until she disappeared from view.

Chapter 10

Nora, December 23

"This was your idea, Daniel! You can't chicken out now."

Nora wanted to laugh at him, because he really was being ridiculous. But he was also honestly frightened. If the skittish look in his eye didn't prove it, the way his hands were shaking definitely did.

"I know. I really thought I could do it, until I put the skates on." She'd had to lace them up, because he wasn't tying them nearly tight enough.

"Don't you trust me? I said I'd help teach you how to skate."

She'd been surprised when he suggested ice skating at Rockefeller Center because he'd never done it before. But as he'd explained, "Isn't that how everybody is? When you live somewhere, you put off all the touristy stuff near you because you can always go there tomorrow, and then one day you realize you never did go at all." She'd never considered that, but it was true. How many of the big tourist attractions back home had she actually seen? Not many.

He'd also mentioned that she'd probably look really cute in a skating outfit. She'd picked out a dark green sweater from Rachel's closet, a knee-length black skirt from her suitcase and a pair of leggings she'd left at Rachel's two years ago and forgotten about until this morning. And she did, immodest as it was to say, look very cute.

Right now, though, her main concern was getting Daniel on the ice. She stood, quickly finding her balance on her own skates, took his hand and tried to pull him up. He wasn't budging.

"I trust you with my heart, Nora. But not with my ankles."

Well, at least he was trying to joke. That was progress.

"Daniel, I worry about your body as much as your heart, or have you forgotten that?" That snapped him to attention. She debated her next words for a moment. When she said them, it was in her sweetest, most innocent voice. "And you remember how quickly you learn when I'm teaching you, right?" His eyes went all unfocused for a moment, and she knew exactly where his mind had gone.

Maybe it was playing dirty, but it worked, because he blinked a few times and then stood up himself, barely relying on her touch to help him balance on his skates.

It took a little more coaxing to actually get him on the ice, and a lot more to convince him to let go of the wall and just trust his own balance and her hand to keep him upright. But he finally did.

And afterwards, sitting in the little café beside the rink and enjoying a hot chocolate, he said, "My ankles are killing me. But it was totally worth it. I guess I really can trust you with all of me."

Daniel, December 24

"Is this the movie theater you told me about?" Nora had asked to do something indoors today, after ice skating outdoors yesterday.

Daniel knew exactly what his girlfriend meant. "Yeah." The only difference between now and two and a half years ago was that they were parked a lot closer to the theater than he and Peggy had been. He didn't want to make Nora walk across a slushy parking lot. Besides, it was the middle of the day and the windows of Dad's car weren't tinted, so even if they'd both wanted to, they couldn't really get up to much.

She was thinking along the same lines; her head was turned, she was gazing at the back seat. But she finally shook her head and turned back to him. "Shall we go?"

"Sure." He got out of the car, came around to the passenger side and opened her door. He grabbed her as she got out, just in case she stumbled on a bit of ice. "But are you sure you really want to see *Working Girl*?"

"Yes! It looked really fun from the preview. And Harrison Ford is hot."

But two hours later, it was clear that *Working Girl* had been the wrong choice. Nora was sniffling for the last fifteen or twenty minutes of the movie, and she began crying—sobbing, honestly— by the time they were outside and walking through the parking lot. Daniel had no clue what had upset her.

It wasn't until they were almost back to the car that she finally spoke. "He was just like my Dad! Why didn't you tell me the movie was about a guy dating somebody half his age?"

Daniel started to say that he'd had no idea what the movie was about, so how could he have known? But then he replayed her words, and things started to make sense.

She'd told him her parents were divorced, but she'd never said very much about them beyond that.

And she hadn't been planning to come to New York over Christmas. She'd believed they wouldn't see each other for twenty-three days as surely as he had. So something had to have changed when she got home.

When she got home to her father.

Her divorced father. Who was probably dating Melanie Griffith.

Well, obviously not Melanie Griffith, but someone as young as her. And when Nora found out about her father's new girl-friend—or maybe actually met her—she couldn't deal with it, so she called her Aunt and begged to be allowed to stay with her in New York.

It all sounded very logical, but he was pretty sure logic wasn't what Nora needed right now. "I'm sorry," he said. "Let's get back to the car and we can drive over to Wendy's and get you a choc-olate Frosty and we can talk about it."

"How will that help?" She nearly shouted it.

"Trust me. I always felt better after my Mom got me a Frosty, no matter what was wrong. I trusted you yesterday with the ice skating. You can trust me now."

Nora, December 25

"I'm sorry about yesterday," Nora said, sitting down on Daniel's bed. It was really comfortable.

He sat down next to her. "There's nothing to be sorry for." With his arm around her, looking around at his childhood bedroom, she could almost make herself believe it.

Almost. "Yes, there is. And not just yesterday. I should have told you about my Dad. And my Mom. And a lot of other stuff. You told me so many personal things. So many secrets. All this stuff that had to be so hard to talk about. And I haven't." Maybe Christmas day, with Daniel's family and his neighbors waiting downstairs, wasn't the time to talk about all her family baggage. Or maybe that was just another excuse not to trust her boyfriend with seeing parts of herself that she wasn't very proud of. There'd always be some reason not to be honest with him.

"Nora, you don't have to talk about things that are hard, or that hurt. If you want to, I'm here, and you know I love you. But it's up to you what you do or don't share. Not me."

She put her arms around him, kissed him quickly, but she pulled away before he could kiss her back. They were in his childhood bedroom. And the door was open. Anybody could come walking by and see them.

"Sorry. I shouldn't have—this isn't the right time for that." She took a moment to collect herself. "Anyway. I do want to share. I just ... I'm not real happy with how ... with the way I ended up at Rachel's." She took his hands in hers, squeezed them, and he squeezed back. That helped. It gave her the strength to tell it all.

How ugly her parents' divorce was. How she'd started acting out—sneaking off to parties, drinking, meeting boys, all of it—just so she could have something to feel besides how much she hurt when her parents kept hurting each other. How she'd learned about both Joelle and Jean-Paul within a couple of hours of getting home from school. How she came down to Rachel's apartment even though Rachel wasn't there. How lonely her apartment was at night.

Daniel listened to all of it, never looking away, never letting go of her. When she was finished, he hugged her, tighter than he ever had, and then he got up and went to his closet. She heard him grunt as he got on tippy-toes and searched around for something on the top shelf. He came back with an old, ratty teddy bear. She guessed its fur had been a rich brown once upon a time, but it was a sad beige now. Daniel had to have had the bear from kindergarten. Or maybe even before that. She wondered when he'd stopped sleeping with it and exiled it to the closet.

If she asked, he'd tell her. But she was never going to.

"I can't do anything about your parents, or all the awful stuff you had to go through. But, here." He handed the bear to her. "That's Mr. Fuzzles. I want you to have him. Take him back with you to your Aunt's place, and maybe you'll feel a little less lonely."

Before she could answer—and thank God, because the only answer she could think of was kissing him like she'd never kissed him before—there was a knock on the door, even though it was already open. Mrs. Keller was there.

"Nora, you shouldn't be sleeping all alone in a strange apartment on Christmas night. You'll stay here tonight. You can have Lisa's room, she won't mind." She laughed. "Well, we won't tell her, anyway. Once everyone goes home, I'll put clean sheets down for you. And Daniel is right. When you go back tomorrow, please take Mr. Fuzzles with you. It's kind of nice to know he's needed again."

Nora had no words; she just jumped up, tears streaming down her face, and hugged Daniel's mother for dear life.

Daniel, Christmas night, bedtime

Daniel didn't know how to feel. Nora was sleeping in Lisa's room, not even ten feet from him. And Mom was fussing over her like Nora was her own daughter. Mom must have fussed over Lisa just as much—but he'd never noticed.

He was noticing a lot of things now, seeing a lot of things differently—more clearly—since he'd met Nora.

But at the moment, nothing felt clear at all.

He was an adult. Almost twenty. He had a girlfriend. They'd slept together. Made love.

But he was also lying in his childhood bed, with all his old toys in his closet and Mr. Fuzzles down the hall in Lisa's Cinderella bedroom. And Mom was tucking Nora into bed. It felt like he was eight years old again.

It was just weird. Too weird.

Nora, at the same time

Much later, after dinner and dessert and coffee and goodbyes to all the visitors, Nora sat on Lisa's bed, clutching Daniel's—her—teddy bear to her chest.

Mrs. Keller knocked at the door and let herself in. "I saw the light was still on." She put a stack of towels on the dresser, and handed Nora a bathrobe. "I don't know if you like to shower at night or in the morning. Either way, here are some clean towels. And, well, you and my daughter aren't exactly built the same. I think you'll do better with one of my bathrobes."

She wanted to cry again, but she'd embarrassed herself in front of Daniel's mother quite enough already. "Thank you, Mrs. Keller."

"I've told you a dozen times tonight, Nora. Call me Marie. Please."

"Okay. Marie. I'll try to remember." She looked over at the phone. It seemed like a big imposition, when she already owed Daniel's parents so much. But she asked anyway. "And—uh—

you've already done so much for me today, but—would it be alright if I made a long-distance call?"

She patted Nora on the head. "Of course! Your mother or your father?"

It was obvious, wasn't it? "Both. But I guess Dad first. He probably feels worse about how I ran out on him."

Marie shook her head. "He'll just be happy to hear from you, Nora. I'll leave you to it. You have a good night, honey." And then Marie kissed her forehead before leaving and closing the door behind her.

She did owe it to him. Maybe her father wasn't perfect, or even in the same zip code as perfect, but he loved her. And despite everything she felt about him—all the different emotions she couldn't even name—she loved him too.

Still, it took her three tries to actually dial the phone. She kept asking herself—what if he was angry with her? What if Joelle answered the phone? What if he hung up the moment he realized it was her?

She finally did it anyway, and he answered on the first ring. "Hello? Who is this?" She had forgotten about the caller ID. He had to be wondering why some random person named Keller was calling him from New York City on Christmas night.

"Dad, it's me. I'm ..." She couldn't start this conversation with a lie. "I'm at my boyfriend's house. His parents invited me for Christmas dinner, and I'm staying in his sister's old bedroom. But I'll tell you all about that later." The tears started up again, and her voice caught a couple of times before she could go on. "I just wanted to say I love you. And I'm really sorry. It was so crappy to run away to Aunt Rachel like I did. And it was mean to Joelle, and I'll apologize to her too, because she was really nice and I liked her, and I hope—I don't even know what I hope, Dad. But you know I love you, right? Please tell me you know."

She heard his voice catch, and what she thought—knew—was sobbing from him. "Of course I know, Pumpkin! Of course I know ..."

Daniel, December 26

His father had volunteered to drive Nora back to her aunt's apartment. Well, insisted. Or, really, demanded.

He assumed Dad wanted to see what kind of place Nora's aunt lived in, and, by extension, what that said about her family. And he probably also wanted the chance to talk to Nora without Mom around to deflect any hard questions.

But Dad surprised him. He did ask a lot of questions, but they weren't intrusive or harsh or anything. It was all basic stuff that anyone would ask of someone they'd just met recently. Dad was as polite and ... well, as nice as Daniel had ever seen him be.

His father did whistle when they parked in front of the apartment building, right there on Central Park West. "That's some place, Nora. I have to ask, what does your aunt do to afford it here?"

"She works for a travel company. Like, corporate travel. Her boss just quit in October so she's been taking up the slack." She laughed. "But you know what, Mr. Keller? I wondered about how much it must cost, too. I never thought about it all the times I was here before, but—I guess now that I have to watch my own money, I've been thinking more about stuff like that."

"Smart girl," his father said, then he turned back to Daniel, "Go and see her to the door."

Daniel got out, opened the passenger door for Nora and took her hand. "I hope Dad wasn't too—well, you know. Too much, I guess."

She chuckled. "No. He was great. So was your Mom. And you, but you knew that already." When they got to the front door, a doorman opened it for Nora. "I guess that's my cue." She embraced him, kissed him—much too quickly, but with his father watching, that was probably for the best.

"I'll call you later. I love you, Nora."

She turned to go inside, but turned back, took his hands in hers. "I love you, too. And I'm—God, yesterday was so nice. It meant so much to me, you don't even know. I'll be waiting by the phone."

And then she disappeared inside, and he walked back to the car.

"She's a lovely girl," his father said once they were on their way back home. "I understand what you see in her. But you need to understand."

This is what Daniel had been dreading. He tried to keep his voice calm and level when he asked, "Understand what, Dad?"

His father didn't look over at him; he kept his eyes firmly on the road as he talked. "What real love is. Adult love. It's not about kissing a pretty girl, or hugging her when she's crying because she failed a quiz or whatever." Daniel wanted to protest, to shout at his father, but he held his tongue. "It's about being there for someone when the worst happens. When they're sick—I don't mean a cold or a sprained ankle. Or when money is tight and you don't know how you'll pay the rent. All the things that you can't fix with a kind word and a smile." Now he did glance over towards Daniel. "And it's about protecting them from things they don't need to see."

That sounded crazy. And horrible. "Dad, I don't know what you mean."

"Did you ever wonder why we sent you and your sister to visit Aunt Carla and Uncle Sebastian back when you were eight or nine?" They were Bianca's parents; that had been a fantastic two weeks.

"I thought they just wanted to see us." That sounded lame—beyond lame—but he had never given it any more thought than that.

"Your mother was in the hospital. She had her gall bladder out. We were pretty worried for a couple of days there, and we didn't want you or your sister to have to be afraid for her, or feel like you had to take care of her. You were just kids. And that's how we loved you." That didn't sound like love. It sounded like fear, more than anything.

"I would have—we both would have helped! We would have wanted to take care of Mom. Why would you put it all on yourself, Dad?" He didn't ask the other question he wanted to—what if it had all gone wrong, and Mom had—no, he couldn't even think that.

"That's what love is. Protecting, even if it means pushing the ones you love away at times. You take it on yourself so they don't have to." His father sighed, and went on with a weary voice. "You don't understand yet. I know you don't. You say you love Nora. You really think you love her. But you've never had to make a really hard choice. I don't wish it on you, but what I want, or what you want, doesn't matter. The world doesn't care what you want. It's going to sucker punch you, and you're going to have to do things you don't want, make choices you never thought you'd have to. And when that day comes, you'll know what love really means."

Daniel didn't answer that. He didn't agree with his father, but he didn't know how to argue against any of it. Or if there even *was* an argument against it.

♥ 🖤 ♥

Nora, December 30

She hadn't seen Daniel since the morning after Christmas. They'd talked for at least an hour every day, but it wasn't the same as being with him. And at times during those calls, he'd seemed—not distracted, but like there was something he couldn't tell her. He'd hesitate just a second or two too long, especially when she asked something about his parents.

But that was probably just because they were right down the hall. That had to be it, right?. Tomorrow was New Year's Eve—maybe they could get together, and then he'd tell her whatever it was.

That would be perfect. They could go down to Times Square and watch the ball drop. She was certain he'd never done that despite living in New York his whole life. And then maybe ...

The phone was in her hand and ringing and she hadn't even realized she'd picked it up. And then Rachel was on the other end of the line.

"Nora? Is everything all right?"

"Uh—yeah. I—I just wanted to call you." This was ridiculous. Rachel probably already knew why she was calling.

"You never 'just' do anything, Nora. You want to have Daniel up to the apartment tomorrow night, don't you?"

There was no point pretending otherwise. "Yes. I really—God, Rachel, I need to see him. Away from his family, away from every-body. Just us together, somewhere safe and quiet and—please?" She was clutching Mr. Fuzzles; how had that happened? She didn't even remember picking the bear up.

There was silence for a moment from Rachel. "And if I say no, are you going to do it anyway?"

No! As much as she was aching—burning!—to see him, to be with him properly, she couldn't do that to Rachel. "You know I never lie to you, Rachel. Anybody else, yeah, I'll say whatever. But you, never. You and—and Daniel. If you say 'no,' then it's no."

More silence, and when Rachel finally spoke it was in a careful, hesitant tone. "Fine. Bring him over for New Year's Eve, but that's it. And after that, you say goodbye to him and you fly back to Providence. You should spend at least a little bit of your break with your father. And with Karen, too. I know she's not great at showing it, but deep down she loves you, Nora. You owe it to her."

Very deep down. Like one of those mineshafts where it took twenty minutes for the elevator to get to the bottom.

Chapter 11

NEW YEAR'S EVE—BRONX, NY/MANHATTAN, NY

Daniel, early afternoon

"It's one night, Dad!"

His father was not budging on letting him meet Nora for New Year's Eve in Times Square.

"I'm not stupid, Daniel. It's not about the night. It's about the morning. We let you go and watch the ball drop with her, and then it'll be an hour before you can get through the crowds to take her back to that apartment, and by then it'll be two o'clock in the morning and wouldn't we rather you stayed over there? So you don't have to go back to Grand Central to catch the last train and then walk back here in the cold at three or four in the morning."

"It's not like that!" It was *exactly* like that, and they both knew it.

Dad had been nineteen once. He'd probably had this same argument with grandma and grandpa—or not. His father had already had a job and his own apartment by then. There was nobody to tell him where he could or couldn't spend New Year's Eve.

The whole family was in the living room for this horrible conversation. Mom was—if Daniel was reading her expression correctly—silently pleading with Dad to give in and let him go. And Lisa, who was here for the day to "get away from my roommate's neurotic friends for a few hours," was completely unreadable.

She spoke up now. "Dad, it's not like he hasn't spent the night with her before. You know he hasn't had a roommate all semester. What do you think they've been doing?"

"Lisa, please!" He and his mother said it in unison. Mom was horrified, and he wanted to—he wasn't sure. Either kill her, or himself. Or maybe both. How could she say that?

His father stared at Lisa, his face going red. But it was Mom who spoke up first. "She shouldn't have said that. But Daniel is an adult, Tony. He's nineteen years old. You remember what you got up to when you were nineteen. Your brother told me some stories over the years. We should be grateful he's asking permission, and telling us exactly where he'll be. That's what we taught him, isn't it?"

Daniel was both intensely curious, and also thoroughly grossed out, at the prospect of hearing details about his father's activities back then. Thankfully it didn't come to that. Between them, Mom and Lisa talked his father into giving in and letting him go; Dad's shoulders gradually slumped as they beat down his resistance.

Later, when he was dressed and ready to head out, he knocked on Lisa's bedroom door.

"Come in, Danny."

"I owe you one, Lisa." What else was there to say?

"We're even. I remember what you did after I came home from Jack's birthday. Besides, I saw at Christmas how you are with her. I'm just glad somebody in this family isn't embarrassed to show some affection in public."

He hugged her, holding her close. She wasn't expecting it, and he couldn't remember the last time he'd done it. It felt really good to hold his sister. "Let's talk tomorrow. You come over here, or I'll come to you, or we go out for lunch. Whatever. We don't do it often enough. Okay?"

"Okay, Danny." And she kissed him on the cheek. When was the last time she'd done that? Or smiled at him without anything sarcastic or guarded or whatever else behind it? Much too long. But that was the past, and it didn't have to be that way anymore.

Nora, about eight o'clock

At first, Nora didn't think it really mattered what she wore tonight. She'd be wrapped up in a heavy coat in Times Square and Daniel wouldn't see it. And if—when—they came back up to the apartment, whatever she wore would end up taken off and tossed on the floor in short order.

But what about dinner? They'd have to eat somewhere, and she could hardly keep her coat on inside the restaurant. So she was going through Rachel's closet looking for just the right dress. Nothing seemed exactly right; there were several good dresses, but none that were *great*.

Except, maybe—there was that red dress in the back. She'd skipped over it the first time—it seemed too dramatic, too much.

She pulled it out, held it up to herself, stared into the mirror. It was definitely too much. But maybe, tonight, too much was just right.

This was New Year's Eve, in Times Square. Their first new year together. The first big holiday date she'd ever had with a boyfriend. If that didn't call for drama, what did?

Daniel, half an hour later

Daniel wasn't sure if the leather jacket objectively looked better on him than when he'd bought it a year and a half ago with his high school graduation money, or if he simply saw himself differently now.

Older, more adult.

Between the jacket and the cologne, he felt—he wasn't honestly sure. He went back and forth between thinking he was legitimately well put together, and that he was simply playing dress-up.

Mom had insisted he wear the cologne—and then supervised the application, "So you don't overdo it and smell like you dumped a whole bottle on. Your father used to do that." She had gotten it just right, as far as he could tell. He smelled it, but just barely, a faint scent of pine combined with—the best word he could think of was cleanliness, but not the kind after you cleaned the kitchen. He hoped Nora would like it.

He got his answer a half hour later when he stepped out of the subway and walked the half a block to her building. She came running out—she must have been waiting in the lobby—and hugged him. Then she sniffed, and leaned in closer. "Oh, that's nice. You should wear that all the time."

As understanding as Nora was, as much as she could laugh at almost anything, Daniel didn't think telling her Mom had picked out the cologne was the right approach, so he just thanked her and then took stock of her. She had her hair up, sort of how she'd had it on their first date, but fancier. Had she gone to a salon just for tonight? Just for him?

She was wearing perfume, too. It had to be the same as that first night, she smelled like jasmine and vanilla and something else he couldn't identify. But it was—well, it put him in mind of that night, so it was obviously doing exactly what it was supposed to do.

"It's only eight-thirty," he said. "Let's get something to eat. Is there any place around here you like?"

He took her hand and they started off down the sidewalk. "There's a great Chinese place over on 82nd and Columbus. It's only four blocks or so." Then she hesitated. "You like Chinese?"

As long as it wasn't from the crummy takeout place Dad liked over on 233rd street. "Yeah. That sounds great." But when they got to the restaurant, and Nora unbuttoned her heavy parka, he no longer cared about food. All he could do was stare at her; she wore a stunning red dress that could have come straight out of a fashion magazine. She must have noticed him staring, open-mouthed—how could she not?—and did a little twirl before she sat down.

How was he expected to eat, or make conversation or even think coherently, when she looked like *that*?

Nora, an hour later

Nora was nearly as overwhelmed with Daniel as he clearly was with her. He'd been nervous—not quite jumpy, but almost—from the moment she'd taken off her coat, straight through the egg rolls and the General Tso's Chicken to the fortune cookies sitting unopened on the table.

She wasn't showing her own nerves; she supposed she'd had more practice at covering up that kind of reaction. But it was right there under the surface. His cologne was—well, sexy. There wasn't any other way to say it. And he'd put on just enough that it made her want to nuzzle right up to him to get a better whiff of it.

He couldn't have done that on purpose. It wasn't his style, and, anyway, seeing how he'd never worn cologne in the two months they'd been dating, she doubted he could have applied it that perfectly on purpose even if he had wanted to.

She wondered if it had been his mother or his father who'd done it for him. Another question she'd never ask him.

Well, not unless there was a serious uptightness emergency and she needed to change the subject immediately. That was a "break glass in case of fire" kind of question if ever there was one.

Besides the cologne, she loved that jacket. It fit him perfectly, and the brown was such a good color on him. "Did you get that jacket for Christmas?"

He shocked her with his answer. "No. I've had it for a while. I bought it myself, after high school graduation." She would never have guessed he picked it out himself. It suited him so well, but buying an expensive jacket like that didn't fit with anything he'd said or done since they'd met.

"Why am I only seeing it now?"

His next answer wasn't surprising at all. "I thought it looked *so* cool in the store, but when I got it home and I put it on and looked in the mirror—it didn't feel like me. It was like, the jacket was cooler than I was. Like it wouldn't want to be seen with me."

That was stupid. And sad. And exactly how she imagined the boy he'd been a year and a half ago would think. "Well, you can tell the jacket from me that you're more than cool enough for it." She laughed. "But I guess you figured that out for yourself already."

He reached across the table, took her hand. "Well, you helped. But I think the jacket probably feels kind of underdressed tonight, compared to you." And then he grinned. "I'll give it a little pep talk later, maybe I can boost its confidence, you know?"

The Daniel she'd met in October wouldn't have made that joke. She clearly wasn't the only one being changed—for the better, she hoped—in this relationship.

Daniel, almost eleven p.m.

After dinner they walked to the subway station over on 86th and shoved their way onto a train. Daniel had never seen the subway this crowded; there was barely room to breathe. Not that he really minded; Nora was pressed against him more tightly than she'd ever been when they were together in his dorm room. Her face was buried in his neck, and she whispered, "This is really nice. Except for the part where I'm losing feeling in my legs."

Thankfully it was only a few stops before they had to switch lines, then only one more stop—on an even more packed Number Seven train—and they were at Times Square. They were carried out by the tide of New Year's revelers, and when they got to the top of the steps, the sudden cold was a shock.

They clung to each other as they made their way through the crowds, searching for a good spot to watch the ball drop, and people-watch until then.

It was just after eleven o'clock when they settled on the corner of 45th and Seventh Avenue, right in front of a McDonalds. When they got there, Daniel noticed the bottle of champagne in Nora's hand. "Where'd you get that?"

She shook her head. "Somebody handed it to me a minute ago. I guess they thought we deserved it."

"Or they thought you were somebody else."

"Whichever," she said. "It's ours now." She handed it to him. "You want to do the honors?"

Daniel had never opened a bottle of champagne before, but he'd seen it done in movies. It couldn't be that difficult, could it?

It wasn't; he squeezed the bottle, just like James Bond always did, and the cork popped off. They both got sprayed, and all he could do was laugh. So what if he got champagne all over his fancy leather jacket? He was here in the middle of the biggest party in the world, with a beautiful girl he loved, who loved him back and smiled at him the way nobody else ever did. Or ever could. "They said the jacket was waterproof when I bought it. Think that applies to champagne too?"

She gave him a quick kiss. "If not, I'll pay for the cleaning. Well, I'll ask my Dad, and he'll pay for it, anyway."

They took turns drinking from the bottle and dancing with each other—well, shuffling around in each other's arms, anyway—as the clock ticked closer to 1989.

Nora, 11:55 p.m.

It was five minutes to midnight. The champagne was gone, and Nora heard the music. She didn't even like "Tell It to My Heart" but wherever it was coming from, it was loud enough to hear clearly. And it had enough of a melody to dance properly to.

She pushed Daniel away, just a few inches, enough to hold him for a real dance. She thought she'd have to lead, but he surprised her again. He knew how to do a box step!

She gave him a questioning look.

"Mom sent me and Lisa to dance class when she was thirteen. I was ten. You can imagine how awkward it was." He twirled her as he said it. Maybe it was the champagne that was bringing this out in him.

"Awkward for who?"

He laughed, twirling her again. "Both of us. But definitely her more than me." Now his eyes went distant for a moment, the way they always did when he was remembering something. "I know you're an only child, but imagine if you had a little brother who was four inches shorter than you and kept tripping over his feet, and you had to dance with him for an hour and a half every week in public."

"Wow," she said. "That ought to be against the Geneva Convention or something."

He twirled her again, and then he dipped her. This was a whole new Daniel; she would never have imagined he had all this in him. "Yeah," he answered finally. "It's a miracle we didn't kill each other before I made it to high school. You'd never guess it now, but..." He hesitated for a second, then went on. "She's the one who talked Dad into letting me come down here tonight."

"What did she say?" Daniel's sister had been tight-lipped at Christmas dinner; Nora hadn't gotten any real sense of what she was like.

"I'll tell you later," he said. "It's almost time!" He was right; she could hear the crowd counting, tens of thousands of voices coming from all around. They both joined in, until the countdown got to ten.

That's when Daniel pulled her close and kissed her, eyes wide open. She kissed him back, and all she could see was the love shining in his eyes. All she could hear was her heart beating. When they finally came up for air, the new year was already a minute old.

♡ ♥ ♡

Daniel, two o'clock in the morning

They took a taxi back to Nora's building. The drive took twenty minutes, and they spent most of the ride making out in the back seat.

When they arrived, Daniel gave the driver a twenty and told him to keep the change.

It seemed only fair; it couldn't have been pleasant for him to see them going at it every time he checked the rearview mirror.

The doorman—a different one than earlier this evening, Daniel noticed—stopped them. "Happy New Year, Miss Nora. Does Miss Rachel know you have a guest?"

Nora sighed theatrically. "Yes, Ike. *Miss Rachel* knows. I think it's eight in the morning in London if you'd like to call her to make sure. I've got the number."

Ike shook his head, not meeting Nora's eyes when he answered. "That's quite all right, Miss Nora. I just have to check, you understand."

She patted his arm. "I understand. I'll tell my aunt you asked. And Happy New Year to you." Ike opened the front door, and Daniel mumbled a Happy New Year greeting as well as they went inside.

It was a very well-kept building. Everything in the lobby gleamed. The elevator door opened without a sound. When they came out on the fourth floor, the carpets looked freshly vacuumed. He echoed his father's question from a few days ago. "How does your aunt afford this place?"

"Rent control," Nora answered, and now it made sense. "She could never live here otherwise. Anyway, here we are." She stopped in front of apartment 406, turned to him and smiled. "I hope you didn't come all this way just to make sure I got home safely. I'd be *so* disappointed."

"I'm here because I want to be." Just like she'd said that first night two months ago. And just as true.

She had the perfect answer. "There's nowhere I'd rather be than here with you." She turned the key in the lock. "Well, not in the hallway. That would be weird." But she kissed him out there anyway, as if she couldn't wait the two seconds to get inside. He didn't mind. How could he ever mind kissing her?

Nora, 2:15 in the morning

Nora let Daniel look around the apartment for a moment before she took her coat off. It seemed only fair to let him get his bearings before she distracted him.

He was looking at the photos on the living room wall—Rachel had pictures from every major European capital up there. "These are really good. Is your aunt a photographer, too?"

"Just amateur. She always tries to set aside a few hours for pictures when her company sends her out on trips. But is that really what you want to talk about right now?" She threw her coat onto the couch, and just like in the restaurant, Daniel went wide-eyed. "That's better," she told him. "Now, here's the quick tour." She pointed to the rooms in turn. "Kitchen. Bathroom. Living room, you're in it. Rachel's bedroom." She took his hand, led him to the one door she hadn't pointed at yet. "And, last but not least, guest room. My room. *Our* room for tonight."

She pushed the door open with one hand, and he followed her in. "Look at that, I remembered to make the bed this morning."

"Yesterday morning," he said.

"Last year."

"Yeah, that too," he answered. Somehow she was in his arms; when had that happened? It didn't matter, because that's exactly where she wanted—needed—to be.

Daniel, 2:20 in the morning

They were sitting on the bed now.

"If this is our room tonight, is it *our* bed, too?"

Nora knew exactly what he meant. Not *his* bed, like in the dorm. Or *the* bed, like it could be any bed anywhere. "Yeah. Ours." She kissed him, slowly, deeply. "I really like how that sounds. I like having things that are ours. I like being an us." Another kiss, and then one more. "I was never an us before I met you."

"I was." But not like this. "This is different, though. It's *our* us. Not something we were born into. Not something that happened by accident. We chose it. We found each other, and we made ourselves into an us." He kissed her this time. "And it's the best thing I've ever had."

She'd unbuttoned his shirt. "For me, too. I never knew anything could feel this way. I never knew I could even be an us." Her dress was—somewhere, he hadn't seen where she'd thrown it.

It didn't matter.

The only thing that mattered was that she was right here, in his arms, pressed up against him. No. There was no him or her in this room, this bed, this moment. There were only the two of them together.

Nora, the morning of January 1st

If it had been up to Nora, they'd have stayed in bed all morning. All day. Hell, all year.

But Rachel had been very clear. And just in case she tried to back out of their deal, her aunt had bought her a ticket to Providence, flying out of LaGuardia at two o'clock this afternoon. So she'd need to be on her way to the airport by noon at the latest. And while Daniel had said there was no specific time he was expected home, his parents—especially his father—surely wouldn't be happy if he sauntered through the door in the middle of the afternoon.

"That reminds me," she said, pouring coffee for the both of them. "You promised you'd tell me what your sister said to convince your father to let you come out last night."

Daniel took a sip of coffee and a bite of toast before he answered. "I did, didn't I?" More coffee, more toast, and no more words.

"You're not really going to hold out on me, are you?"

He went a little bit red; he hadn't done that in a while. But he finally spoke. "Okay. Dad knew I'd want to—we'd want to come back here after Times Square. And he didn't like it."

And this was why Nora had made it a point since tenth grade to say as little as possible—ideally nothing at all—about boys to either of her parents. "I can see where he'd feel that way."

"So that's when Lisa jumped into the conversation. She said something like, 'You know they're sleeping together already, don't you? He doesn't have a roommate, what did you think they were doing?'"

"Oh, my God! She did not say that."

"Cross my heart," Daniel said, but he made the little crossing motion over her chest rather than his.

"I think you're a little confused." Of course he wasn't—but she still wanted to hear him say it.

"Not a bit. I know exactly where my heart is now. And I know you'll always take care of it." Now he crossed his own chest. "And I'll always treasure yours. I love you, Nora Langley. And I wish more than anything that we didn't have to leave today."

She leaned over her aunt's kitchen table and kissed him. He kissed her back, and it took all of her willpower—and his—to remain here in the kitchen.

"I love you, Daniel Keller. And I hate it too that we have to go." She sighed. "At least now it's only eleven days. That's not so bad."

"It feels like forever," he said.

"Yeah. But last night felt like forever, too. Let's both hang on to that."

She hung onto it walking Daniel downstairs and to the subway. And then while she finished packing. And for the taxi ride to LaGuardia. And for the whole flight to Providence.

She was still hanging onto it when her father drove up to the pickup area in his corvette. He took one look at her, and he sighed. "I've never seen you like this, Pumpkin. You must really love this boy."

"More than anything, Dad. I love him more than anything."

Chapter 12

VALENTINE'S DAY—ALBION COLLEGE

Nora, early afternoon

It was hard to believe a month had passed since the start of the semester. Between classes, working on the school paper and helping Kim through the traumatic breakup with her high school boyfriend over Christmas, Nora had barely been able to carve out any time to spend with Daniel.

This afternoon was a rare exception. She sat on his bed, waiting for him to return with snacks from the vending machine down in the lobby. She flipped idly through a notebook, not really seeing the words she'd written there.

She was startled by the phone. Who would be calling him on a Thursday afternoon? She wondered if she should answer it. He didn't have an answering machine. That had surprised her. She'd figured if anyone would have one, it would be Daniel. Heck, he could probably build one himself.

Regardless, he didn't have one. And what if the call was important? He'd want to know, wouldn't he?

She picked it up, and she was immediately greeted by a woman's voice, not that much older than her, if she was any judge. "Hey, Danny!"

It wasn't his sister, but she knew of one other woman who might call him. "Uh, hi. Is this Bianca?"

There was a laugh. "That's me! You must be Nora. It's nice to put a voice to the name."

Nora heard the warmth in her tone. A few words were enough to see why Daniel trusted her so much. "Same here. He told me all about you on our first date. He said your name, and he didn't even realize he'd said it out loud, and I thought for a minute he was talking about some other girl he liked."

More laughter. "Yeah, he told me about that. That's my Danny. Well, I guess he's *our* Danny now." There was a pause, and Bianca's voice was suddenly quieter, more serious. "He really loves you. I mean, with all his heart, Nora. I hope you know how lucky you are, because he's ...he doesn't know how great he is. He never has. I really hope you see it."

For a moment, Nora was offended. A dozen sarcastic remarks passed through her head, but she dismissed them all. Bianca was just looking out for someone she'd known and loved for twenty years. Someone who saw all the amazing things about Daniel that she did; probably the only other person besides her who did.

And there was one more reason not to be offended. If it wasn't for Bianca, he probably wouldn't even *be* the Daniel she loved. So she owed Bianca. She owed her more than she—or Daniel—could ever repay.

"I do see it. And I know how lucky I am, Bianca."

She could practically hear Daniel's cousin smiling at that. "He's lucky, too." Then another pause. "I'm really happy for the both of you. Just ...promise me. Please don't ever break his heart. And when I talk to him next, I'll tell him he better not break yours or I'll never forgive him."

She could never break his heart. Or he, hers. It was unthinkable.

It could never happen.

After Bianca hung up, and before Daniel returned with the snacks, a thought occurred to her. Her father had probably said the exact same thing, nineteen years ago.

Daniel, a minute later

Daniel opened the door, expecting a question or a snarky remark from Nora about how long he'd taken to supposedly run down to the vending machines.

He didn't expect to find her sitting on his bed, hands on her lap and a vacant expression on her face. It took her a moment to notice him. "Oh. Hi. I was just ... I was thinking. Not about anything. Just—not thinking, I guess."

He couldn't begin to guess what was going on. But maybe the flowers would help. "I'm sorry I took so long. I wanted to surprise you," he said, holding out the bouquet to her. She blinked a couple of times, and then she seemed to finally see them.

"You didn't get these out of the vending machine," she said.

"I was going to bring you flowers tonight, when I came over to get you for the dance, but then I thought, you'd have to go back upstairs, put them in water, it would be a whole thing. So I figured, better to give them to you now."

She took the bouquet, brushing a finger over the roses. "You got different colors."

There'd been a little stall set up outside the Whitman building, run by the owner of the flower shop a block over from the Green Lantern Café. She'd had roses in several colors, and a sign describing what each color meant.

"Red, well, you know what that means." Half of the dozen were red. Then he'd gotten two each in other colors. "Pink is for elegance and sweetness, lavender is for enchantment and wonder, and the blue is for mystery and uniqueness. I think that pretty much covers you."

She rolled her eyes at him. "And you knew all that how?"

He couldn't fake anything with her. He had to admit, it was kind of nice to know that. "They had a sign explaining it. I had no idea the different colors meant anything until fifteen minutes ago. But I did pick them out myself."

She got up from the bed, kissed him. "And I picked you out. I guess we've both got good taste." She kissed him again. "Oh, by the way, your cousin called while you were out."

"Bee?" Nora nodded. "And you talked to her?" Another nod. "And ..."

"And now I know what you meant when you were talking about her on our first date. She loves you so much, Daniel. She made me promise to never break your heart."

Of course Bee would say that. "She's got nothing to worry about. You could never do that." As he said it, he saw, just for a moment, something different in her eyes. Something like sadness, maybe? And then it was gone as quickly as it had appeared. "Hey. Did she say anything—did she upset you? Because if she did, I'll talk to her. Nobody's allowed to say anything to upset you, no matter how much I love them."

Nora shook her head, but there was still a hint of that sadness—or whatever it was—in her expression. Or maybe he was seeing things. "No. No! I just ... I guess I'm in a weird mood today, that's all. Maybe it's a blood sugar thing. Or maybe I'm just thinking too much. Or not enough. One or the other, anyway. But I really do want a candy bar."

Maybe that really was all it was. When he got too hungry, his brain got funny. Or dehydrated. A candy bar and some water, and she'd be back to herself right away. They'd be laughing about this later. Of course they would.

Nora, early evening

"For the fifth time, Nora, you look fine! Your makeup is fine, your hair is fine, the dress fits fine. Everything is fine, okay?"

Nora knew she was driving poor Kellyanne crazy. She'd wanted a second pair of eyes just to be sure her outfit and everything else was just right, and Kim was home for the weekend so she'd been forced to look for someone else on her floor to help out. Kellyanne from three doors down the hall was unlucky enough to be in her room when Nora came knocking, and kind enough to agree, which she was surely regretting now, twenty minutes later.

"I'm sorry. I just ... I want it all to be perfect tonight."

Kellyanne rolled her eyes. "You know what your boyfriend is doing now, right?" Nora knew no answer was expected. "He's looking at his clothes for about two seconds to make sure there aren't any stains big enough to see from a hundred feet away, and then he'll run a comb through his hair for about two more seconds. And that's it. That's all any of them do, but we sit here for three hours and obsess over details you couldn't see with a microscope. You tell me how that's fair."

Well, she was wrong about Daniel. He might not take three hours, but he definitely obsessed over details that nobody else would ever notice.

On the other hand, there were plenty of things he didn't know to obsess about. When she'd asked what he was wearing to the dance tonight, so she could make sure they didn't clash, he just stared blankly at her. "I only own one suit," he'd said. "And one tie." And then she'd had to ask what color the tie was, because it hadn't occurred to him she'd want to know.

"I know," Nora said. "But even with all that, he's worth the effort. And I'll make it up to you. Whatever you need, next time you need a favor, it's yours." She laughed then, thinking about how Daniel would react to her words. Once he stopped blushing over her saying he was worth the effort, he'd probably tell her that making open-ended promises of future favors was how people got killed in every gangster movie he'd ever seen.

"Yeah, sure." Kellyanne said it with a laugh, at least. "If you can ever tear yourself away from him. I assume the roses are from him?"

"They are. He even knew what the different colors mean." There was no point in mentioning he'd only learned that earlier today.

"Okay, I'm a little bit impressed now. Maybe he *is* worth all the trouble."

"He is. More than you can imagine."

Daniel, fifteen minutes later

The moment he saw Nora walking out of Morris Hall, Daniel's first thought was, *She must be freezing.*

"You look—God, that dress is amazing. But don't you want to go back upstairs and get a coat?"

She shook her head. "After everything I went through to look like this tonight, I'm not covering it up." He certainly couldn't argue with that. Her dress was emerald green, low cut, and it went down almost to her ankles. And she wore gloves, green to match the dress, that went nearly to her elbows. As if she'd stepped out of an old movie.

He could barely get out the words, "Whatever you did, it was worth it." He took her hand and led her towards the main quad. Just like their first date, the sky was clear and lit up with stars, but her eyes were brighter and more beautiful than all of them put together.

"I'll be sure to tell Joelle." She said it with a smile that was somehow both joyful and sad at the same time. "She'll be thrilled."

She hadn't mentioned that name before. She wouldn't call her mom by her first name, and she didn't have a sister. "Joelle?"

"I told you about my Dad's girlfriend." She laughed at herself. "I guess I never actually said her name." Now she sighed, and her smile was much more sad than joyful. "I ended up asking her to go dress shopping with me. That's not—my Mom doesn't do stuff like that, and Aunt Rachel's still in London, and I ... I wanted somebody with me. So I swallowed my pride and I asked her. She was thrilled and Dad—oh, my God, Daniel. He almost cried, he was so happy I was being nice to his girlfriend."

It made Daniel want to cry, too. It sucked that Nora couldn't ask her mother for something as simple as taking her shopping for a dress. As much as things could sometimes be strained with his father, he knew he could go to Dad for anything he really needed help with. It must feel so awful to know you couldn't trust your parents, or rely on them.

He couldn't do anything to change Nora's circumstances. All he could do was make sure she knew she could rely on him.

Nora, a little later

Nora looked over at Daniel as they walked into the Whitman building. There was so much emotion showing on his face. She could see his pride shining out—he would never say the words, not in a million years, but she could read him perfectly. She knew he felt like the king of the world right now, just for having her on his arm.

Well, he would say that last part, but only at the end of the night when they were alone.

That was for later; right now she wanted to enjoy this dance. It was already fairly crowded, and it was weird to see her class-mates all dressed up. She'd felt the same way at her senior prom, except here nobody needed to spike the punch or rent a hotel room using their parents' credit card for afterwards.

No, that was the past. No hotel rooms, no getting drunk to forget about all the crappy things she didn't want to remember. Tonight was about dancing in the arms of her boyfriend, laughing at his silly jokes, feeling like a queen for a little while—not just in Daniel's eyes, but everybody else's too. And even more importantly, her own.

Why not? Didn't she deserve to feel that way just as much as anybody else?

Daniel's voice cut through her thoughts. "Do you want to dance?" She wasn't sure why he was even asking; he had one hand on her waist and the other in the middle of her back and he was leading her onto the dance floor.

"I think we already are," she said. And as they danced, her boyfriend holding her close and his eyes fixed on hers, she did feel like a queen.

Maybe even the queen of the world

Daniel, a bit later

The last formal dance he'd gone to—the only one he'd ever gone to—was Peggy's prom, almost three years ago. It had been nice when he'd been dancing with her, but awkward otherwise. He hadn't known anyone there but her.

This was different. He didn't know everyone—Albion wasn't *that* small of a school—but everywhere he looked, he saw someone he recognized. And every one of them saw him with the most beautiful girl in the room.

He couldn't deny that it felt good to be seen that way. But it was all because of Nora. The only reason anyone else could see this more confident, more together version of himself was because she'd seen it first, and made him see it too.

"You clean up pretty good, Daniel." He turned to see Phil passing behind him on the dance floor. Phil was wearing—good God, a tuxedo? He'd never seen Phil in anything but a T-shirt or sweatpants in the year and a half he'd known him. And he was dancing with Jeannette Morgan; Daniel thought they'd broken up before Christmas. Well, that wasn't for him to worry about.

Jeannette spoke up. "Nora, right? You look lovely. You guys make a great couple."

Nora nodded her thanks, but before either she or Daniel could say anything, Phil spoke again. "You two are never apart anymore. When's the wedding?"

Daniel tripped over his feet and nearly fell into Nora. She caught him, held him up, but she had a deer-in-the-headlights look in her eyes. The same look he knew was in his own. Because what if it wasn't a joke?

Of course it was a joke. A wedding? That was ridiculous! That was absurd! That was ... not even as bad as his wild thought about having a baby, back before Christmas.

He heard Phil yelp, and cry out, "What did I say?"

"Something really rude and stupid," Jeannette said. "Ignore him, Daniel. You already know Phil has the manners of a rabid squirrel."

"It's fine," Daniel said, looking into Nora's eyes, willing her to think it was fine, too.

"Yeah," she said, after a moment, the fear in her face shifting to a mischievous expression. "And if we ever do get married, I'll ask you to be a bridesmaid, Phil, since you're the first one to suggest it. You'd look great in pink taffeta."

If he hadn't already loved Nora, that remark by itself would have been enough to capture his heart.

Nora, three hours later

They were back in her room. It felt a little strange. Daniel had been in her room before, of course, but he'd never *been* in her room. It wasn't intentional; they'd only come here instead of his dorm because it was a shorter walk from the Whitman building, and she really should have worn a coat tonight.

He was sitting on her bed, bouncing up and down. "I forgot how thin the mattresses were in Morris Hall. I can't believe I slept on one of these for a whole year." She glared at him, and it took him a moment to realize why. "Oh. Sorry." Then he grinned. "Please tell me you're not just dating me to get access to my mattress."

She grabbed her pillow and hit him with it. "Very funny, Keller." It *was* kind of funny, though. She teased him enough, she could take a joke now and then. She sat next to him, and felt the mattress sag noticeably. It really wasn't meant for two people. "I wonder if they purposely bought crummy mattresses so freshmen wouldn't try to sleep together."

Daniel turned to her, kissed her. "It's not working." And then his hands were on her, all over her. Exactly what she wanted. It only took a moment of his touch, everywhere she needed it, and all conscious thought was gone—there was only feeling. Only him. Only right now.

Daniel, the next morning

"I just remembered," Nora said. "I had clothes in the dryer yesterday, and I never got them. You mind waiting up here for a minute?" Of course Daniel didn't mind. There was nowhere else he'd rather be. "And if the phone rings, pick it up. Tammy was going to call this morning to pick a time to study later."

It rang about fifteen seconds after she left. He answered it, and it wasn't Tammy on the line.

"Good morning, Pumpkin!"

It was Nora's father. He took a deep breath. He could do this. Nora had put up with being interrogated by his whole family for hours. The least he could do was to talk to her father for five minutes.

"Uh—this is Daniel, Mr. Langley."

Oh, God.

He wasn't just talking to Nora's father. He was in Nora's dorm room, before eight o'clock on a Saturday morning, talking to her father. He might as well have said "I slept with your daughter last night, how are you this morning?"

But luck—or something—was with him, because there was a little chuckle on the line. "*The* Daniel? The one my daughter is in love with?"

He didn't know Nora had told her father that. "Yes, sir." What else was there to say?

Another chuckle. "You can skip the sir, and the Mr. Langley. Call me Richard. And where is Nora, by the way?"

"Down in the laundry room. She left her clothes in the dryer yesterday." Well, it was true.

"That sounds like her. She probably gets that from me." There was a pause. "She got a lot from me, Daniel. Good and bad."

"Sir? Uh—I mean, Richard? I don't understand."

Another pause. "That's a good sign. Maybe she doesn't take after me as much as I thought. Maybe she learned what not to do."

Daniel had no idea what the man was trying to say, and he wasn't at all sure he really wanted to know. "Uh ... okay?"

"It's fine, Daniel. Forget everything I just said. Just—take good care of her. She deserves—she *needs* love. More than she even knows, I think. She needs somebody she can believe in, no matter what. If it's you, I can't ask more than that."

"I love her. And all I want to do is take care of her," he said, and Nora picked that moment to come back, so—thank God—he didn't need to say anything more. He took the laundry basket out of her arms with one hand, and gave her the phone with the other. "It's your father," he told her.

She looked like she couldn't decide whether to laugh, cry or scream. He didn't blame her one bit.

Chapter 13

Daniel, March 16

Daniel sat on his bed holding Bianca's birthday card, squinting to read his cousin's tiny writing. She'd managed to squeeze three or four pages worth of questions and advice and birthday wishes into the inside of a single Hallmark card. She ended it with a postscript:

I assume Nora's got something big planned for you. I hope it's amazing, Danny. But remember, don't do anything I wouldn't do!

"No promises, Bee," he whispered, setting the card aside. He was curious exactly what Nora had planned. She hadn't given him the slightest hint, and that in itself was surprising. She was a lot of things, but good at keeping secrets generally wasn't one of them.

It was cute, actually, the way she got so excited, bursting to share whatever she was trying to keep quiet, until she lost the last little bit of willpower and she blurted it out. More than cute, really. Like that time right after Thanksgiving, when she found that poetry book over at Turn the Page. "It's perfect. Rachel will love it," she'd told him. And then she proceeded to call her aunt, telling her how she had the best Christmas gift ever for her, and she couldn't wait to give it to her, and all in all it had taken less than five minutes before her aunt knew exactly what she was getting.

All she'd said about tonight was that she'd come over as soon as she finished her paper for Intro to Financial Reporting, and she hoped to be finished by dinnertime. And that it'd be worth the wait. He had no idea what that meant, he just knew it was true. Because everything about Nora had been worth the wait, from the very first moment.

Nora, the same night

Nora buttoned the last button on her coat when Kim walked in. Her roommate looked her up and down, uncomprehending. "Nora, it's seventy degrees out. What are you doing?"

She couldn't help herself. "Gift wrapping."

Kim stood there, mouthing the words, looking very lost, and then recognition dawned. "Oh. Sure. But where's the gift ... oh!"

"It's Daniel's birthday."

Kim nodded. "And you're going to surprise him. I hope he appreciates it."

"He will." She would make sure. She'd tried something similar for Halloween, and that had been a wonderful night—better than it would have been if it had gone the way she'd initially imagined.

But she still wanted to do what she'd intended that night. She wanted to surprise her boyfriend with a gift only she could give—and one he'd never, ever forget. "And don't wait up. I won't be back tonight."

Daniel, the same night

It was just after eight-thirty when there was a knock on his door. He'd been here the whole time; he hadn't wanted to even run to the dining hall in case she picked that moment to show up. But he was a big boy; missing one meal wouldn't hurt him. Anyway, he'd gotten caught up on his reading for Intro to Data Structures for the week, so it wasn't a total loss. He set the textbook aside, and called out, "It's open!"

There she was.

She smiled at him as she walked in, closing the door behind her. He couldn't take his eyes off of hers, flashing with humor and mischief, maybe? And love. Definitely that. He did, just barely, hear the lock clicking behind her as she said, "Happy birthday, Daniel!"

"It is now," he told her, only now looking down and seeing— why was she wearing an overcoat? It had been almost seventy degrees today, she didn't need a coat. But she noticed his gaze moving. She stepped over to the bed, cupped his chin in her hand, redirected his eyes back up to hers.

"Don't you know? Presents are supposed to be wrapped."

He gasped, whether at her touch or her words, he wasn't sure. And then it didn't matter, when she leaned down and her lips touched his, and the whole world disappeared for a moment. When it came back, his hands were tangled in her hair, and his heart was pounding.

She pulled his hands away from her head, guided them to the top button on her coat. "Usually the birthday boy unwraps his own presents." His fingers didn't want to work. Or maybe his entire nervous system was misfiring after that kiss. But Nora helped him with the first couple of buttons, and then he remembered how the process worked. He took his time, savoring her closeness, her touch, the scent of jasmine and vanilla, savoring everything about this moment.

When the last button was undone, she shrugged the coat off in one motion, and what he saw then took his breath away.

Nora—his girlfriend—stood there, in *his* dorm room, wearing that dress. Blue, picking up her eyes, perfect against her skin, and fitted everywhere, every curve. How was this even possible? How was this for him? How was this his life?

"You know it's not enough to unwrap the gift, right? You're allowed to touch it. You're supposed to." And then she kissed him again, and he kissed her back, and eventually she backed away and laughed gently. "Please tell me you weren't one of those kids who never took your Star Wars action figures out of the package so they wouldn't get broken. Because I don't believe in that. You should always play with your gifts." He didn't know how he was still capable of conscious thought at this point.

Another kiss, another touch, another moment where he barely knew who or where he was, and then, not knowing how it had happened, he was sitting in his desk chair, the swively one he'd rescued from behind Addison Hall. And she was turning him around slowly, kissing him again, and somehow, with every revolution, another button on his shirt came undone too.

Sometime after that, she still wore the dress, but his shirt was on the floor, and his jeans appeared about to join them. And then there was another kiss, and this time when he kissed her back she didn't stop, didn't break away, didn't let him breathe. And then there was no noticing or thinking or anything except pure sensation and it seemed to go on and on and on ...

♡ ♥ ♡

Nora, much later that night

He had the cutest little half-smile as he slept. Nora had stirred awake a few minutes ago, and she'd been watching him. Just watching, not moving a muscle.

Daniel was on his side, his left arm flung over his head at a weird angle. Any other night, Nora would have wondered how he could possibly sleep in that position. But after what she'd done for him—with him—he was well and truly wiped out. She doubted she could wake him up now if she wanted to, not that she did. He deserved this peaceful rest and, she hoped, sweet dreams to accompany it.

She'd surprised herself as well as him. Unlike Halloween, she'd stayed "in character" all the way through. And he'd let her, put himself completely in her hands, in a way he hadn't done before.

As she watched him not quite snore, she thought back. Nobody had ever done that before with her, not in a bedroom—or any other context. Nobody had ever trusted their body, or their heart or their *anything* to her so completely, without even a word, just with the absolute belief that she would take care of them.

It hit her then. For all she'd done last night, for all that it was his birthday, the most important gift was the one he had given her, and he didn't even know it. She only hoped she could hold on to it when she really needed it, some night that wasn't as perfect as this.

Daniel, the next morning

Daniel awoke to the phone ringing. He had been dreaming—or maybe remembering.

When he opened his eyes and saw Nora lying next to him, a bright smile on her face, he knew it was no dream. "You'd better answer that. Whoever it is probably isn't expecting me to pick up."

She was right; his father's voice greeted him on the line. "Hey, Daniel. Good morning."

Why was Dad calling? He and Mom had called to wish him a happy birthday yesterday. Was something wrong? It couldn't be. His voice didn't sound upset or alarmed; he sounded excited, if anything.

"Hey, Dad. What's up?" Nora was looking at him curiously. He had to turn away from her; there was no way he could look at her wrapped up in his sheets and talk to his father.

"I've got news for you, son. I wish I'd had it yesterday, it would have been a great birthday present for you. Remember how I told you there was a chance for a summer job with Bill Metzger's brother?" Bill Metzger was his father's boss. Dad had mentioned something about his boss' brother at Thanksgiving, but Daniel hadn't put any stock in it. People talked about possibilities and chances all the time, but they usually amounted to nothing.

"Yeah?"

His father was definitely excited, there was no mistaking it. This must be the one possibility in a thousand that had actually come through, but Daniel still had no idea what kind of possibility it was.

"Leo—that's the brother—owns a textile company in Pittsburgh. Bill was telling me how he got suckered into buying all these new computers to modernize everything, he must have spent $50,000, and he has no idea what to do with all of it." Professor Maddox had told a couple of cautionary tales along those lines in class. "So I guess Leo talked to a consultant, and they told him they'd sort it all out for him for $50 an hour, four months of work."

"Dad, what did you tell your boss?"

His father chuckled. "I told Bill that my genius son could do a better job than those thieves in less time and half the cost, as soon as you finish the semester, and all his brother had to do was find someplace for you to stay over the summer."

Daniel almost said, "You should have asked me first," but thought better of it. This was such a huge show of faith from his father. "Wow, Dad."

"Wow is right. Bill talked to his brother. Leo will pay you $25 an hour, off the books, all cash, the whole summer. And you can stay with his aunt. He says she's kind of fussy, but supposedly she's a good cook and there's no rent. What do you think?"

$25 an hour, off the books. So no taxes. Forty hours a week, thirteen weeks of summer break, that was $13,000.

"I don't even know—Dad, that's amazing! Of course I'll take it!" He had never set up a whole network of PC's, let alone configured them to run a small factory. But he'd have two months to talk with Professor Maddox and his other teachers about it. He'd be ready for whatever Leo Metzger needed him to do by the middle of May. Of course he would.

And then he turned back to Nora, saw the curiosity on her face fading away, replaced by an expression he couldn't read, and everything changed in an instant.

How could he go a whole summer—thirteen weeks!—without seeing her?

Nora, five minutes later

"You're going where?" Nora had to hear it again. She must have been mistaken. He couldn't have said what she thought she'd heard.

"Pittsburgh. Dad set it all up. I'm going to make $13,000 this summer! Do you know what I could do with that kind of money?" The room suddenly felt ten degrees colder, and she pulled the sheets—his sheets—more tightly around herself.

She *had* heard him correctly. He was going to abandon her for the summer. Just like her parents always did. And he was doing it the morning after she'd given him a night he would never forget.

She was shaking, and she felt her heart racing. How could this be happening? How had her boyfriend turned into a selfish, thoughtless jerk out of nowhere? How could he just make huge plans like that without even asking her?

"But I might be in New York this summer!" It took all her self control to stop there.

He didn't know that. He *couldn't* know that. He wasn't a thoughtless jerk.

She hadn't said a word to him about her summer plans. He didn't know that one of Rachel's neighbors was an actress on a soap opera. He definitely didn't know that Rachel had been talking to the neighbor, and she'd promised to talk to a friend who worked at *Soap Opera Digest* to try and set up a summer internship there for Nora.

She hadn't been hiding it from him. She was just waiting until it was a sure thing. She didn't want to jinx anything by talking about it too soon, that was all.

"I had no idea, Nora."

"But did you know about this thing your father was working on for you?"

Daniel reached over and took her hands. "He mentioned it right before I came back to school after Thanksgiving. But all he said was that his boss' brother might have a job for me. I didn't think it would amount to anything." He chuckled. "And anyway, I assumed it would be in the area. I had no idea this guy was in

Pittsburgh." He took a deep breath before he went on. "I would hate to not see you for the summer. But this is huge. With that much money, I could pay for next year's tuition, whatever the scholarship doesn't cover. So my parents wouldn't have to pay it. Mom's been wanting to redo the kitchen for years, but they've been paying tuition for Lisa, and now me, and if I could pay for myself ... Mom deserves her new kitchen. And it would pay for books for next year. And a halfway decent used car. And I could buy you ..."

He trailed off, but she could guess what his next words would have been. He'd use some of that money to buy her an expensive gift. Real jewelry, probably. Real gold, not just gold plated. With a real gemstone.

Maybe even a ring? Was he—could he be thinking about that already?

She'd been ready to scream at him, curse at him, call him every awful name she'd ever heard her mother call her father. And he'd been thinking about what kind of fancy jewelry he could buy for her.

She tried to force a smile, and to clear all the ugly, ridiculous, unfair thoughts out of her head. She was pretty sure she didn't manage it.

What the hell was wrong with her?

Daniel, later that morning

"Bee, I don't know what I'm supposed to do." Daniel didn't understand anything that had happened after his father called. Nora had freaked out, she'd been angry—really angry. It was the first time he'd seen her like that.

She stayed for another half hour afterwards, and they talked and joked like usual. Except something was still off with her, even when she'd kissed him, and he'd kissed her back, right before she left. It felt—he didn't even know how to describe it.

So he'd called Bianca, and told her everything that had happened this morning. He didn't know what else to do.

"This is still new to you. And to her too, I think. Five months isn't that long, but it's long enough to think that the other person must know what you're thinking even if you never said it. And then get pissed off when it turns out you're not psychic after all."

That made sense. A lot of sense. "She acted like I should have known she was going to try and get a job in New York for the summer." *Should* he have known? Should he have assumed she'd want to be closer to him during the summer?

Even if he had, he'd told her the truth. He hadn't thought his father's talk about a lucrative job would work out, and he'd had no idea it wouldn't be in New York anyway.

"Yeah. But I guess—I could have told Dad I needed to think about it, and then talked it over with Nora."

Bianca sighed. "Give yourself a break, Daniel. You were surprised. Uncle Tony told you you'd be making thirteen grand this summer, all in cash. Who would say no to that?"

She made it sound so reasonable. And as much as he hated to see Nora upset, it was reasonable, wasn't it? And while his girlfriend had been angry at him, he'd been thinking about how nice a gift he could buy her with $1,500 or even $2,000. It wasn't fair—it wasn't *right* for her to be angry at him. "Exactly, Bee! But I—now *I'm* getting angry and she isn't even here." Getting angry at her when she wasn't there to speak up for herself wasn't fair or right either, was it? "I don't want to be mad at her. I love her."

Bianca laughed, but he didn't hear much humor there. "Those two things aren't mutually exclusive. You think Uncle Tony and

Aunt Marie never get angry at each other? Or my parents? Like I said, you're new at this. It's just—it's something you have to learn as you go. And there isn't anything I can tell you to make it easier to figure out, Danny."

And isn't that what his father had tried to tell him the day after Christmas? That love wasn't easy?

"I'm getting that idea."

"You always were a quick learner." Bianca was silent for a moment. "You know what, maybe there is one thing I can tell you that might help. You can not like something she *did*, but still love *her*. And I bet she'll figure that out, too."

"I hope so, Bee. Thanks for listening to me."

"Always, Danny. You know that."

That all made sense, right? It was just one misunderstanding. Compared to everything they had, it was nothing—wasn't it?

Chapter 14

Nora, April 4

Nora was in the middle of rereading—for the third or fourth time—this week's assignment for Mass Media & Society. It wasn't getting any clearer, and she was starting to wonder if the problem was with her rather than the material.

She was interrupted by the phone. Why was it ringing at two o'clock? It was weird. Nobody ever called her—or Kim, for that matter—in the middle of the afternoon.

She answered it, and didn't immediately recognize the voice. "Nora? Is that you?"

"Yeah," she said. "Who is this?"

There was hesitation on the line, then, "It's—uh, this is Joelle. Your father's—well, you know. I'm sorry to bother you, I know it's probably weird, but I'm kind of ... I don't know what's going on."

Was Dad sick? It couldn't be an emergency, because surely Joelle would have called 911 if—no. She wasn't even going to think about any of the reasons you'd call 911 for a middle-aged man who had a crappy diet and still smoked even though he told you a hundred times that he'd quit for good.

"Joelle, he's not sick, is he?"

More hesitation. "I almost wish he was." Then a sort of panicked giggle. "I don't mean that. Just—at least I'd understand why he's acting the way he is if he was sick. I'd know what to do. I mean, my sister is a nurse and everything." The words came faster as she talked; Nora recognized nervous babbling when she heard it; she did it often enough herself. "I think ..."

What did she think? What would make her father suddenly act weird?

Joelle didn't need to say it. It was the same thing that always made her father act weird. He fell in love, then after a few weeks or a few months something broke. *He* broke.

She didn't know why, but she'd seen it enough times. It had happened, obviously, with her mother. The weirdness had started long before Nora was old enough to even see it. If her mother hadn't gotten pregnant, they would probably have split up within a year. And it had happened with Grace, and Ellen, and Tabitha. Those were just the ones she knew about. There were probably more.

But should she tell Joelle? Was it better to tell her what was coming, or wait for Dad to break her heart by surprise?

She couldn't do that to Dad. There was always a chance, however slim, that this time would be different. Right? "I haven't talked to him in a few days, Joelle. I don't know anything." There she went again, telling a truth that was a complete lie. "I think you should talk to him. Be honest with him." That was a laugh, coming from her.

"I guess you're right. Maybe it's nothing. Maybe I'm just too nervous. Thanks so much, Nora, I appreciate you listening to me."

After Joelle hung up, Nora wondered if she should have just told Joelle the truth after all—Dad was going to rip her heart out. Just like he always did. Just like her mother did, too. Even Aunt Rachel had done it, when she freaked out after her last boyfriend proposed to her.

Oh, God. Everyone in her family broke the hearts of the people they loved. Every single time.

She sat down heavily on her bed and stared hard at her reflection, asking it if she was doomed to do it to Daniel, too. The girl in the mirror didn't speak, but Nora was afraid she knew the answer anyway.

Daniel, April 8

The last time Daniel had been summoned to Professor Maddox's office, it had been to praise him and offer him a job. He doubted it would be nearly as pleasant this time. He walked up to the fourth floor of Ellis Hall, steeling himself for the criticism—or worse—that was about to come his way.

But when he got there, his advisor was—well, not quite smiling, but close to it. "Close the door, please, Mr. Keller." Daniel did so, and then took a seat across from Professor Maddox. As always, the man's desk was perfectly neat; exactly the way Daniel liked to keep his own.

"Thank you. I assume you know why I asked to speak with you, Mr. Keller?"

Right to the point. His advisor wouldn't appreciate him trying to sugarcoat things. "I haven't been doing as well this semester," he said. But that wasn't all of it. "And I've been distracted in class and I've missed some shifts in the lab."

Professor Maddox nodded. "Thank you for your honesty, Mr. Keller." There was a pause. "Daniel." He'd never called Daniel by his first name before. What did that mean?

"I'm very sorry, sir."

"I already know that. I wouldn't have asked you here if I thought otherwise. What I want to talk about is why, although I'm virtually certain I know. If I may ask, what is the young lady's name?"

What? What was he talking about? Why would he think—how would he know?

"Daniel, please. I know students like to think that their elders were never young themselves. I assure you, I was your age once, and I had the same feelings you are having now."

"Sir, I—I'm not sure what ..."

Now Professor Maddox did smile, for real. "For this conversation, you can dispense with the sir and the Professor and call me Scott. We are talking man to man here, not teacher to student. It's only appropriate."

"Sir—Scott." It felt wrong to call him by his first name, even if he'd been told to do it. "You're right. I've been—I love her. Her name is Nora. And most of the time, she's all I think about. All I *can* think about."

It was beyond weird to tell this to a professor. But the man had already guessed, denying it would only be stupid. And kind of cowardly, too.

"Let me tell you a little story. It's about a shy, somewhat sheltered twenty-one year old student called Scott, and a beautiful, vivacious redhead named Emma. This was the spring of 1962, before the Beatles hit it big." Now he actually did smile; Daniel didn't know the man's face could do that. "As an aside, if you ask me who the Beatles are, I will make it my mission to have you expelled." Daniel laughed, but he didn't add that his parents both preferred the Rolling Stones. "Anyway, as I was saying. It was the spring of 1962, and I fell head over heels in love with Emma. I had never felt anything like it before. I hadn't known I *could* feel it."

"That's exactly how it is with Nora."

His advisor nodded. "I thought so. Things between us were—I assume you can imagine. Until one night in April, when Emma came to my apartment in a panic. She was afraid she was pregnant."

Daniel hadn't once thought about that with Nora.

Except he had, hadn't he? Over Christmas, the idea had popped into his head out of nowhere. But not the way his professor was talking about. He and Nora hadn't had that kind of scare; they'd always been careful.

But now he wondered, what would he do if it happened anyway? Careful wasn't always enough. Accidents happened.

"What did you do?"

Professor Maddox—Scott—sighed. "Nothing, as it turned out. It was a false alarm. But it scared both of us. Myself more than her, to tell the truth. I thought long and hard about what I would have done if it had gone the other way." He was lost in thought for a minute, and Daniel didn't dare interrupt. "If it had, I would have dropped out of school, and gotten whatever job I could, to support her and the baby. I'd have married her, if she would've had me. And it would have ended in disaster."

He couldn't believe his advisor was telling him all this. He'd never had any adult talk this personally, or this frankly, to him. "Why a disaster?"

"Because, Daniel, like you, I am a man who cannot do anything but give my full effort to the things that are important to me. I could not have supported Emma and a baby as a student, and I would not have stood for her working while she was pregnant." Daniel just stared blankly at that, and his professor nodded. "It was a different time. It did not help that she was on poor terms with her parents, and they would not have supported her having a baby. My own parents would have given moral support, but that's all they had."

"But she wasn't pregnant."

"She could have been. And it could have happened again. Without being indelicate, I doubt you could simply cut out the physical aspect of your relationship with Nora, any more than I could have with Emma." No. He was absolutely right.

"But you could have gone back to school, once the baby was three or four, couldn't you?"

"As I said, it was a different time. Perhaps if it had been a decade later, or even five years, that might have been possible. But as it was, I knew I would give up my education for her. And— perhaps it would have taken a few years, or only a few months, but I would have come to resent her, and the child, for what I had given up. I could not do that to Emma. And I knew what I had to do. Better to break her heart then and there, and mine, cleanly and quickly, than to come to hate her, and she me, for years to come."

Was he suggesting what Daniel thought he was? That it wasn't enough just to love someone? That you could love someone completely and still have to walk away? "You're not telling me to break up with Nora?"

His advisor shook his head. "I am not telling you anything. Except that you do have a choice to make. You love this girl, it's plain as day. You cannot do less than commit completely to her. It's in your nature, and that is to be commended. But you are also committed to your education, and the last six weeks notwithstanding, you have been an exemplary student and a tireless worker. So we come to a fork in the road. To quote a movie I'm sure you have seen a dozen times, 'Do, or do not. There is no try.' It is not me telling you that a choice is required. It is your heart, and I think you know it."

"That's a lot to think about, Scott." And yet, he knew already that the man was right. Daniel hadn't ever thought about it in those terms but there was no way to deny it.

"Indeed. And that is all I will say on the subject. Now, onto practical matters. You have been, as I said, an exemplary student and I have no wish to put a C, or, God forbid, a D on your transcript. So regardless of what you decide in a larger sense, I will offer you a bargain. Come to every class these last two weeks of term with your full attention. Come to every shift in the lab—unless classwork conflicts, and you give advance notice. Study diligently for my final exam, and score at least 85%. If you do all that, I will give you a B for the semester, and I will keep you on at the lab for the fall. Do we have a deal?"

Despite his crummy—he couldn't call it anything else—work the last few weeks, his advisor was offering him a way out with a decent grade. "Yes, Scott—I mean, Professor." He extended a hand for his advisor to shake. The man grinned again. It really was weird to see.

"Excellent, Mr. Keller. I shall expect you in the lab tomorrow morning." The grin faded away, and Professor Maddox appeared lost in thought for a moment. "One more thing, and I am not sure I should tell you this. But I am your advisor, and as much as you probably won't like hearing it, it is the truth. Whatever choice you make, it will be difficult. And you will always question whether you were right, regardless of how you decide." He gestured towards the photos on the bookshelf behind him—presumably his wife and children. "I love my family with all my heart. I would like to believe that I have been a good husband and a good father. I have never been disloyal or unfaithful. And yet, after all these years, if Emma were to show up in my doorway right now and ask me to run away with her, I cannot honestly say what I would do."

Nora, April 11

How had she fallen so far behind?

Nora knew she wasn't feeling 100%—and hadn't been for a week—but a stupid little cold was no excuse for sleeping through her eight o'clock class this morning, or forgetting about two different assignments, or collapsing into bed before nine o'clock every night this week.

Schoolwork wasn't the only thing she was missing. Rachel had called twice this week and she'd meant to call back but something had always interrupted her before she could. And she hadn't seen—or even spoken to—Daniel since last Thursday.

She knew he'd called, because Kim gave her the messages. And she knew he'd come by, because Kim left his handwritten notes, and the container of chicken soup he'd brought by yesterday, on her side of the desk.

She hadn't even recognized her own voice when she heard herself last night yelling about the soup. "I can take care of myself! I don't need anybody to tell me what to eat or when to go to bed or how to blow my nose!"

Kim had stared at her like she was a Martian or something, but she didn't actually say anything. Nora could only imagine the freakish look she must have given her roommate. It was only now, a day later, thinking about it, that she realized she'd heard that exact rant before. It was her mother's words coming out of her mouth, with a combination of her mother's vicious sarcasm and her father's anger. And it was even worse because she didn't know why she was feeling any of it.

Thank God Daniel wasn't there to hear it. All he was doing was trying to help. That's all he ever did, and she had lost her mind over it. If she didn't pull herself together, she was going to drive him away—maybe for good.

It was a small mercy that she hadn't thrown the soup container against the wall. Kim must have been afraid of that, because the soup had disappeared right after Nora went into the bathroom to cough up brownish-green gunk for fifteen minutes.

All this craziness—ignoring her boyfriend, blowing off her aunt, neglecting schoolwork—for a little head cold? How was that possible?

Daniel, April 16

He hadn't properly spoken to Nora in almost two weeks. He'd been so busy trying to honor his promise to Professor Maddox, and to catch up on all the other classwork he'd neglected, he hadn't even had time to miss her.

Except at night, when he lay there alone, remembering how it felt to fall asleep with her in his arms, her laughter at some silly joke the last thing he heard before drifting off.

What if he forgot what that felt like?

What if she did? What if she *wanted* to forget it? He'd been busy, but if she'd knocked on his door, or just called to talk for an hour or three, he would have made time.

He had a key to Ellis Hall, and the code for the alarm system. If making time for her meant he had to get up at four in the morning and walk over there in the dark to get his work done, he would have done it. But she didn't knock, or call or anything else.

She'd been sick, that was true. But he'd tried to bring her cold medicine. And hot soup. And even a chocolate Frosty, which cost him $40 counting the taxi fare to the nearest Wendy's and back. But he hadn't even been able to give any of it to her in person; it was always her roommate answering the door.

Nora hadn't thanked him; hell, she hadn't even acknowledged him at all. It was like she'd become a completely different person overnight.

Maybe his father had been right, and he'd just been pretending he was ready for love when he obviously wasn't. If he couldn't even help her through a cold and feeling overwhelmed by classes, how could he ever take care of her if something serious happened? Maybe he didn't even know what love meant at all.

At least he could control his schoolwork. He could finish the semester strong, earn back Professor Maddox's trust, and get ready to do a good job in Pittsburgh over the summer. He could make his father proud, and help pay next year's tuition, and start to build the future everybody wanted him to have.

Until—unless—Nora knocked, or called, or did anything to reach out, that would have to be good enough.

Nora, April 18

Last night, she finally got the call she'd been expecting for two weeks. The only thing that surprised her was that it had come from Rachel, not her father.

He'd broken up with Joelle, and he hadn't even had the nerve to tell her about it directly; he left it to his sister to break the news to Nora.

She had known it was coming. They'd been dating almost six months, and his relationships never lasted longer than that.

"He said they started drifting apart, just stopped talking, and he didn't want to hurt her any worse than she was already feeling," Rachel had told her. That's how it always seemed to go with her father.

But on the phone with her aunt, Nora had lost her temper. She didn't even remember everything she'd said, except that it had been ugly and horrible and she hated herself afterwards for it.

That, and after she hung up on Rachel, she'd screamed loud enough that it hurt her throat, and long enough that it brought Karen Quinn all the way from the other side of the floor to see what was wrong.

If only Daniel were here, if only she could talk to him. He'd make everything better.

Except he wouldn't. Couldn't. Because she'd been dating him for six months, too. And apparently that was the expiration date for love in her family.

She'd already been pushing him away the whole month, just like her father had done to poor Joelle. A very sweet woman who'd done nothing to deserve what happened to her, any more than Daniel deserved her ignoring him and brushing off every kind thing he tried to do.

She had to at least be stronger than her father and be honest with Daniel about what a disaster of a girlfriend—a human being—she was. But she had an insane amount of schoolwork to get through, and final exams to prepare for, before she could tell him what a mess she'd become, and how much better off he'd be without her.

She could tell her father to his face that she was just as good at hurting people she claimed to love as he was, but she couldn't face telling him she'd flunked out of school, too. If she couldn't be a good girlfriend, or even a good person, at least she could be a good student. That had to count for something, didn't it?

Daniel, April 23

Another week, and he still hadn't seen his girlfriend.

Was she even his girlfriend anymore?

He'd thought about going over to Morris Hall and banging on her door until she answered. But that only worked in movies. In real life, it would just get him escorted out of the building by campus security, if not something worse.

Then he'd thought about lurking around Addison Hall and catching her by surprise after she got out of class. But that felt creepy, bordering on stalkerish. Whatever had gone so wrong between them wouldn't get better if she thought he was spying on her.

His last idea was to call her aunt. He remembered the phone number for her apartment from Christmas—he never forgot phone numbers. She might not be home, and she might not speak to him if she was, but he felt like there was at least a nonzero chance that something good might come of it.

It still took him half an hour to work up the nerve to dial the phone.

She answered right away. "Hello?"

"Uh, hi. Rachel? You don't know me, but I'm Daniel. Nora's boyfriend?"

She made a sound that he couldn't place—partly a sigh, partly a curse she barely suppressed. "It's nice to finally talk to you, but I wish the circumstances were better."

What did she mean by that? "I know she's not doing well, but she won't talk to me. I want to help—I couldn't think of anything else to do, so I called you."

She cursed again; he heard it for sure this time. "I know she's not talking to you. She isn't talking to anybody." There was a bitter laugh. "I know she loves you, Daniel. And God knows she needs you right now. But—I hate to say this—I don't think she's going to let you in. Or anyone else."

"I don't understand."

Yet another curse. "She learned some very crappy lessons from her parents. I shouldn't be saying any of this, but you deserve to know. She learned that people who love her always end up hurting her. So I think she's decided to push you away before you hurt her, too."

"I wouldn't ever do anything to hurt her!" Not on purpose. But she was hurt the morning after his birthday, when he found out about the summer job, wasn't she?

"No, I don't think you would. But she doesn't know that. Maybe she'll figure it out one day. But—I am so sorry, Daniel—I wouldn't hold my breath if I were you."

Nora, April 27

The phone rang a dozen times. Usually Kim answered it by the third ring, but now she just sat on her bed staring back and forth between it and Nora. When whoever was calling finally gave up, Kim asked her, anger in her tone, "Are you *ever* going to answer the phone, Nora? Or talk to anybody?"

Why? What was the point? If it was Rachel, she'd only be calling with another lecture. If it was her parents, there wasn't anything they could possibly say that she'd want to hear. And if it was Daniel, he'd probably be calling to dump her, and while she didn't blame him—she had been the crappiest girlfriend imaginable for the past several weeks—that wasn't something she was prepared to hear now.

"It was probably for you anyway."

Kim growled—Nora had never heard her roommate make that sound before. "God, Nora! What the hell is wrong with you? I mean, I've been patient because you were sick, and you were really swamped for a while, but you're not the only person who ever had a bad couple of weeks."

She didn't understand. She didn't have everybody who was ever supposed to care about her let her down. She wasn't doomed to let down everybody she cared about. "It's easy for you to talk, as if you know anything about me."

"Only because you never let me know anything real about you! Not once! You talk and joke and make sarcastic comments, but the second something *real* happens, you shut down like it's a crime to feel anything!" Kim stopped for a second, catching her breath, then she went on. "Except with your boyfriend, and you've been pushing him away, too. It's like you *want* to be miserable, just so you can say you were right all along about how rotten everyone is."

How could she say that? That was the most vicious, the most awful thing anybody had ever said to her. She hated Kim for saying it.

And maybe the truest thing, too. She hated Kim even more for that.

Chapter 15

THE LAST DAY OF SPRING SEMESTER—
ALBION COLLEGE

Daniel, May 15

Daniel had never broken up with someone. Peggy didn't count; there hadn't been an official breakup, just something quietly dying that—in hindsight—hadn't ever been what he'd thought it was in the first place.

He couldn't let that happen with Nora. He owed her the truth, delivered face to face, and he owed it to her to stand there and take whatever her response was. Whether it was tears, or shouting, or the cruelest words imaginable or a slap across the face—did girls still do that, or did it only happen in movies?—he would deserve it.

But whatever happened, it would be better than letting this go on when there was no future. It would be better than breaking her heart even worse three months from now, or six, or a year.

♡ ♥ ♡

Nora

Nora had never broken up with anyone. She had no idea how it was supposed to work, except that she owed it to Daniel to go over to his room and tell him in person. She'd ignored him for weeks, but she couldn't do that anymore. She had to stand there and watch his heart shatter when she said the words.

She could have apologized and tried to fix things, if that was possible after how awful she'd been. But even if he did forgive her, which she didn't deserve anyway, she knew what would happen afterwards. She'd just end up leading him on for a few tense months where every conversation was a minefield, until she said or did something so horrible that it would wreck him forever.

That's what her parents had done to each other, and nearly two decades later they both still had ugly jagged wounds where their hearts used to be. She couldn't do that to Daniel.

Daniel

He should go to her. He knew her roommate was already gone for the semester, so she'd be alone. The least he could do was allow this to happen on her turf.

He put on his sneakers, grabbed his keys and he was almost to the door when there was a knock.

Nora

The door opened, and there he was, keys in hand. Was he about to come over to see her? Did he somehow know what she was thinking?

Daniel

It was Nora. Wearing a faded T-shirt and a colorful skirt. Her favorite warm-weather outfit: cool, comfortable and, as she said, "not too ratty looking."

What was she doing here? Had she somehow guessed what he was thinking, what he was going to do?

Nora

She stepped inside and closed the door behind her. Then, just to be safe, she locked it. It seemed like half the rooms on Daniel's floor were empty, but no point in taking chances. He didn't deserve to be publicly embarrassed.

He didn't deserve this at all.

But she didn't deserve him. She'd thought she did. She'd thought she could be someone different, someone worthy of what she saw in his eyes. But at the end of the day, she was still the old Nora she'd hoped she'd left behind. She was still her father's daughter, and breaking hearts was just what Langleys did.

Daniel

"Nora," he started. He had to find the words. He wasn't the man his father, and Dr. Maddox, had told him he needed to be, the kind of man who could step up for the woman he loved. But he could at least be the man who looked her in the eye and told her the truth.

"Nora, I—we can't ... I love you. But it's not enough. I'm not enough. I can't be who you deserve. I wish—I wish I was different. Better."

Nora

She heard the words, and they were all in English, and they all went together in a sentence. But Nora couldn't make any sense of them. What was he talking about? Not enough? Her Daniel?

Was he—he couldn't be, could he? *Had* he guessed what she was going to do, and decided that he would say it first so she didn't have to? Make himself the bad guy to spare her feelings? He *would* do that, wouldn't he?

"Daniel, what are you saying?"

She couldn't let him. He deserved better than to feel guilty on top of everything else he'd feel once she said what she had to say and she closed the door behind her for good.

"Never mind. You're just being you. Being noble. Trying to take care of me. But you can't. I'm a mess, Daniel, and I can't let this go any farther. You deserve a girl who's not a complete walking disaster. Somebody who ... who isn't me. We have to—I have to end it. I love you too, Daniel, but love isn't always enough."

Daniel

She was just trying to shift the blame to herself. She'd been so careful of his feelings, of his heart, from that first night. Any other girl probably would have dumped him the next day, after he hadn't known what he was doing with her right here on this bed. And she'd have told everyone on campus about it, too.

Not Nora. She'd been patient with him and she'd come to meet his parents when she had to be *so* uncomfortable about it, even if she'd never said so. And she was protecting him now, making herself the villain so he could feel better about himself for wanting to break up with her.

Maybe he didn't have to go through with this. Maybe he could do something so big, so grand that she'd have to believe it, and that he'd have to live up to. He could ask her to marry him, right now. He'd have a week at home before he went to Pittsburgh— plenty of time to go to Bassini's Fine Jewelry on Arthur Avenue and find the perfect ring and put it on layaway.

But even thinking that only proved that his father had been right, the morning after Christmas. It was childish thinking, that some fancy gesture could fix real problems. Or that he could magically become more mature, more capable, more deserving of a woman like her.

No. He'd been right all along.

He reached over and took her hands. Probably for the last time. "Nora, neither one of us is the bad guy. We're just—too young, too whatever. We should have met two years from now, and maybe it would be the right time. Maybe we could have made it work then. I love you with all my heart. And I know you love me. But..."

Nora

"But our hearts aren't grown up enough yet, are they?"

He was right. Obviously he was right, if they'd both come to the same conclusion at the same exact time.

"I wish ... I don't even know," he said, still holding her hands. Squeezing them. "I hate this. But I'd hate it more if we ended up hating each other. And I know you would too."

She pulled him close, hugged him to her, felt his arms around her, felt his heartbeat through his shirt.

"Daniel, I—if this is it? If we're really doing this, if we're never going to be together again, if we'll spend the next two years avoiding each other so we don't have to feel weird, then ... then I want one last memory. One good memory."

One perfect memory nobody could ever take away.

Daniel

He knew what Nora meant. "You want to..." He gestured his head towards the bed, and she nodded.

"I want to make love. One last time. I want that to be the last thing we ever do together."

He did, too.

She was right. One final perfect moment, to hang onto while he tried to put his heart back together again, however long that would take. If it was even possible at all.

"I want that too, Nora."

Nora

They went together to the bed, not letting go of each other for a moment.

It happened slowly, carefully. She took the lead, just like that first night. But he was so much more attuned to her than he'd been then. That night, and the first few times afterwards, he'd been reacting to her. But now he knew her body, her responses, well enough to anticipate, to do exactly what she wanted—

needed—before she even realized she needed it. She did the same for—to—him.

And the whole time, his eyes never left hers. Neither of them looked away, or lost focus for a second.

Daniel

Afterwards, they lay there together, still holding each other, still gazing into each other's eyes. He was trying to commit all of her to memory, every detail of her face, every inch of her body, every goosebump she raised on his flesh with her touch. And the whole time—during the act, and for an hour afterwards—neither of them said a word.

And then she slowly, gently kissed him one last time, and she stood up and got dressed. She went to the door, and unlocked it, and, not looking back, she stepped through it and closed it behind her.

She closed it gently, but in his ears that tiny sound echoed like a sledgehammer, and it stayed with him the rest of the night.

Part 3

Chapter 16

SPRING BREAK 1989 (DANIEL)—SNYDER'S LAKE, NY

Daniel, March 13

Snyder's Lake was just visible off in the distance. The water looked almost gray, but hopefully that was just a trick of the light. The trees dotting the shore definitely looked pretty bare, though. Barely any signs of life at all.

"Remind me why I agreed to this," Daniel said. He wasn't asking anyone in the car in particular, but Phil answered from the passenger seat anyway.

"Because outside of classes, you've been sleepwalking through your life since the fall, and it's depressing to watch, so me and Bob thought a spring break trip might snap you out of it."

Bob, behind the wheel, chimed in. "I get that you had a good thing with that girl, and she was gorgeous. But it's been a year now, and you're the one who broke up with her."

"Nine months and 24 days," Daniel answered. It came out almost automatically. And they'd broken up with each other, but there was no point getting into a pedantic debate about that. "But—you know what, I really appreciate you guys inviting me. I know I haven't exactly been the most fun guy to be around."

"You don't even play *Battletech* anymore," Phil agreed. "I brought my set, by the way. Just in case we get bored looking at the lake and drinking cheap beer."

Daniel hadn't given much thought to what they'd be doing at the house on the shore of Snyder's Lake that Bob's brother's girlfriend's father was letting them use for four days. His family had rented a beach house in Ocean City a couple of times, but there were plenty of things to do in Ocean City, and obviously you could swim in the Atlantic. He didn't know if you could swim in the lake here. There might be—he didn't even know what sort of dangerous amphibian things might live in Snyder's Lake.

It might end up being four days of *Battletech* and cheap beer. Maybe that *would* shake him out of the funk he'd been in since last May. It wouldn't make him forget Nora, or stop missing her, but maybe he could enjoy something—anything—for a little while. He was allowed that, wasn't he?

Bob's shout of, "Hey, Daniel!" cut through his thoughts. "I was just saying to Phil when you zoned out, we won't be the only ones there. You met my little sister, Emily—she just transferred to Albion for this semester. She's coming up with her roommate. She's a redhead—very cute. Kim. She lived over in Morris Hall last year. So that'll be fun, right?"

Kim? Redheaded Kim? Who lived in Morris Hall last year?

Nora's roommate.

Daniel had to laugh; what else was there to do? Even when he actually made an effort to move on, the universe worked against him.

Daniel, later that day

Daniel had forgotten how much he enjoyed playing *Battletech*. It had started raining five minutes after they got to the lake house, so there really wasn't much else to do, but he got into the swing of it almost immediately.

The phone rang, but Daniel ignored it; this wasn't his house. A moment later Bob called out, "The girls will be here in ten minutes. They're bringing pizza."

"We're almost done anyway," Daniel said. He had methodically crushed Phil's forces, and now Phil's last 'mech was pinned in a corner of the map waiting to die. "Actually, this might be it right here." He picked up the dice, and rolled two sixes. A hit. "Do we even need to roll for location?"

"No point," Phil said. "Anywhere will be fatal now." He laughed. "You were never this ruthless before, Daniel. But it was fun to play with you anyway. Rematch later?"

"Maybe you and Bob against me." He grinned. "You might have a chance that way." That was the sort of thing Nora would have said, if she ever played *Battletech*. If she was still in his life.

Phil shook his fist at Daniel. "Gloat now. I'll have my revenge!"

It had been fun, and it was hard to recall the last time he'd just had fun for its own sake. Probably a year ago, on his birthday. But there was no point thinking about that night.

The girls showed up right on time. He would have known Emily was Bob's sister even if he hadn't been told; they had the same nose, the same eyes. Just like him and Lisa.

And Kim looked the same as she had last spring. "Hey, Daniel," she said. She sounded wary. He couldn't blame her; she probably expected him to ask about Nora.

"Hi, Kim. Please don't worry—I'm not going to ask about her." He knew there wouldn't be any point even if he wanted to. Kim wasn't living with Nora this year anyway, so what could she tell him anyway?

"Good," she said. "I've barely spoken to her all year. She's living in her own world, and I don't think she really lets anybody in. But that's all I want to say about her. Let's just pretend she doesn't exist while we're here. Deal?"

Daniel extended his hand, and she shook it. "Deal."

Daniel, March 14

Daniel opened the back door and took a look outside the house. There was a trail down to the lakeside, and it looked like you could walk all the way around it. Despite yesterday's rain that had continued until after midnight, the trail was dry, at least as far as he could see.

It might be nice to go for a walk in the fresh air. There was a little breeze, and plenty of sun. Why not? It would even be healthy, especially after last night's greasy pizza and the prospect of whatever alcohol Bob picked up at the liquor store later today.

Bob had complained about being volunteered to go to the store.

"Why do I have to go?"

Phil told him, "It's your family's house, so you're responsible."

"It's not actually my family's. And even if it was, Emily's family, too, so it's her house as much as mine." he'd protested.

She pointed out, "You're the oldest, so you're responsible."

Bob turned to Daniel. "Why can't you go?"

"I'm not twenty-one yet." Daniel threw up his hands. "Ask me on Wednesday when I'm legal."

Bob finally looked at Kim. "What about you?"

"It's not my house either, *and* I'm not twenty-one. Sorry, Bob." And that ended the debate.

But maybe he'd go with Bob anyway. It wasn't really fair to make him go by himself. In the meantime, though, the outdoors was calling. Or at least whispering.

He was only two steps out the door when he heard Kim call out to him. "Hey, you want some company?"

He didn't, really. But that was rude, and not fair to Kim, wasn't it? "Sure, come on."

They set off, and Daniel quickly discovered that the trail wasn't quite as dry as he'd thought. "Watch where you're walking," he said to Kim after he stepped into a patch of mud up to his ankle. He was glad he'd worn his ratty old sneakers that probably should've been thrown out six months ago.

The trail curved out of sight of the house very quickly. There was nothing else to see except nature all around them, and no sounds except their footsteps. It was almost as though the rest of the world had vanished. Like in that movie he'd seen a couple of years ago, where the hero woke up and everyone was gone.

It was kind of unsettling.

"Are you okay?"

He felt Kim's hand on his arm. He must have been showing his nerves.

"I'm fine," he said. He didn't push her hand away, though. He wasn't sure why. "Just feeling lonely." He realized as soon as he said it what Kim would think. "Not like that! Not about *her*. Just—just this weird quiet, like I'm the last person on Earth. I felt creeped out for a minute, that's all."

She had been starting to frown, but now she just looked scared instead. She punched his arm, not quite playfully. "God, why did you have to say that? Now you've got me thinking it, too. I'd rather talk about her than feel like I'm in a horror movie or something."

"Do you want to go back?"

Kim still looked scared, but she shook her head. "Your friends were trying to teach Emily that stupid robot fighting game. I'm not letting them drag me into that."

"Technically they're not robots," Daniel said. He knew that would annoy her, but if she was annoyed with him, she'd forget about being scared. That seemed like the chivalrous thing to do.

Daniel, two hours later

"They're going to send out a search party for us if we don't head back soon," Kim said.

Daniel shook his head. "I don't think Phil or Bob are going to venture out of sight of the house. Neither one of them is exactly a nature lover." Of course, he wasn't one either. This was the longest he could recall ever being in any kind of wilderness. Not that this even counted as wilderness, really. "Besides, we're three quarters of the way around the lake. It won't be that long."

Kim was silent for a couple of minutes. Then she grabbed his arm to stop him. "Maybe it wouldn't be so bad if we took a little longer." She wasn't letting go. Daniel didn't understand why she was hanging on to him.

Unless she was—what? Flirting with him?

"Kim?"

She let her fingers trail down his arm, and then she was holding his hand. And staring into his eyes. "This has been really nice."

It was nice, to clear his head a little, to breathe fresh air and actually force his body to move properly for the first time in a while. And Kim was good company. "Kim, I'm not—I mean, you're really sweet, and you're pretty." God, that sounded horrible. She deserved a better answer. "It's not anything about you. It's just that you're not ..."

"I'm not Nora," she finished for him, with a sad smile. "I guessed you would say that. But I wasn't sure. It was worth a shot, you know?"

"You're not angry?" She didn't seem to be, but it would make the rest of this trip very awkward if she was.

"Not angry. Just a little disappointed. But I get it." She was still holding his hand. She squeezed it. "You had something real with her, and ... I've never had that, but I'm sure it's hard to get past. But if you don't mind a little free advice, you aren't ever going to get past her until you start trying to."

She looked almost nervous then, as if she thought she'd over-stepped. He squeezed her hand back before pulling away from her. "That's what I'm doing here."

"Miniature robot wars with Bob and Phil isn't really trying, Daniel."

He gave her his own sad smile. "It totally is, compared to how I've been doing since we broke up. And don't knock *Battletech* until you've tried it."

Daniel, March 16

Daniel was officially twenty-one years old. He didn't feel any different than he had last night, when he was still just twenty.

Sure, he could buy liquor now, but he rarely drank, so that didn't seem like a big deal. And as of this morning he could go to Atlantic City and gamble in a casino, but he didn't want to do that anyway.

Even though he'd known intellectually that nothing would really change, he was a little disappointed that he didn't feel … something. He couldn't say what it should have been. Just *something*.

On the plus side, he didn't feel hungover, unlike everyone else in the house. He'd had one cup of last night's drink of choice: the cheap vodka Bob had bought mixed with orange Tang that Phil had found in the back of a cupboard. One cup had been more than enough.

Well, Kim wasn't really hungover. She was the only one who listened to his advice to take three aspirin and drink as much water as she could stomach before going to sleep, and she was the only one who was even halfway functional this morning.

"Thanks, Daniel," she said while he poured out Cheerios for the two of them. It wasn't quite stale, and it was also the only breakfast food in the kitchen. Luckily, there was also just enough milk to share between two bowls. "For last night, I mean. And for the breakfast, such as it is."

He shook his head. "Sure thing. Next time,"—if there *was* a next time—"I'll insist that we stop for groceries on the way. This really is a pretty sad meal, isn't it?"

Kim gestured towards the back door, and he followed her outside with his sad bowl of almost-stale cereal.

"It could be worse," she said, sitting down on the steps that led to the trail to the lakeshore. "At least the company's pretty good." She tapped her bowl against his. "Oh, and cheers to you. Happy birthday!"

"Thanks Kim. It's weird," he said, staring out at the lake. It was perfectly still this morning, and silent. "I thought I'd feel—I don't even know what. But it's just another morning, and I'm still just me."

"A person could do a lot worse than being just you"

He didn't say anything for a while, and neither did she. They both just watched the serene lake. There weren't even any birds this morning, or squirrels or whatever else lived out here. After a while, she tapped his shoulder, and when he didn't immediately respond, she grabbed both shoulders and turned him to face her. "I know what I said when I got here. But do you want to talk about her? You can call it a birthday gift."

He looked at her, and saw nothing except kindness—and maybe some sadness mixed with it in her eyes. "I don't know. I—I still love her, Kim. She's still here," he put a hand over his heart. "I don't think she'll ever not be there, you know what I mean?"

"Like I said the other day, I've never felt that. But I can imagine what it's like." She hesitated for a moment and her voice caught before she went on. "I *do* imagine it. A lot. And sometimes I want to go downstairs to Nora's room and scream at her because she did have it and she let it go." Daniel didn't answer. What could he say? He waited for Kim to go on. "Except—I guess this is what you want to know—I don't think she *has* let it go, any more than you have. I don't think she can."

Daniel didn't know how he felt about that. This whole year had pretty much sucked. There wasn't a day that went by— sometimes not even an hour—where he wasn't reminded of her. He'd see something she would have joked about, and he'd hear her laughter and then he'd turn around and expect to see her. And always—every time—be disappointed that she wasn't there.

If she was feeling that, too—he didn't want that for her. It was bad enough that he lived with the constant ache of her absence, she shouldn't have to hurt every day, too.

"I'm sorry to hear that," he said, after a while. "If she's going through what I've been ... I wouldn't wish that on anybody."

There was another silence, and after—he didn't even know, maybe ten minutes?—Kim finally said, "If I talk to her—I'm not promising, just if—do you want me to tell her that you're doing okay?"

"Yes." It was a lie, but the truth wouldn't do anything except hurt Nora even more than she already was. "Maybe if she thinks I'm okay, she'll let herself feel better. It's the least I can do, right?"

Kim leaned over, hugged him. "I don't think you owe her anything, Daniel. But I'll tell her. I promise." He wished he could believe he didn't owe her anything. It would be so much easier. But maybe he didn't owe her *everything*. That, he could probably make himself believe.

He held on to Kim for a moment or two longer. He hadn't realized how much he'd been missing simple human contact. Not sexual. Not romantic. Not anything except *kind*. Just touching someone else, and being touched, because they were another person who knew you were hurting and they wanted to make it better, even if it was just for a minute.

"Thanks, Kim. It—all of this, it means a lot." He let her go, and grinned at her.

Chapter 17

Nora, March 13

Nora was already regretting this. She hadn't stayed over at her mother's condo in nearly two years, for many good reasons. She'd put all that aside when Mom asked her if she had any spring break plans.

She'd asked Mom if she was going to be in Providence, and if she wanted company for a few days. Naturally, she couldn't just say "Yes, my daughter, whom I love, please come and stay with me," like a reasonable person. Still, she had made it clear in her own convoluted and self-involved way that Nora could come and visit.

Mom hadn't been there when Nora arrived, so she'd had to find the building manager and beg him to let her in. He'd made Nora show her driver's license and sign a form before he'd unlock the door for her.

For a while, Nora just sat in the guest bedroom—it was her bedroom once upon a time. It had been redecorated at least twice that Nora knew of, since she went away to college. Right now it was all pastels—baby blue paint on the walls, delicate pink sheets and blanket on the bed, a light green chair in the corner and a lavender torchiere lamp with a soft white bulb installed. It didn't look as if it gave enough light to read at night, not that anybody who stayed in this room probably did much reading.

It definitely wasn't her style; it hadn't really been anybody's style since 1986 or so. She wondered if one of her mother's boyfriends had sold her on this décor, or if it had been Mom's own idea.

She sat in the awful green chair, lost in thought, until she heard her mother in the living room. "Nora, darling! Are you here?"

Nora had a sudden urge to open the window and see if she could climb down to the sidewalk. It was only four floors up, she might be able to get away without ever having to talk to Mom.

"I'm in here, Mom." If she went out the window and fell, she'd break her leg and then she'd be trapped here with her mother for several weeks.

Karen Langley came in. Swept in, really; she liked to do that. Her hair was shorter than the last time Nora had seen her. And blonder. And the little lines under her eyes were gone. And was her nose different? Had Mom gotten plastic surgery?

"Why are you sitting in the dark like a sad, unloved flower?" Her mother turned the lamp on; it didn't make much difference, and Mom shrugged. "We can buy another lamp. But come out with me into the light so I can see you properly." Nora's hand was grabbed, and she was hauled up and led into the living room, where her mother looked her up and down.

"You aren't eating enough, and you need to use a proper face cream every day. You're only young once, Nora, it would be a mistake to waste it." Nora thought she might have heard something close to kindness there; probably as close as her mother could get. And even then it was all superficial.

She bit back her first several responses, and settled for. "I hear you, Mom,"—with the nearest thing to a smile she could manage.

She hadn't expected much from this visit. All she really wanted was one conversation—one moment—that was real. One chance to tell her mother what she was feeling, and get an honest answer. But five minutes with Mom and that already seemed impossible.

Unless some kind of miracle was forthcoming, it was going to be a very long four days.

Nora, March 14

The phone rang at eight o'clock in the morning. To Nora's surprise, it only rang once before her mother answered it. Nora listened to her mother's side of the conversation from the guest room, and to her further surprise, Mom sounded—she couldn't recall ever hearing it from her—professional and competent. She wasn't making airy pronouncements, she was giving orders in a calm tone, as if she was utterly confident they'd be obeyed.

"Yes, I said unload the truck and clear out the blue room. Make sure it's completely empty. I'll be there by ten, I want a full crew ready to go so we can get everything installed by lunchtime." There was silence for a minute, then, "Yes, that's what I said. I have lunch plans with my daughter, and I am *not* going to disappoint her again. Am I clear?" A momentary pause, then, "Good. See that you do." Nora heard her mother hang up the phone, and then footsteps—probably Mom heading into the kitchen.

Nora had to replay her mother's words several times. Did she—could she—really mean what she'd said? She thought for a moment about just going into the kitchen and telling Mom she'd heard everything. But maybe that wasn't the best plan.

Her mother had said things like that before, hadn't she? Better to just let the morning unfold and see if her mother's actions backed up her words.

If they did—maybe a miracle really would happen this week.

Nora, two hours later

Nora had convinced her mother to let her come along to the gallery. Honestly, it hadn't taken much convincing; Mom seemed almost excited about the idea, but of course she couldn't actually say that.

When they arrived, and Nora saw how the staff reacted to her mother, the way they carried out her orders quickly and without question, she couldn't help but be ashamed of herself.

She'd always thought that running the *Galerie Coeur Nouveau* wasn't a real job. That the gallery was something she'd sweet-talked an old boyfriend into letting her take over, paid for by the generosity of subsequent well-off men.

It had never occurred to her that her mother was actually interested in art, and knowledgeable about it. And competent—more than competent—at making a living displaying and selling it.

All this time, all these years, she'd viewed her mother as little more than a—no, she wouldn't even think the word.

She wasn't merely ashamed of herself. Nora was totally disgusted.

No wonder she'd blown things with Daniel. It just proved that the only decent thing she did for him was to let him go, before she could be as ugly to him as she'd been for so long to her mother.

She wandered around the gallery, hating herself more with each passing minute. Until she stopped in front of one of the new paintings that had just been hung. It was very abstract, really just vague shapes and blocks of color. The sort of thing she usually laughed at, and wondered how dumb someone would have to be to pay thousands of dollars for.

One afternoon, a month after they'd started dating, she and Daniel had been walking around off campus, headed nowhere in particular, and they went into a little art gallery, and then they'd spent two hours at the Green Lantern Café talking about exactly that—who was buying the ridiculous modern art that didn't even look like anything, and why, and what were they doing with it?

But looking at this painting, really looking at it, Nora saw something. It wasn't just random shapes and colors. There was yellow, very bright, almost a circle, partly obscured by dark shapes. Clouds. So the yellow was the sun, and it was shining out, and rising above dark clouds.

The sun was always there, even if you couldn't see it. And it would always be there. It would always, sooner or later, shine through the clouds. No matter how dark it was—how dark *she* was—there would always be light.

Just because she'd been horrible to her mother for years, didn't mean it had to always be that way. Maybe today could be the day the sun finally came up.

Nora, two hours later

"Didn't this used to be an Italian restaurant?" Back in high school, her father had taken her here a few times in its previous incarnation.

"They went out of business last year. Chef Michel took over two months later," her mother said. "Amazing man. And the most gentle hands—never mind, I'm sure you don't want to hear about that." That was new; usually her mother would go on for several minutes about the latest man in her life. It was as though her mother was a completely different person today.

And then it got even stranger. When the waiter came, her mother ordered wine for the both of them. Nora didn't question it, but apparently her expression did it for her. Mom laughed. "You're not going to pretend you've never had wine before, are you? I know you started drinking when you were thirteen."

"No! I never—I didn't ..."

Her mother was still laughing. "You weren't really—excuse me—dumb enough to think I didn't notice, were you?" She didn't give Nora a chance to answer. "Oh, of course you were. Exactly as dumb as I was at that age, when I thought my parents didn't notice everything I got up to." And now she was smiling, but it was—not gentle, exactly, but as close as Karen Langley could get to it. "And as dumb as my future grandchild will be one day, I'm sure." Where had any of that come from?

"Mom, I—I don't know what's going on here."

Her mother reached over, patted her hand. "You wanted to talk. You wanted to really communicate. That is why you came to stay with me, isn't it?" Now she sighed deeply. "I know I haven't always—ever—been the best mother, but I'm not blind. And I do love you, regardless of what I've probably given you plenty of cause to believe."

How had her mother known? How had Mom guessed what she'd been thinking, what she wanted—needed—to hear? And—whatever joy she'd felt at her mother's words was gone as quickly as it came—if she was that perceptive, why hadn't she ever shown it before? Where had this version of Karen Langley been for the past several years? Where had she been a year ago, when Nora had needed her—needed anybody who could rescue her from herself—more than she ever had?

No, that wasn't fair. Or, even if it was, it didn't matter. There was no way to change the past, but Mom was trying here and now. She had been given exactly what she asked for, and it would be the most ungrateful thing imaginable to turn her back on it.

She argued with herself until the wine was served, and she drank her whole glass before she felt like she could safely speak. "I love you, too, Mom. I always have. I just—you're right. I wanted to talk. I hate how things have been with us all this time." She hesitated, debating whether to say anything more, but the words poured out of their own volition. "And I—I need you. I need somebody, because I miss him so damn much. It's been almost a year, and I think about him all the time still, and it's hell. I don't know what to do." She fought back tears, but she heard herself make a choked, sobbing sort of sound, and she felt her mother's hand squeezing hers. She couldn't remember the last time she'd felt that. "I need you—I need you to be the kind of Mom who fixes everything, because I can't fix anything myself."

Nora, that evening

They had talked—really talked, properly talked—all through lunch, and the drive home, and for several hours after that. Nora had never said so much to her mother. Not even before the divorce, when her parents were still trying to coexist and pretend to her that everything was normal.

She'd told Mom all about Daniel, everything except the most intimate details, and she'd probably said enough that her mother knew all about them, too.

They were in the living room. Mom had made margaritas for both of them—another sign that she'd seen far more than Nora ever thought she had.

"Mom—can I ask you—what really happened with you and Dad? Why didn't it work?"

Her mother considered the question for a while, then downed half her drink before she answered. "We didn't really—I'll speak for him too, because I think it was the same story for both of us. We didn't know how to be in a relationship. Your grandparents, they weren't the most talkative people. It was how they grew up. They were kids during the Great Depression, my father fought in World War II, and then after the war, they had me. And—neither one of them was emotional. No, that's not fair. They felt everything, they just made sure never to show it, because you didn't back then."

That made sense. It fit with everything Nora knew about that era, and with the little she remembered of her grandparents as a kid. "And then you grew up with Elvis and the Beatles and then—oh, God, I can't believe I'm saying this to my Mom—the pill and free love and all that stuff. Right?"

Her mother laughed, and finished the rest of her drink. "Pretty much. They didn't know what to do with me. I didn't know what to do with me. None of us did. The world was changing and all the rules my parents knew were out the window, and nobody knew what the new rules were. So I never learned how to be a girlfriend, a real, loving, proper girlfriend. Or a wife." She hesitated, then cursed under her breath. "So we made each other miserable, we learned to hate each other. And with all that, how could we ever teach you to do any better?"

Nora couldn't think of anything to say to that. They were both silent for a moment, then her mother went on. "Well, you did better in one way. At least you didn't get yourself pregnant and have a child to disappoint for the next nineteen years."

How many times had Nora felt disappointed by her parents? How many bitter and ugly thoughts had she had about them? How many times had she told herself she hated the both of them?

It was all still there. Every bad memory, every moment of pain, every time she burned inside because she'd needed them and they weren't there—none of it went away.

But right here, right now none of it mattered.

She went over to her mother, hugged her tightly, and they both cried until they didn't have any tears left.

Nora, March 16

She'd gotten her miracle, and more. Nora had gotten her mother back this week.

It wasn't perfect; Mom had lapsed back into her old self at times, and there'd been the incredibly awkward dinner last night with her latest boyfriend. But despite that, things were infinitely better between them than they'd been since—well, ever.

Mom even drove her to the train station.

"Before you go, there's one more thing I'll tell you. This may not help—it might make you feel worse about that boy." Mom had not referred to Daniel by his name once all week. "But I think you should know it."

Nora couldn't begin to guess what was coming. "Mom, if it's that bad, maybe you don't need to tell me."

Her mother gave her a sad smile. "It's not so much bad as it is history repeating. You're my daughter, you can't get away from it, so the least I can do is tell you what to expect." A pause, and Nora imagined her mother wished she had a drink in hand to steady her nerves. "I never did get over your father. Not really."

"What?"

"Don't get me wrong, Nora. I don't want him back. That will never happen. It never has, since we divorced. But there's part of me that will always love him. Part of his heart I'll always hold, no matter how much we hurt each other. And I'm afraid it'll be the same for you and that boy. It doesn't mean you won't find another love—I hope you will—but you will never be totally free of him. I'm sorry, but it's just who you are. You're your mother's daughter." She took a deep breath before she finished. "And your father's. If you could ever get him to be honest, he would tell you the exact same thing."

She'd never get over Daniel? She'd always feel this way about him, even ten years from now? That's what she had to look forward to?

"Mom—I wish you hadn't said that. But ... thank you anyway."

"I love you, Nora. I'll try to always tell you the truth from here on. Even if it's something you don't want to hear."

She kissed her mother, said her goodbyes, and then she spent the next few hours on the train praying that her mother was wrong about her.

Chapter 18

Nora, September 6

"Happy birthday to our brand new assistant editor!"

The whole staff of the *Albion Observer*—all six of them, not counting Nora—was here in the paper's office in the basement of the Whitman building. It was touching that somebody had remembered today was her birthday—and then the rest of Ben's words hit her.

"What? What did you just say, Ben?"

Ben Francis was the editor of the Observer. He was a senior, and tall, and his hair was blonder than Nora's. Maybe even blonder than her mother's, which was saying something. "Well, I thought we'd celebrate two things at once. Efficient, right?"

"That's amazing! Thank you! I promise I'll do a good job." She hadn't expected a promotion, or even really thought about it. If you'd asked her, she would have said that obviously Marcia Bennett—a senior, an intern at the *Albany Courier* last year, an actual grown-up—would have gotten it.

"Don't thank me yet," Ben said with a laugh. "The biggest part of the job is keeping this lot,"—he gestured to the rest of the staff—"in line. You've heard the phrase 'herding cats?' It's like that, but worse."

That wasn't true. Or was it?

She'd been late on articles more than once last spring, and Ben—he'd still been assistant editor then—had to harass her to get them done. She couldn't have been the only one who needed a push now and then to meet a deadline.

But she could do that. Although, maybe it wouldn't hurt to sit down with Ben for a chat, and pick his brain about the best way to go about it. But first, there was a candle to blow out, and a cupcake to eat.

And then she could head over to West Hall and tell Daniel her news.

He was probably planning some big surprise ...

No, he wasn't.

He wasn't planning anything, and she wasn't going to share her news with him. Because they weren't together. They hadn't been for over a year.

They wouldn't ever be together.

Why couldn't she just accept that already?

Daniel, September 6

"I assume you've begun researching possible employers, Mr. Keller?"

He had, but not today. Today, he'd been trying to figure out what to do for Nora for her birthday. She'd made his twentieth birthday special—beyond special—and he owed her ...

He heard himself curse under his breath, and Professor Maddox stared hard at him. "Excuse me, Mr. Keller?"

How could this still be happening? How did Nora still have this much of a hold on him almost sixteen months after they'd broken up?

"I'm sorry, Sir. I think I finally understand what you told me, when we had that long talk."

"Ah. Your Nora. I suspected that might be it." Now his advisor smiled softly. "I wonder if you even know that you doodled her name in the margins of your final exam book last spring."

"Sir?" How could he have done something like that? "Oh, God. I know what happened. I finished in an hour, and then I went over every answer three times, and everyone else in the class was still writing and I didn't want to be the first one to hand in my exam, and I must have zoned out."

Professor Maddox laughed—a real belly laugh. "You truly are just like me, Mr. Keller. I also hated being the first to turn in my paper. It felt so awkward, everyone's eyes on me, and I'd wonder if somehow there was a whole other page of the exam that I'd missed. So I would sit there, trying to calculate the appropriate moment, and on occasion I, too, would become thoroughly lost in thought."

That was exactly how it felt! Daniel had never met anyone else who knew about that; but, then again, he was almost always the first to finish exams, going all the way back to grade school. "Thanks, Sir. But I am sorry—I can't believe I did that. But it's like you told me—I guess she'll always be in here," he put a hand over his heart. "Never mind. You were asking me about job searching?" Except, how could he build a future when he couldn't let go of his past with her? It had to be possible—Professor Maddox had done it, hadn't he?

"I would like to suggest a company to you. Quantum Networking Solutions. They are based in Chicago, and they are one of the largest companies in fiber-optic networks. It will be a huge growth field, and you can get in on the ground floor. Do some research on them, and if you like what you see, let me know. A reference from me would certainly not hurt you. An old fraternity brother of mine is a Vice President there."

Daniel's eyes went wide at that last comment, and his advisor noticed. "Don't be so shocked, Mr. Keller. I did not always wear tweed jackets with elbow patches. You said you remembered our talk, so you know I, too, was young once."

He'd have to take Professor Maddox's word for it. There were no fraternities or sororities at Albion, so his knowledge of Greek life came entirely from "Animal House" and "Revenge of the Nerds." It was impossible to picture his advisor doing anything from those movies.

Then again, if you asked Daniel's friends from high school, they'd all say it was impossible to picture him ever having a serious girlfriend, let alone aching over her sixteen months after they'd broken up.

Nora, September 15

God, Ben was handsome.

He obviously spent a lot of effort styling his hair so that it looked like it didn't take any effort at all. It was like an art form, one that Nora herself had never come close to mastering. And he knew exactly what colors to wear and how to wear them.

"Hey, Nora, are you okay?"

What she wanted to say was "no," because how could she be expected to concentrate on this week's articles when he was sitting there like he'd just stepped out of a Benetton catalog?

"Sorry, I just got lost in thought for a minute."

It hit her then; this was the first time she'd thought that way about anyone since Daniel. Sure, she'd swooned over the pottery scene in *Ghost* and imagined Patrick Swayze's arms around her, just like every other girl with a pulse, but that didn't count.

This did. Ben was an actual human, sitting four feet away from her, and he looked—well, hot—even under the horrible fluorescent lights of the *Observer* office.

"Nora? Are you sure you're all right? We can do this tomorrow, if you're not feeling well."

No. Ben would still be hot tomorrow. Hot, thoughtful, smart, and worst of all he acted like he didn't even know it.

Being his assistant editor was going to be a lot more difficult than she'd thought.

Daniel, September 20

Daniel sat at the desk watching over the brand new Macintosh lab in Ellis Hall. A dozen Mac SE's for anyone on campus to use, as well as anyone at the nearby Albany College of Law. Apparently the law school didn't have their own computer lab.

He didn't mind. The law students were very quiet and—well, studious. They never asked for help or advice or anything. It left him free to catch up on his classwork, which was a mercy because Data Communications was proving to be a struggle to keep up with.

For the last hour, though, he hadn't been doing schoolwork. He'd been staring at the birthday card he'd bought two weeks ago for Nora and then stashed in the back of his desk instead of giving it to her.

Even two weeks late, he could give it to her. She'd probably think it was hilarious. But he hadn't even written in it; what could he possibly say?

He was snapped out of his distraction by an angry grunt, followed by a woman's voice not quite shouting, "Oh, my God! You're supposed to be smarter than I am!" Then there was a light thump, like a fist hitting a table, and finally, "I give up! Can somebody please help me?"

Daniel looked up, and other than the owner of the voice—a blonde woman with her hair tied back in a ponytail—he was the only somebody in the room.

She should have checked in with him and left her ID, so he could hand her a disk with whatever software she needed, but she must have just grabbed a disk right off his desk without him noticing. He could mention that to her later; there was no point making a big production out of it when she was the only other person here.

He went over, and she turned to face him. He wasn't great at guessing ages, but she seemed a little older than him—she might be one of those normally quiet law students. She had brown eyes, and she was trying not to smile. Her smile was probably warm and inviting and—God, where had that thought come from? He needed to get a grip; he hadn't thought about anybody's smile since ... Nora.

"Hi," he said, trying to forget about soft brown eyes and a warm almost-smile. And about Nora, too. "What's going on?"

"MacWrite isn't cooperating."

He grabbed a chair and sat down next to her. "You'll have to be a little more specific."

She pointed. "See here? It's not centering my name. It should look like this," she handed him a paper—someone's resume, obviously not hers. "Carrie said she did her resume here in five minutes, and it looks great and mine looks like garbage so far."

Hearing it out loud jogged his memory. He'd been working on an assignment while Bob was covering the desk last week, and Bob had spent the better part of an hour formatting a resume for a girl named Carrie. He'd never looked up, but he'd heard the whole thing.

"I hate to tell you, but your friend Carrie stretched the truth a little bit. My friend Bob did it for her, and it took him nearly an hour."

The woman laughed. "I should have guessed. She's been known to exaggerate from time to time." She took the resume back from Daniel. "Look, right here." She pointed. "Summer Intern, Fitch & Calabria. Duties included assisting in the strategic preparation and execution of multi-jurisdictional litigation with direct impact on corporate compliance." She rolled her eyes dramatically. "Do you know what Carrie actually did there?"

Daniel shook his head. He was pretty sure she didn't expect him to answer.

"She filed the contract with the caterers for the firm's Fourth of July party. That was the sum total of her strategic litigation experience."

Daniel chuckled. "Well, at least she's creative, right?"

"Are you one of those glass half full people?" She didn't wait for an answer. "Well, I guess the world needs you guys, too." He wasn't sure if that was a compliment or not, but he smiled anyway. She smiled back, and it was as pretty as Daniel had thought it would be. "I'm Valerie, by the way. Valerie Vance. In case you didn't read it off the screen."

"Daniel. It's nice to meet you." He extended a hand, and she shook it. And held it for a second or two longer than he expected her to. But maybe that was just how she was. "Let's see if we can't get your resume looking better than Carrie's, okay?"

Nora, September 28

"Get your stuff together, Nora. You're coming with me."

Nora looked up from the article she was editing—a funny piece Marcia Bennett had written about how commuter students occupied themselves while riding the bus to or from campus—to see Ben standing over her.

"What?"

"The mayor's press conference. I got a second press pass. Come on, it's a fifteen minute drive, and then we have to find parking and get a good seat once we get there."

She didn't know there was *one* press pass. How had Ben even managed to get one pass for the *Observer* to cover a City Hall press conference, let alone two?

It didn't matter; he was in a rush, so she had to keep up. She grabbed her purse and followed him out of the office, up the stairs, out of the Whitman building and two blocks to the student parking lot. And then—"Holy crap! How do you have a Jaguar?"

It was green. Almost emerald, but even darker than that. And very well kept, at least from the outside. "It's eighteen years old and my father got sick of the repair bills, that's how. He replaced it with a Toyota, and I drive it as little as possible." He didn't quite laugh. "And pray every time I do."

The car didn't seem to have any problems on the drive over to City Hall. And Ben turned out to be a whiz at parallel parking, something Nora had barely managed on her road test and avoided whenever possible.

They even managed to get decent seats—in the second row, right behind a reporter from *Government Affairs Monthly* and a freelance writer for the Associated Press.

Ben turned to her and whispered, "OK, Nora. You're just here to watch today. I probably am, too. I doubt I'll have the chance to ask anything, but it's still good experience just to be here." She nodded. But she saw his notebook, with several questions scribbled in his nearly unreadable handwriting.

Mayor Kinsey and his press secretary came out, a few minutes late, and gave a short statement about progress on building a new runway for the airport, and then they took questions. Nora wasn't sure why she and Ben were even here—nothing that was being discussed seemed at all relevant to Albion College.

But then the transportation reporter from the *Albany Courier* asked about proposed cuts to the city bus system. The Mayor gave a dodgy non-answer, and Nora saw her hand shoot up before she even realized she'd done it. Ben glared at her, but it was too late—she was being called on.

"Yes, Miss ..."

"Langley, *Albion Observer.*" She paused for a moment, trying to recall the exact figures in the article she'd been working on just an hour ago. "Over 40% of students at Albion are commuters, and most of them rely on the number 23 bus route to go to and from campus. If you cut that route, how will they be able to complete their education? These are local people who will become local employees and local taxpayers when they graduate. *If* they graduate, given the impact of your transit cuts. What do you say to them and their families?"

She couldn't believe herself; her heart was pounding too loud for her to even hear the Mayor's answer. But it must have been another dodge, because she saw a dozen raised hands to follow up on her question, and several more reporters frantically jotting down the Mayor's words. And hers, too?

But better than that was the way Ben's glare had transformed into a proud—almost triumphant—grin.

Daniel, October 10

Daniel was at the desk in the lab, as usual on a Wednesday. And the lab was almost empty, also as usual. The only difference today was that he was caught up on all his classes, so he could actually pay attention to the one person who was working in the lab.

It was Valerie. She was here a lot. Almost every day he worked in the lab, come to think of it. And she had a question almost every visit. It was weird that she couldn't get the hang of things he'd explained three or four times.

"Hey, Daniel," she said, seemingly on cue.

He went over to see what she needed.

"I can't get the footer to look right. It keeps messing it up."

He'd shown her how to fix that last week. And two weeks ago. "You have to use the format menu. You can't just click in the footer like you did there."

He grabbed the mouse to show her, and her hand brushed against his. He expected—he didn't know what, maybe for her to jump away? But she didn't. She smiled at him instead, and then watched him demonstrate—again—what she needed to do.

"Thanks. Maybe I'll remember this time. Unless something,"— she glanced up at him, smiled—"distracts me." She shrugged. "Or maybe there's only so much room in my brain, and it's filled with case readings and statutes. No room for anything else."

Daniel doubted that. He was pretty sure there was room in Valerie's brain for whatever she wanted to be there.

And then a thought occurred to him, so absurd that he couldn't imagine where it had come from. Maybe she *did* remember about the footers—and everything else she kept "forgetting"—and she just wanted his attention.

Except—why? What could a twenty-four year old woman, months away from being a lawyer with a high paying job and everything else, possibly want with him?

"I'm sure you will," he said, dismissing his idiotic notion.

"Yeah," she said, giving him an inviting smile. "Some friends of mine are meeting for lunch over at the Green Lantern Café. Why don't you come along with me?" She waved a hand at the computer. "I'm sick of corporate partnership compensation structures anyway. I'm not going to get anything else done. Let's go."

Daniel tried to decline, but there was no arguing with a lawyer. Or even an almost-lawyer. So off they went.

When they got to the Café, her friends were already there. Six of them, in one of the big circular booths in the corner of the restaurant.

"Shove over," Valerie said, pushing Daniel in ahead of her, so he was squeezed between her and a short, pale-looking man who was already starting to lose his hair.

She named all her fellow law students, which Daniel doubted he'd remember. Then she introduced him. "This is Daniel. He's my computer guru. And my graphic designer. You want a resume that'll stand out, or anything else formatted and designed perfectly, he's your man. And he only charges $25 a page."

She poked him in the ribs, he assumed to stop him from protesting. But she didn't need to bother; he was too shocked to say anything anyway.

"I bargained him down from $50. And honestly, he's worth more than that."

There was plenty of scoffing at first, until Valerie pulled her resume out of her bag like she was performing a magic trick.

It was a good trick. By the end of lunch—she paid for his—he had every one of her friends asking when he was available to design their resumes.

On the walk back to Ellis Hall, he was still shellshocked.

"Valerie, what just happened?"

"I just helped you make $150, that's what. I remember undergrad. Money is always tight—I figured you'd appreciate it. And after all the help you've given me, it's the least I could do."

It wasn't the least she could do. The least she could have done was nothing—helping users in the lab *was* his job. And he was happy to do it, especially for people who were friendly and fun to talk to.

But her words led him back to his ridiculous thought from earlier: what could a smart, pretty, funny twenty-four year old almost-lawyer possibly want with him?

He still didn't know. But here she was, walking right beside him. Treating him like she considered him her equal. Like he wasn't just a twenty-one year old kid who spent Saturday nights playing *Battletech* in the dorm lounge and had no idea what his future held.

Chapter 19

THANKSGIVING 1990—BRONX, NY/MANHATTAN, NY

Daniel, November 20

Daniel dragged his suitcase up the three steps to the front door of his house. He was about to put the key in the door when he heard a shout behind him, followed by muttered curses.

It was Mr. Barnaby, under the hood of his old Toyota up to his waist. Daniel left his luggage and went across the street. "Is it acting up again? I thought they fixed your engine over the summer."

His neighbor extricated himself from the car and grunted. "So did I." The man brushed brown hair away from his eyes with an oil-stained hand, and did his best to smile. "I'd just call AAA to tow it, but I need to go to Cross County this afternoon. I was hoping I could fix it myself. I guess I'll call a cab and worry about the engine later."

Daniel had planned to go up to his childhood room and collapse on the comfortable queen bed for a couple of hours. But Mr. Barnaby needed help. That's what you did for neighbors.

"Forget the cab, Mr. Barnaby. Mom's car is in the garage, let me bring my stuff inside and I can drive you over there."

His parents were both with his sister, touring the condo that she hoped to buy. They wouldn't be home until dinnertime, probably.

He went inside, brought his suitcase upstairs, came back down and drank a glass of Coke in ten seconds flat. A minute after that, he was behind the wheel of his mother's twenty year old Cadillac—inherited from *her* mother—and driving out of the garage.

The Cross County Shopping Center in Yonkers was only a ten minute drive away, and there was almost no traffic at all on a Tuesday afternoon. "Where do you want me to park?"

"Wanamakers, please." That was one of the two big department stores at the mall.

"What do you need there?"

His neighbor didn't answer for a moment, and when he did, it was in a low, almost hesitant voice. "A new suit. For—God, if I can't even say it out loud, what the hell am I doing? A date. My first first date in twenty-five years."

Daniel didn't know what to say to that. Mrs. Barnaby had passed away four years ago. That was a long time—in the movies, people started dating again, or even got married again, faster than that.

Why shouldn't he? He didn't need to be alone the rest of his life. And he had plenty to offer someone. He owned his house outright, he had a good job, he was a great father as far as his kids said. And he was—not that Daniel was a good judge of this—decent looking. He had all his hair, anyway. That seemed like a big plus at his age.

"That's great," Daniel said. "I hope it goes well."

It took a half hour in the men's department for Mr. Barnaby to find something he was satisfied with. He kept asking Daniel's opinion, and it was weird the way he wanted to know, "What's the style today? What are guys your age wearing?"

"Why are you so worried about that?"

"Because that's what she's probably looking for. Because—God help me—she's twenty-six years old, okay?"

Daniel didn't know how he managed to keep silent at that. That was only a couple of years older than his daughter Jane. It was bizarre. It was freaky. It was totally wrong.

No, that wasn't for him to say. Mr. Barnaby had been kind to him his whole life. He'd obviously loved his wife deeply, and he'd been mourning her for four years now. If this girl wanted to go out with him, that was her business, and good for Mr. Barnaby for having the courage to ask her in the first place.

It was more courage than Daniel himself had. He'd broken up with Nora a year and a half ago and he hadn't even thought about another girl.

Except that wasn't true, was it? There was Valerie. He'd thought a lot about her. It was just that all his thoughts were about why she couldn't be interested in him despite all the evidence to the contrary.

If his neighbor could work up the nerve to ask out a woman half his age, then the least he could do was to stop concocting ever more convoluted reasons why Valerie didn't actually like him.

Nora, November 20

Nora was at Aunt Rachel's apartment for yet another holiday. It was different this time, though. Dad was here, too, in the guest room while Nora shared a bed with Rachel.

Her father had been here for two weeks already; a plumbing disaster two floors above him had destroyed his ceiling and flooded half his apartment. It would be at least two more weeks before it was livable again.

This morning, Rachel was showing Dad around her office, so Nora was on her own. She took the subway down to Times Square, and without realizing it, ended up in front of the McDonalds on 45th and Seventh Ave.

"Get a grip," she muttered to herself. That night was almost two years ago, and it wasn't ever going to happen again.

Not with *him*.

She finally turned away from that spot. She spent an hour people-watching, window shopping, and finally found herself on Madison Ave., right in front of Ann Taylor.

A black skirt-suit in the window caught her eye. It wasn't her style, not at all.

But maybe it should be. How many TV journalists did she see wearing flowery dresses or colorful skirts or leggings? None.

If she wanted to be taken seriously, maybe it was time to look serious, too. And Dad had told her she could use the emergency credit card to buy herself something as a much-belated birthday gift. So—what the heck—in she went.

It didn't take long to find something even better than the suit in the window: a similar suit, except in dark pink and with a more flattering cut. She grabbed her size, took it into the fitting room and tried it on.

It felt great. And in the three-way mirror it looked perfect. But for $450—even if it was Dad's money—she needed an outside opinion.

She took her purse and went back out into the store, looking for a sales clerk. Instead, she was approached by a redheaded woman probably around Rachel's age, looking somehow both desperate and hopeful at the same time.

"I have a date tonight," she said, "and I need something fantastic."

Clearly she thought Nora worked here.

And equally clearly she needed help.

Nora remembered needing help herself. She remembered standing in front of her closet for a half hour before her first date with Daniel, until Kim saved her. Why not pay it forward now?

"Where are you going?"

"A little Italian place in the Bronx." She looked down. "It's our first date."

Nora smiled. "How do you feel about dresses?"

The woman hesitated. "That's not my usual style. I work in a restaurant, so it's a chef's jacket and slacks every night. But—maybe? He'd probably like it."

"He'll love it," Nora took her by the arm and led her over to a rack of dresses. "I say go with black. It's classic. And it'll set your hair off, too."

Fifteen minutes—and a lot of hemming and hawing—later, Nora convinced her to try one on. When she emerged from the fitting room, she looked very uncertain.

"That's fantastic," Nora said firmly. "It's totally you. Just, you know, hold your head up and smile. Wear it like you own the place, right?"

The woman tried. And for a second, she almost pulled it off, just as a real sales clerk came over. "That's lovely, ma'am," the clerk said. "I can help you when you're ready to check out. And you too, Miss," she said to Nora, "That suit fits you perfectly."

The redhead blinked. "Wait, I thought you ..."

"I don't work here." Nora laughed." You just looked like you could use a hand."

Five minutes later, they both stood at the counter, bags in hand.

"Thank you," the woman said. "I was really freaking out, you're a lifesaver." She laughed nervously. "Still freaking out, I guess. I never even told you my name. I'm Cassie."

"Nora. Nice to officially meet you," she said with a laugh. "And good luck tonight."

"You too. That suit is fantastic, do you have a job interview coming up?"

"Not yet," Nora said. "But I'll be ready when I do."

Cassie hugged her. "Well, good luck whenever that is."

As she watched Cassie walk away, armed with a killer dress and—hopefully—a little confidence, Nora wondered when she'd have a first date of her own again.

Daniel, November 21

Daniel sat on his bed, wondering how long he could stay up here in his bedroom before he'd be missed.

Dinner last night had been stressful. It shouldn't have been—nothing Dad or his sister asked him was unreasonable, really. Did he have any prospects yet for a job after graduation? Was he enjoying his senior year? Was he dating anyone?

All totally normal questions. But he hadn't answered any of them. He'd deflected and dodged and—well, flat-out lied. And he wasn't even sure why.

As childish as it was, he wished he had Mr. Fuzzles right now. Stuffed animals didn't make you feel like you were betraying them because you were hoping to get a job in another city. And they didn't judge you for not being able to get over the girl you loved, even eighteen months after you broke up. He hoped Nora had kept the bear, and that it was comforting her whenever she needed it.

There was a knock at the door. "Daniel, can I come in?" It was Mom.

"Sure," he said, although he wasn't at all.

His mother came in, closed the door behind her, and sat down next to him.

"I know it's hard, Daniel," she said. "You're trying to figure out your whole life, and you're scared we're all judging you for not having it all figured out already. Right?"

Of course she knew.

"I know it's stupid. You *weren't* judging me. You were just talking, you and Dad. And Lisa, too. But that's how I felt anyway, like I couldn't say ..."

She put an arm around him. "You didn't want to say that you're thinking about moving away when you graduate. Or maybe you already have a job lined up."

He didn't quite laugh. "Almost. They want to fly me out to Chicago in January for an interview. Nothing's final—I can still say no."

Mom grabbed his shoulders, turned him to face her. "Daniel, look at me. I—both of us, me and your father—the only thing we want for you is to have a good life." There was sadness in her voice, but also steel. "That's all. Whether it's here, or Chicago, or anywhere. Of course we'll miss you if you get that job. But we'd miss you just as much if you moved across the street. That's how life works. You raise your kids the best you know how, and then you let them go. That's why they call it leaving the nest."

Daniel looked down. It felt less like leaving the nest and more like jumping out when he didn't know if he could fly or not.

But Mom believed he could.

He hugged her. "I'll miss you if—it's not a sure thing, but I think they really want me. If it happens, I'll miss you and Dad. And even Lisa."

Now she laughed. "She'll miss you too, even if she'd sooner die than say it out loud." Mom sighed, and the sadness was back in her voice. "And the other thing—you didn't say it, but I can see it. You're still aching for her, and I hate that for you. But—this is from experience, Daniel—there is life after your first love. You know I didn't marry your father until I was twenty-five. Did you ever give that any thought?"

No, he hadn't. Who thought about their parents' love lives?

"Mom, I don't know what you mean."

His mother shook her head. "Yes, you do. I had a first love, too." She hesitated for a moment, probably lost in memories. "He wanted different things. Or maybe I did. All I know for sure is, it broke my heart. And afterwards, I thought about him for months. I ached, just like you do for Nora. But I had a good friend who was honest even when I didn't want her to be, and—well, after far too long, I listened to her advice, and I put myself back out there even when I didn't really feel like it."

"And that's when you met Dad?"

Now she smiled. "That's when I had two years of terrible first dates, and maybe one second date. And *then* I met your father."

Nora, November 22

This was the first home-cooked Thanksgiving dinner Nora had had in at least a decade.

There had been plenty of love in the kitchen, and laughter as she and Dad and Aunt Rachel did their best to make turkey, gravy, stuffing and glazed carrots. Sadly, the end result on Rachel's little dinette table looked bad and tasted worse.

"I hate to say it, but I think we have to call this a failure," Dad said after he'd taken two bites of each dish.

"Yeah," Rachel agreed. "I think if Mom was around to taste this, she would have disowned us."

She knew Dad had lived at home for a while after college, but it was still strange to imagine him and Rachel under the same roof. She'd only have been a toddler then—how much could they remember together?

Regardless, she thought their mother—her grandmother— would have been thrilled they cooked Thanksgiving dinner together, no matter how bad it turned out. And it really had. Nora could only stomach one small piece of turkey, and that had been an effort.

"Let's go out. We can have dessert somewhere nice, where we don't have to clean up after ourselves," her father said.

"No!" Nora surprised herself. "I mean—I like it here, the three of us. It's really nice. Can we sit a little longer? I like feeling like a family." Where had that come from? It was true, she just hadn't thought about it that way.

Both Rachel and her father stared at her. "Of course, Pumpkin," Dad said. "But you should always feel like family." He looked down, sighed. "Maybe you wouldn't have to say it if I did a better job of making you feel that way. But you are. I love you, and you know Rachel loves you. And—your mother, too."

Nora knew that. She even felt it most of the time. But it was never like this, getting together on a holiday, doing the traditional things, being silly with each other.

"I think it hit me when you threw the flour at Rachel. That's what families do, right? They can be as stupid and goofy as they want with each other."

Rachel didn't quite roll her eyes. "So food fights are how families show love?"

No. Yes. "It's more like, knowing you *can* throw food at them and they'll still love you just as much afterwards." At Christmas two years ago, there hadn't been any food fights at Daniel's house. But there had been jokes and awkwardness and people insulting each other one minute and hugging the next, because there wasn't anything you could do to drive them away. Because family—whether blood or people you chose, like Daniel's neighbors across the street, or his not-a-cousin he loved more than the rest of them—family wouldn't abandon you no matter what.

Family, like Daniel should have been.

"Hey, Pumpkin, are you still with us?"

How long had she been lost in thought there? "I'm fine, Dad. Just—just thinking, I guess."

"You still love that boy, don't you? Daniel." She didn't answer. What was the point? "I'll tell you a secret. You might not believe it, but one day you'll see for yourself. You can love him and still move on. Meet someone else. Go on dates. All of it."

She knew that. She even almost believed it. But she didn't know if her heart would let her do it.

Chapter 20

Nora, January 7

"Mom, if we don't leave now, I'll miss the train!"

Nora's relationship with her mother had been infinitely better since last spring, but some things about Karen Langley hadn't changed. Her lack of punctuality was one of them.

"Nora, darling, you worry too much."

She didn't say what she wanted to, something along the lines of, *Because you don't worry enough.*

Mom had insisted on one last breakfast out at Nora's favorite diner, which was thoughtful, but it had left Nora only fifteen minutes to pack her suitcase and find her train ticket before they absolutely had to be out the door. Those fifteen minutes, and another fifteen too, were gone now.

"Okay, Mom. But the train's not going to wait and the next one isn't until ten o'clock tonight."

Ten minutes later, they were finally in her mother's car.

"Don't worry, dear. I know a shortcut. And Steven—lovely man, I'm sorry you didn't get to meet him—bought me a radar detector for Christmas, so I can drive as fast as I like and not worry about tickets."

Nora was pretty sure that wasn't how radar detectors worked, and she absolutely didn't trust her mother's "shortcut." But she just smiled and nodded anyway.

Somehow, they arrived at the station in one piece, and with five minutes to spare.

"I want you to enjoy yourself, Nora," Mom said, walking ahead of her up the steps to the platform. Nora started to point out that you were supposed to walk behind someone, so that if they tripped, you'd be able to catch them before they fell backwards. But she thought better of it. "Perhaps you'll find some time to see that boy you kept changing the subject about for the last two weeks."

Nora sighed. There was a reason she hadn't told her mother about Ben. She wasn't sure what she thought about Ben herself, other than that he was very handsome, and smart, and her boss; but she knew her mother would have thoughts, and plenty to say about him—and she wasn't at all prepared to hear it.

Daniel, the same time

Daniel was in his bedroom, checking the closet for the tenth time. There wasn't any point; he was all packed and ready and he knew he hadn't forgotten anything. It was just nervous energy, he supposed.

Dad was going to drive him all the way downtown, to Penn Station in an hour. He'd be back at Albion by this afternoon. Back in his dorm room. Back in the lab in Ellis Hall tomorrow morning.

Back to seeing Valerie three times a week.

He'd been thinking a lot about her over the break. Going over and over all the reasons why she wasn't flirting with him, she wasn't interested in him, he was just deluding himself.

Or was he? Maybe it was time to think logically about it.

He was only twenty-one, she was twenty-four. That was a huge difference. But his birthday was in two months; he was almost twenty-two. And he was just assuming she was twenty-four. Maybe she had a really late birthday. Or she'd been skipped a grade as a kid. Or she had a ton of AP credits and worked like a dog and finished undergrad in three years. They might be almost the same age, really.

She was nearly a lawyer, and far more knowledgeable than him. But was she really? Yes, she'd asked him to proofread a paper once, and he'd only understood about twenty percent of the words and maybe two percent of the argument. But that didn't mean she was smarter—just trained differently. She lived in a world of case law and legal theory. His world was wires, code, and logic gates. Could she build a computer from scratch? Configure a company-wide network? Not likely.

He was a dork who played Battletech *on Saturday nights.* Yes, that was true. But she might have hobbies that most people would consider equally silly. Maybe she was an obsessive soap opera fan. Or she secretly loved knitting. Or anything, really. She could be just as much of a dork as he was, in her own way. And she might appreciate *Battletech* anyway—you had to think strategically as a lawyer, didn't you?

All the things he thought were flirting were just his imagination. But she did make a point of always sitting closer to him than she needed to. And she touched his hand when it wasn't at all necessary. And she never came in the lab except when he was there. It stretched credibility to believe those were all just coincidences.

He still wasn't over Nora. There was no counterargument for that. Except—his mother had sat right here on his bed a few weeks ago and told him how she'd had her heart broken, and she went out and dated before she really felt ready. And it wasn't like he was contemplating marriage or something. He could go out on a date—whether with Valerie or anyone else—without it being anything more than hopefully a fun couple of hours and maybe—or not—a kiss at the end.

And if it wasn't fun, and there was no kiss, so what? It wouldn't be the end of the world. He would have tried. That had to count for something.

Nora, January 8

Nora was just starting to unpack when the phone rang.

"Nora? I'm glad you're back." It was Ben. What could be so important that it couldn't wait until the first staff meeting of the semester next week? "Want to meet me over at Sammy's Grille in half an hour? There's something I want to talk to you about."

It was weird that he called her dorm room; he never did that. So it had to be urgent. "Sure. Can we make it an hour, though? I literally just got in the door five minutes ago."

"It's a date. See you then!" And he hung up.

Maybe it was about replacing him as editor-in-chief next year. If he was going to push for her, he'd want to tell her first, and privately. And if that was the case, she needed to look the part.

She had the skirt suit she'd bought over Thanksgiving, but that was overkill for a meal with Ben. She'd wear it for a formal meeting with their faculty advisor, but for today? A good, solid blouse—maybe the red one that Rachel had given her for Christmas—would do nicely. And wasn't red supposed to be a "power" color? She got it out of her luggage, paired it with a conservative dark skirt, threw her coat on and headed over to the restaurant.

He was already there when she arrived, sitting at a table in the back of the restaurant. He stood up until she sat. "I'm glad you came, Nora," he said. "Just to get the important business out of the way first, I ordered sweet potato fries to share, but I didn't know if you'd want iced tea or a soda."

She'd prefer a milkshake, but the Green Lantern Café did them much better. "Iced tea is always safe," she said. "So what's the big deal? What did you need to talk to me about?"

He was staring at her; almost a searching sort of look. "I already said it on the phone. It's a date." Now he looked away, just for a moment. "I hope so, anyway." He lowered his voice a little, and was there the tiniest hint of nerves there? "A date. Me and you."

She only now paid attention to what he was wearing. A light brown sweater that set off his eyes. Slacks that were perfectly creased, as though he'd ironed them just before he got here. And when he'd stood up, she'd caught a glimpse of his shoes—shined to the point that you could see your reflection in them.

He was serious. Had he been thinking about this—about her—all during Christmas break? Were the shoes new? Had he bought them just to impress her?

"Uh—I wasn't expecting that, Ben." But the question was, did she *mind* it?

He laughed. "I wanted to catch you before classes started—and the paper—and you got too busy. I even came back to campus a day early. You're worth the $50 it cost me to change my flight."

She wasn't sure whether she believed him.

But even if it was a lie, it was a flattering one, and also pretty harmless. It was the kind of thing she might have said herself, once upon a time.

It was also flattering that he'd gone to all this trouble. And he was handsome. And smart. And a great editor-in-chief. And hadn't she been thinking about him this morning—and all through Christmas break?

If she wanted to see what could happen with him, here was her chance. If she wanted it.

"Well, then, I agree. I guess this *is* a date."

Daniel, exactly the same time

It was going to happen!

Quantum Networking Systems was going to fly him to Chicago, a week from tomorrow.

He'd known at Thanksgiving that they wanted him to come out—but it wasn't finalized. It wasn't official. There wasn't an actual plane ticket. The whole thing could have fallen through, for any of a thousand reasons.

Now, though, it was set in stone. Not an hour ago, he'd spoken with Francine from the Human Resources department. She confirmed the date, and all the arrangements. His ticket would be waiting for him at the airport, they'd have a car to pick him up when he landed at Midway and take him to the hotel—which they were also paying for. Then in the morning, another car to take him to company headquarters for the actual interview.

He hadn't been able to think straight on the walk over to Ellis Hall; he'd nearly ran into two light posts and a tree.

And now that he was here in the lab, he couldn't think about anything but the trip. He was lost in his own world. He was …

"Hey, Daniel, are you all right?"

It was Valerie. She looked concerned. Worried, even.

"Oh. Hi." He knew he still had a mindless grin on his face.

"I called your name ten times. What's wrong?"

He shook his head, tried to focus. "Nothing. Everything is good. I mean, really good. Like, amazingly good."

She pulled over a chair from the nearest desk and sat herself next to him. "Well, I want to hear it."

He wanted to tell it. Shout about it.

But before today, he'd been thinking about Valerie. Thinking about asking her out. Or stuck in a loop about asking her out, really. But it wasn't unrealistic now, was it? He wasn't some 21 year old kid with nerdy hobbies. He was an almost 22 year old man who was being flown halfway across the country for a job interview. Someone like that could totally ask out a law student, couldn't he?

"I will. But I need to say something first. I was thinking about you over Christmas."

She smiled, just as prettily as the first day they'd met. "I've been thinking about you too. And today I thought—why don't we grab dinner? My treat. And we can tell each other everything we've been thinking about." She paused for a moment, which he was pretty sure was for dramatic effect. "And, yes, I'm officially asking you out on a date, just so we're both on the same page."

♡ ♥ ♡

Nora, three hours later

"So I've got three interviews in two days. I'm heading down to Manhattan tomorrow. I'm glad we could get together beforehand."

"So am I," Nora said. It had been—nice. Not magical, not amazing. But nice. Comfortable, mostly. Ben had talked more than she had, quite a bit more. But he did have a lot to talk about and it was all interesting—the story with his brother and the yacht captain, and how Ben had snuck into a press conference at Gracie Mansion, and the ridiculous Christmas gifts his family gave each other.

She definitely knew him better now, and she wanted to keep knowing him—one new story at a time. That could start right now; they were outside the front door of North Hall. It was quiet out, and dark; only a handful of lights on in the windows of her dorm. If ever there was a moment to seize with him, it was this one.

"Well, here you go. Home safely." She could absolutely invite him upstairs; her roommate wasn't back on campus yet. Or at least she could kiss him goodbye; maybe that would be enough for now.

Or not; she leaned in, and he turned his head so that all she could reach was his cheek. She kissed that, and he patted her on the arm.

"I'll call you when I'm back. I had a great time, Nora. See you soon."

And he was gone. What the heck had just happened? What had she done to turn him off? She'd thought he liked her—he was the one who'd asked for a date, out of the blue. And then he didn't even want to kiss her?

Nora didn't know what it meant, except that it definitely wasn't good.

Daniel, the same time

They were at the Green Lantern Café. Daniel had made a point of not sitting at the same booth he and Nora had sat in for their first date. That felt disrespectful, somehow.

But other than that, he was completely focused on Valerie. And she seemed to be equally focused on him. She listened to him go on and on about the interview in Chicago. He'd stopped himself several times to apologize for talking too much, until she finally said, "Daniel, I'm going to be a lawyer. If there's anything I'm good at, it's speaking for myself. If I didn't want to hear what you've got to say, I'd tell you."

He blushed a little at that, but he couldn't argue with her words, or the smile that went with them. "Okay. Objection sustained—is that right?"

She chuckled. "Close enough. Go on, counselor."

"So, yeah. It's next Wednesday. They're flying me out, putting me up in a hotel, all expenses paid. And then three interviews the next day. I think one is with human resources, and then one with the team I'd be working with and then just one on one with the guy—well, it could be a woman, I don't know—anyway, the person I'd be reporting to."

"Three interviews in one day? Sounds to me like you're a finalist."

That's what it sounded like to him, too, but he didn't want to say it out loud, so he just nodded.

"How do you feel about all that?" Her smile faded a bit as she asked it. "I lost my cool a little with my first serious interview. I know it's hard to believe, but even I get nervous sometimes. But part of that was, I wasn't really prepared, and I tried to fake it and I could see they weren't buying." The smile came back. "Never again, though. Every interview afterwards, I made sure I was ready for anything. I might make mistakes, but never the same one twice."

It was hard for Daniel to picture her making the same mistake *once*.

"I am nervous, yeah. But I've been reading up, I think I'm ready. And I have this whole next week to make sure."

She nodded. "You know what? I'm going to help you be *absolutely* sure. The next few days are kind of busy for me, but next Tuesday, you'll come over to my apartment and we'll do a practice interview. Deal?"

They weren't even through their first date, and she was offering to do that? It was hard to believe; why would she go through all that trouble for him?

Because she liked him. Hadn't he gone over all that yesterday? Why should it be so impossible to believe that Valerie could be interested in him, could want to spend time with him? Could want good things for him?

Maybe Nora wasn't the only girl in the whole world who saw more to him than he saw himself in the mirror.

"Deal."

They sat there for another hour, talking and laughing, and then he walked her to her car.

"This was—it was great, Valerie. I'd really like to see you again, and not just for interview practice."

She gave him the big smile, the prettiest one. "I'd like that, too, Daniel."

He leaned in, and kissed her then. On the lips, just for an instant. So quickly that it barely counted as a kiss at all.

Except it definitely counted.

Nora, January 15

Ben had said she wouldn't hear from him for a few days, but after the way he hadn't let her kiss him goodbye last week, she assumed he was just being polite. She figured the next time she saw him would be at the Observer office—probably during a staff meeting, where he'd go out of his way not to look at her.

But to her shock, he called an hour ago and asked if she wanted to go to a movie with him. *"Home Alone* is playing. I know it's cheesy, and I'm sure you've seen it already, but it's fun, and two hours in the dark with you and a bucket of popcorn sounds like a pretty good afternoon to me."

She'd agreed, and now here they were, in the back row of Theater Three at the AMC Campus Hills. The popcorn was in her lap—she'd insisted—and his arm was around her. And at some point while Macaulay Culkin was torturing poor Joe Pesci, he leaned over and kissed her.

She'd wondered if he would do it. Honestly, it was all she was thinking about once they'd stopped talking when the movie started. She'd tried to kiss him last week. But now, after a week of thinking and mixed signals, she wasn't sure if he wanted to—or if she wanted him to.

If she was being brutally honest, she was almost—maybe dreading wasn't exactly the right word, but it was the closest she could come to it. She hadn't kissed anyone since Daniel. And she hadn't realized until this moment how much that mattered. It felt weird to even think about it, almost like she was cheating.

But how could you cheat on someone who you broke up with almost two years ago?

She didn't respond when he kissed her—the first time.

But ten minutes later, the second time he did it, she kissed him back. And it wasn't nearly as weird as she had feared it might be.

It was only later, sitting on her bed, with Mr. Fuzzles on the pillow next to her, that she realized how weird it was that it wasn't weird.

Daniel, that same night

He was in Valerie's apartment.

He'd been in Nora's dorm room. And her aunt's apartment. And back in high school, he'd been in Peggy's house—even her bedroom once. With the door open and her parents ten feet away.

But he'd never been in the actual home that a woman actually lived in and paid for herself, alone with her.

Maybe it shouldn't have felt like a big deal, but it did.

He was sitting on the futon she used for a couch, waiting for her to—he didn't even know what. When they'd gotten there, after another long meal at the Green Lantern Café, she'd headed into her bedroom, saying, "I'll be out in five minutes."

"Mr. Keller," she said in a cold voice, when she stepped out. She was wearing a suit—black blazer over a crisp white blouse, and slacks. "I hope you're prepared. We spent a lot of money bringing you out to Chicago."

She wasn't smiling—or even looking at him. Just staring down at a clipboard.

She'd said she wanted to help him practice interviewing, hadn't she? Clearly, she wanted to make it as realistic as possible.

Well, he was definitely off balance now, which he was pretty sure was how he was going to feel in Chicago. "Uh, yes, Ms. Vance. I'm ready."

She started with vague questions—why was he interested in this particular job, what were his career goals, and so forth. He had decent answers for all of them. Then she got into more technical topics, which he had no trouble at all with, but he did wonder how she knew what to ask.

And then, half an hour into it, she asked, "Are fiber optic networks covered by the Telecommunications Act of 1934? And do the privacy provisions of the Telecommunications Act of 1986 apply to signals transmitted over fiber optic lines? And how is all of that impacted by local cable operator monopoly contracts, Mr. Keller?"

"Uh—what?" What in the world did any of that even mean?

She suddenly broke character and burst out laughing. "I'm sorry. But it was worth it to see your face just now."

He laughed as well; it *was* kind of funny. "I can imagine. But I guess, if I got a question like that, I'd just say that I'd refer it to the corporate counsel, it's their job to deal with all that."

"Good answer." She took off the blazer and came over to sit next to him on the futon. "I think you're going to nail it, Daniel. You were ready for everything I threw at you. Not that I have any idea if you answered the tech stuff right or not, but you sounded very sure of yourself."

"How did you even know what to ask?"

She put an arm around him. "Two hours in the engineering library at Albion. I'm really good at research." She pulled herself closer to him. "And you're worth the effort."

And then she kissed him, for real.

And he kissed her back.

It wasn't until half an hour later, after she drove him back to campus and dropped him off in front of West Hall, that he really thought about the kiss, and wondered if Nora could forgive him for cheating on her.

It wasn't until the next morning that he was able to convince himself you couldn't cheat on someone you broke up with exactly twenty months ago.

Chapter 21

Nora, February 25

Nora had been staring at her phone for ten minutes. Things were so much better—mostly—with her mother, but this was something different. Asking her mother for practical work advice wasn't something she'd ever thought she'd do.

But who else was there to ask? Normally this was the kind of thing she would have asked Rachel, but—as far as she knew, anyway—Rachel had never been anyone's boss, and Nora needed to know what Ben was thinking. She needed to know if she should be grateful or angry at the way Ben was delegating—or dumping off—so much work on her.

They'd been dating for six weeks now, and every week, as they got closer—although not yet close enough to spend a night together—he assigned more and more of his usual duties to her.

The phone wasn't going to dial itself, was it? If she was going to call, she needed to just do it already.

It only rang twice before her mother picked up. "Hello?"

"Mom, it's me."

"Nora, darling! How is my future world class journalist this morning?"

Well, she was in a good mood. That was promising. Maybe she'd actually have some useful advice.

"Confused, mostly. I need—I need your—I don't know. Insight, I guess? I need to figure out what my editor is doing."

Her mother laughed. "I'm no journalist, Nora. I wouldn't know anything about it."

Nora sighed. "It's not a journalism thing, Mom. It's a boss and employee thing. You manage people. I need to know how you think when you're giving out assignments. Like, when you hand off annoying tasks, are you just doing it because you don't want to deal with it yourself, or are you trying to help them build up their skills and—I don't know, teach them something?"

Saying it out loud, it sounded ridiculous. Was she that insecure? That clueless?

Who was she kidding? *Insecure* and *clueless* ought to be tattooed on her forehead.

"Is your editor male or female?"

"Ben's a guy. What difference does that make?"

There was silence for a moment. No, not quite silence; Nora thought she heard her mother suppressing a laugh and rolling her eyes.

"You did not just ask me that, Nora. Please tell me you aren't that ... unaware." Nora imagined her mother had mentally run through several far harsher words before settling on *unaware*. Another word they could tattoo on her forehead.

"I guess I am, Mom. I mean, I just didn't think about that."

More hesitation on the line. The silence was uncomfortable and went on much too long before her mother finally spoke again. "I don't want to disillusion you. Or discourage you. But this Ben, there are only two reasons why he'd assign all his unwanted tasks to you. Either he's simply lazy and wants to do as little work as possible, so he's dumping them on you." Another pause. "Or he wants to sleep with you, and he hopes you'll become so tired of the work that you'll trade yourself to him in return for better assignments."

"Mom!" She yelled it out, probably loud enough to hear in the lobby of the dorm two floors below.

"You asked for my advice, Nora. I have worked with countless men, and they all boil down in the end to lazy or horny. And I hate to say this, but you'll have to learn for yourself how to tell the difference."

That was—well, *horrifying* didn't even begin to cover it. And the men her mother had been with over the last ten years didn't inspire confidence in her judgement. But she had been running her gallery all this time. Successfully. She had to know what she was talking about, right?

But if she did, then that meant Nora had been completely wrong about Ben going back not just to six weeks ago, but to last year. And if that was true, what else—who else—had she also been wrong about?

"Thank you, Mom. That's ... a lot. But I'll think about it, I promise."

She hung up the phone and stared at the wall for a full minute, unsure if she wanted to scream, cry, or laugh. Maybe all three.

Daniel, February 26

"Any news yet?"

Daniel gripped the phone tightly. It was all he could do not to scream at Bianca. But they hadn't talked in three weeks. She had no way of knowing that he held his breath every day when he got back to his room and the day's mail was waiting for him under the door.

"Not yet, Bee. It's driving me crazy. I keep thinking, if they wanted me, I'd already know. And if not, it shouldn't take this long to send a rejection letter."

The interview with Quantum Networking Systems had been almost six weeks ago, and he'd thought everything had gone great. Valerie had asked him tougher questions in her apartment than anyone had in Chicago. Unless he'd completely misjudged everything, which was possible. This *was* the first real interview for a serious, professional job he'd ever had. What basis did he have for comparison?

"Big companies can take forever sometimes, Danny. It took three months for them to get back to me before I got my job, remember?" That wasn't as comforting as she probably thought it was. But he didn't need to tell her that.

"Yeah, I remember. I'll just be patient and keep hoping for the best."

His cousin chuckled. "Then we can talk about something else. Or *someone* else. Anything to share about this mysterious girl you barely mentioned last time we talked?"

"She's—she's great, Bee. Her name is Valerie, and she helped me prepare for the interview, and we've gone out a bunch of times."

There was silence on the line. He should have known he wasn't going to get away without more than that.

"And—and we've kissed. Well, made out, I guess." He sighed. "Remind me why I'm telling you all this?"

Now Bianca laughed. "Because who else are you going to talk about it with? So you've kissed her. And obviously that means you've managed to convince yourself you're allowed to move on only two years after you broke up with Nora. I guess congratulations are in order."

He wished she hadn't put it that way. Not because it was unfair but because it was exactly the truth, and it stung worse coming from someone who knew him so well.

He didn't feel remotely like he'd moved on. Yes, he could spend time with Valerie, and laugh with her, and kiss her and in the moment it was fine—better than fine. But afterwards, every time, he still felt—not guilty, exactly. But definitely not fine.

"Thanks, Bee. I really do appreciate it. And when I have news about the job, or Valerie or anything else you should know, I'll call you right away. Fair?"

"Sounds fair, Danny. You take care of yourself. I love you."

"Love you, Bee."

He hoped there *would* be news soon. About the job. About Valerie. About anything that might feel like a step forward.

Nora, February 27

Here she was, in Ben's apartment. Nora had come up with a half a dozen excuses not to be here alone with him over the last month. She hadn't even realized herself they were all excuses until afterward.

But there weren't any more excuses. He was in the kitchen opening a bottle of wine, and she was sitting in the one comfortable chair he had, facing the TV.

It was a studio apartment; the bed was right out in the open. Nora didn't like that. There was no way to ease into things—you couldn't pretend that anything else was intended. Especially because she could smell that his sheets had just come out of the dryer. He'd done laundry just for her visit.

Was that flattering, or creepy?

Was he, as Mom had put it, lazy or was he horny?

What had happened to her judgment? Back in high school she'd done a lot of things she wasn't proud of—but she always knew where she stood. Almost every rotten situation she'd gotten into, she'd walked into with her eyes open.

And now, almost three years later, she couldn't recognize what was going on right in front of her? She didn't trust herself anymore.

It was all Daniel's fault. She'd never needed to trust herself with him; never needed to make snap judgments on his intentions. It was all there on the surface. No pretense, no subterfuge. Just him, for better or worse—and always better.

She'd lost the ability to spot trouble because she'd never had to use it with him. So what did she do now?

Ben came over, handed her a glass, clinked his against it. "To next year's editor-in-chief, Nora Langley."

What? She knew she was up for consideration, and she wanted it desperately—but wasn't this too early to announce it? Ben hadn't officially gotten the job until the final week of the semester last year.

Was this a test? Did she have to sleep with him to clinch the job, as her mother had implied?

She wanted to sleep with him anyway—at least part of her did. He was ridiculously handsome, he had great eyes—maybe not as pretty as Daniel's, but still great, and he was incredibly sharp. He was everything she *should* want.

And now he was taking the glass out of her hand, when she'd only had one sip. And holding both of her hands in his. And ...

"Ben, I can't do this." She pulled her hands away from him. "I—God, this is hard. I like you. But I have to be honest. I don't trust ..."

He looked—not quite hurt, not quite angry. Sort of a combination of the two, with half a dozen other emotions she couldn't even guess at mixed in.

"You don't trust me. That sucks, Nora." He looked like he wanted to use a stronger word. "But—look, I'm not a jerk. I don't want to be with somebody who doesn't want to be here."

She cursed under her breath. "It isn't you I don't trust, Ben. It's me. My judgment. I can't go to bed with you if I don't know how I feel. How I should feel."

He was silent for a while. She wished there was something she could say to make this less awkward. Less horrible.

"I know there's more going on with you, Nora. You've been cautious with me—with us. Not like you are at the paper, or in the classes we've had together. I kept hoping you'd relax, or whatever you want to call it."

She sighed. "The last relationship I was in. It's been over for a long time, but I guess I'm still not over him." She took a breath to steady herself. "And that makes me question you. Doubt you, even when you don't give me any reason to. I'm sorry. I—I thought I was ready."

He didn't quite laugh. "Well, that explains everything. I can't compete with a ghost." He stood up, paced around for a minute or two. "Fine. Let's just call it a day, then. But just so you know, you're still going to be editor-in-chief next year. And I'm still going to be working you like a dog so you're ready for the job come September. You're not getting out of it by breaking up with me."

So she was wrong all along. He wasn't pressuring her, or using the editor job as bait, or anything else she'd feared.

But she was also right. She wasn't ready, and she had no idea if she'd ever be.

Daniel, February 28

"Still no word?"

Valerie stood in front of Daniel's desk in the lab.

"What gave it away?" At least he was able to manage a smile, even if it was half-hearted.

Before she could answer him, the phone rang. Which was weird, because nobody ever called the lab phone. "Hello, Mac Lab."

It was Jack McKenzie from the dorm. Daniel didn't really know him well, except that he'd been pestering Jack every day for the past few weeks; Jack picked up the mail for the dorm from the Administration building and delivered it under everyone's door.

"Daniel. You've got a letter. From *them*."

He didn't need to say anything more. Daniel hung up the phone, jumped out of his chair and grabbed Valerie's hand. "Please—just come. I need someone with me for this."

He'd dragged her out of the lab, down a flight of stairs and nearly to the door of Ellis Hall before he stopped, and blushed furiously. "I'm sorry. It's just—that was the guy who delivers the mail."

Valerie laughed, and started off again. "Well, what are you waiting for? Let's go!"

They jogged all the way across the quad and to West Hall, and once they got inside, Daniel took the stairs three at a time. They were both panting when they got to the door of Room 318.

He fumbled with his keys until Valerie grabbed them out of his hand and unlocked the door for him. Then she shoved him inside and locked the door behind her.

The letter was there, on the floor. He could see the logo for Quantum Networking Systems in the corner where the return address went. He bent down slowly, picked it up gingerly, held it in his hands, not daring to open it.

After a minute, Valerie said, very gently, "Would you like me to open it?"

Yes.

No. He was almost twenty-two years old. He was nearly a college graduate. He was dating a beautiful lawyer—well, almost a lawyer, anyway. He was mature enough, confident enough, to open a letter, no matter what it might say.

He slit it open with a finger, pulled out the letter—two pages, surely that was a good sign?—unfolded it. He started reading aloud:

"Dear Mr. Keller, we are pleased ..."

He wasn't sure if he or Valerie shouted first. All he knew was that, suddenly, she was in his arms, and her lips were on his, and his on hers, and then, almost without transition, they were on his bed, and his shirt was unbuttoned down to his navel and her hands were working that very last button.

It had been almost two years since this had happened. Since he'd been with a girl. Since a girl had looked at him the way Valerie was right now, with desire. With ... love?

Two years since Nora had looked at him that way, since they'd made love without ever looking away from each other.

No, not two years. Twenty-one months and thirteen days.

And if he could still count it like that, from memory, then his heart was still with her.

He took her hands, gently but firmly, and pulled them off of that last shirt button. Outside of breaking up with Nora, and maybe his freshman year calculus final, this was the most difficult thing he'd ever done.

"I can't. I'm so sorry, Valerie. I want to—God, I can't even tell you how badly I want to. You're amazing. And beautiful. You helped me believe I could get the job. You didn't just change my life, Valerie—you changed how I see myself. But ..."

She was panting; it took her a moment to settle herself. "But what?"

He owed her the truth. Even if she would hate it. "There was— two years ago I broke up with her. She was—she was my first girlfriend. And I loved her. We were in love. But—the timing was wrong, and we were—too whatever. Or not whatever enough. We both knew it. The last day of the semester, my sophomore year, we broke up. And it's all this time later ..." He didn't need to tell her he knew it to the exact number of days. She probably already figured that.

"All this time later, and you're not over her. She must have been something." She wasn't angry. Why wasn't she angry? He tried imagining how he'd feel in her place, and angry was the first thing that came to mind. "I wish you weren't so—whatever you are." She laughed, and there was a trace of bitterness in it—but only a trace. "But I don't think I would have been interested in you if you weren't. I understand. I don't like it, and I'm going to need a cold shower when I get home. But I understand."

She wasn't looking away from him. And he saw in her eyes that she did understand.

"I—like I said, I'm sorry. You deserve somebody who's totally with you. Their heart is completely yours. I wish it could be me, because you're—seriously, whoever you do find is going to be the luckiest guy in the world."

She reached over, started buttoning his shirt back up. "Right back at you. If you ever do get over that girl, you'll make somebody a pretty fantastic boyfriend. But," now she laughed again, without any bitterness at all. "This doesn't get you out of helping me in the lab the rest of the semester. I've got a 20 page paper next week I'm going to need you to proofread."

When she finished with his shirt, she got up and retrieved the letter from the floor, read it quickly, muttering approvingly to herself as she did. "And you're going to need my help, too. Bring the letter to the lab tomorrow, and we'll talk about negotiating their offer." She waved it in front of his face. "This isn't bad, but we can do better for you. Don't call them or write them until I tell you what to say. Okay?"

He hugged her, held her for a couple of moments. "Okay. And thank you. For everything. I'm glad—even if I blew it with you,"—he nodded towards the bed—"I hope we're still friends."

"You bet we are, Daniel. It's not that easy to get rid of me."

Just like Nora.

Some people were with you forever.

Chapter 22

Nora, March 7

Nora was sitting in Addison Hall, Room 303 for Media Ethics and Law, but her mind was 160 miles away.

Specifically, in the workshop of Uncle Bruce's jewelry shop back in Providence. She was picturing him working on the pendant she was sketching right now in her notebook. She could see the tiny pliers, the miniature torch and that curved, pronged thing she never remembered the name of.

He could do it. He could turn her design into reality—if she ever got it right. She'd been making sketches—and then tearing them up—for three days now. This had to be perfect. If it was going to embody everything she felt for Daniel, everything she hoped he still felt for her, everything she couldn't put into words ...

"Miss Langley?" Professor Morrison's voice cut through her thoughts. "Is there something you'd like to share with the rest of the class?"

She could have—should have—mumbled an apology and sunk into her chair like a normal person. Any other day, if she'd been thinking about anything else, she probably would have.

"Sure." She stood up, notebook in hand, and walked to the front of the room. She stood eye to eye with her teacher—well, eye to hairline; she was a good three inches taller than the man. She showed him what she'd been working on while he'd been lecturing. "I'm designing a necklace. For—for someone who's really important to me."

Professor Morrison blinked in confusion. "Did I hear you correctly? A necklace?" Nora heard chuckling—and sniggering—behind her. She didn't care.

She flipped through the notebook, letting him see the dozens of previous versions. "Yes. Like I said, for someone special. Someone who's always going to be in my heart. So it has to be perfect."

Now she heard a couple of gasps from her classmates. They had to know who she was talking about.

"And you think this is the best use of your time here in class, Miss Langley?"

She laughed; what else could she do? "No. But also yes. He's graduating in May, and it'll take my Uncle a few weeks to make it. He's a jeweler, he makes custom designs all the time. See?" She pointed to her latest sketch. "Two stones. Sapphire for me, aquamarine for him. Together, always. If it wasn't so important, I wouldn't be doing it during class."

Her professor looked almost impressed despite himself. Almost. "I think I understand. And I must say, you do have some artistic talent. That's quite a sketch. And—your honesty is refreshing, if perhaps a bit misplaced." He paused for a moment. "But perhaps we can all return to the finer points of libel law for the remaining ten minutes?"

Nora nodded and went back to her seat. She was sure she'd be the talk of the class for the next few days, but that didn't matter. The only thing that mattered—well, after the next ten minutes, anyway—was making sure the necklace was absolutely, positively perfect.

Daniel, March 10

"So tell us about the job already," Dad said. "We've been waiting two weeks to hear the details, Daniel."

He was sitting at the kitchen table, Mom and Dad both looking at him expectantly. Daniel had only gotten the final, renegotiated offer on Friday and faxed back his acceptance. He hadn't wanted to tell his parents over the phone. Really great news—not just bad news—should be delivered in person.

"Valerie helped me—she told me what to counteroffer, and exactly how to say it. Otherwise it wouldn't have been nearly as good. But they're going to pay me $41,000 a year, plus a $2,000 bonus with my first paycheck. *And* they're paying $2,500 for moving costs—I'll get that first week in May."

His father looked like he was about to cry; he opened his mouth but couldn't seem to think of any words to say. Mom, though, focused on one word. "Valerie?"

Daniel hadn't mentioned her at all—he wasn't sure why. Mom, at least, would have been supportive. "She's a law student—she's in the computer lab a lot, and we got to be friends. So she offered to help me negotiate. She got them up from $34,000, and there wasn't any starting bonus at first. Oh, and she got them up to three weeks of vacation instead of two."

"Is she single? That's the kind of girl you should be going for, Daniel," Dad said, finally finding his voice. Daniel thought—hoped—he heard teasing in there somewhere.

"I don't think that's going to happen, Dad," he said. "But I definitely want to get her a thank-you gift. If it wasn't for her, I would have taken the first offer on the spot."

Later, after he'd answered every question his father had about the job—or tried to answer; Dad had asked about some important details Daniel hadn't even considered—he went up to his room to unpack. He was just about done when there was a knock at the bedroom door, and his mother walked in.

"Daniel, if you want to talk about her, it'll be between us. I won't say anything to your father."

She sat down on his bed, and he joined her. "There's not that much to tell. She started coming into the computer lab in the fall, and she needed help ..."

It took him an hour to tell Mom "not much to tell." When he was done, she hugged him, and kissed his forehead.

"You know something, Daniel? Now I know for sure we did a good job raising you. I'm *so* proud of you. You've grown into *such* an amazing man."

"Because I can't get over Nora?"

Mom sighed. "Well, I guess we still need to work on a couple of things. I'm proud of you because you put yourself out there for Valerie even though you weren't sure. And then when you knew you weren't ready to be more serious with her, you told her honestly. And kindly. You didn't lead her on, and you didn't hurt her. *That's* how a good man behaves."

It hadn't felt good or kind in the moment—but he and Valerie were still friends, weren't they?

"I guess."

Mom sighed again, this time with full dramatic flair. "*You guess.* I'll take that for now." She hugged him again. "And it goes without saying, but I am so proud of you about the job, too. I'll miss you—you'll have to come home for Thanksgiving and

Christmas. You can afford it with the extra money your law student negotiated for you, right?"

"Right, Mom. I promise."

As if she needed to ask.

Nora, March 13

"This is beautiful, Nora. If the journalism thing doesn't pan out, you can come work for me."

Nora sat with Uncle Bruce in the workshop in the back of his store. "It took, I don't even know, a hundred tries to get it right? Or two hundred. I lost count."

He patted her on the back. "That's how it works, honey." He laughed. "Well, I've got it down to ten or fifteen versions for a custom piece before I'm ready to show a customer. But I've been at it a long time."

She wondered if Mom had ever ordered anything custom from her brother. And if she had, how many different versions she'd made him go through before she was happy with the final design. But she wasn't going to ask him about that.

"Can you make it?"

He nodded. "You already knew I could." He gave her a look. "You want to know if I can finish it before you go back to school this weekend."

She hadn't wanted to say it that bluntly, but Uncle Bruce was like that, always getting to the heart of things without much small talk. "Yes. I knew you were closed this week, so I was hoping."

He finished his coffee before answering. "You didn't know I was supposed to go on a cruise this week, but your Aunt Dorothy got chicken pox—who knew you could get that when you're fifty? So instead of being in—I think it's the Bahamas today—I'm here helping my favorite niece out."

Wow. That sucked. And she hadn't known that adults could get chicken pox, either. "I'm sorry. If you don't want to do it …"

"I was just giving you a hard time, Nora. I'm happy to do this for you. And since I've got all this free time, I can definitely get it done by the end of the week. Especially with your help."

She hadn't been expecting that. "But I don't know anything about making jewelry!"

He gave her a kindly smile. "Neither did I, once upon a time. You'll learn." He paused. "We didn't talk about paying for it, by the way."

"I don't care. Whatever it costs, that's fine. I've got money saved up."

He closed his eyes for a moment, mumbling to himself and tapping his fingers one at a time. "Since you're going to work on it, and because you're family, I'll just charge you for the materials. Depending on the stones, it'll be around $400, give or take. But something like this, if I was selling it, I'd probably charge $1,500. Maybe $2,000."

He waited for her to react, but she just stared back at him. She would have paid the $2,000 if she had to. She didn't know where it would have come from, but she'd have made it work somehow—this was too important. "I've got $400 in my savings account, Uncle Bruce."

"Okay, honey. Then let's get to work."

Over the next two days, she got a crash course in creating fine jewelry. She'd never really watched her uncle before, and it amazed Nora how he was able to do such exacting work with his huge hands.

He had her do the final adjustments on the heart—while he used the torch to soften the metal, he had her shape it as she'd drawn it. It took two hours to get it exactly right.

"Now all that's left is putting the clamp on for the chain. I'll do that—it's tricker than you'd think. And then we have to set the stones. And you're going to help with that, too. First we have to pick them out."

He opened a drawer, pulled out two little trays filled with precious stones—sapphires and aquamarines. She went through them slowly, picking up each stone in turn before she finally found two that were just right.

"Very nice. You've got a great eye, Nora." Neither stone was huge—Uncle Bruce estimated them at just over one carat each—but they were cut perfectly.

It took another two hours to set the stones, with Nora doing the final step herself.

"Now we let everything cool off and settle overnight. Tomorrow morning we look it over, polish it, and put it in a pretty box for—you never did tell me who this is for."

No, she hadn't. "Daniel. His name is Daniel. We broke up two years ago, but he's—he's still in my heart, so I have to give him this. That way my heart will always be with him, even if we never see each other again after he graduates. I think it already is, but I have to be sure."

He gave her a searching look. "Your mother—she used to talk like that. Not always, just once in a while. And then not at all." He looked down, sighing. "I wish she could have held on to it. I think she'd be a lot happier if she had." Another sigh. "I'm glad you're doing this, Nora. Even if this Daniel doesn't appreciate it—he'd have to be a moron not to—you hang on to how you're feeling. Love isn't ever wasted. Ever. You remember that."

She already knew that.

Because of Daniel.

Daniel, March 16

They'd just been wandering around Manhattan all afternoon. Bianca was being very patient, just following him around wherever his feet took him.

"Enjoy it now, Danny. Who knows when you'll get to spend any time down here, once you start that job."

That's exactly what Daniel was thinking. That, and the thing he hadn't told his cousin—he hoped he'd see inspiration for a gift for Valerie somewhere, in one of the countless storefronts they'd passed by. But so far, nothing had caught his eye.

They were on Madison, just crossing 59th St., and something jumped out. He stopped in his tracks, and shouted, "Mont Blanc!"

It was perfect—except not for Valerie.

He hadn't even been thinking about Nora until this instant. But he had to give her something—something special. Something she'd always carry with her, always remember him by. She was in his heart; he had to make sure she'd have something of him with her no matter where she went.

Bianca gave him a blank look. "Mont Blanc, like the fancy pens?"

Daniel pointed at the window—the Mont Blanc boutique. "Let's go in."

"This place is really expensive, Daniel. Are you sure?"

One other thing he'd never told Bianca: two years ago, when his father had told him about the summer job in Pittsburgh and how much it would pay, he'd mentally set aside $1,500 to buy a proper gift for Nora. And even after they broke up, he'd kept that money set aside. He couldn't even say why he had, but now he knew. It was for this moment.

He went all through the store; he had no idea there were so many kinds of pens, or so many designs. But in the end he decided something simple and classic was best. It was black with a cap and gold accents—real gold.

"I think this one," he told the sales clerk, an older man in a well-tailored suit.

"Are you certain, sir? It is $720, plus tax."

Daniel just stared at him. "Yes, I saw the price."

Bianca stared at him. "Daniel, that's a lot of money. I know this girl helped you with the job offer ..."

"No, it's not for her. It's for Nora. And I was ready to spend twice that much on her." He turned back to the clerk. "I'll take that, and let's get two—no, three refills. I wouldn't want her to run out of ink. And I believe you'll engrave it?"

The clerk nodded, not looking Daniel in the eye. Well, it was his own fault for making assumptions.

There was one problem, though—the little sign announcing free engraving also said you could only have twenty characters on the pen. That wasn't really very much space for a message. "Bee, I need your help with this. It has to be short, but it has to say everything."

It took fifteen minutes for them to come up with a message he was satisfied with. He gave it to the clerk and then remembered that his original goal was a gift for Valerie, and that still wasn't accomplished.

"I need one more thing. Another gift. I think ..." He looked over to Bianca. "What about—I think I saw business card holders. She's about to graduate, she'll need that, right?"

"You're crazy, Daniel. Buying an expensive gift for one ex-girlfriend is nuts already, but for two of them?"

"It's my money, Bee. And they both deserve it. So what do you think? Business card holder, yes or no?"

"Yes. And I'd better get something fantastic from you at Christmas this year, Danny. Remember, I've loved you way longer than Nora or Valerie or anybody else."

He hugged her. "Count on it, Bee."

He found a pink leather card holder that he thought Valerie would love, and they personalized that, too—although there was only room for her initials, and he'd had to wrack his brain to remember the one time she'd mentioned her middle name. "You can put VAV—Valerie Angelica Vance."

When he finally checked out, between both gifts and the pen refills and sales tax, he ended up spending over $1,200. But they were both worth it.

And even if they didn't appreciate it—impossible as that seemed—it was worth it because he'd kept a promise to himself.

That was worth everything in the world.

Chapter 23

Daniel, May 14

"She's the girl you bought the card holder for? You never said she was a lawyer!"

Daniel stood with Bianca on the edge of East Capitol Park, in the shadow of the state capitol. It seemed fitting that the Albany College of Law had their graduation here. And on the makeshift stage only feet from the capitol steps right now, Valerie Vance was receiving her diploma.

Daniel clapped for her, even though the audience had been instructed not to cheer for individual graduates but to wait until the end of the ceremony. And even from a couple of hundred feet away, she heard, and saw him, and smiled.

"Technically, I don't think she's a lawyer until she passes the bar exam. But, yeah. That's her."

"Are we staying for the whole thing?" It shouldn't be much longer. They were calling people up alphabetically, how many graduates could there be left? But it would be awkward to go up to her afterwards with her family there, wouldn't it? How would he even introduce himself? "Hi, I'm Valerie's computer guru and proofreader and boyfriend for about six weeks earlier this year?"

He'd gotten to see her graduate, and she'd seen him. That was good enough. "No, let's go. My parents are probably getting restless." He and Bianca were already at the very back of the crowd; it was easy to slip away without causing any commotion.

A little later, on the taxi ride back to the Albion campus, Bianca turned to him and said, "Someday you're going to meet a girl where the timing is right, and everything is right. And she's going to be the luckiest girl on Earth."

"What are you talking about, Bee?"

"You dated one girl for a few weeks, and after you break up, you still go to her graduation—and you didn't even know if she'd see you there. You dated another girl for six months, and two years after you break up, you buy her a $700 gift just so she'll remember you. I can't even imagine what you'll do for the right girl when she comes along."

Daniel sighed. He didn't say the words that came immediately to mind, but he didn't have to. Bianca said them for him. "I know. You think you already did meet the right girl, and you'll never have anything like what you had with Nora." She put her arm around him. "Danny, I hope to God you're wrong. Because if anyone deserves for things to be right, it's you."

Nora, later that day

Nora sat on her bed, staring at the little velvet box. She had been going back and forth on when to give it to Daniel. He was probably with his family right now—his parents must be here for his graduation—but he'd be in his dorm room tonight. The last night he'd ever be on this campus.

But this gift shouldn't be opened in shadows, in a mostly packed up room. It really ought to be given in the daylight, under the open sky, with the sun shining brightly on it—on *them*. She knew for sure where he'd be tomorrow at eleven o'clock. And he'd be there early, because he always arrived early for anything important. She'd learned that about him the first week they were together, and she was sure he hadn't changed.

Tomorrow was better. She'd find him on the quad, waiting for everyone to start lining up for the ceremony, and she'd give him the necklace and—if she could hold her nerve—make her promise. And ask for one in return.

Daniel, around nine o'clock at night

He hadn't wanted to lie to his parents—and he'd really wanted the Raspberry-Chocolate Torte—but Daniel had complained that he was too full as an excuse to finish dinner and get back to the dorm.

His mother had asked, "Since when do you say no to dessert, Daniel?"

"Since never, Mom. But I have to fit into my graduation robes tomorrow."

Everyone had accepted that—well, except Bianca; she knew why he was really cutting the evening short, and she winked at him when nobody else was looking. And now here he was back in his room, holding the gift in his hands. It felt heavy, as though it was weighed down by all his memories.

He hadn't spoken to Nora in two years, almost to the day. What would he say to her when she opened her door?

Maybe he should have thought more about that before spending $700 on a gift he had no idea how she'd react to.

No. It didn't matter how she reacted. He hadn't bought it for that. He bought it because she deserved something beautiful—because she'd given him something beautiful. And maybe it was selfish, but he needed her to know: he still loved her.

And also for her to know that even if they never saw each other again, if they never got closer than a thousand miles to each other after tonight, he'd always be rooting for her.

The night wasn't getting any younger. If he was going to do it, now was the time.

Nora, fifteen minutes later

She might as well go to bed early. She'd packed up all her books, so there wasn't anything to read; most of her friends were already gone for the semester, so there wasn't anyone to talk to; and going downstairs and sitting on the filthy old sofa to watch late-night reruns by herself seemed pathetic.

She was about to get undressed when there was a knock at the door. Who would be coming to see her now?

She wondered for a moment if she should just ignore it, and call campus security if they kept knocking. But that was paranoid thinking. Silly thinking.

She went over, opened the door.

It was *him*.

She didn't think. She didn't hesitate. It was all instinct, as though the last two years hadn't happened.

She grabbed Daniel, pulled herself to him and kissed him.

Daniel, thirty seconds later

She'd kissed him, he'd kissed her back, and now they were somehow sitting on her bed, breathless. Their faces were only inches apart, and her arms were still wrapped tightly around him. He held her with one hand, the other awkwardly dangling behind her back clutching her gift.

He needed a second to catch his breath before he could speak. "Nora. I—I needed to see you tonight. I don't know if we'll ever see each other—I've got a job. In Chicago. I start week after next. But I wanted to—I have something for you."

It was hardly eloquent, but she seemed to follow it well enough. "You have something?"

He pulled back from her far enough that he could show her the little box. "I know we're not together. I know we'll be a thousand miles apart. Maybe two thousand, I don't know. I know it won't work—we both already knew that. But I want you to remember me. To remember us. I want you to know, wherever you are, I'll always be hoping for the best for you."

He handed it to her. She turned it over, examining it from every angle. Then she noticed the Mont Blanc label on the box, and she smiled—the smile he had never forgotten. "You gave me a pen? Does that make me John Cusack in this scenario?"

He laughed. "Believe it or not, I never thought of that. And I *have* seen *Say Anything*. Twice, actually." How was this possible? Joking with her, laughing with her, just *being* with her as though they'd never broken up, as though the last two years hadn't happened at all.

She opened the box, and gasped when she saw the pen. "Oh, my God, Daniel! That's real gold. And—you had it engraved, too?"

She held it up to him, read the words aloud:

To N with love - D

He shrugged. "It was the best I could do with less than 20 characters."

She kissed him again, and when she finally pulled back, she said, almost whispering, "It's the best thing anybody could ever do, Daniel."

Nora, a minute later

The shock of the gift had worn off. But the shock of his presence hadn't.

Daniel was here.

Here, with her!

Alone with her.

"How did this happen? How are we here now?" he asked as though he couldn't believe it.

"You came over here, Daniel," she said. "If you don't know, nobody does."

He shook his head. "That's not what I meant."

She knew exactly what he meant. But joking was safer than crying over everything they'd lost—everything they'd thrown away—two years ago.

"Yeah," she muttered. "I guess I wasn't very funny just now, was I?"

He didn't answer, but she knew what his silence meant. She'd always known—almost always—when he agreed with something self-deprecating she said but didn't want to say so aloud. That was one of the many things she'd loved about him.

Still loved. Present tense.

Future tense, too.

"Nora," he said, reaching over and gently taking the pen from her hands, then squeezing them. "I don't know if anything's really changed. I'm going to be in Chicago, and you'll still be here next year, and then—who knows? You could be anywhere. You can write your own ticket. You'll have your pick of jobs. But we'll be far apart. And all the stuff I was afraid of, all the things I didn't understand back then ... they're still there."

He was right. Every word of it.

"I hate this," she whispered, as much to herself as to him. "Why can't we be smarter? Or braver? Or more—whatever the hell it is we're supposed to be?"

There were tears in his pretty—*so* pretty—eyes.

"I wish I knew," he said. "God, I hate this as much as you. But we—" His voice broke. He steadied it. "We survived. I'm graduating. I've got a great job. You're going to be editor of the paper next year. You're a star. Let's just—let's never forget each other."

He didn't believe it. She hadn't heard his voice in two years, but she still knew how it quavered when he was trying so damn hard to convince himself of something. And she knew—if she tried to answer—he'd hear the same tremble in hers.

"I'm never going to forget, Daniel."

That, at least, she could guarantee.

Daniel, a moment later

Did he dare say it?

Two years ago, she'd said it.

This moment was the same.

Or maybe it was even more. He couldn't say more *what*—just more.

If he knew anything at all in this world, he knew she felt the same way he did right now.

"Nora, if this is the last time we'll ever see each other, really the last time," his voice caught and he blinked away a tear, "I want to—I want one more memory. One more perfect memory with you."

She didn't blink, didn't turn away.

Instead, she leaned in, until her lips were only an inch away from his. "You're asking me to make love with you," she said softly. "One more time. One last time. Just so I'm clear."

He nodded ever so slightly, leaned in that last inch and kissed her. Gently at first, barely brushing against her, and then more fully. She kissed him back without hesitation.

When she pulled back, there were tears in her eyes, but there was also a smile—*his* smile, the one she only ever gave to him.

"Okay, that was pretty clear. So I guess I should be clear, too. I want that, too, Daniel. I want one more perfect memory. I want to make love with you. Right here and right now."

And then neither of them needed any more words.

Nora, around midnight

They'd made their memory.

Afterwards, they lay together in her bed, not speaking, not really doing anything except holding each other.

"Daniel, I don't want you to go. Not now. Not like I did the last time."

He caressed her cheek and kissed her gently. "I wasn't planning to. I know—*I know* this has to end. But not yet."

Not yet.

They were both silent a while longer. It was so peaceful.

This was how it had always felt afterwards with him.

And during the act—it felt the same as it always had with him, too. As though no time at all had passed.

She reached over, put her hand on his chest. "The body always remembers," she whispered.

Like—what did athletes call it? Muscle memory.

"And the heart never forgets."

How could it?

He kissed her again, just for a moment. "Is that from a poem or something?"

She kissed him back. "No. It just came to me. It's us. How we'll always be, no matter where we go after tomorrow. Even if we never see each other again."

Her voice dropped to a whisper again, her hand still on his heart. "I'll always remember. You'll never forget."

He didn't say anything. But his eyes—and another kiss—answered for him.

Daniel, the next morning

He opened his eyes, and there she was, watching him. Smiling.

"Good morning, sleepyhead."

There was no disorientation, no confusion. Daniel knew where he was. Exactly where he should be. "Good morning, Nora."

He leaned in to kiss her, but she was too quick, putting a finger to his lips. "Not now. We took care of that last night. Now you have to get dressed and go back to your room."

What? She was kicking him out after last night? After *everything*?

Then he saw the clock on the desk behind her. Of course she was kicking him out. She knew what today was just as well as he did.

"You've got to finish packing up, shower and get dressed—and do it all in time to be on the quad a half hour before you're supposed to be there."

He laughed. "Am I that predictable?"

"It's one of the things I fell in love with," she said. "Now, get your clothes on. I'm not going to be responsible for you being late to your graduation, Daniel Joseph Keller."

She used his full name, exactly how his mother did when she was thoroughly annoyed with him—and almost managed to keep a straight face. But not quite.

"You nearly got the tone right. You need to put a little more exasperation into it."

Now she was laughing uncontrollably. This was as good a moment as any to get out of bed and start dressing.

A minute later, he was done, and she'd gotten herself under control. She stood up, took his hands in hers. "Thank you. For last night. For coming over. For the pen. For never forgetting. For always—always being you. My Daniel."

She leaned in, kissed him. He kissed her back.

"Now go."

He started to answer her—even though he had no idea what he could possibly say. But again she pressed a finger to his lips. "Just go. Maybe—never mind. Just ... maybe."

Maybe she'd be at the ceremony?

Maybe that would be the real, true, for-good-this-time goodbye?

He didn't think there was any maybe about it.

Chapter 24

Daniel, May 15

"Wow, I don't miss college at all," Bianca said. "Your whole life in a hundred square feet. And the lobby downstairs? A travesty. They should take that sofa out somewhere and burn it."

Daniel chuckled. "You're not wrong about the lobby. It is pretty awful." He glanced around the room. Everything was boxed up, ready to go in the back of Dad's car. But that's not what he saw in his mind's eye. "Still, some really good things happened in here."

She raised an eyebrow as she headed to the door. "You mean *she* happened."

He didn't answer; he just followed her out, locking the door behind him.

They went down the stairs, through the travesty of a lobby and outside before she spoke again. "I'm sorry," she said, in a quiet voice. "I shouldn't have said that."

"There's nothing you can't say to me, Bee. You should know that by now." He took a deep breath. "It's just—I don't know why

I haven't told you. I went to see her last night. I gave her the pen. And—and then ..."

She slipped an arm around him as they walked. "Yeah. I know all about *and then*, Danny. You keep forgetting I'm older than you."

He laughed. "You keep forgetting to act like it."

She grinned, jabbing him lightly in the ribs. "You mean like that? I could give you a wedgie, too, if you want."

"No thanks, I'll pass." He paused. "Anyway, yeah. You can guess what happened. It was like we were still back two years ago. Like New Year's Eve. Or my birthday."

He blushed at the memory of that night. Of course she noticed.

"You never told me what happened with her that night."

"And I never will," he said, still blushing. "Some stuff you can't even tell your favorite cousin."

"Danny!"

"Well, I guess I can say this much. Remember what you wrote in my card? *Don't do anything I wouldn't do?*" She nodded. "I'm pretty sure I did."

Nora, a few minutes later

There he was, sitting on a bench on the north side of the quad. She was at least a hundred feet away, and seeing him from the back—but it had to be Daniel. Of course it was—she'd known he'd be there, ready to go in his graduation robes, half an hour before he was supposed to be there.

Who was he talking to? A woman. Not his mother or his sister, but that's all Nora could tell from the back. The woman had her arm around him and they were leaning close—there was only one person it could be.

"Daniel!" Nora called out when she was just a few steps away.

They turned in unison, and she saw she was right. The woman was a little older than him, but not much. Dark haired, like Daniel, with the same nose. "And you have to be Bianca."

The woman stood up and—Nora hadn't expected this—came straight up to her and hugged her. Tightly, the way you hug someone you love but haven't seen in months.

"Nora! It's so great to meet you. I mean, in person. I feel like I know you from everything Daniel's told me, but ..." Bianca let her go, took a step back, and gave her a long, appraising look. "Wow, you really are beautiful. He showed me pictures, but they don't do you justice."

Nora wasn't sure how to respond to that. "Uh—thanks?"

Bianca smiled and it was nothing but honest and kind. "It wasn't a trick question, Nora. I'm just telling you what I see." She turned to Daniel. "And I'll tell you what else I see. I see how much you love my Danny. *Our* Danny."

She leaned in again, kissed Nora on the cheek. "Thank you for that. For loving him. You changed his life, Nora."

"Bee, that's enough," Daniel said, but there was no edge to it. Just fondness. "I think Nora and I need a moment alone."

Bianca patted Nora's arm. "I'll go check on Uncle Tony. But I want to hear all the details later. Promise?"

Daniel nodded. Bianca gave Nora a wink, and headed off.

Once she was out of earshot Nora sat down on the bench, and gestured for Daniel to join her.

"I see why you love her so much, Daniel," she said. Then she grinned. "Or should I start calling you Danny now?"

Daniel, a moment later

What Daniel wanted to say was, *You can call me whatever you want, for the rest of our lives.* But that was impossible. Their time together—last night, and now—was one final gift, and that would have to be enough.

"I never liked being called that. Except by her."

She nodded. "I get it. I'd probably be okay with Rachel calling me a nickname, even if I hated it. Not that there's anything you can do with my name. You can't shorten it or make it cute or whatever. It's always just Nora."

Again, he couldn't say what he wanted to. So he settled for, "There's not a thing in the world wrong with just Nora. Except that you aren't *just* anything."

She blinked, and he wondered if she was holding back tears.

"That's sweet. Just like you always are. But—God, this went so much easier in my head. I don't want to do this, because once I do … then it's goodbye."

Daniel saw what she wasn't saying. Her hand was halfway inside her purse, and her eyes were darting back and forth from him to it. She had something to give him.

She didn't do it last night. Of course she didn't. She didn't want to upstage his gift to her.

"Nora, it's all right," he said gently. "We said it last night. You'll always remember. I'll never forget. Even if this is goodbye."

She blinked again, but this time the tears came.

"You're right. You're always right. I have to do this now."

She took a deep, shuddering breath, and a small velvet box from her purse, tied with a little blue bow. A jewelry box?

"Nora, you didn't have to give me anything. You already gave me everything."

But he took the box from her anyway, untied the ribbon, opened it.

"I had it made. Specially made. Just for you. For us, really. You're just the one who'll wear it."

Inside was a necklace. The pendant was a silvery heart. But not silver. Platinum, maybe? Or white gold. Probably white gold, because it was an alloy—gold and something else, he couldn't remember what, but fused together. Two things made into one.

Set on the heart, side by side, were two blue stones. A sapphire, her birthstone. And the other one ... aquamarine. His.

"Like I said," she whispered, barely able to speak. "For us. So you'll always remember me. I'll always be by your heart." Her voice cracked. "I wanted you to always remember. Because I'll always love you."

He leaned over, kissed her. Her tears were on his face.

And then, so were his.

Nora, two minutes later

She finally stopped crying, and so did he. He was holding the necklace up to look at it more closely. The stones glittered in the sunlight exactly the way they should.

"It's beautiful, Nora." Daniel turned his back to her, and for an instant she was confused, but then she realized what he was doing. "Would you—please, would you put it on for me?"

She took it gingerly from his hand, draped it around his neck and closed the clasp. "There, let's see."

It sat there, maybe a couple of inches above his heart, and it looked perfect. Like it had always belonged around his neck.

"I can't believe you did this, Nora. I mean—I do believe it, just ...
I don't know how."

Her fingers were still playing with the necklace. "I don't think
I ever mentioned my Uncle Bruce. He's a jeweler. I drew the
design myself, and he made it for me. I had to give you something.
Something real. And symbolic, too, I guess."

He took her hands in his. "It really is. And not just the stones,
or even the heart. I love that you picked white gold. Two different
metals, together into one new thing."

What did he mean? White gold was an alloy, she knew that.
Uncle Bruce would have thrown her out of his store if she didn't
know something as simple as that. But she'd never thought about
what that really meant.

The tears started again, suddenly. She had to fight to make
any words come out.

"I never—I mean it. I didn't even think of that. And *you* did! I
said it should be a symbol, and you made it even more of one."
Last night, she'd told herself she would make the promise, and
ask for his, if she could hold her nerve. It was now, or never.

He started to speak, but she pressed her finger to his lips. Then
she took a deep breath, and another, and wiped her tears away.
"Daniel, I don't know how to say this. I've been thinking about
it for weeks. I want us—I want to make you a promise. And then
you make one to me."

He was looking into her eyes, all the way into her heart. But
as well as he knew her, she didn't think he knew what she was
asking.

"Say it, Nora. Whatever you're thinking, you can say it."

Now or never.

"I promise, Daniel. Ten years from today. May 15, 2001. If I'm
still single, if I'm not with anyone. Ten years from today I'll be
here. Right here. Waiting for you."

He laughed. How could he laugh at that? She was—she wasn't just baring her soul, she was tearing it open, and he was laughing?

And then she understood why, and she laughed, too. Not just because it truly was funny, but because—just like the white gold—she hadn't even realized the other meaning of her words.

"The first time we ever spoke," he said "The first time I heard your voice, you were talking about *2001: A Space Odyssey*. And that's when you want us to meet again."

She knew he'd make the promise now. He had to.

"I promise, Nora. Ten years from today. If I'm not with anyone, I'll be here. I'll be waiting for you."

She kissed him, one more time. One last time. He kissed her back, and didn't let her go until there was a sound off in the distance, way on the other side of the quad. Trumpets blaring.

"That's your cue. Go, Daniel. Go and graduate. Go and be amazing." She hugged him, this time for the really and truly last time. "Go with my love. And come back to me ten years from now."

So he went.

She watched him go, watched him disappear into a crowd of blue robes. But he'd be back. Ten years from now, he'd be back. How could he not?

The body always remembers, and the heart never forgets.

When he came back, she'd be here waiting for him.

Part 4

Chapter 25

Nora, July 8

"Hey, Langley, the boss wants to see you." It rankled Nora that Jack Elliott still called her by her last name, even after a year here. And that he shouted across the office rather than walk over to her desk like a normal human being. But he was unlikely to ever change, and he did have seniority, so she ignored the first three or four responses that came to mind.

"Thanks, Jack."

It was kind of pathetic that her boss refused to use email to communicate in the office, but that was also unlikely to ever change, no matter how much time it would save everyone. Ninety percent of the things Mr. Brooks summoned people to his office for could be handled with a one sentence message.

She made her way through the maze of cubicles to Mr. Brooks' cluttered office. When she sat across from him, she had to crane her neck to see him over the pile of books, magazines, and God only knew what else on his desk.

"You wanted to see me?"

He was shorter than her and had to stand to see over the junk and look properly at her. It had taken two months for Nora to train herself not to laugh at that.

"Yes, Nora. Your work has been exemplary recently."

She hadn't expected that. She hesitated for a moment, weighing her words, then she ignored her better judgment and said the first thing that had come to mind. "I don't think Mr. Elliott thinks so."

Her boss chuckled. "Has he thrown anything at you recently?" Nora gave him a blank look. Was he joking? "If Jack doesn't throw a stapler at you—or his phone, if he's in an especially foul mood—then he is satisfied with your work."

"Couldn't he learn to—I don't know—behave like a grownup?" Nora regretted that as soon as she said it, but Mr. Brooks didn't appear to be offended.

"That would be nice. But I've learned to live with his—let's call them peculiarities. First, because he actually is an outstanding editor. And, second, because his uncle is on the board of our parent organization."

That explained a lot. And, Nora supposed, it was almost a point in Jack Elliott's favor that he hadn't ever mentioned his family connection. Almost.

"Understood. And thank you. It's encouraging to know you think I'm doing well."

Mr. Brooks smiled, the sort of kindly smile she remembered her grandfather had, on the few occasions she'd seen him. "Oh, I didn't call you here merely to feed your ego, Nora. I have an assignment for you." He looked down, rummaged through the pile on his desk, and pulled out a brochure, which he handed to her.

"The *National Technology Solutions Conference*?" Mr. Elliott always assigned articles. Why was Mr. Brooks asking her to write one?

"Yes, Nora. You're going to be covering it on-site for *Modern Computing*. Twelve pages. Maybe sixteen, depending on the photographs."

"I'm no photographer." Why had she said that? Why didn't she just thank him?

He still had that kindly smile. "I'm sure you're selling yourself short. But we are sending a photographer. You'll be supervising him." He chuckled. "Well, he'll be on his own most of the time, but you'll direct him as needed."

"Uh—thank you. It's an honor. I'll do my best."

"Of course you will, Nora. If I ever thought you were doing less than that, you wouldn't be here."

She wasn't sure if she'd just been praised or chastised. Maybe both. Could you do both at the same time?

Daniel, July 9

Daniel took his dinner out of the microwave, to the disapproval of his roommate.

"There are a hundred restaurants you can walk to from here. Why do you insist on that TV dinner garbage?"

He and Jeff had had this conversation a hundred times. "Because it's quick and easy and there's one little tray to throw out afterwards." It sounded lame to his own ears, but he didn't want to tell Jeff the real reasons.

First, because every dollar he didn't spend eating out went into his savings; the same reason he was sharing an apartment when he could afford to live on his own with his salary. And second, because he hated the loud, pushy crowds in this neighborhood; honestly, he kind of hated Chicago in general but the job was too good to think about trying to leave and move somewhere he'd actually enjoy living.

"You just want to get back to your computer and do work nobody actually asked you to do," Jeff said. Well, that was true. "But maybe you're the smart one after all. I shouldn't be telling you, but you're going to Kansas City next week."

Daniel forgot about his dinner, and stared at Jeff. "For the conference? The *National Technology Solutions Conference*?"

"I saw your name on the travel list," Jeff told him. Jeff worked in accounting, so it made sense he would be involved in travel planning. "You're down as Team Lead for the main booth."

He was supposed to go two years ago—only a few weeks after he'd started the job—but at the last minute, there'd been a change in plans and he—twenty-two years old and not two months out of college—had been left behind to supervise the whole office for the week. Then, last year, he'd gotten the flu the night before he was scheduled to fly out for the conference and his boss, Mr. Kincaid, had said, "Maybe next year, Typhoid Mary." And that was that.

"You're kidding," Daniel said. *Team Lead?* He hadn't even managed an intern, let alone six people. Why would Mr. Kincaid put him in charge of the company's biggest booth at the company's biggest conference?

"Something else I shouldn't tell you—Kincaid put the paperwork through last week—you're getting a raise, too. I may have read the letter to justify it, and, well, he is *seriously* impressed with you. And I don't blame him. I can't pretend to understand anything you're working on, but I see you're working your ass off on it. So you can skip the false modesty, and you can dump that fake food into the trash and let me buy you a real dinner to celebrate. Okay?"

Daniel didn't think Jeff would allow him to refuse. And, honestly, as much as he disliked the crowds, he didn't want to refuse.

He was well aware of how hard he worked. And—maybe it was bragging, but it was still true—how good his work was. If his boss was noticing, why shouldn't he celebrate? His parents and teachers had drilled it into him all his life: hard work, and good work, would eventually be rewarded.

Maybe it was time to start believing that.

Nora, July 12

It went against everything in her nature. Nora never packed ahead of time for a trip, and she certainly never made checklists of everything she needed to do before she headed to the airport.

Only obsessive weirdos did that; but then again, they didn't show up at the major conference they were supposed to cover without everything they needed to do their job properly.

So she had to act like one herself. Checklists it was.

Plane ticket? In her purse already.

Conference badge and press credentials? Same.

Pager number for Kenny the photographer? Written in her little notebook, along with the external numbers for Mr. Brooks, Jack Elliott, and Arielle from the company travel office. And the notebook was in her purse, too.

The Mont Blanc pen? Right there in her purse as well, just as it had been ever since Daniel had given it to her. Not a day went by that she didn't use it.

But that wasn't what she needed to be thinking about now, was it? Back to the list.

Map of the convention center, and full conference schedule? In her carry-on bag, along with her travel makeup kit and toiletries.

Pager. Pager? It was somewhere in her apartment. She'd picked it up from the travel office yesterday, and she clearly remembered bringing it home, and testing it out. But what had she done with it after that?

It could wait. She still needed to pack her suitcase—the brand new one Dad bought for her over the weekend when she told him about the conference. He'd driven down from Providence, took her shopping, and refused to let her pick any of the cheaper models she pointed out.

"You worked hard, and you earned this opportunity, Pumpkin. I won't have you going around like a hobo on your first big opportunity." So she had a top of the line Samsonite wheeled carry-on bag. It was even a lovely shade of pink. "And make sure you do carry it on the plane," her father had said when they got back to her apartment. "You've seen how they throw the bags around when they're loading the plane up. Carry it on, and find some strong young man to help you put it up in the bin when you get to your seat. Let him throw his back out instead of you."

Nora had wondered whether Dad's words came from a sense of chivalry, or because he'd thrown his own back out a few months ago. Either way, obviously she could load her own luggage in the overhead bin.

But it was probably chivalry. Daniel would have loaded the bag in the bin for her, no question.

Daniel, July 13

"Daniel, do you think anything has jumped out of your bags in the ten minutes since you checked them over?"

Jeff was exaggerating. It had been at least fifteen minutes. And he was just making sure he hadn't forgotten anything. That was completely normal. Responsible, even.

"What? I'm just being thorough."

"There's thorough, and there's obsessive-compulsive." Jeff's tone left no doubt where he placed Daniel on that scale.

He sat down, took a deep breath. Maybe his roommate was right. Everything was there, between the suitcase and the carry-on bag. And if—God forbid—anything wasn't, he'd be at the hotel by noon, he could call the office and have them FedEx whatever was missing overnight.

The rest of his team wouldn't even be there until tomorrow afternoon anyway. He'd asked if he could fly out a day early so he could get to the convention center at seven a.m. Wednesday morning, the minute it opened up for exhibitors. That way he could make sure all the materials for the booth were where they were supposed to be, and he could get a head start on setting up before everyone else arrived.

The other reason he'd wanted to go a day early was to avoid any possibility of a flight delay or cancellation or anything really crazy. Even if that happened, he'd still have Wednesday to fly to Kansas City.

Not that he'd tell anyone that. It sounded paranoid, even to his own ears.

He touched the necklace, hanging just a little above his heart. *She* would have understood. She would have laughed and asked why he hadn't flown out yesterday, just to be extra sure.

He shook his head. It was no laughing matter. This was a huge responsibility, and he was going to do absolutely everything in his power to make sure the Quantum Networking Systems booth ran perfectly.

Short of a plague of frogs or locusts at the convention center, he was pretty sure he had every possibility covered.

She would have laughed and asked him what his plan for the frogs and locusts was.

Nora, four hours later

Everything had been easy, so far. There was no traffic on the taxi ride to Logan Airport, which was unheard of. There'd been no line at check-in. Nora had even been upgraded to first class.

She had one glass of champagne on the flight. It was free, and, anyway, she wouldn't start working until tomorrow. She had all afternoon and evening to herself, and when was the last time that had been true?

Her senior year of college had been a blur. She'd juggled her position as editor-in-chief of the *Observer*, her honors thesis and what had felt like hundreds of job interviews. Then she'd been hired at the Livingston Scientific Network, and she'd had to move to Boston, find an apartment, furnish it and actually learn her job.

Livingston had three dozen publications, and over her first year there, she'd been rotated through most of them. Nora lugged home books and journals to study every night, so she wouldn't sound like an idiot in staff meetings—or, far worse, when interviewing world-renowned scientists. She felt like she hadn't sat down to rest in more than two years.

Eight hours with zero responsibility sounded like heaven.

But she had to get to the hotel first. Once she landed, she followed the signs from the gate, through the terminal and to the taxi stand. She had to walk by the baggage carousels, and as she went past Carousel #2, just as a tinny voice announced over the PA system that baggage for Flight 387 from Chicago was arriving now, she thought she saw something.

Someone.

Dark hair, crisp blue button-down shirt.

From the back, it looked like ... *him*. The way his head tilted just a bit to the side, the way his shirt bunched up in the back if he didn't stand up straight, the way her heart was fluttering just like it always did when she'd been with him.

But it couldn't be. What were the odds that he'd be here, now, at the exact moment she was walking by? One in a million? No, worse than that—one in a million was generous.

Obviously it wasn't him. She wasn't going to see Daniel again. Not for another eight years, at least, and then only if he hadn't met someone else.

It was just her imagination. She shook her head, muttered to herself, and headed for the taxis.

Daniel, that exact same moment

The flight had been okay. He had a window seat, which he always preferred, and nobody next to him. He'd spent the whole flight going over the booth schedule—so focused that the flight attendant had to call him three times before he looked up.

Once he landed, he headed straight for baggage claim. Daniel had packed brochures, spare giveaway items and an extra laptop he'd had to beg the Logistics office for—just in case one of the freight trunks arrived at the convention center late, or someone on the team forgot their computer. You never knew what might happen.

He couldn't see any signs to indicate which carousel he needed to go to, but a voice over the PA system announced that the bags from his flight were arriving on Carousel #2.

He was almost there when he caught a glimpse—dark-blonde hair, a flicker of blue and orange, a skirt brushing against her knees. His breath caught.

It couldn't be.

It was exactly how Nora liked to dress.

But obviously it wasn't her. Why would she be flying to Kansas City, landing at the exact same time he did?

No. If he was ever going to see her again, it would be eight years from now, back at Albion College. If she wasn't married by then—but of course she would be. She was too funny, too beautiful, too … *everything*. She was probably already dating someone, maybe even engaged. Of course she was.

He shook his head, laughing at himself. He was here to work, not to chase shadows. Not to chase *her*.

Nora, half an hour later

Her good luck was continuing. Nora got to the reception desk just ahead of a busload of tourists.

"Welcome to the Marriott Downtown, Ms. Langley. You'll be with us for five nights?"

She had to take a moment, and count the days on her fingers to be sure. "Right. Checking out Sunday. But I'm still working Sunday afternoon—can I leave my luggage somewhere after I check out?"

The perky girl behind the desk smiled. "Of course." She tapped away at her keyboard. "And here you go. Twentieth floor, Room 2020. Enjoy your stay!"

The girl handed over a plastic card.

"That's my key?" She knew that some hotels used keycards instead of good old physical keys, but she'd never stayed in one that did.

"Yes, ma'am. We switched over last winter."

"Sure you did," Nora muttered, looking a bit suspiciously at the card before tucking it in her purse and heading for the elevator. As she did, she heard a voice behind her. A familiar voice, talking low, as if he didn't want to disturb anyone else in line to check in.

"Yes, Dad. I'm allowed to call home on the cell phone. The company isn't that cheap!"

It sounded exactly like Daniel—same tone, same rhythm, even that low chuckle at the end. But, just like at the airport, it obviously couldn't be him. She started to turn, just to prove to herself that, of course, he wasn't here. But the elevator dinged open at just that moment, and with three other people behind her, she let herself be swept inside—without turning around.

Daniel, the same moment

Daniel walked into the lobby of the Marriott, shivering a little at the blast of air-conditioned cold. He was right behind a crowd that poured out of a tour bus—a dozen people all talking at once as they got in line ahead of him to check in. It would probably be ten minutes before he'd get to the front of the line. Plenty of time to call home—just long enough for Mom and Dad to tell Mrs. Parlato that their son, the business traveler, had phoned from the lobby of a Kansas City hotel.

Dad answered on the first ring. "Daniel? Is that you? Are you calling from your work phone? You won't get in trouble, will you?"

He shook his head, and kept his voice low as he reassured his father he wouldn't be reprimanded for a five minute call home. The whole lobby didn't need to know his business.

"You just do a good job, son. Make sure they see what a star you are."

"I will, Dad. Don't worry about that. I just have to figure out what to do with myself tonight. Nobody else from my team is here yet." He hadn't spent any of his meal allowance today, so he had $60 for dinner. That would go a long way, even at a fancy downtown restaurant.

He said goodbye to his father and hung up, and just as he slid the phone back into his pocket, a voice floated up from the front of the line—bright, clear, a little sarcastic

It could have been Nora. The tone was exactly right. But it couldn't be. Of course it couldn't.

What was wrong with him? He was seeing her at the airport, hearing her here at the hotel. Why was she in his thoughts so much today?

Maybe it was the prospect of being alone in a strange city, no plans, no clue what to do with himself. Nora would've had a dozen ideas. All of them fun. All of them uniquely *her*.

That's all it was. Had to be. Just loneliness. Just nerves.

Chapter 26

SETUP DAY FOR THE CONFERENCE—KANSAS CITY, MO

Daniel, July 14

Daniel woke up fully refreshed and ready to go. He didn't bother to shower; there wasn't much point when he was going to spend the next few hours getting sweaty and filthy crawling around the convention floor. He'd even packed ratty clothes specifically for the task—an old, faded Yankees T-shirt and a pair of jeans that probably should have been thrown out two years ago.

He got to the convention center right at seven o'clock, the moment the doors opened. The show floor was honestly a little eerie. The lights were dim, but not dim enough that he couldn't see the dust in the air. Hundreds of big freight trunks were set up in rows, waiting for their owners to arrive and unpack them.

And in this whole huge, almost cavernous space, there were only a handful of people besides him. He could hear a group of them, off in the distance, grumbling and complaining; and there was a forklift beeping as it drove through the aisles of trunks, delivering still more of them to their proper spot.

Thankfully, the row markers were already hanging from the ceiling, and he followed them to where the QNS booth was supposed to be—spot number 505. And there they were, all sixteen ... no, there were only twelve trunks here. He'd have to talk to someone—the forklift driver, maybe?—to track down the missing ones.

But that could wait. He could start with what was here. He'd made sure that all the trunks were numbered so it would be easy for the team to set things up. And right there was trunk number one.

An hour later, with the help of a convention center employee—Larry, according to his nametag, who'd clearly taken pity on the lone nerd in the Yankees shirt—they had the frame standing and the canopy bolted into place. Daniel made a mental note to buy Larry lunch.

Stepping back to look at his progress, he had to admit that it actually looked pretty good. And it was oddly satisfying to accomplish something purely physical—no code or screens or slide decks. Just metal and plastic and his muscles.

And—where had the thought come from?—he wondered what Nora would say if she could see him now.

Nora, later that morning

Nora wasn't proud of herself for flirting her way into grabbing the last seat for the pre-conference demo of Windows NT.

But what was that saying—all's fair in love and war? This demo was a hot ticket; Microsoft was billing this new operating system as a game-changer. And, anyway, flirting was kind of a strong word; it was more like strategic charm deployment. All she'd done was smile brightly and bat her eyes at a Microsoft employee who looked like the last time he'd seen sunshine was back in the 1980's.

The important thing was, it worked. And the cherry on top? Not only did she get the last seat, she had the pleasure of seeing the door shut right in the face of Annette Goddard. Annette had started at Livingston the same week as Nora, but she'd been a bad co-worker and a worse human being. She'd left three months later.

Nora had heard through the grapevine that she'd landed at PC Magazine. So taking her spot was a double victory—sticking it to a rotten person, and also getting the edge over a major rival publication.

A little to her surprise, Nora found that she was able to keep up with the demonstration, and even jot down a few questions for the Microsoft people later. All those nights of reading up instead of having anything like a social life were definitely paying off.

At the end of the session, Nora wondered what Daniel would have thought about it. This was his subject—his world. Would he be amused that she was—tangentially, but it still counted—part of it herself now? Or jealous?

The one thing he wouldn't have been is surprised, because he'd told her that she could do anything.

Would she have believed that if he hadn't believed in her first? She didn't know. And right now, she didn't want to find out.

Daniel, late afternoon

The booth was finished. Daniel had done probably eighty percent of the work himself, but he'd had help for the last two hours. The whole team was here—Bryce, Edward, John, the two Kristins, and Thomas.

The ongoing argument over how to differentiate the Kristins cropped up again as soon as the last workstation was set up and the last brochure rack was filled.

They'd joined the company within a week of each other, so "Old Kristin and New Kristin" didn't really work. They were eight months apart in age, so "Young Kristin and Old Kristin" only led to acrimony. They were both blonde and within an inch of each other in height, so physical descriptions were out. And neither of them wanted to use their last initial.

Daniel had anticipated the problem, though. "Guys! Look in the small trunk. Down at the bottom, there's a paper bag." Bryce went over and leaned into the trunk—almost disappeared into it, if he was five foot four, that was being generous. He emerged a moment later and brought the bag to Daniel.

Daniel reached in, pulled out three blue polo shirts with the QNS logo over the left breast pointed to Kristin Zachetti. "You're Blue Kristin." He pulled out three more shirts, exactly the same except red, and handed them to Kristin Chambers. "You're Red Kristin. Problem solved." It was exactly the kind of thing Nora would have come up with, probably with a more sarcastic twist than just red and blue.

Blue Kristin shrugged and took her shirts. Red Kristin asked, "That's fine for now, but what do we do when we're back in the office?"

Daniel hadn't thought that far ahead. But he wasn't their manager back in Chicago, so it really wasn't his problem. "You can call each other every morning and coordinate outfits, I guess." Both women glared at him, until Thomas—the senior employee on the team at the ripe old age of twenty-nine, stepped in.

"Let's not kill Daniel before the show even starts, okay? Or else,"—he looked at Red Kristin—"I'll tell everyone what your middle name is." That settled them down, although now Daniel was curious how bad her middle name could possibly be.

"More important question," Edward piped up, "Where are we going for dinner? The Team Lead always takes everyone out after the booth is done."

Mr. Kincaid had warned Daniel about that tradition—and also that the company credit card would cover it.

"That place across the street looked good," Daniel said. "Hickory Moon? The concierge at the hotel raved about it."

John spoke up. "Of course she did. They probably pay her under the table to send people over there."

Once John got started on his conspiracy theories, there was no stopping him. You had to cut him off right away. "Fine. I saw in the guidebook, there's Smoke and Embers. It's a couple of blocks from here, but it's supposed to be really good, too. Let's just go there. Call it a command decision. Everyone good?"

Thankfully, everyone *was* good. They all wanted free food more than they wanted to argue.

Nora, fifteen minutes later

Nora was back in the lobby of the Marriott. She'd been working nonstop since eight o'clock in the morning—four demos, six interviews, and an hour sneaking around the show floor, one step ahead of security the whole time.

She deserved a reward. Her per diem was $50 a day, and she hadn't spent any of it yet. A nice dinner would be just the thing now. She'd be by herself, but she was used to that. She would have asked Kenny the photographer, but he had family nearby, so he was booked tonight.

The guidebook in her room had mentioned a local barbecue joint that sounded interesting. Smoke and Embers, three blocks away. All the better she was eating alone—she wouldn't have to worry about making a mess with an order of ribs.

"Hey, Nora."

She turned to see who was calling her. It was a redheaded woman, taller than her and wearing an ingratiating smile. Annette Goddard.

"Hi, Annette. Sorry you missed the Windows NT demo this morning. Maybe you heard some of it from the hallway?"

Yes, that was obnoxious, but did Annette really deserve anything better?

Maybe that was unfair. Annette had behaved horribly in the three months Nora knew her, but sometimes people had stuff going on that wasn't apparent from the outside. She wouldn't want to be judged forever for the way she'd acted the spring of her freshman year.

"Sorry, forget I said that. How's life at PC Magazine?"

Annette's smile hadn't wavered at her catty remark, or her semi-apology. "It's great. I'd love to talk with you about it. What are you doing for dinner?"

Well, that was suspicious. She'd just tried to give Annette the benefit of the doubt, but clearly the woman wanted something from Nora. But that was fine. She could be wary, and still polite.

"I was just trying to figure that out, actually."

Annette grabbed her arm and pulled her towards a window. "I've heard Hickory Moon is fantastic," she said, pointing at a flickering neon sign across the street. "And I've got a company credit card, so dinner is on me. Do you want to change and meet me back down here in half an hour?"

Nora didn't, really. But it would be a free meal, and, knowing that Annette was searching for dirt, she'd be on her guard, so there wasn't any downside. She might even get some good information about a competitor, in addition to some genuine Kansas City barbecue.

"Sure, Annette. See you in a half hour."

Daniel, an hour later

The team dinner was officially a success. It would have been nice to think it was because of his excellent leadership, but Daniel knew better. It was the pitcher of margaritas he'd ordered that was making everything go so smoothly at the table in the dimly lit back corner of Smoke and Embers.

But that *was* leadership, wasn't it? Knowing what the team needed? And as far as the rest of them knew, he was paying out of his own pocket, so that was bonus points for him.

The Kristins had even gone along with his idea—they'd dressed in their assigned colors for dinner. Kristin Zachetti didn't even grumble when Thomas asked her to, "Pass the ketchup, Blue."

But at the end of the meal, while Daniel was waiting for the waitress to come back with the company credit card, Edward said, "Well, this was a great start to the conference. But I'm looking forward to seeing what the booth babes look like tomorrow."

Both Kristins spoke in unison. "We're right here!"

"I didn't mean you guys," Edward said. "I mean, not that you aren't babes ..."

Thankfully, Thomas stepped in again to defuse a potential problem. "Stop digging, Edward. You're already six feet deep."

That wasn't why the Kristins—either of them—had been assigned to the team, had it? Daniel didn't work too closely with them back in the office, but he'd been in meetings with both of them, and they were both really smart and always ready with an answer. If Mr. Kincaid only wanted them here to provide sex appeal to the booth—that wasn't right.

Even if that was what his boss wanted, it wasn't how things would be on the show floor. They'd be wearing the shirts Daniel had brought for them, and he'd made sure to get the right sizes. They wouldn't be parading around in clothes two sizes too tight on his watch.

"Thanks, Thomas," he said. "Let's just get this straight. Every one of us is here because we're good at our jobs, we know our products, and we're hard workers. I don't want to hear anybody suggest otherwise." Daniel said it with a firmness he didn't remotely feel, but maybe that didn't matter—they heard him all the same.

On the walk back to the hotel, Thomas walked a few steps behind the rest of the team, and gestured for Daniel to join him. "You did a good job back there," he whispered. "I don't think Edward will do anything else stupid, but I'll keep an eye on him." Daniel nodded his thanks. "And one more thing. I know they gave you the company credit card. But I won't tell the rest of them. Kincaid did the same thing for me first time I was Team Lead."

Daniel had wondered why Thomas wasn't the Team Lead this time, but now it made sense. It must be Mr. Kincaid's way of slowly grooming young staff. Give them responsibility, but have an older, more experienced employee there to quietly support them.

When they got back to the hotel, while the team waited for the elevator to go up to their rooms, he whispered to Thomas, "Come back downstairs in fifteen minutes. I'll buy you a drink in the hotel bar. With my own credit card."

He was too focused on his teammate to notice the pretty dark-blonde woman chatting animatedly with the redheaded reporter from PC Magazine he'd seen escorted off the show floor by Security earlier in the afternoon.

Nora, around the same time

It was irrational to be annoyed at someone for eating neatly, but Nora couldn't help it. It was really bothering her the way Annette had gone through a whole helping of ribs slathered with barbecue sauce and her mouth and hands were somehow completely clean.

It made her think of the beginning of *Gone with the Wind*, when Mammy tells Scarlett to eat before the big barbecue because young ladies weren't supposed to eat in public. She wondered if Annette practiced how to eat perfectly, so she'd make the right impression at business lunches.

No, she was right. It *was* irrational. Annette was being perfectly pleasant. She'd asked a lot of questions about how Nora was doing at Livingston, how she'd gotten assigned to this conference and so forth, but that could have been normal conversation with someone you used to work with.

"How about you, Annette? How's life at PC Magazine?"

"Great! It's great. Like a dream." Annette said it much too quickly, and too firmly. Like she knew it was a lie but hoped Nora wouldn't notice.

Nora didn't cooperate. She just raised her eyebrows and looked Annette in the eye, and it only took a few seconds for her former co-worker to give it up. "It's not great. And it's more like a nightmare than a dream."

Nora wasn't surprised, but she didn't say that. "I'm sorry to hear it. I mean, I know we weren't exactly best friends when you left Livingston, but I wished you the best." That wasn't true, but there was no need to rub salt in a paper cut. "If you want to talk about it, I'm here, and,"—she waved a hand towards the bottle of merlot on the table—"my advice sounds better after a second glass of wine."

Annette told what Nora assumed was a sanitized version of her story. PC Magazine was much more fast-paced than Livingston, and everyone there was cutthroat; it was impossible to make any friends in the office. "This is my last chance," she said. "I need to come back with something big, or I'm toast."

Despite herself, Nora felt a twinge—more than a twinge—of sympathy. Maybe Annette had just been afraid during her three months at Livingston. Maybe she didn't trust her own talents, or that her co-workers would be willing to help her.

She took a deep breath. She wasn't at all sure this was the right approach, but how many people had taken chances on her? "Check in with me tomorrow, and if I see anything that might help you, I'll let you know." She gave Annette her pager number. "I should be on the show floor around lunchtime, but if you don't see me, page me."

"That's really—that's going above and beyond, Nora. I wasn't sure you'd even have dinner with me." She chuckled. "I didn't even tell you the worst thing today. After I missed the Windows NT demo, I snuck into the show floor, just to see—I don't even know what I expected to find. The only thing I did see before I got thrown out was this poor guy with Quantum Networking Systems. You know, the fiber optic people?" Nora nodded. She knew who they were; they were on her list of companies to check out tomorrow. "There was only one guy working, putting the whole booth together by himself. Skinny guy, dark hair, kind of cute, just working like a dog."

Nora's jaw dropped. Daniel hadn't ever mentioned the name of the company that had hired him, only that they were in Chicago. Which was where QNS was based. And *skinny, dark hair and cute* was a fair description of him.

No. She shook her head violently. She had to clear these insane thoughts away. It wasn't him. Obviously it wasn't. How could Daniel be here? Coincidences like that only happened in movies, not in real life.

"Nora?" Annette was looking at her with something very much like concern.

"Sorry. I was just remembering something. It's not important." She finished her glass of wine in one swallow. "I'll check them out tomorrow. I haven't had a date in forever—I've almost forgotten what a cute guy looks like."

She had forgotten nothing. Every detail about him was burned into her memory forever.

Chapter 27

Daniel, July 16

"I shouldn't have had that second drink downstairs," Daniel muttered to himself, staring at a bleary-eyed reflection in the mirror.

He hadn't felt it at the time, so he skipped the extra water and aspirin when he got back to his room. Now, of course, he was paying for it.

The bathroom light was far brighter than it had any right to be, and his mouth was all cottony and dry. He wasn't properly hungover, just generally crummy. Enough to be moving and thinking a little too slowly. No doubt enough for his team to notice.

This didn't have to be a disaster, though. He could drink water now, and take the aspirin. That would keep him from feeling any worse. Then plenty of coffee, and maybe once he got over to the show floor, adrenaline would kick in. Then more caffeine around nine o'clock, and plenty more water.

That was a solid plan. By lunchtime he'd be his normal self. Their big demo today wasn't until two o'clock anyway. Once that was over, there'd only be another two hours at the booth, then he could retreat back to the hotel for an early dinner, a couple of hours of mindless TV watching, and to bed by nine o'clock.

Yes, that sounded like a typical evening for his grandfather—dinner at five, *Wheel of Fortune* and *Jeopardy*, an hour of whatever cop show happened to be on, then straight to bed. But it was just one night. Tomorrow was the most important day of the conference—three demos, two meetings with vendors and a panel session he'd be on stage for. He had to be at his best for all that, and if the price was his team mocking him for acting like an eighty year old, so be it.

Nora, an hour later

Nora woke up completely refreshed. She felt better than she had in—well, longer than she could remember.

It would have been nice to think that it was good karma from her conversation with Annette last night. But that wasn't true; she'd gone to bed thinking about Daniel.

Uneasy thoughts about Daniel—missing him, wondering if it really was him Annette saw yesterday, and what she'd do if she saw him herself.

It had taken her a good hour to actually fall asleep once she'd gotten into bed, with all those thoughts whirling around in her head. A year ago, those thoughts would have kept her up all night. That was progress, wasn't it?

The bed itself must have been the reason she felt so good this morning. A really good mattress obviously made all the difference. Maybe if she got a bonus at the end of the year, she could upgrade from the clearance-sale bed she'd bought when she moved into her apartment last year to something halfway decent.

She could start earning that year-end bonus this morning. She'd managed to snag an interview with a senior engineer from

Intel, thirty minutes with him at nine-thirty, right before the show floor opened.

A quick shower, a decent breakfast and she'd be all ready. She'd show Mr. Brooks—and Jack Elliott, and everyone else—that she didn't just *belong* at Livingston. She was going to be a star there.

Daniel, two hours later

The water and aspirin and caffeine were definitely helping. Daniel felt like he was operating at a good 70% of his normal capacity, which should be enough to get through the morning.

The team was doing their part to help. Everyone was at the booth on time, all wearing their QNS logo polo shirts—the men in dark gray, and the Kristins in their assigned red and blue. It only occurred to him now that by giving them different colored shirts, he was calling extra attention to them. He hadn't meant to single them out, but he'd unwittingly done exactly that.

No. They were still loose-fitting polo shirts. Nobody could mistake them for anything other than well-qualified experts on the company's products. Besides, anybody who did would get a—very polite—earful from either Kristin.

"I think we're doing great," Daniel told the team. "Let's just check all the computers again, make sure everything is ready to go, and everyone give their station one more cleaning—the Lysol is on the shelf behind the back podium."

Everything was ready to go, and when the crowd started pouring in at ten o'clock, his adrenaline definitely kicked in. He talked to a hundred people—well, probably not, but it felt like that many—just in the first hour. And he had a great fifteen minute conversation with the Technology Infrastructure Manager for

Los Angeles County. If QNS could get a contract there, it would be a massive win—not just for the company, obviously, but for his team. And, maybe for him personally.

He was so excited after that conversation, he didn't even get annoyed when a photographer for the Livingston Scientific Network asked him to pose in front of the booth, as ridiculous as it made him feel.

Kristin Chambers—Red Kristin—came back from a bathroom break just in time to see the photographer walk away. When Daniel told her what had happened, she said, "They publish *Modern Computing*, didn't you know that?" He didn't.

Then she ran after the photographer, and dragged him back to the booth. "If he's going to be in the magazine, we should all be. Everybody get up front!"

So Daniel posed for another photo. If it made the team happy, he could live with it.

Nora, two hours later

The interview with Dr. Patel from Intel had been great. Nora could see it being the centerpiece of her coverage for the whole conference. If she'd understood him correctly—and she was pretty sure she had—their new Pentium chips would be a real game-changer for the whole industry. And the powerful new software those chips could run would change a hundred more industries in ways nobody was even thinking about yet.

Telling that story was exactly why Mr. Brooks had sent her to this conference. She'd show him his confidence in her wasn't misplaced.

Nora didn't have any other interviews scheduled this morning, so she decided to explore the show floor. She had a list of companies to check out, and after the Intel interview, she had better questions to ask them.

Right there in row 500 was one of those companies. Quantum Network Systems. They had a double-sized booth, and several computers set up running slideshows showing the benefits of their fiber optic networks. They didn't seem to have anyone skinny, dark-haired and cute working their booth, though.

She stepped into the booth, and examined the display model of an actual fiber optic cable. Nora hadn't actually seen one before.

"Here, let me show you," a very short, brown haired man said. He flipped a switch on a little box attached to the cable, and light began to pulse along it. "Of course, normally it's insulated, but this way you can see how it works."

Nora knew the theory of how they worked, but it was pretty cool to see it in action. "So how much faster is this than internet through DSL?"

The man—Bryce, she saw on his nametag—said, "Right now, under good conditions it's ten times faster. But that's only because there aren't modems to take advantage of the speed. We're working on that end of it, and then you'll see speeds maybe up to a hundred times faster."

That was impressive. It certainly beat dialing up to AOL over her phone line at home. "I assume you also provide software for end users to take advantage of all that speed?"

"I'm not the expert on the software." He raised his voice. "Hey, Blue, can you come over here?" A blonde woman in—naturally—a blue QNS shirt ran over. "Can you talk to her about the software?"

The woman talked for ten minutes about software. Nora could just about keep up. "So are you going to be coming out with updated software to take advantage of the new Pentium chips, once they hit the market?"

She shrugged. "Nobody's talked to me about that yet. If anybody would know, it's our Team Lead. Tall guy, dark hair—you can't miss him. Well, you can right now—he had to take Red to first aid. She sprained her ankle. Hopefully that's all it is, anyway. I'm not sure when he'll be back, but it shouldn't be too long. Maybe check back in an hour?"

Before Nora could ask the Team Leader's name, there was a shout and a suppressed curse from another podium. "Oh, God," the woman in blue said. "Excuse me, I have to go see what Edward did."

Nora had other companies to visit; she couldn't wait here to ask someone else if the missing Team Leader was really her ex-boyfriend who'd been on her mind from the moment she landed two days ago.

But she could come back in an hour and see for herself.

Daniel, the same time

Daniel sat with Red Kristin in the little room—more like a walk-in closet, honestly—that served as the conference's first aid center. They'd been waiting for someone—surely not a doctor, maybe not even a nurse—for ten minutes.

"You don't have to sit here with me, Daniel. I'm a big girl."

She'd said that half a dozen times already. But he was Team Lead, and that meant taking care of everyone. "I'm not going any-where, Red." That really did sound stupid. How had he thought it was a good idea? "I mean, Kristin. And you couldn't put any weight on your ankle, what were you going to do, hop on one leg all the way across the convention center?"

"If I have to, yes. You sound like my big brother right now, you know that?" She chuckled. "Actually, I don't mind that so much. You *are* kind of like Bill, come to think of it. He's quiet, too, but there's a lot going on under the surface. And you know what else? I'm sort of getting used to the whole Red thing. I've had worse nicknames before."

Daniel wondered if those other nicknames had anything to do with the middle name she didn't want anyone to know. He wasn't going to ask; if she wanted to tell, she would. If she didn't, he had no right to make her feel uncomfortable.

The nurse—or whatever he was—showed up then. "Sorry for the wait. There's one of me and ten thousand people out there. What's the problem?"

"My ankle. I twisted it hard."

"Let's get your shoe and sock off so I can take a look," the man said. Daniel saw his nametag—Andy Thompson, RN. Definitely a nurse. That was encouraging.

The way Red's face went purple and she cursed when he touched her foot was less encouraging. Daniel took her hand, squeezed it. "It's okay, Red. I'm here with you." She squeezed back harder, her nails digging into his hand as the nurse managed to get her shoe and sock off.

Her ankle looked swollen, but not horribly. Daniel had read somewhere that if you broke a bone, there'd be huge swelling you couldn't mistake. The nurse felt around, with more cursing from Red, before he announced, "It's a sprain. I'll put some ice on it for ten minutes, then I'll wrap it and I think I've got a plastic splint in here somewhere. Keep it wrapped, keep icing it, keep it elevated, and you'll be back to normal in a couple of weeks."

"Weeks?" Daniel didn't know Red's voice could go that high. "What am I supposed to do the rest of the conference?"

"I just told you," the nurse said, with exaggerated patience. "Keep it wrapped, keep icing it, keep it elevated. And obviously don't put any weight on it."

"It's fine, Red. We'll take care of you. There's a CVS a block away—remember, we passed it coming back from dinner last night? I'll send someone over to get everything you need."

Twenty minutes later, with Red on one leg and Daniel supporting most of her weight, they made their way back to the booth. It wasn't until they got there that he properly looked at his hand. She'd actually drawn blood with her nails. And in the back of his mind, he heard Nora's voice: *You should claim hazard pay for that.*

Nora, late afternoon

She never did get back to Quantum Networking Systems. After lunch, she went to a demo of the Digital Compliance Library. It was run by the National Regulatory Institute—they published all those looseleaf binders of laws and regulations, the kind they mailed you new pages every month to update with.

It was a lot more interesting than she'd expected. They were replacing the binders with CD-ROMs—one disk instead of twenty books on a shelf, instantly searchable.

Livingston had several of their products, and for her first month on the job, it had been Nora's job to swap out new looseleaf pages for old.

She'd ended up talking to their sales rep for half an hour after the demo was over. She had enough material for two pages in her coverage, and she could probably tie it into the Pentium chips, too.

Then Annette had found her, and they'd debriefed each other. Nora suggested she check out the Intel booth, and if she could corner Dr. Patel, she could drop Nora's name to help things along. In return, Annette told her she'd heard that the CEO of Gateway 2000 was here at the conference, but they were keeping it secret until their big presentation tomorrow.

"Thanks," Nora said, surprised. "You didn't have to tell me that. You could have kept it to yourself."

"I probably should have. Before last night, I think I would have. But you didn't have to take time for me. Fair is fair."

Nora knew that was an exaggeration. Last night's dinner might have been the final straw that turned over a new leaf—she had to laugh at herself for that thought. Her high school English teachers would've had a stroke over that metaphor, and Jack Elliott would probably fire her on the spot if she said it out loud.

But whichever metaphor she wanted to use, Annette must have been stewing over things for a while, and Nora had only given her that last little push she needed to start acting more like a halfway decent human being.

"Okay, in that spirit, if I manage to catch him and I get anything good, I'll give you a heads-up."

Annette smiled—a genuine, heartfelt smile. "Thank you, Nora. I've got one more thing for you. Totally not work-related, but you did say last night you haven't had any fun in ages." That wasn't what she'd actually said, but there was no point in being pedantic. "I hear there's going to be a big crowd from the conference at this karaoke bar—a little place called Second Verse, it's on Walnut Street, four blocks or so from the hotel. A room full of tech geeks singing off-key all night—how can you beat that?"

That did sound like fun. It sounded like the kind of thing she and Daniel would have gone to, back at Albion. They'd have sat at the back of the room, laughing at the terrible singing, and at some point Nora would have gone on stage, dragging him with her kicking and screaming.

Not that Daniel had ever kicked or screamed. He would have pouted, and then surprised everyone by singing better than anyone would have guessed.

She'd never heard him sing, come to think of it. They'd dated for eight months, and that was something that had never come up. What else had they missed out on?

Never mind. That was then.

She shouldn't dwell on him—no matter how often he crept into her thoughts on this trip. "You sold me. I'll go. Want to go over together?"

Daniel, the same time

The big demo was over, and it had gone better than Daniel could have hoped.

The room had been full—a hundred people, most of them city and county executives with real authority to make decisions. He and Thomas made the case for the benefits of contracting with QNS to install fiber optic lines throughout their localities: how it would improve property values, make local businesses more efficient and more profitable and make them personally appear more decisive and forward-looking. Blue came in at the end with ten minutes about why QNS wouldn't interfere with any local cable TV and phone contracts they had, not to mention the potential federal subsidies they could qualify for.

Still riding the high, they walked back to the booth—only for Daniel to stop short when he saw Red. She was sitting on a stool, her leg propped up on one of the podiums.

"I thought I told Edward to take you back to the hotel."

"You did," Red said. "But as the senior person left at the booth ..."

Edward snorted. "By three days!"

"Whatever," Red said. "I made a command decision. I didn't want to leave Bryce all alone for twenty minutes."

She *was* an adult, and a sprained ankle wasn't exactly life-threatening. "Well, the floor closes up in five minutes, so let's get everything shut down for the night, and then Edward and I will both help you back to the hotel."

It didn't even take five minutes to close the booth up. They really were a good team. Daniel was trying to think of something fun for them to do tonight, but Bryce beat him to it. "I heard from one of the AOL guys, there's going to be a party at this karaoke bar, a place called Second Verse. It's not far from where we ate last night. What do you all think?"

A room full of tech geeks singing off-key? Thomas spoke up, saying pretty much what Daniel would have, "Could be either hilarious or a couple of hours of torture, depending how much you have to drink."

"Let's go—I mean, it's not required or anything, just if you want to. But I think it'll be fun." Daniel looked over to Red. "I'll get a cab for you so you don't have to walk all that way, and no arguments."

Karaoke was something he and Nora hadn't ever done—why did he keep thinking about her? She'd been in his mind this whole trip.

But she would have loved karaoke. He could picture it—she'd be laughing at every butchered song, until she got up the nerve to take the stage herself. And she would have dragged him up there right alongside her.

And he would have loved it.

Chapter 28

Nora, July 16, eight o'clock

The karaoke bar was right in between a diner and a used bookshop. "Of course it would be," Nora muttered to herself.

Annette gave her a look.

"Sorry, just talking to myself." It was like a tour of memories with Daniel; the day at Turn the Page when she'd read out loud from that ridiculous romance novel with him on the other side of a bookshelf, and the night a couple of weeks later at the Green Lantern Café where they'd had their first date.

Even if he was somehow at the conference—which of course he wasn't, why couldn't she just accept reality already?—what were the odds that he'd be here to listen to terrible karaoke?

No. She needed to forget about him, and just enjoy tonight for what it was. The past was the past. They'd each made a promise, but if he even remembered his, it wouldn't come true for another eight years.

"Come on, Nora. There's a table over there, by the window." Nora let Annette lead her over, and she let her order the drinks, too. "Two Mariah-garitas," Annette told the waitress, then she looked over at Nora. "Salt?" Nora nodded. "Salt for both. Thanks!"

Nora thought she knew the answer, but she asked anyway. "What exactly is a Mariah-garita?"

"According to the sign by the door, it's a margarita with extra drama." That was pretty much what she'd guessed. The name went with the décor—lighting that was just a touch too soft, neon musical notes on the walls in garish colors and a stage that was too small—surely to force groups of singers to huddle together for maximum embarrassment.

Still, it could be worse. She was out for a fun evening with someone who wanted her there—when was the last time she could say that?

Their drinks came just as the first act of the night went up on stage. It was one of the junior Microsoft reps who'd run yesterday's Windows NT demo. He sang—well, tried to sing— *Video Killed the Radio Star.* Honestly, it was less singing and more howling, sort of like a cat getting chased up a tree by foxes.

But everyone clapped when he was done anyway. Or maybe *because* he was done.

Nora glanced out the window, just in time to see a taxi stop at the curb outside, and a man get out.

A slim, dark-haired man with the prettiest eyes. A man who looked exactly like Daniel.

Because ... he *was* Daniel.

She didn't even register the glass slipping from her fingers until it hit the floor and shattered. All she could see was *him.*

Daniel, one minute later

Just for an instant, when he got out of the cab, but before he turned around to help Red out, he thought he saw someone in the window. Someone dark-blonde and beautiful, shining green-blue eyes and a smile on her face.

But it wasn't Nora. Obviously it wasn't. She was—he didn't know where she was living or working now, but she couldn't be here at the conference, at this bar. He didn't know why he was obsessing about her all week, but it had to stop. He had a job to do, a team to lead and right now a couple of hours to just relax and watch other people embarrass themselves while he had exactly one drink.

"Here you go, Red, I've got you." She grabbed his arm, balanced herself on her good ankle, and then put an arm around him.

Why couldn't he think about someone like her instead? Not Red herself, obviously, or Blue, or anyone back in the office in Chicago.

Dad had drilled it into him, and so had Dad's boss. And Lisa. And Bianca. And about a million movies and TV shows. Never date anyone at work—it was a recipe for disaster. And even more so now that he was a Team Lead.

But why not someone like her? He could go out with Jeff, or with other guys from the office, and maybe meet someone that way. Or there were the personal ads in the paper. Or even church. There was a Catholic church three blocks from his apartment. That was still a way to meet people, wasn't it?

There were countless things he could do to meet an actual girl, rather than losing himself in memories of someone who—no matter how amazing she was—he hadn't seen in over two years. And wouldn't see again for another eight, if they both kept their promise.

Except, the moment he stepped inside the bar, he saw her, right here and now, not twenty feet away.

It was her. Nora. In the flesh.

She sat at a table by the window, with a shorter, redheaded woman. Just like the first time he ever properly saw her, in the Green Lantern Café sitting with her freshman roommate.

She turned and saw him. Their eyes met. And the expression on her face, a mix of confusion and fear and a dozen other things he couldn't even guess, changed instantly, and she smiled. *That* smile. The one she only ever showed to him.

If he hadn't been holding poor Red up, he would have run to her. But he had just enough presence of mind to call Thomas over to take her, and the moment she grabbed hold of his teammate, Daniel went to Nora.

She was already standing, already coming towards him.

And then she was there, her arms were around him, and his around her, and they were kissing, and nothing else in this bar, or the rest of the world, mattered.

Nora, a moment later

She pulled away from him, finally, only because she needed to breathe. And because, no matter how much she wanted to, she couldn't make love with him right here on the floor of the bar.

No, that wasn't what she wanted. She wanted to talk to him. To know everything he'd been doing for the last two years, all the good and the bad. And to tell him everything she'd done, everything she'd felt since the moment she'd last seen him, up on the stage receiving his diploma.

But before they could talk, before anything else, there was one thing she had to do. Her hands were ahead of her; they'd already unbuttoned the two buttons on his polo shirt.

And there it was. She pulled the necklace out, held it up to her face.

"You're still wearing it." She knew he would be.

"I haven't taken it off since you put it on me." She hadn't known that. But she probably should have guessed it.

Nora only now realized that everyone in the bar was staring at them. She didn't care, but Daniel might. Except he wasn't paying any attention to anything or anyone except her. His eyes were locked on hers.

"You want to sit down?" Out of the corner of her eye, she saw Annette get up from their table, clearing out to give her space with Daniel. But before they got halfway there, a voice boomed out from the speakers by the stage. "Stop right where you are! If you're going to give us a floor show, then you have to sing, too!"

She turned away from Daniel to see the emcee pointing at them, beckoning them to the stage.

"I guess we have to," Daniel whispered to her. He didn't look nearly as hesitant as she expected. "I can't sing, but if we're up there together, it doesn't really matter, does it?"

No, it didn't. She took his hand and walked up there. The emcee wasn't all that much older than her, maybe mid-twenties, and he wore the most hideous multi-colored sportscoat she'd ever seen. "Sorry for making a scene," she told him, although she wasn't at all.

He handed her the songbook, and she opened it, holding it up for Daniel to see, too. "You pick," he said. "Like I said, I can't sing, so pick something you're good with and I'll—I don't know. Hum along, I guess."

An image came to her mind then—that stupid music video for *Addicted to Love*. Except she'd be Robert Palmer and Daniel would have to be one of the slinky women in a too-tight black dress.

She had to laugh at that. But her voice probably couldn't go that low anyway. And, anyway, it wasn't the right mood. There was something better, though. She wasn't really a Cyndi

Lauper fan, but it was a pretty melody, and she was fairly sure she could hit all the notes. "Okay," she told the emcee. "We're ready. Number 315."

The emcee gestured for her and Daniel to take the stage, and handed each of them a microphone. He reached over and took her hand, lacing his fingers with hers, and then the music started up.

Daniel, five seconds later

He knew the song, of course. He'd been a freshman in high school when it came out, and it was all over the radio.

Nora's voice was shaky for the first couple of lines of *Time After Time*, but she quickly got hold of herself. She knew the lyrics by heart. She didn't glance at the screen once—her eyes never left his.

He just watched her, listened to her, felt how close she was. He hadn't forgotten how much he missed this—missed her—but the intensity of it surprised him. The way she filled all his senses—not just sight and sound and touch. She still smelled of jasmine and vanilla, and from her kiss he could still taste something tangy and maybe sour—whatever she'd been drinking right before he got here.

She was *everything*.

And she could even sing. Her voice wasn't trained, he could hear that. But it was beautiful and clear all the same.

He had to join in, didn't he? The chorus was coming up, and it was perfect because it was true. He wasn't looking out at the crowd when he started singing, he was focused on Nora and every word was from the heart. He would always catch her if she fell, and for two years now—no, twenty six months and one day—he *had* been waiting.

♡ ♥ ♡

Nora, three minutes later

The music faded, and she hugged Daniel, holding him as tightly as she ever had, enough to break a rib and she could see that he didn't care.

The crowd was clapping, and Nora glanced away from him for a minute to see one table on their feet and shouting, and all wearing the same shirt. His co-workers, they had to be. But he didn't see them, he was completely focused on her. "Let's go sit down," he said, and he led her off the stage. She pointed to the table Annette had vacated.

"That's the first time I've sung in public since ..." Since when? High school. The choir at St. Brendan's. Something else she'd never told Daniel. Not that it was a secret, it was just already part of her past by the time she met him, something she rarely thought about.

There was so much she hadn't told him in those seven months they were together, and just as much he'd never told her. And now there were two whole extra years they didn't know about each other.

"Since when?"

"I was in the choir at my church for a few months, sophomore year of high school. But—it's not a deep dark secret and it's not sad or anything, but I'd rather hear about you now, Daniel. I want to know all about your life."

She didn't say, *I want to be part of it*, even though she did—so desperately that it burned.

"You want to know the truth?" She nodded. "Look over there, see them with the same shirts I'm wearing?" She nodded again.

"That's been my whole life, from the week after I graduated until five minutes ago when I saw you in here."

Was he saying what she thought he was? That he'd been alone all this time, he didn't have a girlfriend, he hadn't been with anyone at all?

"I can't believe that." Except she did believe it. It was equally true of her, wasn't it?

He shrugged. "I mean, I've made friends at work, but—but that's it. I share an apartment with Jeff from accounting, I get into the office by eight, I get home at six, most nights I bring work home or if not I sort of half-watch TV, and on weekends I do laundry and go to the grocery store and if Jeff harasses me enough maybe I go to a baseball game with him or something."

She reached over, grabbed his hands. "That—I don't mean this how it's going to sound—that sucks, Daniel. You deserve so much better."

He almost laughed, but it came out more like a sigh. "Yeah, that's what Bianca says, too. And my mother thinks it, I can tell, but she won't say it. Dad just asks how much money I'm saving up and if I've gotten a promotion yet."

What if it hadn't been that way? What if she'd followed him to Chicago when he graduated? She could have transferred schools—there were a ton of good colleges there. Northwestern had a great journalism program.

Instead of saying goodbye when she gave him the necklace, she could have asked him to marry her, right there on the quad. He would have said yes.

No, he wouldn't have.

He wouldn't have let her uproot herself and change all her plans just for him. No matter how much it would have gutted him to say no to her. And he'd do the same now, if she suggested it.

"You should listen to Bianca. And me. There's more to life ..." Her voice caught, and she looked away from him. "What the hell am I saying? It's exactly the same for me. Work, home, bring work home, errands. Except I don't even have Jeff from accounting."

Now he did laugh. "You're not missing much there."

"Maybe not. But you know what I'm saying. Why are we both like this? Why are we both alone? Did we ruin each other for anybody else that much?"

Daniel, an hour later

"You realize your team has been watching us this whole time," Nora said.

"I figured," Daniel agreed. "But I'd rather spend this time with you. I've got eight hours a day, five days a week to spend with them." More like nine or ten hours, really, which just proved his point all the more.

"I was at your booth this morning. They said you were at first aid, helping—I assume the girl you were with when you got here?"

Of course Nora came by. "Yeah. Red sprained her ankle. I wasn't going to let her hop all the way across the show floor by herself."

Nora clinked her glass to his—their third Mariah-garita each, which he was pretty sure he'd be regretting in the morning. So much for one-drink-only tonight. "That's my Daniel. Always the hero." But then she raised her eyebrows. "But what's the deal with calling her Red? Doesn't she have a name?"

He laughed. "She's Kristin. And so is the one in blue sitting next to her." He told Nora the story of their inability to come up with a suitable way to differentiate themselves, and his solution to the problem.

"Wow," she said, when he finished, barely able to control her giggles. "That's hilarious. The perfect solution. But I bet they both hate it." She paused. "Which makes it even better. It's so annoying it'll force them to come up with something better for themselves."

Daniel hadn't considered that, but it made sense. They'd probably do that once they got back to Chicago. "They're putting up with it for now. I think they're just taking pity on me because this is my first time leading a team."

Nora wasn't laughing anymore. "Daniel, I would have thought you'd be able to give yourself a little credit by now. I don't think any of them are taking pity on you. I think they all see you're a fantastic Team Leader. Your booth looked great, you were taking care of the people under you when they needed it, and you came up with a creative solution for a problem nobody else could solve. When are you going to start seeing in the mirror what everybody else sees in you?"

She was holding his hands; when had she put her drink down to grab them?

That was just dodging her question. He owed her an answer. More important, he owed himself one.

"I do see it—sometimes. There are moments. Flashes. When I got picked to lead the team. When I got the St. Louis contract three months ago." When he'd officially gotten the interview with QNS, January of his senior year, and he'd asked out Valerie.

"Who's Valerie?"

He felt himself blushing. "I said that out loud, didn't I?" Nora nodded. "She was—I guess you didn't know. Valerie's the one girl I dated after we broke up."

♡ ♥ ♡

Nora, a moment later

Nora had known. Not the name, and not for certain. But Kim had told her about the blonde girl—woman—who'd been in the Ellis Hall lab all the time, almost always with Daniel sitting next to her.

She'd made a point of avoiding the building, so she wouldn't have to see for herself.

Well, now she knew. But she could hardly blame him, when she'd been dating Ben at the exact same time.

"What happened with her?"

"We—we only dated a few weeks," he said. He wasn't looking away from her, but she wouldn't have expected otherwise. Daniel had always been honest, even when it was something painful. "She helped me practice for my interview. And she was—this won't make sense, it doesn't to me. She was totally different from you, but everything I liked about her was something I loved about you."

It made perfect sense.

"But we broke up the day I got the letter—the letter with the job offer. I had her come back to my dorm—I needed somebody to be with me when I opened the letter, and when I did, and I read it ..."

Nora didn't need him to say what came next. Except, she did, because she was clearly missing something here. "Wait. *That's* when you broke up with her?"

"We kissed—I mean, really kissed, and then we were on my bed, and—and she wanted to. And I wanted to. But I couldn't." He paused, took a deep breath. "Because she wasn't you."

The same reason she hadn't slept with Ben. "I couldn't, either," she muttered.

And then Daniel truly shocked her. She would have spit out her drink if it had been in her mouth. "Of course you didn't. Valerie totally isn't your type." It wasn't just the words, it was the way he said it completely deadpan.

When she finally stopped laughing and collected herself, she said, "You really have changed. You finally have a decent sense of humor."

"Well, I'm working on it. But," he said, "I know what you really meant. The same thing happened to you, didn't it?"

So she told him—about Ben, about that last night in his apartment, about how close she'd come and why she couldn't go through with it.

"I think you were right, what you said a while ago. We definitely ruined each other for anybody else."

She wished he was wrong. But, really, when had Daniel ever been wrong about anything important?

Daniel, an hour later

After their mutual confessions, neither of them said much for a while, other than joking about the mostly dreadful performances on stage.

It was like they were back in college, back in his dorm room, just being together without having to do or say anything.

He remembered everything about Nora, but he'd forgotten how much he missed the times like these. Comfortable. Safe.

Not in the boring way people usually meant it—safe with Nora had always been the best kind of safe.

"Oh, boy," Nora said, breaking the latest silence.

Daniel saw what she was talking about—the two Kristins were making their way up to the stage, Red leaning on Blue as she gingerly hopped her way across the floor. They huddled with the emcee for a moment, then, when he handed them microphones, Red pointed directly at him. "This one is for our Team Leader. Here's to you, Daniel!"

Then the music came up. He recognized the song, and felt himself blush. This was completely unnecessary and deeply embarrassing—and kind of the nicest thing anyone had done for him all year.

"Go up with them!"

He shook his head. "They don't need any more encouragement." His co-workers were belting out—with a lot of enthusiasm and not much talent—*Holding Out For a Hero*.

"You're right," Nora said. "What they need is voice lessons."

Embarrassing as it was, Daniel couldn't help but be touched. They actually did respect him; they saw him as a leader because of who he was, not just because Mr. Kincaid appointed him. They wouldn't be teasing him like this if they didn't.

Just like Nora always teased him, with not just love but respect.

It came to him then. It was silly, and he'd make a fool of himself on stage, but Nora would love it. He was pretty sure he'd seen the perfect song in the songbook when he'd been dragged up there a couple of hours ago.

"Get ready," he told her. "We're going up next, Nora."

Nora, three minutes later

It was a good thing she didn't gamble. Nora would have bet everything she owned that Daniel Keller would never, ever voluntarily go up on stage at a karaoke bar.

But here he was, the songbook in one hand, his other hand clutching hers tightly.

"That's it," he was telling the emcee. "Number 204."

The emcee clapped his hands. "I love it! You'll bring the house down."

"Are you going to tell me what we're singing?"

Daniel shook his head. "You'll see."

"How do I know what my part is?"

"You'll know." This was a whole new side to him. She didn't have a clue what song he'd picked.

And then the microphone was in her hand, and the music started. "I don't believe you!" It was brilliant—and, again, something she would never in a million years have guessed he would pick.

Daniel launched straight into the first verse of *Don't You Want Me*, looking her in the eye as he sang. His voice was—well, it was pretty bad, honestly, but it was loud and clear. She didn't know how he wasn't laughing his head off as he sang about pulling her out of a cocktail bar and how easy success was for her.

Then her verse came, and she didn't need to follow the words on the screen; how many times had she heard this on the radio back in high school?

She didn't expect to hear her voice break when she sang about still loving him, or for him to hug her when it happened.

When they got to the end, she did expect his kiss, and she returned it, and she was pretty sure he wasn't hearing the crowd or the emcee or anything else as they stood up there on the stage wrapped up in each other, any more than she did.

Chapter 29

AFTER MIDNIGHT—KANSAS CITY, MO

Daniel, July 17, ten minutes after midnight

They were in his room at the Marriott. Nora's room was three floors above him; they'd flipped a coin to decide where to go.

"You've got a bigger TV than I do," she said. "And a better view. I'm looking down at the parking lot."

They'd been talking like this since they got here, dancing around anything meaningful. She probably didn't know what to think, or what she wanted now, any more than he did.

That wasn't true. He wanted to make love with her, and he was sure she did, too.

But if they did, what would it mean? They'd said their good-byes at his graduation, two years ago. He didn't want to mess things up, or make them more complicated, or—he didn't even know what.

"Daniel," she said, sitting on the bed and motioning for him to join her. "We don't have that much time. I don't want to waste it." He sat next to her, but she didn't turn to look at him. "I don't know what I want. I never imagined I'd see you here."

"Me neither." He'd never actually pictured running into Nora. "I didn't dare think about it." He thought about Nora every day, every day for twenty-six months, but he'd never actually given any thought to what a meeting with her would be like, where and when it could happen.

Now she was looking at him, and holding his hands in hers. "I know what you mean. I couldn't let myself imagine how we might find each other. It would've hurt too much. I didn't even try to find out what company you were working at."

Just like he hadn't looked into where she'd gone after graduation. It wouldn't have been hard to do, but then it would have been torture every day having to not call her, not write her, not buy a plane ticket to fly to her.

"We're still not—whatever it is we're supposed to be, are we?" She didn't answer; she just nodded her head ever so slightly, and squeezed his hands harder, waiting for him to go on. "I wish I was. But even if I was, how would it work? I don't think either one of us is ready to quit our jobs and move a thousand miles."

Especially not after this conference, when he was earning the respect of his team, and she was scoring interviews with leading scientists and tech executives.

And yet, if she asked him to, he'd do it. He'd give Mr. Kincaid two weeks notice, apologize to Jeff, pack up his boxes and take his chances in Boston. But she would never ask it, any more than he would of her.

"So where does that leave us?" Her voice was barely louder than a whisper. He could feel how much it hurt her to say it. Just as much as it hurt him to answer her.

"I hate it, but—I think the same place we were before tonight."

♡ 🖤 ♡

Nora, a moment later

Daniel was right.

Of course he was. A few hours, a few kisses, and two off-key karaoke performances didn't change anything. How could they?

She still loved him. He still loved her. They still couldn't be together.

"You remember our promise?"

He didn't answer, at least not in words. He pulled the necklace out from under his shirt.

"Is that really why you're still wearing it? Or do you just not know how to take it off?"

It was a joke; he had to know it was a joke. So why was he blushing?

"The truth?" She nodded, even though she definitely didn't want it. "It's ninety-eight percent our promise, and two percent I can't get it off myself and I didn't want anyone else touching it."

She wanted to laugh. Or throw something at him. Or both. How could he joke about it, especially right now?

Or maybe this was a perfect time to joke. And, anyway, ninety-eight percent was pretty good, wasn't it? "You honestly don't know the trick?" He shook his head. She reached over, grabbed the necklace gingerly, and pulled it around until the clasp was in front. "You've got a computer science degree, and you're a Team Leader and your IQ probably qualifies for Mensa, and you couldn't figure that out for yourself?"

Now he wasn't merely blushing; he was beet red. "Swear to God, I never thought of that. It seems pretty obvious now."

"It was obvious to me when I was seven years old, Daniel." She believed him, though. It was exactly the kind of simple, practical thing that a man who'd never worn jewelry except possibly for his high school class ring, wouldn't know. "But now you know. So you can take it off whenever you want."

He shook his head again. "I don't want to. The only time I even thought about it was a year ago, at Uncle Fred's house. I was going to go in his pool, and I wanted to take it off so it wouldn't get—I don't know, corroded or something. You know, with the chlorine in the water?"

"That wouldn't hurt gold, Daniel. People don't take their wedding rings off to go swimming. You know that, right?" He had been returning to his normal color, but he was back to red again. "Right. You never thought about that. One more question. Why didn't you want to let someone else help you take it off?"

"Because nobody besides you should ever touch it." He smiled, a gentle, loving smile. "Do you honestly not know that?"

Daniel, an hour later

He didn't want this to end. But it had to.

Putting all his emotions aside, it was a matter of practicality. It was already after one o'clock in the morning, almost one-thirty, and he had to be up at six-thirty so he could shower, dress and be at the booth by seven. And he needed to be at his best; it would be the busiest day of the conference.

And surely Nora had a big day ahead as well. She needed her rest just as much.

He could ask her to stay here, sleep here—but regardless of their best intentions, if they were together under the covers, there wouldn't be any sleep. It was difficult enough to keep his hands off of her sitting up and fully clothed, and he could see it was the same for her; she gave it away with her eyes, and in the way her breathing was too fast and shallow and in every bit of her body language.

She was thinking the same thing; of course she was. "I think I should go." She paused. "I don't want to. But ..."

"I know. I feel the same way. I'll walk you down to your room. And maybe ..."

She smiled; it was *that* smile. "Maybe after the show floor closes today, we can have dinner."

He stood up, held out a hand for her. She took it, and let him lead her to the door. "Not maybe. Definitely. Come by the booth at closing time, meet me there." Unless she had a big interview, or something else she couldn't get away from. "Or, if you can't get there right then, call me." The cell phone was right there on the dresser, next to the coffee pot. He grabbed it and read her the number. She went into her purse, pulled out a pen. The pen he'd given her. Of course she still had it.

"Got it," she said, jotting it down in a little notebook. "See, pen *and* paper. You know, I started putting a notebook in my purse that morning, as soon as I got back upstairs to my room."

"You always were a fast learner." They were down the hall, in and out of the elevator and down the hall again to her room in a minute. Much too fast.

"If I remember right, that was you," she said, giving him a look that would have melted his heart if it wasn't already a puddle.

He leaned in, kissed her. She kissed him back, and it was so difficult to pull away. He didn't know where the strength to do it came from, and a part of him wished he didn't have that strength.

"Nora, I—I can't wait until later. Until tonight. I'll be counting the minutes."

One more kiss.

"Me too, Daniel. Until tonight."

She opened the door, stood there in the doorway. After a few seconds—or an hour, it was hard to tell—she pushed it shut.

One of them had to, right?

Chapter 30

THE SECOND DAY OF THE CONFERENCE—
KANSAS CITY, MO/SIOUX CITY/ SD

Daniel, July 16, seven-thirty in the morning

The whole team was already at the booth when Daniel got there. Thomas was directing them, getting all the computers booted up and ready and cleaning all the podiums.

"We weren't expecting you for at least another hour," Red said.

"Yeah," Edward chimed in. "I hope you didn't kick her out of ..." He didn't finish the sentence; Blue smacked him in the head with a stack of brochures. Daniel made a mental note to buy her a drink later, or maybe some flowers.

He took a deep breath, tried to settle himself. "I'm sorry I ditched you guys last night."

"Don't apologize, Daniel," Bryce said. "If I ran into my lost love, I would have ditched everybody for her, too."

"Not exactly lost," Daniel said, as much to himself as to them. "I don't even know how to explain it."

Red beckoned him over, and hugged him when he got to her. "You don't need to explain anything." She raised her voice. "You all hear that? No harassing our Team Leader. He doesn't pry into our personal lives, so we're not going to do that to him."

"Speak for yourself," Blue said. "I want to know what the deal is with that necklace."

Why shouldn't he let her see it? It was proof he was loved, and why should he hide that? He pulled it out from under his shirt and held it up for her to see. Blue came up to peer at it. "She made it for me. Had it made, I mean. But she designed it herself."

"It's beautiful," Blue breathed.

"The aquamarine is for me. My birthstone."

Red hopped over to see for herself. "And the sapphire is hers?"

"So we're always together. She gave it to me the morning I graduated. Two years ago. That's the last time I saw her before yesterday." He didn't know why, but it wasn't nearly as difficult talking about this as he'd expected it to be.

Probably because he was going to see her again tonight. It wouldn't be as easy when he had to say a final goodbye to Nora Sunday when the conference was over.

"I hope you can make it work with her," Red said. "You looked so comfortable with her last night. It was really nice seeing that."

"And the singing," Blue added. "It's a shame we don't have it on tape. Nobody's going to believe it back in the office."

Daniel laughed at that. "I can hardly believe it myself," he said, tucking the necklace back under his shirt. "But let's get back to work. We've got a big day coming up, I want to be sure we're as ready as we can be."

He was sure they weren't done talking about him, but he could live with that. They weren't mocking him, they genuinely seemed to be happy for him. Even Edward, in his thoughtless way.

If they all believed he deserved good things, maybe he could believe it, too.

Nora, two hours later

When she'd closed the door on Daniel, she'd thought she would be up all night with racing thoughts. But she'd fallen asleep the moment her head hit the pillow, and she'd woken up with a clear head at the first buzz of the alarm she'd set.

Was it the three glasses of water he made her drink when they'd gotten back to his room last night—and the aspirin he'd insisted she take? Or was it just the mere presence of *him*—her Daniel?

She knew the answer. It was going to be so hard—so impossible—to say goodbye again, for good again, two days from now.

She didn't have to.

Last night, she'd thought about what would have happened if she'd thrown caution and everything else to the wind, and asked him to marry her that morning on the quad when she gave him the necklace.

She could do it here. There were jobs in Chicago; it was the second—third?—biggest city in the country.

She could give her notice when she got back to the office on Monday, spend the next two weeks packing up and job searching and then go to him, where he'd already have a new apartment ready for them to move into together.

A month from now, they could be buying furniture together as husband and wife. She'd be Mrs. Nora Keller. Or maybe Mrs. Nora Langley-Keller? He wouldn't care if she took his name, or hyphenated or if she kept her own.

She'd care, though. She'd want everyone to know she was his wife. She'd carry his name proudly.

But it couldn't happen. He'd say no—not because he didn't want it, but because he loved her too much to let her make that kind of sacrifice. No matter how much it broke his heart, or hers.

She took a deep breath, tried to clear her head. She couldn't be thinking about Daniel now. She was waiting for the CEO of Gateway 2000 to come out of his meeting. She'd managed to convince his assistant to give her ten minutes this morning, and she needed to be completely on her game.

Daniel would tell her the same thing. *Nora, this is the kind of thing that could get you a promotion. Forget about me,* he'd probably say.

When she saw the man a moment later, stepping out of the Monarch Room in a suit not nearly as fashionable as she'd have expected from a major tech company CEO, Nora found she was able to do exactly that.

Daniel, half an hour later

"You all know what to do?"

Thomas rolled his eyes. "Yes, for the third time. Nobody burned the booth down when you were running the demo yesterday, or when you took Red to first aid. Go tell everyone in that ballroom why fiber optics is the wave of the future."

Red spoke up. "If I didn't know better, I'd say you're looking for excuses not to go get up on that stage for your panel."

"Which would be really stupid," Blue added. "You know everything cold, and you look—well, as good as any skinny twenty-three year old in a polo shirt can look."

Reminding him that he was just a skinny twenty-three year old didn't really help. But he *did* know everything that realistically might come up in an hourlong discussion about *The Future of High-Speed Residential Internet*. The Senior Vice President for National Sales at Comcast, and the Director of Regional Network Marketing at AT&T he'd be sharing the stage with might both have twenty years of experience on him, but there was no way either of them had spent more hours preparing for this panel than he had.

"I get it," Daniel said. "I'll be back in an hour." He wondered if Nora might be in the room to cover the panel. It was something that *Modern Computing* would probably be interested in, and—so long as she wasn't sitting directly in his line of sight to distract him—he liked the idea of her seeing him "in action."

Maybe she could even interview him afterward. It would be cool to be featured in a national magazine. Although there were probably ethics rules against it, now he thought about it.

He shook his head as he headed for the Union Ballroom. Better to put Nora and fantasies about being on the cover of a magazine aside, and just do his job. That approach had gotten him this far, hadn't it?

Nora, the same time

She probably shouldn't have been surprised. Of course the CEO of a billion-dollar corporation would have constant demands on his time. Nora had been sitting next to him for nearly thirty minutes, and they'd had maybe ninety seconds of actual conversation in between multiple calls on his cell phone and interruptions from his personal assistant.

And another call now. "Yes, I heard you," he was saying to whomever was on the other end of the call. "They won't reschedule? You told them that I'm supposed to be announcing this partnership at three o'clock today?" He listened, then made a frustrated, almost grunting sound. "Fine. Call the travel office, have them call the airport and get the jet ready and file a flight plan. I should be able to get to HQ by one o'clock. That gives us two hours to hammer things out and they can put me on speaker in the ballroom here for the announcement."

So much for her big interview with the CEO of Gateway 2000. Unless ...

No, that was insane. She couldn't ask him to let her come with him and do a truly in-depth interview with him on his plane. Why would he ever agree to something that ridiculous? Asking a CEO to let her tag along on his private jet was career suicide. Wasn't it?

"Mr. Whittaker?" He put his phone back in his pocket and turned to her. "I have a proposition for you."

"Make it quick, Ms. Langley. I'm sure you were listening, I have very little time."

Now or never. "There'd be more time to talk on your jet. Let me come with you, answer my questions, let me be there at your headquarters while you finalize your agreement with Intel, and it'll be the cover story for next month's issue of *Modern Computing*."

He stared hard at her. "You can guarantee that?"

Of course not. She'd be lucky if Mr. Brooks didn't fire her for daring to offer it. "If I bring back a good enough story, my editor won't have a choice but to put it on the cover." Even if she did bring back a killer story, Mr. Brooks might fire her anyway. This might be the stupidest thing she'd ever done. But she was committed now.

He kept staring at her for a moment, waiting for her to—she didn't know what. But whatever it was he was expecting, she didn't do it. She returned his gaze with all the confidence she didn't remotely feel.

"What the hell. You've got nerve, Ms. Langley. Let's see if you can back it up. The car will be in front of the hotel in fifteen minutes, and it leaves for the airport in sixteen."

"Thank you," she said, already up and on her way to her room. Fifteen minutes to get there, pack, get back downstairs and check out? She could manage that.

It wasn't until twenty minutes later, sitting in the back seat of the car with Mr. Whittaker, that she remembered her promise to meet Daniel when the show floor closed down later today.

He'd understand. He had to.

Daniel, around five o'clock

Daniel made it back to the booth just in time to help the team shut it down for the day.

Everything had gone well—better than he could have hoped, honestly. The panel was great—he'd more than held his own with the people from Comcast and AT&T. The vendor meetings had been successful—he'd made a strong start that the sales team could follow up on. And all three demos went off without a hitch.

The only thing missing was any word from Nora. She hadn't been in the crowd for the panel, or at any of the demos, and she definitely hadn't come by the booth—his team would have told him immediately if she had.

And no messages on the cellphone. But she was busy—she had interviews lined up, plus whatever else she ran across on the show floor that was newsworthy. There were a couple of hundred booths, that was definitely enough to occupy a reporter all day. Especially when she was the only reporter from her organization here.

But he could page her now. She'd see it was him, and she'd call back when she was free. He dialed the number, heard the tone and left his cell phone number. He punched the digits in casually, as though she'd somehow be able to tell his state of mind when she got the page and a recorded voice read the number back to her.

Now it was just a matter of waiting.

"Daniel," Red said. "If you don't—you know, if you don't have plans, we were thinking of—don't laugh—going bowling. Well, you guys can bowl." She waved her injured leg in the air. "I'll keep score and let you all buy me drinks."

Bryce spoke up. "I went for a run this morning, and passed by a bowling alley—just a few blocks away."

Nora might call at any moment. But the cell phone would be with him, so when she did he could just make his excuses and leave. Or he could invite her to join them. She'd probably love it. And watching her put Edward in his place when he inevitably said something stupid and obnoxious would be hilarious. Not to mention he might actually tone the obnoxious behavior down if he got called out by someone outside the team.

"Sure," Daniel said. "It sounds like fun." He didn't add, *Until Nora calls me back*, but they all knew it anyway.

Nora, an hour later

She finally had time to contact her office, after she'd been dropped off at the Prairie Gate Inn and checked into a room.

She'd spent the last five hours at the Gateway 2000 Headquarters in North Sioux City, South Dakota.

Nora's first call was to the twenty-four hour emergency line for the travel office. They needed to know where she was, both for safety's sake, and also so the company credit card wouldn't be declined when she used it to check out from a hotel in South Dakota instead of Kansas City where she was expected to be.

They also needed to book her a flight home on Sunday morning. After spending most of the day with Bill Whittaker and his leadership team, he'd asked her to stay tomorrow for an in-depth tour of the Gateway 2000 factory, and an extended demo of their new corporate workstation product line. "We already have a strong presence in the home computer market, but we're going to make a big push to get into the business market. You'll be the first journalist to see what we're planning."

She couldn't say no to that; she'd miss a lot at the conference, but this was absolutely a cover story. Even if Mr. Brooks fired her for making a snap decision without consulting him—or anybody—back home, he'd have to give her the cover first.

She had his home number, for emergencies, and this certainly qualified.

But she had another call to make before that. Daniel would understand; how could he not? This was a career-making opportunity. She could hear him now: *I can't believe you just asked him to take you with him on his jet! You're amazing, Nora. Didn't I tell you you'd be a star?*

She had to settle for imagining his words; when she called his cell phone, she got a computerized voice telling her no one was available and to leave a message.

Maybe he was at an early dinner with his team, or maybe the phone battery had run out. Either way, he'd get her message soon enough, and he could call her back here in the room.

So she might as well order room service and wait for that call back.

Daniel, two hours later

Still no word from Nora. He was starting to worry that something had happened to her. She could be sick, or injured. She might be in the hospital.

What else could explain it? Even if she'd been slammed with interviews all day, she would've checked her pager. She would've found a phone. Wouldn't she?

The silver lining—if you could call it that—was that his increasing anxiety was helping his bowling. He was throwing the ball harder than he could ever recall doing, thanks to all the nervous energy. He actually bowled a 160 the last game, which was an all-time high for him, by a lot.

Nobody on the team asked if he'd heard from her. And every time he checked the cell phone for messages, they all pretended not to notice.

After the fourth game, Blue suggested going back to the Marriott for a late dinner at the hotel restaurant. It seemed as good an idea as any, so Daniel settled up the bill using the company card—he could explain it to Mr. Kincaid as team-building—and took Red back in a taxi while the rest of the team walked the five blocks.

When they got there, everyone else sat down at an open table in the hotel restaurant, leaving only one seat for Daniel—a seat with a clear view of the big revolving door they'd just come through.

He didn't thank them; if they were going to the trouble of not calling attention to how badly he was missing Nora, then he wasn't going to mention it either.

He'd mention it in their evaluations back at the office, under the headings of "team spirit" and "going above and beyond."

They lingered for nearly two hours—dinner, dessert, coffee and bad jokes. Every time the revolving door turned, he looked up. But Nora never came through it.

Where was she?

Chapter 31

THE THIRD DAY OF THE CONFERENCE—
KANSAS CITY, MO/NORTH SIOUX CITY, SD

Daniel, July 17, eight o'clock in the morning

When he got back to his room last night, Daniel promised himself he wouldn't do anything weird or obsessive or stalkerish. He'd wait to hear from Nora. There had to be a good reason she hadn't called him back.

But when he woke up this morning, there still wasn't any message on his cell phone. Or his room phone. Or a note under his door. Or anything.

So he paged her again. That was at six-thirty.

At seven, when he should have been heading over to the booth, he called down to the lobby to get the phone number for her room. There was no answer.

He should have gone over to the convention center then, but what if Nora had had some kind of accident in her room last night? She was the only reporter from Livingston Scientific Network here—there wasn't anyone to check up on her or miss her on the convention floor. Except him.

She didn't answer when he knocked on her door, either. But if she'd had an accident and she was unconscious, obviously she wouldn't answer, would she?

So he went down to the lobby—this was definitely bordering on stalkerish, but he didn't know what else to do—and asked them to send someone up to her room to be sure she wasn't bleeding to death on the floor of the bathroom or something. "The guest in Room 2020 checked out yesterday morning, sir," a too-perky woman at the reception desk told him.

There was nothing else to do but go over to the booth, and wonder what the hell was going on with her.

Why would she leave in the middle of the conference? She'd told him how many interviews she had lined up, how many booths she needed to visit and panels and demos she needed to sit in on. She'd been so excited about it; she was going to show what a star reporter she was beyond all doubt.

And then she just ... left town.

Had something happened with her family? If there was an emergency with one of her parents, or her Aunt Rachel, she would change her plans and rush home for that, and calling him would be the last thing on her mind. If Mom or Dad or Bianca were in the hospital, he'd probably forget about Nora until he got there and saw them for himself, no matter how wonderful Thursday night had been. He couldn't blame her for doing the same.

That had to be it. What other explanation could there be—unless it was all his fault. Unless he'd done or said something to scare her off.

No. Not just scare her. Traumatize her—so badly she'd flush a massive career opportunity just to put a thousand miles between them.

When he finally got to the booth, he was completely distracted, replaying every word from Thursday night to try and figure out what he'd said that was so horrible.

"Daniel, is everything okay?"

It was Red.

"Sure," he lied. "I'm fine. What's going on?"

"You've been emptying and refilling that rack of brochures over and over. Usually you're a little more with-it than that." She hesitated; he could see she was debating her next words. "If you need to talk about something, you can carry me over to the lounge and I'll just sit and listen. It's the least I can do for you, the way you've been helping me the last couple of days."

He was sorely tempted. Another perspective—a woman's perspective—might be just the thing he needed. But he couldn't dump all his feelings and fears on Red. It wasn't fair, and it wasn't really appropriate, either. Besides, there was a lot of work to do today.

"Thanks, Red. But I'm fine—well, I'll be fine by the time the floor opens, anyway."

They'd broken each other's hearts before and he managed to function afterwards. It would be miserable, but he could do it again.

What other choice did he have?

Nora, a few hours later

Nora was impressed, both at the demonstration the Gateway people had put on, and also at the way they'd managed to throw it together on almost no notice, on a weekend.

If they could really do everything they talked about, they could be looking at massive growth. Of course, the whole point of today had been to sell her on that.

Well, mission accomplished. What she'd seen today was enough to guarantee them a cover story—and a very positive one. There was no way Mr. Brooks could argue against it.

She was back at the Prairie Gate Inn, in her room overlooking the parking lot. Not that the view from any other side of the building would have been any better. It was just as well she was in a quiet hotel in a quiet neighborhood. She had a lot of work to do tonight, translating all her interview notes into something more legible, then shaping them into a story, before going to bed early so she could be up at four-thirty in the morning to get to the airport tomorrow.

She wondered if it was just company policy to book the cheapest flight, or if she was being punished, because her flight took off at six o'clock, and it went to Dallas of all places, where she'd connect to a flight to Boston and finally land at three-thirty in the afternoon.

She checked the pager; no messages, still. She tried his cell phone again and got no answer, just like last night; so she left another message.

It made no sense. Why didn't he answer her? Had something happened to him? He could have had an accident. One of his team members had sprained her ankle; who's to say he didn't break a bone or something yesterday? Things like that happened every day. If he was in the hospital, or resting in his hotel room whacked out on painkillers he wouldn't be answering his phone.

Or it could be a work crisis—something with his booth, or maybe he'd even been called back to the office. She couldn't imagine why—but before she'd taken her chance with Bill Whitaker, she couldn't have imagined being in a hotel room in South Dakota right now, either.

There were plenty of logical—if unlikely—possibilities. She'd just have to wait and find out which one it was when he finally called. In the meantime—if she could force herself to concentrate—she had a hundred pages of notes to go through.

Daniel, nine o'clock in the evening

His team was at the barbecue place across the street from the Marriott—Hickory Moon—for another team dinner. Daniel didn't really want to go, but sitting alone in his room would have been far more depressing.

It took two pitchers of margaritas for him to finally talk about Nora's leaving. "I don't get it. She was so excited for this conference—and then she just vanishes?"

Edward opened his mouth to say something, but before he could get a word out, Red and Blue shouted, almost in unison, "Shut up, Edward!"

"What? I didn't even say anything?"

"Good," Blue said. "Keep it that way. And, Daniel, I know it's weird, but I'm sure there's a logical reason."

He didn't bother to say that he'd already thought of every logical explanation, and a lot of illogical ones. "Yeah. Or maybe one night was all we were allowed to have. Maybe I should think of it as a gift, and just enjoy it for what it was. Right?"

He could see that nobody agreed with that, but they all nodded along with him anyway, and then Thomas changed the subject. Daniel appreciated that.

But the more he thought about it, while half-listening to the team talk about which other booths they liked the best, the more he felt like he had his answer. God or the universe or whoever decided these things, gave them one night together, just so they could remember what love felt like. And comfort. And safety. And all the other things they'd been for each other.

They both needed that reminder—Nora wasn't having any more luck having a social life since graduation than he was. Maybe they'd been given one night as a gentle push to get out of their ruts and start actually living again.

Or maybe that was nonsense, because it was easier to pretend he believed the universe had a plan than to admit he didn't have a clue what had gone wrong.

They stayed at the restaurant until nearly ten o'clock. When they got back to the hotel, Bryce asked Daniel to borrow his phone. "My girlfriend likes for me to call around this time."

Daniel handed it over. "No problem. But where's yours?"

Bryce shrugged. "Yeah, about that. I kind of slipped on the bathroom floor last night, and it sort of went flying out of my hands into the sink. And the sink was half full of water." He had the decency to look down as he was telling the story. "There were some sparks. And a really loud pop. And then a little bang, and some smoke. I'm pretty sure it's dead."

Mr. Kincaid couldn't blame Daniel for that, could he? He was responsible for his team, but he could hardly be expected to prevent his co-workers from having accidents in their own bathroom, right?

"Stuff happens, Bryce. I'm sure you're not the first one to kill a phone when you're travelling."

Bryce gave him a grateful smile. "Thanks, boss. I appreciate it." He unfolded Daniel's phone, and looked curiously at it. "Uh—this is my phone. That's my number."

Daniel took it back, and he saw Bryce was right. The number written there below the tiny screen wasn't the number he remembered. "Yesterday morning, before my panel. Our phones were both on the main podium. I must have grabbed yours by mistake."

And he hadn't thought about it when he paged Nora. He entered the number he remembered, because of course he'd memorized the number on his assigned phone the first time he saw it. The same number he'd given Nora to write down Thursday night.

So maybe she *had* called back, and left messages on a now-dead phone where nobody could retrieve them.

She probably thought *he* was ignoring *her*.

Well, he could fix that. He still had her pager number. He could page her from the phone in his room.

If she even still had the pager. She'd flown home yesterday; she might have gone straight to the office and turned it back in. But it couldn't hurt anything to try.

Nora, a little later

She needed to get to sleep already.

Nora had been telling herself that for the past hour. But every time she closed her eyes, they refused to stay shut. Instead, they kept stubbornly popping open and focusing on the phone sitting there, unringing, on the night table.

This was ridiculous. Either Daniel couldn't call, due to illness or accident or maybe abduction by Martians; or, as much as she didn't want to face up to the possibility, he was refusing to call on purpose.

Every time she thought about that, she dismissed the idea. She hadn't said or done anything that could have hurt or offended him. Thursday night felt like no time at all had passed; like it was the fall of 1988 all over again, when everything between them was new and easy and wonderful.

And maybe that *was* the answer.

Maybe when he got back up to his room after walking her to hers, he'd had the same thought, felt just as comfortable and loved as she had. And then maybe he laid there alone in his cold bed, in the dark, in a strange city and realized there could only be one more night, or two, and they'd have to say another final goodbye. And maybe he just couldn't face it. Couldn't bear to say goodbye again. So he just ... didn't.

Or he was protecting her from having to say goodbye.

Either way, it made all the sense in the world.

Still, she got out of bed, walked over to the dresser to take one last look at the pager, just in case. But there was no point; it was off.

She tried the power button to no effect. The battery must be dead; and she didn't have a cable to charge it. They'd given her one, but it was—oh, God, she was so careless—sitting on her kitchen table back in Boston.

So even if she was wrong and Daniel wanted to reach her, to say a proper goodbye—or anything else—he couldn't.

But he didn't know that, so if he was trying to call her, he surely thought she was ignoring him. Probably for the exact same reason she'd decided he was ignoring her.

She wasn't sure if this was some sort of message from the gods of love and romance, or their cruel joke. She didn't even know which was worse.

She only knew how much it hurt.

Chapter 32

AFTER THE CONFERENCE—CHICAGO, IL/BOSTON, MA

Daniel, July 21

Daniel thought the post-conference debriefing was over. There had been three hours of meetings yesterday, and he'd written a ten page report detailing everything that had happened—professionally, anyway—in Kansas City. But here he was in Mr. Kincaid's office, going over it all again.

"Well, Daniel, I had very high expectations for you," his boss said. Then he paused; the man had a habit of doing that, making you wait and wonder whether you were about to be praised or chastised. It was incredibly annoying, but Daniel suspected that was the point. Some old boss of Mr. Kincaid had probably told him it was best to always keep his employees off balance. "And you exceeded them. I'm impressed, not just with your results but how you handled the team."

"Thank you, sir," he answered. Daniel expected his team to give him a good evaluation, but it was nice to hear it all the same. "They made it easy. Everyone did a great job." Even Edward; as rude as he could sometimes—almost always—be, he'd consistently come through every time he was needed at the conference.

"How did you feel about it—I mean personally. Did you enjoy being Team Lead? Is it something you can see yourself doing again?"

Was that a trick question? He thought he'd been very clear in the debriefings, and in his written reports. "Uh—yes. Like I said, everyone made it easy for me."

Mr. Kincaid shook his head. "You're misunderstanding me. I mean *you*, Daniel Keller. Not your team, not the results—*you*. Did you like being in charge? Is it something you'd like to do more of?"

"Honestly?" His boss nodded. "I hadn't thought about that. But—I guess I did enjoy it. I—pardon my language—but I worked my butt off beforehand, and it felt good to see it pay off."

Mr. Kincaid laughed. "I like that. All you need is a big cigar and a black van, and you sound like Hannibal from *The A-Team*."

It took Daniel a moment to get it, but then it clicked. At the end of each episode, he always said, *I love it when a plan comes together.* "I guess so." He laughed. "I always liked *Knight Rider* better, though. I'd much rather have a talking car than an old van."

"Well, they were a team, too. The old guy in the suit, and the mechanic, I don't remember her name." Daniel resisted the urge to point out their names—Devon and Bonnie. "The point is, I have another opportunity for you coming up at the end of the year. There's a big show in December in Minneapolis—God knows who thought that was a good idea. But it's an important show. The *National Communications and Connectivity Expo*. The job is yours if you want it. You can pick who goes—within reason, of course. And we're going to be redesigning our booth, so you'll be involved in that. What do you think?"

He didn't need to think at all. "Yes, sir. I'll do it."

Except—what if Nora was assigned to cover that show, too?

♥ ♥ ♥

Nora, July 22

Nora was at her desk, typing away. A shadow fell over her, and she knew who it was, but she did her best to ignore it. If Jack Elliott wanted her attention, he could speak to her like a normal person, rather than looming over her like something from a horror movie.

"Ahem," Jack said, finally. He actually said the word. Who did that?

"Yes, Mr. Elliott?"

"The boss wants to see you." She knew he was hoping she'd blubber in fear. He'd been nothing but hostile to her from the moment she walked in the office Monday morning. But Nora knew—well, she was pretty sure—she had nothing to fear from Mr. Brooks. If he was going to fire her, or demote or discipline her some other way, he'd have done it already. He wouldn't wait four days, letting her go about her work the whole time.

"Thank you, Mr. Elliott." She stood up and headed off to Mr. Brooks' office, making a point of not looking at Jack as she did.

When she got to her boss' office, he told her to close the door, which he never did.

Maybe she'd been wrong. Maybe Mr. Brooks *had* been planning to fire her, and the delay was just him working through the paperwork with Human Resources. He was the kind of man who made sure every "i" was dotted and every "t" was crossed. If he were going to let someone go, it made perfect sense he'd take four days to make sure it was done by the book.

"You should know Jack has been in here telling me to fire you every day this week. He says it was insubordination, and no matter how good your story is, I can't permit reporters to go rogue like you did. I don't think I've ever seen him this angry."

Why was he telling her this? It wasn't surprising; Jack had been cold—beyond cold—to her ever since she got back.

"I'm not sure what to say, Mr. Brooks."

Her boss didn't quite smile. "What I'm about to say does not leave this office. If you ever repeat it, it *will* be insubordination, and I *will* fire you. The reason Jack wants you fired is because he's jealous. It's because he recognizes—as I do—just how good a story you brought back. And because he knows he would never have had the nerve to do what you did to get it. Which is why he will never be in my chair, but—one day, several years from now, *if* you continue to produce excellent work, and create stories where other reporters would not, you may be."

It took her a moment to process that. Was he really saying what she thought he was?

"Thank you. I think."

Now he was smiling properly. "I don't say any of that to swell your ego. Just to let you know you've taken your first step on the path I hoped you would follow. But it is only a first step. You've raised the bar for yourself, Nora. I will expect the same quality of work every time from you, and the same good judgment."

"I'll do my best," she said.

He talked to her a few minutes more, and she did her best to stay engaged with him. But it was difficult; she couldn't stop thinking about Daniel.

About how, by opening the door towards one day sitting in Mr. Brooks' chair she'd also maybe closed the door to the man she still loved, forever.

Daniel, August 28

Daniel stopped by the bookstore when he got home from work and bought the new issue of *Modern Computing*.

And now he knew what had happened to Nora.

He couldn't blame her—a massive opportunity had presented itself, and she'd done the only thing she could have. He could picture how it had probably happened: she would have been interviewing the Gateway CEO when he got an urgent call to return home to deal with a crisis. And she'd invited herself along—not thinking about the consequences or the downside, just seeing her big chance and acting in the moment.

And it had paid off. How many reporters got a cover story and twenty-four pages inside the magazine when they'd been working for less than a year? He'd been right when he told her she was going to be a star, but even he didn't think it would happen this fast.

She wouldn't have had any way to let him know in the moment, and then came the cell phone mix-up, so when she tried to call him from South Dakota, she was really calling the phone that Thomas had drowned to death.

But she hadn't tried to contact him since then. She knew where he worked, it would be easy for her to get his phone number, or his email address.

Just as easy as it would be for him to get hers, and he hadn't contacted her, either.

When he walked into his apartment, the phone was ringing.

Could it be? If she was ever going to call him, this would be the time. He let it ring once more, twice more, before picking it up.

"Hey, Danny." He collapsed on the couch when he heard his cousin's voice. He'd never hung up on Bianca before, but he almost did now. It took all his strength to answer her.

"Hi, Bee."

"Don't sound so thrilled." Then there was silence for a moment. "Oh, crap. I'm sorry. You must have thought ..."

She knew. Bee always knew. "Yeah. I got the magazine just now, and I guess I got my hopes up when the phone rang."

"Of course you did. But you know, *you* could call *her*, too. Except you two are both too—whatever you are. I'd say neurotic, but I don't think that really covers it."

She was right. They both were. If he knew her at all, Nora hadn't called because she knew there was no way anything could work between them now, and it would hurt too much to keep in touch knowing what they both wanted so badly and couldn't have.

"What am I supposed to do, Bee? I still love her. I don't think I can ever not love her. But she's there and I'm here, and we're both—if you read inside, you saw the little sidebar about my company—we're doing great. I'm doing great, and you know I never talk about myself like that. And obviously she's doing fantastic. This just isn't—it can't work now. No matter how much we want it to."

She was silent for a while. "I don't know what to tell you, Danny. I think you're wrong, but it's easy for me to say that. I'm not in your shoes. I just—I love you, and I want *everything* for you. You deserve it."

"I love you too, Bee. Maybe—do you think it would be okay if I thought of it this way? Like it was a reminder, just so we wouldn't forget what we had, so when the time is right someday, we really will be ready?" That was wildly optimistic, but maybe he could make himself believe it, if he kept saying it to himself enough times.

She sighed. "Does it hurt any less when you tell yourself that?"

"No."

"Didn't think so. But maybe—maybe you're right anyway. Just know I'm thinking of you, and you can call me anytime you need to, Danny."

He was pretty sure he'd be taking her up on that.

Nora, the same day

Nora sat on her couch, just staring at the cover of this month's *Modern Computing.* Would it be too obnoxious to have it framed and hang it in her living room?

What a stupid question. She never had anybody up to her apartment; there wouldn't be anybody to call her obnoxious.

Well, except her parents. But Dad would never call her obnoxious—he never had, even though she'd given him a million reasons to back in high school; and the only thing Mom would say about it was that she should have had it enlarged to poster size before she hung it up.

She wondered if Daniel had seen it yet.

Of course he had. He'd been reading the magazine cover to cover every month since college. Even when they were dating, and he was only a sophomore. She could still see it on his dorm room desk—always opened to an article, a pen jammed between the pages.

"It's really interesting," he'd said. "And I need to keep up, if I want to work in the field."

He probably subscribed to it. He might be reading her story right now.

But if he was, why wasn't her phone ringing? It wouldn't be hard for him to get her phone number.

No harder than it would be for her to get his. And his phone wasn't ringing with her on the other end of the line right now, was it?

Maybe he'd never gotten her messages; cell phones could be very flaky. Maybe it was only today when he saw her cover story that he finally knew where she'd gone. And maybe he'd made up his mind about her by the time he flew home from Kansas City; that there was no future, no hope. No reason to risk his heart any more than he already had at the karaoke bar or in his hotel room.

Or, maybe, just maybe, there was a reason they'd been given one night together. Maybe it was just a reminder of their promise on his graduation day. Just enough to make sure they didn't forget how much they meant to each other, so that, come 2001, they'd both be ready, for real and for good.

And maybe, if she kept telling herself that often enough, it would only take ten or fifteen minutes for her to cry herself to sleep, instead of an hour.

Part 5

Fall 1997

Chapter 33

Daniel, January 20

"Is it just me, or was Mike giving off some very weird vibes in that meeting?"

Daniel agreed. They'd just gotten out of an all-division meeting led by the Vice President for National Sales, Mike McGee, and there was definitely something off about him. Not that Daniel had been in that many meetings with the man, but there'd been enough over the last two years for him to have a sense of what to expect.

"It's not just you, Red." Kristin Chambers had never shed that nickname after the conference in Kansas City three and a half years ago. Everyone else who'd been on the team had moved on; Daniel was the only person besides Kristin who knew why she was called that. "I think there's something going on that nobody in management wants to talk about."

"If you hear anything, you'll tell me?"

She didn't need to ask. "You know it. You keep your eyes open, too, okay?"

She nodded, and they went their separate ways; her down to the third floor, and Daniel to the office that had belonged to his boss when he'd first been hired by Quantum Networking Systems, and had been his for the last year and a half.

He'd just sat down at his desk when the phone rang. It was a Washington, DC number. He couldn't think of anyone he knew there personally, or any vendors his team worked with who were based there. But some instinct told him to answer it anyway.

"Daniel Keller?"

He thought he recognized the voice, but he couldn't think from where. It was a woman, and if he had to guess, not that much older than him. Maybe in her thirties?

"Yes, who's this?"

"A voice from your past. I'm kind of hurt you don't recognize me, actually." But he heard humor rather than pouting there. Someone from college? But who would be calling after almost six years?

And then memory kicked in. He knew who she was.

The Ellis Hall computer lab, his senior year. A law student, a friend, and for six weeks or so, an almost-girlfriend. "Valerie Vance? Is that you?"

She laughed. "Yes, but I can't talk on this line. I need you to get out of your office, and call me back in ten minutes at this number. Call on your personal cell, not your work phone." And then she hung up.

What the hell? She sounded like someone in a spy movie. It was ridiculous. Silly. Stupid. Pick an adjective.

But in the few months he'd known her, she had been nothing but good to him, and never anything but truthful. She'd helped him get this job, and negotiate for a better salary—even after he'd broken up with her. Obviously he could trust her.

Ten minutes later, he was sitting on a bench in Cityfront Plaza, well away from anyone else, and he dialed the number back.

"You're out of the office?"

"Yes, Valerie. I'm all alone in the park. What's with the cloak and dagger stuff?"

There was silence for a moment. "Protecting myself. I could get fired for this. Disbarred, even. But—I helped you get your job. I feel like I owe it to you."

That didn't actually explain anything. "Owe me what?"

"Before I say anything, I need your promise, Daniel. You cannot breathe a word of this to anybody. Not friends, not family, and absolutely not coworkers. I need you to swear it to me."

And now he knew.

Not the details of what she was about to say, but what they meant. Something was going on with upper management. Mike McGee knew, and he'd spent ninety minutes dancing around like he needed to pee because he couldn't say anything about what he knew, and how it would impact everyone in the meeting.

"I swear, Valerie. But I think you can probably skip it. Just tell me—I need to get out now, before the layoffs start, don't I?"

Nora, January 22

She was back in Mr. Brooks' office again. Nora had been in here a dozen times the last couple of weeks. He'd been questioning her work in detail, making her explain herself in a way he hadn't done since her first few months on the job.

"Mr. Brooks, can I ask you something?" He nodded. "Do you have a problem with my work? If there's something you're unhappy with, I'd rather you just come out and tell me."

He shook his head. "There's nothing wrong with your work, Nora. But your intuition could use some fine-tuning."

What did that mean?

"Sir?"

"Must I spell it out to you?" She knew she had a blank expression on her face; it was probably all he could do not to laugh. "Apparently I do. Jessica Waybourne is pregnant, I assume you're aware of that?" She nodded. Jessica was the editor of *BioCurrent Monthly*. And she was *very* pregnant. The last couple of times Nora saw her in the hallway, she was surprised the woman wasn't on bed rest.

"And obviously you know—not firsthand, since you haven't needed it yet—Livingston has a generous maternity leave policy. Starting next Friday—possibly sooner, she looks about to pop, if you'll forgive the expression—you'll be stepping in for her while she's out for the next eight months."

He wasn't ...?

Was he?

Had the last two weeks been a test? Making sure he could trust her before ...?

"Are you saying you're putting me in charge while she's out?"

He clapped his hands. "Give the lady a cigar. Or whatever the equivalent these days is; you don't really seem the cigar type to me."

"You can save it for my father," she said. At least he was down to one cigar twice a week instead of half a pack of cigarettes a day. "But—thank you so much!"

He launched into a rundown of the new responsibilities she'd have, in gory detail. She knew there was more to being an editor-in-chief than most people realized, but hearing it all laid out like this? It was ... a lot.

"Two final reminders, Nora. First, this is temporary. When Jennifer returns, the job is hers again, and you go back to your current position. That said, if you excel—as I expect you to—you'll be putting yourself in line for a permanent editorship."

"Understood."

"Second," he added with an apologetic smile, "I'm afraid you'll have to delay that cruise you won at last year's Christmas party."

That had been a shock; she'd never won anything before, let alone the best prize of the night. "That's fine. I don't have anybody to go with right now, anyway."

And then, without warning, *his* name came into her mind, totally unbidden.

I wonder if Daniel would enjoy a cruise?

Daniel, January 23

It only took two hours at the public library for Daniel to confirm everything.

First was the easy part—he found Valerie in the *Martindale-Hubble Law Directory*. She was listed as an associate at Kane and Redfield, a big Washington, DC corporate law firm specializing in mergers and acquisitions.

The harder part was searching the *Wall Street Journal* archives using the library's Lexis-Nexis terminal. It took most of those two hours, but eventually he found what he needed to know: Kane and Redfield had been retained to represent Comcast.

The final piece of the puzzle came in an article about a recent Comcast shareholder meeting. Buried near the end was a single sentence: they were planning a major acquisition to expand their business into fiber-optic networks.

They were going to buy QNS.

And Valerie was probably working on the deal. Writing the contracts, helping to structure the merger or whatever else corporate lawyers did in these situations. Which meant she hadn't been kidding—talking to him about it was a real risk. Definitely a fireable offense, and maybe even an actual crime.

But, technically, she hadn't actually told him anything.

When he'd asked if he needed to leave before the layoffs started, she hadn't answered. Her silence had been all the confirmation he needed, and he'd changed the subject immediately.

If—unlikely as it seemed—anyone had overheard them, all they would have heard was two old college friends catching each other up on their lives after graduation.

There was one other detail he hadn't given any thought to at the time. He'd gotten a call last week from a headhunter at National Technical Recruiters. Based in Washington, DC.

The headhunter said he had a client who needed someone with his skills and experience, and Daniel, thinking it was just a cold call, had blown him off.

But what if there was more to it? What if Valerie had set it up? She could easily have contacts with a company like that, and all she needed to do was give them his name and let them do the rest. And then, when she checked with them a week later and learned he'd ignored them, she'd thrown subtlety out the window and called him directly.

It was possible. And if it was true, that meant the job was real, and Daniel needed to call back today, while he still could. And he needed to let Red know what was going on, so she could make her own plans, too.

Nora, January 25

It wasn't a usual practice for a reporter to buy her source a thank-you lunch, but Nora thought it was appropriate in this case.

Greg Sanders—Dr. Greg Sanders, as of three weeks ago, she really should remember to call him that—had spent hours with her, trying to explain the finer points of Quantum Theory. Not really succeeding, if she was being honest, but she at least understood some of the terminology now. The least she could do was treat him to Thai food.

He was waiting for her at the restaurant. "I took a chance and ordered you a milk tea," he said when she sat down.

"That's exactly what I would have ordered," she said. It wasn't, but she appreciated the gesture. "I'm glad you could meet me. Starting this week, I'll be at a different publication—*BioCurrent Monthly*. I'm stepping in as interim editor."

"Congratulations!" He seemed to genuinely mean it. "So what is the *Livingston Physics Review* going to do without you?" There was something more than just congratulations in his voice, but she couldn't put her finger on what she was hearing.

"We've got a meeting this afternoon to figure that out. If it's okay, I'll put whoever takes over for me in touch with you."

He gave her a look that, again, she couldn't quite interpret. "Sure. That's fine." He hesitated. Was he annoyed? Sad? Supportive? Something else? "I'm happy for you, but—I'm also glad you won't be working on physics stories anymore. I haven't said anything, but I've been thinking about something for a while now ..."

It clicked for Nora then. She knew exactly what he couldn't quite bring himself to say. He'd never expressed any interest in her before, because he knew she couldn't date a source. But if she wasn't going to be writing for the *Physics Review*, then he wasn't a source anymore. And that meant ...

"Greg, are you asking me out on a date?"

She probably shouldn't have just blurted it out like that, but better to just rip the band-aid off.

To his credit, he didn't look away from her; he met her eyes and steadied himself. "Yes."

Did she want to date him, though? He was—well, not precisely handsome but close enough to it. He had piercing brown eyes that lit up when he got deep into the weeds on a physics problem. Just like—no, this was *not* the time to think about Daniel. She owed Greg her full attention; it wasn't fair to him to be thinking about her past. Whether she said yes or no, he deserved that much.

But would it be yes or no?

He *was* close to handsome. And obviously very smart. And funny, when he let down his guard and forgot to be self-conscious. And, anyway, it was only a first date he was asking her on. She didn't need to make a lifelong decision or anything.

"Then I'm saying yes."

Daniel, January 30

The headhunter had been for real, and the job they wanted him for was a perfect fit. The initial conversations had gone very well, and their client—Piedmont Integrated Systems, in Charlotte, North Carolina—wanted to meet him in person.

Just like QNS had in his senior year of college, they were going to fly him out for the interview. This time, he wouldn't need Valerie's help to prepare. He knew exactly what they were looking for—and he even knew some of the people already. They'd been a vendor for a few months last year, until Mike McGee took over as the division Vice President and cancelled all the contracts.

If all went well, though—and there was no reason why it shouldn't—he'd still owe Valerie the job.

"I'm going to go broke thanking her," he muttered to himself as he dialed the phone. There was another reason he believed—knew—this job would work out. It was fate.

"Danny? What's going on? You never call in the middle of the day."

It was fate that the job was in Charlotte because Bianca just moved there herself two months ago.

"You're not going to believe this, Bee, but I'm going to be in your neighborhood on Friday. I've got a job interview."

"What?"

He told her the whole story.

"You're going to buy that lawyer another expensive gift, aren't you?"

He laughed. Of course she knew what he'd been thinking. "I tell you I'm probably going to be your next door neighbor in a few weeks, and that's all you have to say?"

"Am I wrong?"

"No, you're not wrong, Bee. And one other thing ..."

Again, she was ahead of him. "Of course you can stay with me. Lucky for you, I just got a bed for the spare room last week. And you said Friday? That's perfect, I've got a friend I've been meaning to invite over for dinner. She's really sweet. You'll love her."

He should have expected that. "If this happens and I move to Charlotte, are you going to try and set me up with one of your single friends every week?" Maybe that wouldn't be so bad. He hadn't had a first date in months; or a second date in two years. And any friend of Bee's already had a lot going for them just by virtue of her vouching for them.

"Looking forward to it, Bee. I love you."

Maybe all this really *was* fate.

Chapter 34

Nora, November 5

She and Greg were sitting at her kitchen table, enjoying breakfast before they got on the road. "You never said last night, how was your first day back at the *Physics Review*?" He was stirring cream into his coffee almost absentmindedly as he talked.

Nora had been too focused on packing to think about work. "I wouldn't know. I spent the last two days catching Jennifer up on everything. I won't actually be back at my old job until after we get back from the cruise."

It was going to be an adjustment; she had enjoyed her time as an interim editor, and she'd been—all modesty aside—damn good at it. It was hard to explain, even to herself. It wasn't that she liked being in charge; more that she enjoyed being the one people came to knowing she'd have answers—and actually having them. It was almost—as silly as it sounded—kind of intoxicating.

"Good," Greg said. "I mean, I'm going to be a source again for you. I'd hate it if journalistic ethics made you break up with me before our vacation." He laughed, but it was something she'd have to address. She'd need to talk to the Ethics Board, and probably also Human Resources. Nora knew there were ways to work around the rules, but she assumed there would be a lot of paperwork involved. And probably a stern lecture from Mr. Brooks, too.

But it would be worth it. She'd been with Greg Sanders for nine months; the longest relationship she'd ever had. And this was their first proper trip together; they'd gone on brief weekend trips—one night, occasionally two, but that was it.

This was nine nights and ten days onboard the *Empress of the Seas.* That was a serious trip. A serious commitment. And if it went well, it might be just the first commitment of many.

She might even say the words to him that she hadn't said to anyone since Daniel. And mean them.

Daniel, the same time

"Are you excited yet, Daniel?"

Leanne Butler was. She'd been unable to talk about anything except the cruise for the last two weeks. He'd thought he was obsessive about getting ready early for a trip, but he had nothing on her. He'd gone over to her place for dinner three nights ago, and she led him straight to the bedroom to show off her packed luggage with the same proud flourish David Copperfield used when he made a national landmark vanish on live TV.

"I'll be excited once we get to Baltimore." He *was* looking forward to the cruise, even if he wasn't quite as excited as his girlfriend. Honestly, he'd be glad to go on any kind of trip with her. Between their work schedules, her family commitments and the two cats she refused to spend more than one night away from at a time, they had yet to go anywhere together for more than one night.

The reason Leanne was willing to leave the cats now was the same reason she and Daniel had met in the first place: Bianca. His cousin had met Leanne in a pottery class in January and they became fast friends—Bianca had a knack for that. Three weeks later, Bianca introduced him to Leanne, and two weeks after that they'd had their first date.

Two months ago, Bianca and Leanne got to talking, and Leanne lamented that there was a great deal on a cruise, and she really wanted to go, but she couldn't leave Reeses and Hershey alone for ten days. Bianca volunteered to stay at Leanne's apartment for the duration of the cruise, and that was that.

"Then let's get going! Everything is in the trunk, I double-checked already. If we start now, we should make it to Baltimore before dinnertime."

Five minutes later, they were off. Leanne offered to drive, but seven hours on the highway was very taxing, and he wasn't about to let her start off the trip by tiring herself out. Instead, she navigated, and in between calling out directions, she read aloud from the brochure about all the attractions aboard the *Empress of the Seas.*

It hadn't occurred to Daniel at the time, and he only thought of it two hours into the drive north to Baltimore: the day that Bianca agreed to watch Leanne's cats, the same day she'd booked the cruise, was September 6th.

Nora Langley's birthday.

Why did that thought hit him now? He needed to be fully present for Leanne. She deserved that—and so much more—from him.

Nora, around dinnertime

She hadn't really wanted to stay by the airport. Something about it just felt weird to Nora. But Greg had done some research and declared the BWI Airport Marriott the best combination of price, ease of access to the cruise terminal, and amenities.

Who was she to argue, after he'd spent two hours putting together a chart with bullet points?

No, that was unfair. He'd spent two hours to make sure she didn't waste money, her car would be safe for the duration of the cruise, and there'd be no trouble getting to the terminal tomorrow morning. And she hadn't asked him; he'd done it of his own accord. She should be grateful.

It was the kind of thing Daniel would have done. Except with less bullet points and more self-deprecating jokes.

And that was unfair, too. She needed to stop thinking about Daniel. The last time she'd spoken to him was more than four years ago. She was with Greg now, and she wanted desperately to make this work. Greg deserved her full attention, her full heart. And she deserved someone who was ready to accept it.

"What do you think?" They were in their room, and she was ready to collapse. They'd split the driving, but she'd had the bad luck to be behind the wheel for the worst traffic, and it had frayed her nerves. "We can go down to the restaurant, or call room service and just collapse up here. This bed is awfully comfortable, it'll be kind of decadent to sit in bed and eat a fancy dinner in our pajamas, won't it?"

"Sure, Nora. That sounds good to me. Go ahead and order, you know what I like." But he wasn't joining her on the bed; he was sitting in the plush armchair—admittedly, it did look very comfortable, too—and making no move to put his pajamas on.

Maybe he was tired from the drive, just like her. He hadn't slept all that well last night, either. Maybe a good dinner—hopefully the crabcakes lived up to their reputation—would lift his spirits.

Daniel, around nine o'clock

Leanne turned to him as they lay in bed. "Do you know the last time I had an actual vacation? A whole week off?"

Daniel shook his head. It hadn't been since they'd started dating.

"Neither do I," she said. "Maybe—the week after I took my last exam? That was—God, was it really three years ago?"

"That's too long," he agreed. Not that he could talk. He always made sure to use his vacation time, but he either just stayed home and spent a few days zoning out in front of the TV when he wasn't catching up on household chores he'd neglected, or he went back to the Bronx and stayed with his parents.

"But, you know what, it's sort of the same for me. I haven't been on a proper vacation since—wow, Disney World, when I was fifteen."

She stared at him. "I don't believe you."

"I mean a vacation where you go somewhere fun, and you stay in a hotel, and you have no responsibilities at all. Where you eat out every day, and somebody else cleans up after you, and there's no laundry or taking out the garbage or anything. Not just taking time off of work, you know what I mean?"

She thought about that, and finally nodded along with him. "I see what you're saying. If you put it that way, I think the last time

I went on one was probably spring break, senior year of college. Me and my roommate went to South Padre Island." Daniel gave her a blank look; he'd never heard of it. "In Texas. About three hours south of San Antonio. That's where Gloria was from—my roommate, obviously. It was her idea, and I thought it would be—I don't know. Boring? Stupid?"

"But it wasn't?"

"No!" When she got excited, Leanne's bright blue eyes got so wide; you couldn't help but be drawn along with her into whatever she was talking about. "It was a blast. We were almost in Mexico. Margaritas on the beach, live music every night, and the boys ..."

He leaned in and kissed her, and she kissed him back. When they broke apart, he grinned. "What about the boys?"

"Well, it wasn't like *that*." She laughed. "Not really." She paused, just for an instant. "Okay, there was one night, and there was this guy from—Texas Tech, I think?—and we were sitting together on a blanket, and there was a big bonfire, and he had the prettiest eyes. Not like yours are pretty, but—you know, it was a romantic atmosphere, and I'd had a couple of margaritas ..." There was only one other person who'd ever said he had pretty eyes. But—he had to put her out of his mind. It wasn't right to be thinking of her when he was lying in bed with his girlfriend, who he'd just kissed a few seconds ago.

"A couple?"

"Six, if you must know." That sounded more accurate for spring break in almost-Mexico. "And we kissed for a while, until Gloria dragged me back to the hotel room. I yelled at her when we got there, but ..."

Daniel knew what she was going to say. "You thanked her the next morning."

"Something like that," she agreed. "I wonder what she's doing these days. I should try to look her up. She was good people."

Daniel kissed her again. "You know what, Leanne? So are you."

She really was. It was impossible not to see it. So why did he have to keep reminding himself of it?

Chapter 35

Nora, November 6, ten o'clock in the morning

Nora was glad she'd bought Keith from the travel office lunch last week. She'd spent the whole hour interrogating him about every detail of cruising, and it was paying off now.

"Yes, Greg. Really. That's it. That one little card is all you need on the ship." They'd finally gotten to the front of the check-in line, and her boyfriend was having trouble believing that one magnetic card was not only their key to every door on the ship, but also the way they'd pay for everything aboard.

"So do we just get a bill at the end of the cruise?"

Nora reached into her purse for her wallet, and pulled out her American Express card. "No. I give them this," she handed it to the woman behind the counter, "and everything gets billed to it." She laughed. "Technically, I guess you're right, I will get a bill at the end of the cruise. And don't argue—I'm the one who asked you to come, so we're using my credit card."

She didn't want him to argue—mostly. There was a little part of her that hoped he would. And an even smaller voice in the very back of her mind, hoping the check-in clerk would hand her card back and tell her that Daniel—no, Greg! —had already arranged ahead of time for everything to be charged to his card.

Why had she thought of Daniel?

Because that's absolutely what Daniel would have done. If they'd managed to make it as a couple long enough to be able to afford a cruise together.

Daniel, an hour later

"You were right, there was barely any line at all," Leanne said. Daniel had figured—correctly, as it turned out—that most people would rush to check in early, even though boarding didn't start until ten-thirty and continued until three o'clock in the afternoon.

Instead of spending an hour in a slow-moving line, they'd enjoyed a leisurely breakfast at the hotel, with two trips each to the omelet station. And now, at the cruise terminal, they'd only been in line five minutes when they were called up to the check-in desk.

The clerk took their tickets, typed away at her computer, and handed them each their SeaPass cards. "And I see you've already given us a credit card, Mr. Keller. Thank you. Enjoy the cruise."

"Daniel, when did you—we never talked about whose card to use!"

They walked away from check-in and towards the boarding area. "We split the cost for the tickets, but I wanted to do this for you, Leanne. There was a number to call for pre-boarding, and I gave them my card. I hope you're not angry—I know maybe we should have discussed it, but I wanted to surprise you."

She smiled—almost as brightly and joyfully as Nora used to. "I'm surprised. And—I like it. I'm just not used to anyone doing something so ... I don't know. Gallant?"

Nora had called him that once, too.

ღ 🖤 ღ

Nora, two hours later

"Here we go. Room 3146. You ready?" Nora inserted her SeaPass card, heard the little click, and pushed the door open.

She climbed in, with Greg a couple of steps behind her. She was glad all over again that she'd spent that hour with Keith; she knew to expect that the room would seem very small at first glance.

Sure enough, that was the first thing Greg noticed. "This is tiny! There's barely enough room to turn around in here."

Nora stepped away from him and did a twirl. "See? I can turn around just fine." He almost laughed; that was a good sign. "Really, it's bigger than it seems. And anyway, like Keith said, we're not going to be doing much in here besides sleep, so it doesn't make much difference how big it is."

He didn't say anything at first, just mouthed, "Keith?"

"Oh, he's in the travel office at work. I figured he'd know all about cruises, so I harassed him over lunch last week about it. I just wanted to be prepared." He nodded. "By the way, one thing he said—we already saw it a little when we boarded—they're always trying to sell you something. He said to just tune it out. If you let it get to you, you won't have a good time onboard."

Of course, she had let it get to her almost immediately; she gave her SeaPass card to the first person who asked. It was a woman in a snappy Royal Caribbean uniform at a little table in the

Atrium selling the specialty dining package—three dinners in the specialty restaurants aboard ship, supposedly at a discounted fee. "If you'll pardon the pun, that ship has sailed already, hasn't it?"

He said it with a smile, but she wondered—just for a moment, then she dismissed the thought—if Daniel would have said it at all.

Daniel, two hours later

They were wandering the halls of the ship, not going anywhere in particular.

"I just had a thought," Leanne said, "They must have a doctor on the ship, right?"

Daniel stopped in his tracks. She hadn't said anything about feeling bad; had he missed some sign? He looked her up and down, and there didn't seem to be anything wrong with her. "Are you okay?"

She put a hand on his arm and laughed gently. "No. It's just—you can take the girl out of the hospital, but you can't take the hospital out of the girl, I guess."

Why hadn't he thought of that? Of course as a nurse, she'd be curious about medical care onboard. "There was a map by the elevators," he said, and led her through the corridors of deck three to the nearest elevator bank. Leanne stopped him in front of a stateroom door.

"Oh, that's cute!"

There was a handmade sign on the door, held on by magnets: *Caution: Unsupervised Couple on Vacation!* And a couple of little heart magnets on either side of it.

"I wish I'd thought of that," Daniel said. It would have been a nice little extra surprise for Leanne. "They've definitely got the right idea."

"So do we," Leanne said. "Maybe if they're lucky, they'll have as good a time as we're going to have."

He took her hand and led her the rest of the way to the elevators. "There," he said, pointing at the map of the ship. "The sickbay is on deck one. Looks like the only thing that's there." That, and all the machinery and everything else needed to keep the passengers comfortable for ten days.

"We don't need to go down there, I just wanted to know. Just in case."

As she said that, Daniel thought he was hearing something in her voice now. Just a tiny hint of—what? Maybe just fatigue. Or hunger—they hadn't eaten anything since breakfast and it was almost four o'clock now. That was probably all it was.

"Makes sense," he agreed. "I think I heard someone say they've got a little café up in the Solarium. You want to go up there, sit out on a beach chair and have a little something? Dinner isn't for another three hours."

"Sure," she said, and was she forcing more certainty into her voice than she felt? Or was he just hearing things? "The elevator is right here, let's go."

Up they went. Maybe some cookies, or a sandwich or whatever they had for snacks would sort her out. If there even was anything to sort out.

Nora, two hours later

"We can't eat now, we'll spoil our dinner," Greg said.

He was right. Nora knew he was, but she didn't care.

"Dinner isn't until seven-thirty. I'm hungry now. Let's go up to the Solarium. Keith said they've got snacks there all day long."

Greg shook his head. "Nora, dinner is at the steakhouse tonight. We're going to be eating the whole world."

He was just being reasonable. Rational. Maybe some other words starting with "R." That's all it was. There was no call to tell him that whether she ate herself out of fitting into her bathing suit was her problem, not his; or that she was the one paying for the steak dinner. That would be hostile, and hateful and probably some other words starting with "H."

"I know. Just a little snack to tide me over. And the spa is up there, too, we can check out what they're offering. Maybe there'll be a sale, too—you know, two massages for the price of one, something like that."

He rolled his eyes. "You're the one who told me to ignore them trying to sell us something everywhere we go on the ship." Then he paused, collected himself. "I don't need any of that, Nora. I just want to spend time with you. That's what this trip is about for me, not where we eat, or what kind of massages we can get or anything."

She threw her arms around his neck and kissed him. He responded, leaning into her, but only for a moment, then he pulled back. "I'm glad you feel the same way," he said, panting a bit. "But let's save that sort of thing for our cabin. There must be a hundred people here watching us."

She didn't care. He shouldn't, either. All they were doing was kissing—people did that all the time in public. What did it matter who saw them?

No—that wasn't fair, was it? He was entitled to his feelings, and if he was uncomfortable doing anything more than holding hands in public, then that's all they'd do outside of their cabin.

"I understand," she said. "I was just—it really meant a lot to me, what you said. I wanted to make sure you knew." That was the third thought she had.

The first one had been, *I guess we can't ever get married, if you can't kiss me in front of a crowd.*

The second, much worse one, was, *Daniel wouldn't have cared if everybody on the ship, and the Captain, was watching. He probably would've taken a bow afterwards.*

Daniel, around seven o'clock

They walked down the stairs to the floor of the Main Dining Room, and Daniel had three thoughts.

The first, and best one, was that Leanne looked absolutely stunning in her shimmery blue dress that perfectly set off her eyes, and with her long blonde hair pinned up just so.

The second, and sort of disturbing one, was that walking down the staircase made him think of the scene from the trailer for *Titanic* that they played before *Event Horizon* when he'd gone to see it back in September. There'd been a shot of a grand, ornate staircase flooding as the ship sank, and that was definitely not something he wanted to think about now. Not that there were likely to be any icebergs in the Caribbean, so really it was just a stupid thought rather than a legitimately worrying one.

The third, and by far the worst, was that the last time he'd been with a beautiful woman in a dress—not counting dancing with Bianca at cousin Frank's wedding last year—was with Nora at the Valentine's Day dance back in 1989.

Maybe it was the necklace. He still wore it, every day. How could Nora not keep pushing her way into his thoughts when there was a constant physical reminder of her right above his heart?

He hadn't even taken it off the first time he and Leanne had made love, back in July. They'd had a long weekend planned.

They were going to rent a cabin on the shore of Lake Norman, half an hour north of Charlotte. July 4th had been a Friday, and she was supposed to have four days off.

She never showed up at his condo on Friday morning; it wasn't until the afternoon that she left an apologetic voicemail—it sounded as though she'd been in tears, telling him that the whole weekend was shot, there was a crisis at the hospital and she'd be working all day Friday, and also Sunday and Monday.

She knocked on his door Saturday morning, and she *was* in tears. He'd led her straight into the bedroom, got her under the covers, let her sleep for six hours and then brought her lunch in bed.

That night—after the one glass of wine she allowed herself, since she had to be back at the hospital by six the next morning— was their first time. And *his* first time since the night before his graduation.

"Daniel? Hey, are you okay?"

He'd been so lost in those thoughts he hadn't noticed they were at their table and already sitting down.

"I was just—I was thinking about July 4th. About us. I'm so glad we're here. And I was also thinking how lucky I am, to be with the most beautiful woman on the whole ship."

The second part was true.

And maybe—if he kept saying it enough—he could convince himself the first part was, too.

Nora, eight o'clock

"I thought for a minute about renting a tuxedo for the cruise," Greg said, looking around at their fellow diners.

It wouldn't have been out of place—maybe half of the couples in the steakhouse were in formalwear. The men didn't all wear tuxedos, but most of the ones who didn't wore well-tailored suits instead.

Greg's suit was—well, he'd had it dry-cleaned, anyway. That counted for a lot. Didn't it? He could just as easily not have packed a suit at all. There were a few men here in sweaters, a couple in polo shirts and one—his wife, or girlfriend or whatever she was didn't look happy about it—wore a T-shirt.

She wore a green dress; the same one she'd worn eight years ago, at the Valentine's Day dance with Daniel. That had been the last time she'd worn it; she was shocked to find it in the back of her closet when she'd been packing for the cruise. The only thing missing was the elbow-length gloves. She wondered what happened to them.

Maybe they'd fallen into the back of her dorm room closet after she and Daniel had gotten back from the dance, and a few months later, whichever freshman girl had gotten her room the next year claimed them for herself. Nora hoped she—whoever she was—had gotten good use, or at least a good laugh, out of them.

"Nora?"

She shook her head to clear it. "Sorry, I was thinking—I really do like that suit on you." It wasn't totally a lie.

"I was just asking, mashed potatoes or macaroni and cheese for our side?"

He did say earlier that they'd be "eating the world," didn't he?

"Why do we need to choose? I heard the waiter say to that table,"—she waved a hand in the direction of an older man and a redheaded woman maybe half his age—"we can order as many sides as we want, there's no extra charge."

"I guess so," Greg said, but there was a hesitation in his voice she couldn't quite place. "Still kind of wasteful, isn't it?"

Normally, she liked that Greg thought about things like that. She tried to be mindful of herself and not buy food she wasn't pretty sure she'd eat. But this was a vacation. How would they know if they liked the mashed potatoes or the mac and cheese better if they didn't try both?

"Let's do it anyway, just this once. I bet they're both really good."

He gave in with reasonably good grace. She just hoped he wouldn't be glaring at her later if she didn't clean her plate.

Daniel never would've minded. He'd have ordered all the sides just to see her try them.

Chapter 36

**THE FIRST NIGHT OF THE CRUISE—
ABOARD EMPRESS OF THE SEAS**

*Daniel, November 6, around nine-thirty
in the evening*

"Daniel, it's fine. Please, go see the show, I can get back to the room on my own."

He'd thought Leanne was looking a little off even before dinner. The escargots surely hadn't helped.

"I'll walk you back. Let's go down to the sickbay first, though—when you were in the bathroom, I asked the waiter and he said they keep seasickness pills out for people to take. We'll go get some and then get you comfortable."

"I think it's more the snails than the seasickness. And you warned me, I should have listened."

All he'd said was, "Are you really sure you want to eat snails?" And then when she'd affirmed that, yes, she was going to try them, because if she was ever going to, this was the place to do it, he'd eaten one as well.

It was exactly as gross as he'd expected.

"Well, like you said, a vacation is the time to try new things. Now we know we don't like snails, we can check that off the list."

They went down to deck one, and, sure enough, even though the sickbay was closed, there was a rack on the wall with sea-sickness pills in little paper pouches. Daniel grabbed a handful, and escorted Leanne up to Room 4548.

He got her into bed, poured her a glass of water, gave her the remote control for the TV. "You can stop fussing over me, Daniel." She reached out, pulled his head down, kissed him quickly. "Actually, it is kind of nice. You can keep doing it. But *after* the show. You said you wanted to see the comedy act, so go. I'll be okay by myself."

She didn't really look okay, but resting in bed was the best thing for her. He could leave her for a little while, and, anyway, she'd probably be asleep in ten minutes. The show would only be an hour, and he could come straight back here as soon as it was over.

Everything would be fine.

Nora, the same time

"I'm fine," Greg said. "It's just food coma. That was a very heavy meal. I'll pace myself better tomorrow."

They were heading back to the cabin. Nora had been trying to convince Greg to explore the ship by night, but he wasn't up for anything except an early bedtime.

"Would you be okay if I went back up to the Atrium for a little while, after I drop my purse off? There's supposed to be a live band." She felt a little guilty—but only a little. There was so much to see and do aboard the ship, and she wanted to experience it all, not go to bed before ten o'clock. She could—and too often did—do that at home.

"Of course," he said. "I'll be more lively tomorrow, I promise."

He had his SeaPass card out, ready to insert in the door, but he stopped when he saw the message on the door, stuck there with magnets.

"Did you put that up, Nora?"

"Isn't it great?" She'd debated writing a message that included their names, but she decided against it, thinking that Greg might feel self-conscious. But what was wrong with *Caution: Unsupervised Couple on Vacation*?

"It's cute, I guess," he said, not sounding very sure. Maybe she should have asked him first.

He opened the door and headed immediately to the bed, only stopping to take his shoes off. A good night's sleep would do wonders for him, like he said. Tomorrow he'd be ready to explore with her—and she could downshift to a lower gear, and not make him feel like they were in some kind of race to do everything as quickly as possible.

In the meantime, though, he looked comfortable, and she wanted to see the band. "I'll just be an hour or so. I only want to hear a few songs, maybe dance a little depending on what they play. Okay?"

"Have fun," he told her.

She blew him a kiss as she left the room. He didn't look up, but that was okay. There was music waiting for her.

Daniel, ten minutes later

Daniel checked his watch as he got off the elevator on deck five. A quarter to ten, so he still had fifteen minutes before the show started. And there was music coming from deck four, the lowest level of the atrium. Familiar music.

Bon Jovi. It was a cover band, playing a decent rendition of *Living on a Prayer.* He walked over to the railing, looking down at the band, and the little crowd dancing—as much as you could dance to a song like that. Really they were mostly shuffling around and waving their arms a beat or two behind the music.

Exactly like he'd danced to it with Nora, on a Halloween night in his dorm room nine years ago.

And then he looked up, and on the other side of the atrium, standing at the railing just like him and maybe a hundred feet away ... A green dress, and hair a little bit longer than she'd had in college.

But it was her all the same.

No. What was wrong with him? He'd been thinking about her all the time yesterday and today, when he should be thinking only about Leanne. His girlfriend, who had been nothing but sweet to him for nearly nine months, who was lying in bed right now feeling sick.

What kind of jerk was he, to be obsessing about someone else, no matter how much that someone had meant to him once upon a time?

He looked back, and the woman he'd thought was Nora was gone. Maybe she hadn't been there at all; maybe she was just a mirage.

That's all she was. Obviously.

Nora, the same time

The band was playing *Living on a Prayer*, and Nora didn't even realize she was dancing to it until she looked down and saw her feet moving of their own accord.

She'd danced with Daniel to this song once.

Why couldn't she get him out of her mind? Nora had been thinking about him more these last two days than she had in months.

Since July, the first time she'd gone to bed with Greg, after making him wait six months, offering up excuses that sounded pathetic to her own ears but which he'd accepted without question.

She hadn't talked to Greg for three days afterwards; that's how long it had taken her to convince herself she hadn't cheated on Daniel, that it was impossible to cheat on someone who you'd been broken up with for eight years. And he hadn't begrudged her that time, or even asked why she'd needed it.

And now, from the moment she'd woken up yesterday, she'd been comparing him unfavorably to Daniel. Greg wasn't Daniel. That was true. But he *was* himself—kind, and patient, and steady—and that should have been enough.

She kept telling herself that, over and over, as her feet tapped along to the music, right up until the moment she saw him.

Daniel.

Not a hundred feet away, across the atrium from her, watching the band just like her.

Same dark hair, same impossibly pretty eyes—clear even from across the room.

She looked down, closed her eyes, looked up—and he was still there.

It couldn't be him, though. It was just some other random dark-haired man with pretty eyes. Of course that's all it was.

But she had to be sure. She started walking—jogging, really—around the atrium. She was only a few feet away now, and the pretty-eyed man who wasn't Daniel wasn't looking in her direction. He was staring intently at the spot where she'd just been.

And then he turned, and she saw. It *was* him.

It was impossible. He couldn't be here, but he was, and he was walking the last few steps towards her, and pulling her into an embrace, and kissing her and she was kissing him back.

It was impossible, and it was wrong and she wouldn't—couldn't—let him go.

Daniel, a moment later

What had just happened? How was she here? How was Nora Langley in his arms?

Why was he kissing her when Leanne was one deck downstairs and maybe two hundred feet away?

He didn't know. All he did know was that he couldn't let Nora go, couldn't look away from her, couldn't take his hands off her.

"Nora ... how?"

She didn't know either. She just smiled—*that* smile—and kissed him again, and he responded. He was dimly aware that there were dozens of people on this deck, watching the show he and Nora were putting on instead of watching the band down below. He didn't care.

He knew he should have—but he didn't.

Nora, a few minutes later

They were sitting in what was generously called the "Library." It was two half-filled bookshelves and four comfortable chairs.

Thankfully, none of their fellow passengers were in a reading mood, so they had a little privacy.

"What are you doing here?" She shook her head, laughing. "I mean, obviously you decided to go on a cruise. But how did we—what are the odds we'd pick the same cruise?"

It was one thing when they'd run into each other at the conference four years ago. They were both working in the same field; it really wasn't so bizarre that they'd had that night together. But this? There were dozens of cruise lines, and hundreds of different ships which sailed all year long. How did they end up on the same ship at the same time?

"Either the universe has a sense of humor," he said, "or it's trying to tell us something, I guess." It was so good—so comforting, far more than it should have been, to hear his voice.

But if this was a joke the universe was playing on them, it wouldn't be very funny to Greg, would it? Or to whoever Daniel was with.

That thought should have been enough to make her say goodbye to Daniel and go back to her room where her boyfriend was ... probably already asleep.

It wasn't.

She wasn't going anywhere.

Daniel, a few minutes later

The comedy show was starting right about now. That's where Leanne thought he was.

That's where he should be.

But he wasn't getting up. He wasn't saying goodbye to Nora and telling her they had to pretend the last few minutes hadn't happened, and then avoid each other the rest of the cruise.

That's what a good boyfriend would do; the kind of boyfriend he thought he was.

But a good boyfriend also wouldn't still be wearing the necklace his college girlfriend had custom made, right over his heart, and Daniel had been doing that to Leanne for nearly nine months.

His hand was on top of it now; when had that happened?

"You still wear it every day?" Nora already had to know the answer. "Did you forget the way I showed you how to take it off?"

It wasn't fair for her to smile the way she was now. It wasn't fair for her to be here at all. But she was, and—as much as he hated himself for it—he was glad she was. No—not *glad*. That was a horribly inadequate word. Overjoyed, maybe? Heart-burstingly happy?

"I never forgot anything you told me, Nora." Now her hand was over his, and it felt good. Right. Like it should never have been anywhere but there.

And he knew then, with that one touch of her hand, why even after nine great months he hadn't been able to tell Leanne he loved her. Why he'd *never* be able to tell her, and have it be true.

♡ ♥ ♡

Nora, a few minutes later

Nora finished telling Daniel what had happened four years ago in Kansas City.

"That's pretty much what I figured, once I saw your cover story," he said. "And the part you don't know—there was no way you could—was that my phone got switched with somebody else's on my team. They were all loaners from work, same model, no way to tell them apart. So when you were leaving messages ..."

She laughed; what else could she do? "Somebody else was getting them."

Daniel shook his head. "That's the other part you don't know. He dropped the phone—my phone—in the bathroom sink in his room. Nobody was getting your messages, because the phone was fried."

They were still sitting in the plush armchairs of the ship's library, such as it was. His hand was on the arm of his chair, and her hand was on top of it. When had she done that? "Why did he have the phone in the bathroom?"

Now Daniel laughed, too. "I never asked. I didn't really want to know."

That was fair. There really wasn't any good reason to have a cell phone with you in the bathroom. They'd been working a booth at a trade show; it wasn't like Daniel's coworker was a surgeon waiting to be called into the operating room or something.

"But you never called me once you saw the story in the magazine. If you knew why I left ..."

He wasn't laughing anymore. "I couldn't. It would just have been another goodbye, and I—I couldn't. Any more than you could. You knew where I worked, too." He said it without any bitterness, which almost made it worse. Especially because he was right.

"I did. And—yeah. I could have called you, but I didn't want to say goodbye again, either. I still love you, Daniel."

He didn't say anything for a while; he just held her eyes. Finally, he said, "Is that why you wore that dress?"

What did he mean by that? She didn't know he'd be on the ship! What was he saying?

And then it hit her. She was making a statement to herself by bringing the dress from their Valentine's Day dance on the cruise. She was telling herself she wouldn't ever fully be with Greg, that she couldn't ever commit to him because in her heart she was still back in college with Daniel.

"I didn't think that's what I was doing—but, yes, that's exactly it." She laughed gently. "The same reason I'm still using the pen you gave me. And I still sleep with Mr. Fuzzles."

She hesitated for a moment. He didn't say anything. She had to fill the silence. "And the same reason you still wear the necklace."

"I still love you, too," he said, reaching between the buttons of his shirt to pull it out. "So what do we do about it?"

Daniel, a few minutes later

She hadn't answered his question.

He couldn't blame her. He didn't have an answer either. This wasn't like Kansas City, where one of them could leave if they really had to. They were on this ship for ten days. There was no way to guarantee they wouldn't run into each other. No way to make themselves believe they even wanted to.

He was pretty sure she didn't want to anyway, any more than he did. So where did that leave them? She hadn't said she was with someone, but she clearly was. Nobody went on cruises by themselves.

Which meant that, even though he hadn't mentioned Leanne, she had to know he wasn't alone either.

"Nora, we have to figure this out. I—I have a girlfriend. Leanne. She's in our cabin. She's probably asleep by now."

She nodded. "So is Greg. I'm sure he fell asleep two minutes after I left."

"They don't deserve this."

Nora looked down. "We haven't *really* done anything. It was one kiss." Nora had never lied to him, but he remembered the times when she'd lied to herself and tried to make herself believe it was true. She wasn't any better at it now than she had been back in college.

"Yes, we have. It's not about what we're doing right now. It's what I've been doing to Leanne from the day we met. I've been wearing your necklace, and carrying you around in my heart."

Now she was looking at him again. "When I finally went to bed with Greg—and I made up so many ridiculous reasons not to before it happened—but after we did, I couldn't talk to him for three days. Because I felt like I'd cheated on you." She smiled, but it was the saddest smile he'd ever seen. "How stupid is that?"

"It's not stupid at all." He'd felt the same after he'd been with Leanne for their first time, back in July.

"They're never going to forgive us."

No, they wouldn't. "She'd forgive me for the kiss. If she ran into her first love, and she had a moment and she kissed him, I would forgive that. But if she said she'd never stopped loving him, and never told me—I couldn't forgive that. And I could never ask her to."

Daniel had been so caught up in the conversation that he hadn't noticed the music had stopped—the band had probably packed up five or ten minutes ago. But now he heard it again—different music, a slow, jazzy tune he didn't recognize. And Nora was standing up, and reaching down, grabbing his hands, pulling him up.

"Greg is the same. But I just figured it out, what we're going to do."

Her arms were around him, and he followed her lead into a slow dance.

"We're going to have one dance. One last dance," she continued. "And then one last kiss. And then you're going to go back to—Leanne, you said?" He nodded. "And I'll go back to Greg, and we'll forget each other and spend the next ten days reminding ourselves about every great thing we ever saw in them. And we'll go overboard." She chuckled. "Pardon the pun, and do everything we can think of to make them as happy as they deserve to be. And maybe, if we're really lucky, that'll be good enough."

Daniel couldn't lie to her any more than she ever could to him. "And if it's not enough, which we both know it won't be, at least we can give them a good time before we break their hearts. Right?"

She didn't answer for a while. Not until the song ended, and she kissed him, and he kissed her back. "Sometimes I really wish we were better at lying to each other, Daniel."

Chapter 37

Nora, November 7

She and Daniel managed to keep their mutual promise to avoid each other for twelve whole hours.

When Nora got back to her room last night, Greg was asleep, just as she'd assumed. He was snoring gently, and he didn't even stir while she washed her face, brushed her teeth, undressed and got into bed next to him.

He'd awoken refreshed, and it took all her self-control not to burst into tears and confess everything to him. "I know I was kind of a wet blanket last night, Nora. But I'm ready to go now. Let's go and see everything on the ship today."

So they went to breakfast in the Main Dining Room, with no sign of Daniel. She looked up every time anyone walked by their table, and passed it off as idle curiosity. "I always wondered what kind of people come on these cruises," she'd said, and he accepted that.

After breakfast, he suggested going up to the spa. "Maybe they've got couples massages," he said. She could hardly say she wasn't interested, when she'd been the one to mention the spa yesterday.

The spa was located in the Solarium, a huge glassed-in space on deck nine with a small pool, two hot tubs and a snack bar, as well as tons of beach chairs and plenty of tables scattered about, where couples or little groups were sitting and chatting or playing cards or, at one table, some sort of board game. And that, of course, put her mind on Daniel.

She might have dismissed the thought—if he weren't in the hot tub they were walking past. She only saw him from the back, but it was unquestionably him. She couldn't mistake his dark hair, or his build, or the delicate chain draped around his neck. She also didn't miss the arm around him, which was connected to a slim blonde woman chattering away. She remembered nights sitting in his dorm room with her arm around him, how comfortable—and comforting—it felt.

That thought was not helping at all.

He didn't turn to see her as they walked by, thank God. But she was tensed up now, and Greg had to notice that.

"Nora? Are you okay?" His arm was around her, and that wasn't helping at all either.

"I just had a chill," she said, and it wasn't even technically a lie; she definitely felt something cold and upsetting running from her head down to the pit of her stomach. "It'll pass. Let's go get that massage."

With any luck, Daniel and—Leanne?—would be out of the hot tub and somewhere else entirely by the time their massage was done. And maybe after an hour—or however long it actually was—of being oiled down and kneaded by expert hands while lying a few inches from her boyfriend—she wouldn't be thinking about Daniel anyway.

Daniel, an hour later

When he'd heard her name spoken, Daniel tried to convince himself that it wasn't her. There were over two thousand passengers on board. There had to be at least a dozen Noras, right?

He couldn't make himself believe it; it was enough of a victory that he didn't turn to look at her and the man—Greg, she'd said—who was with her.

"You're so distracted, Daniel," Leanne had said. "You're not still mad about last night, are you?"

He hadn't been mad. Well, not at her.

When he got back to the cabin last night, he'd tried his best to quash the bitter anger he felt towards himself, and he thought he'd succeeded. But then, when they'd woken up this morning, Leanne had apologized for spoiling their first night on the cruise. He told her five times she'd done nothing wrong and had nothing to apologize for, but she still didn't believe him.

"I was mad at myself for leaving you in the room when you were feeling bad. Really angry, to be honest." It was strictly true and completely dishonest, and he hated himself for saying it. But she'd finally accepted it, and suggested some time in the hot tub after breakfast to make them both feel better.

And it had worked until he heard *her* name. But then her footsteps trailed away, in the direction of the spa, and he managed to sort-of relax for a few more minutes of soaking.

Now they were up on deck ten, standing on the elevated railing that ran around the deck, looking out at the ocean. It was peaceful at the moment; nobody else was up here, and the shouts of little kids splashing in the main pool one deck below were just background noise.

And as a bonus, Nora would almost certainly not come up here. She wasn't exactly acrophobic, but she also didn't love high places, especially when they were fully exposed to the elements as this spot was.

Leanne, on the other hand, was in heaven. "This is great, Daniel! You can feel the wind, and smell that air—it's so clean. I get why people love sailing."

She had a point. The view was beautiful, and the air *was* clean. You never noticed the pollution and the random smells of the city—even in a smaller city like Charlotte—until you were somewhere where there was none of that.

"I'm not sure about a sailboat, with all those ropes and everything. But this is really nice. I could get used to this."

He turned to Leanne. Her hair was blowing in the breeze, and so was her sundress, and she was absolutely glowing, just radiating joy. All she wanted in the whole world right now was to enjoy this moment with him.

It should have been good enough for him. But—as hard as he tried to convince himself otherwise—it wasn't.

Nora, an hour later

The massage had been nothing short of a miracle. Ten minutes into it, Nora had forgotten not only Daniel, but her own name.

The only thing she could think about was how the hands of the masseuse felt as they worked what seemed like every muscle in her body; and the strong, warm pressure of Greg's hand holding hers between the tables they were laying on.

When it was over, it had taken her five minutes to summon up the strength to stand, and Greg had to support her out of the spa and all the way down to deck six and the art gallery by the atrium.

"I thought you'd want to see this," Greg said.

Her brain still wasn't fully engaged. "Pretty colors?" That was all she could comprehend. Pretty colors hanging on the walls.

They stopped in front of a painting of a brightly-lit cottage. Greg was admiring it. Nora stared for a good minute or two while she slowly regained the capacity for rational thought. "I like it," she finally said. "But Mom would disown me if I put a Thomas Kinkade up in my apartment."

He was confused at that. "I thought your mother ran an art gallery?"

"Exactly. But modern art. The more abstract, the better."

Greg took her hand and led her around the little gallery. "Something like this?" He was pointing at a garish, almost neon-colored painting. "We could buy it for her. Christmas isn't too far away."

She threw her arms around his neck and kissed him. Unlike yesterday, he didn't pull away from her. "Oh, my God. That's the nicest thing. But ..."

His shoulders drooped at the word "but." All she could do was laugh. "No, really. It's such a sweet thought. But there's no way you could know. Mark Kostabi,"—she gestured at the little plaque showing the details of the painting—"Mom actually knows him. Despises him, is more like it. Something happened when she worked on an exhibition at the Museum of Modern Art back in 1992. I have my suspicions, but obviously I can't ask her and I don't really want to know the truth anyway."

Greg perked back up with her words. "I wouldn't want to remind her of—whatever went down with her and this guy," he said. "Maybe tomorrow in Charleston—there's the big market, right near the port. We can find something there for her."

She kissed him again. "That would be fantastic, Greg. She'd love it." The market was already on her list of must-dos in Charleston, so even if they didn't come across anything that Karen Langley would actually like, which was pretty much guaranteed, it would still be a good time.

Maybe she could keep the promise she'd made last night after all.

Daniel, late afternoon

Right after lunch, the weather took a sudden turn towards cold and wet. There weren't too many options indoors this afternoon; the shops were kind of overpriced, neither of them wanted to go to the casino and, as Leanne said, "If I spend any more time in the hot tub, I'll turn into a prune." But then she saw something they'd both missed earlier—the big theater on deck four was showing a movie, and the choice was made.

It turned out to be *Grosse Pointe Blank*, and two hours later, Leanne was still grinning when they walked out of the theater. "That was great! How did we miss it when it came out in the spring?"

He didn't remind her of the truth, which was that he'd very much wanted to see it at the time, but the way the commercials emphasized the violent shootouts had turned her off. "I don't really like movies with all that bloodshed," she'd said.

Apparently the charm of John Cusack overcame her feelings about movie violence, which he supposed was good to know for the future. But there was something else about the movie that was occupying his thoughts just now. This was 1997. He was the same age as John Cusack's hitman in the movie. And his ten-year high school reunion was—coming up? Or had he missed it already?

"Daniel, what's up? You're getting distracted again."

At least it wasn't about Nora this time; he had nothing to feel guilty for. "I'm sorry. It's the movie—it got me wondering if I missed *my* reunion. This is ten years for me, just like John Cusack. I don't think I ever gave them my address when I moved to Charlotte."

They wandered out to the atrium. Deck four was the lowest level, and there was a bar located there. Leanne beckoned him to sit on a stool next to her. When the bartender looked their way, she told him, "Two champagne cocktails for us, please." Then she turned to him. "It's ten years for me, too. So this can be our own little high school reunion. What do you think?"

He leaned over and kissed her. "I think it's perfect."

They toasted each other with their first round of drinks, and swapped embarrassing high school stories for the next three rounds. And an hour later, as they didn't quite stagger their way back to the cabin to rest up before dinner, Daniel wondered if, just maybe, he might be able to keep the promise he'd made last night after all.

Nora, nine o'clock in the evening

It had been a good day, and so far a good night. They'd had a surprisingly good lunch in the buffet up on deck nine, then Greg spent an hour swimming laps in the solarium pool while she watched. He'd invited her in, but the waves in the pool from the motion of the ship were a little too big for Nora's comfort.

Later, they'd sat in the back of the big South Seas Lounge on deck six and enjoyed cocktails and watched a spirited session of bingo. Then, before they knew it, it was time for dinner in the Main Dining Room. And this time, when Nora wanted to order three different appetizers, Greg didn't say a thing.

No, that wasn't true. He'd suggested a fourth one. "Let's try the shrimp cocktail, too." he'd said. So they stuffed themselves, waddled back to their cabin, and now she was sitting on the little sofa, her arm around Greg and leaning into him while she idly flipped through channels on the remote control.

"I don't care what's on TV," he said. "I'm just glad to be here with you."

She was glad, too. She hadn't thought of Daniel once today, after the near-miss this morning. Maybe that was the key—take it a day at a time. There was no need to make promises for the future, or even for the rest of the cruise. She just needed to focus on Greg and how she felt about him *right now*. And then in the morning, do it again, and tomorrow afternoon, and so on. Step by step. That's how everything else in life worked, right?

She could manage that.

Hopefully.

Daniel, November 8, ten o'clock in the morning

The bad weather from yesterday afternoon was gone, a couple of hundred miles to the north. It was a bright, clear morning in Charleston when Daniel stepped off the ramp and onto the pier, hand in hand with Leanne.

It was chilly, though; he was glad he'd brought a jacket on the cruise. Leanne had given it to him for his birthday, the first gift she'd bought him. He wore it whenever the opportunity presented itself, even though he didn't actually like it that much. It looked good; that wasn't the problem.

What he didn't like was that it was too heavy for a day like today, but not heavy enough for anything colder than today. He hadn't said anything about that to Leanne—you didn't criticize gifts. No matter what you really thought, you acted like they were great, because someone cared enough to buy them for you.

Just like the Members Only jacket he'd desperately wanted back in tenth grade, and Mom finally bought it for him and then it turned out to not fit quite right, and he didn't look nearly as cool wearing it as he'd imagined he would. But he wore it anyway, so she knew how much he appreciated it.

"You want to go to the market first?" Leanne was looking back and forth between the map in her free hand, and the street up ahead.

"Sure," he said. Honestly, he didn't care that much what they did. He was, first of all, glad to be on solid ground, and second, happy to enjoy Leanne's company wherever she wanted to go. "Look, there's a sign, we're headed the right way."

It was only two blocks until they got to the open-air portion of the Charleston City Market. There were tents on either side of the street for two more blocks, leading up to the main building.

"Let's get something for Bianca," Leanne said. "A thank-you gift for getting us together."

Daniel nodded. That was a great idea, but he had no idea what to buy his cousin. He knew her better than anyone, but she could be very finicky and her hobbies changed with the season. Just this year, she'd taken up and quit pottery, quilting, and stained-glass painting.

"Maybe clothes. Those sweaters look nice." There was a table on their right with what he assumed were hand-knitted sweaters, in a variety of bright colors. "She might like one of them."

He and Leanne were going through the stack of sweaters looking for something in Bianca's size, when he heard *her* voice, bright and clear. There was no mistaking it.

"Rachel would love one of these!"

And then Leanne was pulling him aside, politely making room for Nora. "Daniel, let them look too." He had no choice; he had to scoot over, and look up to see Nora's face, maybe six inches from his.

Nora gasped, but caught herself before she could do or say anything more. At least he'd had a moment's warning, but the way he was bent over looking at the sweaters, she'd had no idea it was him until he stood up straight.

She jumped away from him, and the man with her was looking at her curiously. So Daniel did the only thing he could think of to protect her. "It's okay," he said. "You didn't quite step on my foot."

Nora patted his arm, touching him for just a split second. "No, I did, but thanks for trying to make me feel better. We can come back here later, I think I need a snack now anyway. Have a nice day." She said it all without taking a breath, the way she always talked too fast when she was nervous or excited.

And then Nora and Greg were gone. "That was really sweet, Daniel," Leanne said. "You always look out for everybody, don't you?"

He wanted to believe her words. But he didn't feel like he was doing a very good job of looking out for the person right next to him.

♡ ♥ ♡

Nora, an hour later

Nora was still rattled, an hour after blundering into Daniel. Thank God he'd been alert enough to come up with something on the fly that let her escape the situation without unraveling her relationship—and his—as though it was one of the handmade sweaters he'd been looking at.

"Nora, what's going on with you?" Even the glass of wine she'd ordered at the little café across the street from the market wasn't helping, and Greg was growing more concerned as the morning went on. "Did that guy you bumped into—did he do something to you?" Anger was just creeping into his voice. She had to calm down, and calm her boyfriend down, and she had to do it now.

"No, Greg. I stepped on his foot, and—this is stupid, but it brought back a bad memory. I did that in high school, to one of the other girls on the volleyball team, and she tripped over me and sprained her ankle, and everybody blamed me."

It hadn't happened like that at all; she'd injured herself because she hadn't stretched properly, and it had been her calf rather than her ankle, but the anger and shame from her disastrous week on the high school volleyball team was still there thirteen years later, and she used it now.

He pulled his chair closer to hers, put an arm around her. "I guess it's true what they say—high school never really ends. It must have been really bad, if you still get upset about it all these years later."

Nora wasn't sure which was worse: that it was so easy for her to lie to Greg, or that one crummy week in 1984 still hurt as though it had just happened.

What stung even more was another realization: the only time she'd been able to put the volleyball incident in its proper place, was when she'd told Daniel about it back when they were dating.

It was a couple of weeks before Thanksgiving, 1988. They'd been sitting in his dorm room, and they'd somehow gotten onto the topic of the horrors of high school gym class. She'd started telling the story, and she got panicky and then the tears had started, and Daniel took her hands in his, and said, "You're not her anymore. You never were. It's not worth crying over a bunch of jerks who couldn't see how great you were, and besides, you're probably never going to see any of them again anyway."

And that's all it had taken. His hands and his pretty eyes staring at her with love—and so much more than love.

Daniel had been able to talk her down when she was so much closer to that episode, and to the girl she'd been; why did the hurt and shame burn so strongly now, so much farther away? Why couldn't Greg's touch, and his words, do what Daniel's had back then?

She knew. Of course she knew. But she couldn't accept the answer.

Daniel, around six o'clock

By the time they'd finished lunch, at a great little seafood restaurant tucked into a side street near the City Hall, Daniel had—mostly—managed to put the meeting with Nora out of his mind.

He and Leanne spent the rest of the afternoon wandering the streets and admiring the gorgeous old houses. Leanne surprised him with her knowledge of architecture and building techniques. "My uncle restores old houses," she'd explained. "My first high school job was helping him out. I guess I picked up more than I thought."

When they got back to the ship, she insisted on a soak in the solarium hot tub, to ease her—and his—sore legs. And now they were in the Main Dining Room for a relatively early dinner.

While they waited for their appetizers, he asked her, "So what do you want to do tomorrow?" They'd be at Port Canaveral—close to both Orlando and the Kennedy Space Center, and the ship offered a dozen different excursions.

She had an immediate answer. "I figure you want to see the space center."

He absolutely did, but he didn't think it would be her top choice. "I mean, that would be cool, but there's also Disney World. I know we'd probably only get four or five hours in the park, but that's enough time for a few rides, and maybe we can get a picture with Cinderella. Or the mermaid ...?"

"Ariel," Leanne said with a laugh. "Or Woody and Buzz. Actually, forget them. My nephew has *Toy Story* on video, and the last time I babysat, he made me watch it with him three times in a row." The waiter interrupted their conversation momentarily to bring her French onion soup and his salad. "Actually, I'm not sure about Disney. We'll have to wait on lines everywhere. What about the beach instead?"

There was a bus from the ship to Cocoa Beach, only fifteen minutes away according to the brochure that had been left under their door this afternoon. They could sunbathe, swim in the ocean, enjoy colorful overpriced cocktails with umbrellas in them, and there were supposed to be plenty of shops right off the beach.

He could live with that. "Sure, that sounds great. We can stop by the excursions desk after dinner." Except—what if Nora chose the beach, too? They'd barely avoided disaster this morning when they were both fully dressed. He had no illusions that he could keep his composure if she was laying out in a bikini ten feet away from him. And he was certain Nora would lose her cool if she saw him wearing only a bathing suit and the necklace she'd made for him.

He'd just need to figure out where Nora would go after dinner tonight, and come up with some way to get her alone for five minutes to plan out where they were both going tomorrow. It would probably mean yet another lie to Leanne, but better that then an ugly public scene tomorrow.

Maybe they could plan out the whole rest of the cruise, and make certain they wouldn't encounter each other anywhere. That could work.

It had to work. If it didn't ... an ugly public scene probably wasn't even in the top ten worst things that could happen.

Nora, nine o'clock

She was sitting by herself, near the back of the South Seas Lounge, waiting for karaoke to start.

And also waiting for Daniel.

She would have come anyway; when she saw on the daily schedule that there was karaoke, she'd told Greg she wanted to see it, and maybe even get up and sing herself. But he was wiped out from all the walking today, which she couldn't blame him for. Most days at work, he didn't get out of the lab or the classroom much, while she made a point of taking a long walk every day, if not at lunchtime then before work. So he was in the cabin, and she was here—and if Daniel was going to try and find her, well, he remembered their performance at that karaoke bar in Kansas City just as well as she did.

And here he was now. He sat down next to her just as a couple who were probably in their fifties began butchering *Summer Nights*.

She whispered, "Are we safe?"

"Leanne's taking a shower and going to bed early. I told her I wanted to see how bad the singers were. She said she'll come tomorrow night if they have it again."

She nodded. "Same here, except I don't think Greg would come at all. Karaoke is totally not his thing."

They just listened to the rest of the song in silence. When it was, mercifully, over, Nora said, "Olivia Newton-John would turn over in her grave if she heard that."

"She's not dead," Daniel reminded her.

"She'd want to be if she had to listen to that." But they had more important things to talk about. "Before the next song starts, where are you going tomorrow?"

"Cocoa Beach," he said. "I figured she'd like that better than Kennedy Space Center."

Nora chuckled. This might work after all. "I guessed you'd take her there, or Disney. We're going to Kennedy—Greg will love it. He's a physicist, so it's right up his alley."

Daniel looked—not quite pained, but something close to it. It had probably been a mistake to say anything about Greg at all. "Okay. So that just leaves us five more days to avoid each other."

She sighed. How were they going to manage that? "Wait—I have an idea." Hadn't she seen a notice board, around the corner from the customer service counter on deck five? "You know where the note board is?"

He nodded. "Deck five. I saw it yesterday." For a moment he seemed confused, then he smiled and his eyes—God, they were even prettier now than they'd been back in college!—lit up. "We can leave our plans on there for each other. We just need to come up with names—I know!" *Say Anything*. "Lloyd and Diane."

That was perfect. How did he always know the right thing to say, to do? "Except you gave me the pen, so you're Diane and I'm Lloyd." Why hadn't either of them thought of that the first night? It would have made things so much easier.

With that settled, they sat back and enjoyed—if that was the word—the performances. At a quarter to ten, though, there were no more volunteers, and the very energetic young woman hosting the event was pleading for someone to come up and sing. "Fifteen minutes left—come on, someone's got one last song in them!"

If this was going to be the last time they were together, the last time she'd be able to be this close to him and look into his pretty eyes and listen to his voice, then they needed to mark the occasion.

She got up, took his hand and dragged him to the stage. The hostess handed her the songbook, and she quickly flipped through it. There—that would work! "Number 106, please."

Daniel looked both excited and resigned; she wouldn't have thought both of those things could show on someone's face at the same time. He took his microphone from the hostess, and put an arm around her, and then the music started.

When he realized what she'd picked, he burst out laughing. But he sang *Don't Go Breaking My Heart* with just as much enthusiasm as she did. And when it was done, he tossed the microphone over to the hostess, pulled her into the shadows in the far corner of the lounge, and kissed her for all he was worth.

Daniel, a moment later

She didn't pull away from him; she was still in his arms, her face still only a couple of inches from his.

"I'm sorry," he whispered. "I couldn't say goodbye without that—I just couldn't."

She held him even closer. "I know. If you didn't do it, I would have. But—this *is* goodbye, right? We're not going to see each other again. We have a plan. We'll stick to it. We'll stop being selfish and rotten to Greg and Leanne, because they deserve better. And we are better. Aren't we?"

Daniel didn't think it had much to do with being better; they were still in love, and you couldn't get rid of emotions by unplugging yourself and rebooting your system, as nice as it would be if that were possible. But he nodded along with her anyway, because everything else she said was right, and they absolutely owed it to Leanne and Greg.

"We are. So—I love you. I'll always love you. But, yeah. This is goodbye."

He pulled himself away, walked out of the South Seas Lounge, and started back to his cabin—to his girlfriend—and to the second or third attempt at keeping his promise.

To her.

And to himself.

Chapter 38

Nora, November 9, early evening

They were sitting in Giovanni's, the fancy Italian restaurant on the ship and Greg asked her, "How can something be so amazing and still be disappointing at the same time?"

Nora felt the same way about their visit to the Kennedy Space Center today. There'd been so much to see, and their tour guide had been fantastic. Everything was fascinating. But, as they'd discovered, the timing of their visit was awful.

There'd been a rocket launch yesterday morning. And there was a space shuttle launch scheduled in just ten days—the next cruise would probably visit here just in time to witness it. At least they got to see the space shuttle sitting on the launch pad, which she couldn't deny was an awesome sight.

"I know. And I should have thought of it when I picked the date for the cruise. I work for a science publisher, for God's sake." Not to mention, if she'd booked the next cruise instead of this one, she wouldn't have run into Daniel, and she wouldn't have had to spend the whole trip lying to her boyfriend.

But what was done was done. She hadn't thought of Daniel—well, not much—today.

Except during the quiet moments when Greg was standing there staring up at the space shuttle, totally enraptured, or geeking out at the Apollo 11 display, and she imagined Daniel doing the same thing.

That was mostly a victory, wasn't it?

Daniel, a little later

It had been a great day. Cocoa Beach was everything he'd hoped for. The weather was perfect, it wasn't too crowded, and on a more shallow note—hey, he was only human—Leanne looked amazing in a bikini.

He felt a little guilty, because her view of him in a swimsuit couldn't have been as appealing to her; he hadn't realized just how pale he was until he saw the tans on nearly all the men and women sunning themselves. And also because he'd had a fleeting mental image of what Nora would look like in Leanne's bikini.

He'd managed to banish that thought and focus all his attention on Leanne, which she had enjoyed as much as he did.

They were in the Main Dining Room now, waiting for dessert, and thinking about the beach, and all the scantily-dressed beachgoers brought an old story back. He'd never told it to Nora; if he told Leanne now then there'd be something that was just between them, something he didn't share with anyone else. It was worth a little embarrassment.

"I've never told anyone this. Not even Bianca," he said. "But being at the beach today made me think about it. You know I went to an all-boys school, and I was pretty shy. So the first time

I really started noticing girls—I mean, I noticed them, but this was the first time out in the world, if that makes sense. It was that trip to Disney World, sophomore year of high school. It was March, spring break time, I guess, and a lot of the girls there were wearing long T-shirts, you know what I'm talking about, they go down to their thighs?" Leanne nodded. He could feel himself going red as we went on. "And all I could think was, were they wearing shorts under them, or just underwear?"

"Daniel!" She reached across the table to punch his arm, mostly playfully. "That's so juvenile!"

"I *was* a juvenile!" he protested, then grinned sheepishly. "And it's not like I did anything about it—just stared from a distance, and blushed a lot."

She laughed at that, and then she shared her own story, slightly racier, about really noticing boys for the first time.

It involved her first high school dance, her first kiss, the most mortifying talk with her mother afterwards, and—inevitably— her first properly broken heart.

"I've never told anyone that, either. Well, except my mom. But otherwise just you."

Shared secrets—even if they were a decade old and nobody else would even care about them—was something to build on, wasn't it? Maybe he could be the man Leanne deserved after all.

Nora, November 10, around eleven o'clock

"I'm nervous about this," Greg said as they boarded the tour bus to Sanctuary Bay. He'd been saying it all morning.

"If you really, really don't want to do it, you can stay on land and go to the bird patio. The brochure said there are all kinds of exotic birds." She hoped he'd overcome his anxiety and go in the water with her. Swimming with dolphins was the thing Nora had been looking forward to more than anything else on the cruise, and she wanted to share it with him.

He didn't relax any during the ten minute bus ride, and she couldn't understand why. He liked swimming; he'd done laps in the pool aboard the ship almost every day. She'd showed him the brochure, which had laid out all the safety measures—there was a dolphin trainer right there in the water with you at all times. Besides, it was a protected lagoon—there were no dangerous currents, no jellyfish, no surprises.

She couldn't make him do it. That would be selfish and awful, and he wouldn't enjoy it anyway. One thing about Greg she'd learned was that—unlike Daniel, or herself for that matter—he didn't laugh at himself afterwards when you pushed him to do something he thought he wouldn't enjoy and it turned out not to be nearly as bad as he'd feared.

It was not his best quality. But then, she had plenty of those herself. She could hardly begrudge him one tiny flaw.

"I can't. I'm sorry, Nora," he said, once they went through the gate and a guide led them to the changing rooms. "I'll make it up to you tomorrow in Nassau—whatever you want to do, Okay?"

She pushed down her disappointment, and gave him a quick kiss. "There's nothing to make up for. Go enjoy the birds, and I'll meet you there when I get out of the water."

Daniel, a few minutes later

He was disappointed the moment they stepped off the boarding ramp and saw no tour bus waiting where it was supposed to be—just a man in a Royal Caribbean uniform surrounded by a small group of frustrated passengers.

"Again, we apologize for this inconvenience," he was saying. "There won't be any snorkeling today—the water conditions are poor. But as an alternative, we've made arrangements to have your tickets honored at the Dolphin Experience. Anyone who would like to take part, please head over to bus number six, to my left."

Leanne squealed with joy. "That was my second choice. Let's go, Daniel!"

Nora would be there. She'd written it on the note board last night, just like they'd agreed.

Leanne was already heading to bus number six, almost skipping. She was so excited, and he couldn't think of a single good excuse to say no, or suggest something different.

So he followed her onto the bus, sat next to her, let her take his hand—and prayed that he'd somehow be able to avoid Nora.

But on the bus ride over, all he could think about was how hurt and betrayed Leanne would feel if he couldn't.

Nora, ten minutes later

Nora stood on the edge of the lagoon, watching the lucky first group of swimmers enjoying their time with the dolphins.

Belle, one of the staff at the Dolphin Experience, had explained that only six guests were allowed in the water at a time, along with a trainer, so the dolphins wouldn't be overwhelmed. Nora had been seventh in line, so she'd have to wait until the first group finished their half-hour session.

Luckily, only three other people were waiting with her—maybe that meant more attention from the dolphins when it was her turn.

Everyone, both humans and fish ... no, she knew better than that! Dolphins were mammals; she'd never hear the end of it if she slipped up like that at work.

Anyway, both the mammals with legs and those without seemed to be having a great time.

A loud voice called out in the distance. "Belle! We've got another bus, come help check them in."

So much for a smaller group. Apparently the next round would be full after all.

Daniel, ten minutes later

Leanne was as excited as Daniel had ever seen her. If not for the staff of the Dolphin Experience leading them towards the changing rooms, he was pretty sure she would have run straight to the dolphin pool—or enclosure, or whatever it was called—and just dived right in, clothes and all.

When their guide—Belle, she'd said—pointed out where they had to go, Leanne pulled away from him, took three steps towards the women's changing room, lost her balance and went down hard.

He ran to her to help her up, but she was already on her feet. "It was nothing," she said. "I'm fine." But she wasn't fine; there was a nasty cut on her left leg. She was putting weight on it, so she hadn't broken a bone or probably even twisted anything. But she would still need first aid for the cut.

Daniel guided her to a little stone ledge to sit down. "Daniel, I said I'm fine," she protested.

There was a voice behind him—Belle. "I'm sorry, ma'am," she said, walking past him to take a closer look at Leanne. "You'll need to come to the office. We have a first aid kit there, and Jacques is trained."

"I'm a nurse! I know what a serious wound looks like." Leanne's voice was raised; she was barely keeping it below a shout. He'd never seen her this upset. "This'll stop bleeding in a minute, I'm completely fine."

Belle wasn't having it. "It's regulations, ma'am. No one can go into the lagoon with an open wound. It's unsafe for you, and also for the dolphins."

Leanne's face was redder than the blood on her leg. "No! They cancelled the snorkeling, and now I can't swim here, either? It's not fair!" He didn't blame her; this was frustrating, even though he understood why they had the rule.

Maybe there was a way to salvage this. "What if we get her first aid right now, and then after they clean it up, could she go with the next group?"

Belle shook her head. She only seemed to have bad news. "There isn't going to be a next group. Yours is the last one today. The weather report is unfavorable, and they are cancelling the rest of the sessions today." She sighed. "Please don't blame me, this comes from the management, they have to take special care with the dolphins."

Leanne cursed under her breath, and Daniel's eyes went wide. He hadn't known she even knew that word. Belle pretended she hadn't heard it.

"Daniel, you go. You swim. One of us ought to enjoy it," Leanne said, forcing her voice into something close to her usual calm tone. But he couldn't. She was injured, he had to go with her to first aid.

"Leanne ..."

She grabbed his hand, squeezed it hard. "I mean it! This sucks, but I don't need any moral support to have a cut cleaned and taped up. Please. Go and swim, and you can tell me all about it afterwards, so at least I'll be able to enjoy it vicariously."

She wasn't going to change her mind—and he doubted he could change it, either. So he kissed her forehead, apologized to her, and went off to the changing room.

Nora, ten minutes later

The previous swimmers were out of the water, and now it was her turn. In just a minute or two, she'd be nose to nose with a dolphin.

The trainer, a tall, redheaded man who looked like he was barely out of high school, beckoned her group over.

"Right, I'm Mitch, I'll be with you in the lagoon." The Australian accent didn't surprise her; after five days aboard a ship with crew from thirty different countries, she was used to it. "I hope you're ready for the experience of a lifetime, but first, some very simple rules ..."

He didn't finish; Belle's voice rang out from behind her. "I've got two more for you, Mitch! And then you're done for the day."

Nora turned to see the two new arrivals: a young woman in a red one-piece swimsuit, and ...

Oh, God.

Daniel.

They had a plan! She left a note, exactly like he'd said! What was he doing here? He wasn't supposed to be here! He was going to ruin everything!

And yet, in the midst of her panic, another thought rose up. It was clear and it was bright and it was the most true thing she'd ever known:

She was glad he was here.

Overjoyed.

If this was going to be the experience of a lifetime, she wanted to share it with the love of her life.

And that man wasn't Greg.

She couldn't pretend anymore. She couldn't keep lying to herself.

It was—it had always been—it would *always be* Daniel.

Daniel, the same time

He said a quick prayer that Nora had already finished her swim, that she was already drying off in the changing room, anywhere but here.

No such luck.

There she was, standing by the water in a blue two piece bathing suit, staring right at him. Her face was full of fear and confusion—and then it changed.

That smile appeared suddenly—the one that was only for him. Her eyes lit up, wide and bright and shining. And he was smiling back at her before he even realized he was doing it.

Whatever had been on his face an instant ago—worry, guilt, fear—it was gone. There was no way to deny it anymore.

He loved her. Only her. Only ever her.

He wanted to share this experience with her. Only her.

Leanne was an amazing woman. She was sweet and generous and smart and funny and a thousand other great things. She'd been nothing but kind and loving to him. But she had one over-riding flaw none of that could overcome: she wasn't Nora.

For nine months, he'd convinced himself that didn't matter. That he could learn to love her. That she could be *the one* for him. That they could build a life together.

He'd kept trying to believe it even after he saw Nora in the atrium on Thursday night.

But it wasn't true, and he had to admit that it never had been.

All he could do now was surrender to the truth. Swim with Nora. Share this moment with her.

And then tell Leanne the truth. That he couldn't give her his heart. It wasn't his to give. It had belonged to Nora from the very first moment they'd met.

Nora, five minutes later

The moment she jumped into the lagoon, hand-in-hand with Daniel, all her worries and fears vanished.

The cold water shocked her; she'd expected it to be warm as bathwater. But even that surprise faded an instant later when the dolphin swam up to her.

"Benny likes you!" Mitch the trainer called out. "You can touch him, don't be afraid!"

She was anyway, despite his encouragement. What if he didn't want her to?

But she felt Daniel grabbing her hand, gently placing it on the back of Benny's head. The dolphin's skin felt strange, slick and almost rubbery; her hand sliding as the dolphin bobbed in front of her. That made sense, though. Smooth skin meant less friction in the water, right?

Forget science. This was about being in the moment.

She put her other hand on Benny, and then before she even realized it, she was loosely hugging him, and he was letting her. At the same time, she felt Daniel's arm wrap around her.

"You totally made a friend, Nora," he said softly.

Benny was beautiful. He—Mitch had said it, but how did you even tell with dolphins?—was light gray, which surprised her a little. Weren't dolphins supposed to be black?

It didn't matter. Benny was perfect exactly as he was.

Just like Daniel.

Daniel, a few minutes later

Daniel didn't notice the second dolphin until it swam right up and nudged him in the ribs.

"Say 'hi' to Annie," the trainer called out. He assumed that meant this one was female, not that he could see any difference between Annie and Benny.

It didn't matter anyway. It was more than enough that she wanted his attention. Her skin was sleek and cool, and he could feel her powerful muscles underneath.

"The boy came to me and the girl went to you," Nora said, splashing water at him. "What do you think that means?"

"I guess Annie has the same good taste you do," he said, grinning.

That earned him another splash, right in his face. He laughed as he wiped the water from his eyes. He definitely deserved that.

"What about Benny having good taste, too?"

Benny hadn't left Nora's side the whole time. Daniel didn't blame him one bit.

"That goes without saying."

But not everything could go unsaid. Not anymore.

He paddled slowly beside her, Benny and Annie bobbing between them.

"Nora," he said, barely above a whisper. "What do we do when this is over?"

Nora, a few seconds later

Why did he have to ruin this moment?

Because he knew, just as well as she did. This was their only chance to talk about what had to happen. And he was right.

"I hate it, but ..." That was all she could get out.

He met her eyes. "I do, too, Nora. It's horrible. I don't even want to think how much it's going to hurt Leanne."

It would break Greg's heart, too. Wouldn't it?

He loved her. He'd never said the words. She suspected he was waiting for her to say them first. How could he have known she never would? *She* hadn't known it herself, not until she saw Daniel across the atrium a few nights ago.

"It's going to be just as bad with Greg."

What would he do? Would he scream, or cry or just take it in quietly and walk away to collect himself?

He'd shown a flash of jealousy in Charleston, when she'd crossed paths with Daniel at the market. Just a flash, but that was more than she'd ever seen from him. Then again, she'd never given him any cause to feel jealous—until this cruise.

Which only showed how much she didn't know about him. And how much of herself she'd kept hidden from him.

Somewhere deep down, she must have always known: Greg wasn't the man she could trust with her whole heart. There'd only ever been one man, and she'd handed him her heart—all of it—in a dorm room nine years ago.

"We have to tell them," Daniel said quietly, "no matter how hard it is."

Annie was nuzzling up against him again. Of course she was. Even the dolphins knew they belonged together.

"When? There are still four more days after today."

And four more nights.

If she told Greg this afternoon, he wouldn't want to spend another minute with her. She wouldn't, in his place. It wasn't like they could switch cabins, or hop off the ship and drive home separately.

Daniel nodded; he must have thought the same thing. "It would be—I don't even know a word for how awful it would be, making Leanne stay in the cabin with me for four more days after I tell her it's over."

She chuckled, not that there was anything funny about any of this. "If this was a movie, you'd switch cabins with Greg, and the Captain would perform a double wedding on the last night of the cruise."

He smiled, but there was no humor in it. "Yeah. I could see that. But—there's not going to be any wedding at all."

No, there couldn't be. She loved Daniel with all her heart. But they couldn't jump into a relationship after this. How could they?

"Nothing good could come of it," she said. "It would be poisoned from the start."

She ran her hand along Benny's back, in hopes he'd somehow pass on some dolphin wisdom. "But that still leaves the question—when do we tell them? If we don't tell them today, then, what? We keep lying to them for four more days?"

He was quiet for a long time. Then he paddled the last couple of feet over to her, and wrapped his arms around her. She melted into him; nothing bad could happen with him holding her.

"Maybe—if we can do it—we make it like that last night before the semester ended." The night they'd broken up. "You said you wanted one last memory. Maybe we can give them that. Four days instead of a couple of hours." He squeezed her tight, and she could feel *everything*—his love for her, but also his anxiety, his fears. And his sadness. "We owe them that much."

She squeezed him back, and then she kissed him. She meant it to be just a momentary brush of her lips against his, but that was impossible for both of them.

When she finally pulled away, she whispered, "We can do it. You're right, we owe them."

She rested her head against his chest. She felt the necklace against her cheek, and she heard his heartbeat, strong and steady. He made anything seem possible. "Four days, and then we tell them, and then ..."

"And then we go our separate ways," he said. "And maybe—if we can ever forgive ourselves, we can keep our promise."

Maybe three and a half more years would be long enough.

Chapter 39

Daniel, November 11

Last night had been, without question, the worst one of Daniel's life.

Worse than the night in the hospital after he broke his arm when he was nine years old, and the painkillers had stopped working and he couldn't even cry because Dad had told him to "be tough."

Worse than the drive back from the movie theater after he hadn't slept with Peggy, sitting in the passenger seat while she wouldn't look at him and he imagined every insult he'd hear from the guys at school if they ever found out.

Worse than the night Nora closed the door behind her and never came back.

It was the worst because Leanne had no idea what was in his heart. Because she'd believed him yesterday when he told her he was just overwhelmed by the Dolphin Experience, and it was hard to put into words how he felt. And because that was completely true and completely dishonest at the same time.

How could he do this for another three days? Or even three hours? He already felt nauseous; how much worse would he be when it was finally time to tell her the truth?

The ship was docked this morning in Nassau, and they hadn't scheduled an excursion. Leanne wanted to just walk around the town. It would just be them, with no distractions, no group around them, nothing to concentrate on except each other.

She was already dressed, in an orange sundress that looked fantastic on her. And she was just radiating excitement. "It's supposed to be beautiful," she said. "And everyone says the shopping is great—tons of bargains." She took his hand and opened the cabin door. "And I get you all to myself, all day. How lucky can a girl be?"

He had to calm down, get control of himself. One conversation at a time. One hour at a time. One minute at a time. He could do that. He could try to be the man she thought he'd been all along, just a little bit longer.

Nora, a little later

Last night had been horrible.

Nora already felt guilty enough, but Greg made it a thousand times worse with his repeated apologies for backing out of the Dolphin Experience.

She'd almost laughed at one point, because he actually should have been sorry—but he had no way to know why. If he hadn't backed out, there would only have been one space left in her group rather than two. And when Daniel had walked up to the edge of the water, without Leanne, and seen her there holding hands with Greg, he'd have let the brunette in the red swimsuit have his place.

She wouldn't have shared that time with Daniel, and maybe—just maybe, if nothing else happened to screw up their system of notes—they'd have both been able to avoid each other the rest of the cruise. Both of them might have been able to salvage their relationships. Or at least keep them going past the last day of the cruise and, if they still had to end, it would have been cleaner and easier.

"Nora?" She looked up from her thoughts, and her omelet, to catch Greg's eye. She noticed her fork was midway between the plate and her mouth; how long had it been there, frozen in midair?

They were at a table by themselves in the Main Dining Room; she'd have preferred one of the big circular tables with strangers to talk to and keep her from getting lost in her thoughts, but Greg—again, he couldn't know—had picked a table for two.

"Sorry. I was just—you know I get lost sometimes."

He was about to apologize yet again. It had to stop. And she had to stop rationalizing her own choices. She had no right to blame her cowardice, or how little she knew her own heart, on him.

"Greg, please. You didn't do anything wrong yesterday. Let's just concentrate on today. We'll finish breakfast, go back to the room and freshen up, and then it'll be time to go ashore and do the pirate ship thing."

That had been his choice. It sounded silly, but fun. Ridiculous costumes, swordfights and plenty of "Arrgs!" and "Ahoy, mateys!" and "You scurvy dogs!"

Considering what she was going to do to him in a couple of days, he deserved all the silliness and fun and scurvy dogs she could give him today.

♥ ♥ ♥

Daniel, shortly after lunch

They'd been in a dozen shops already, or at least Daniel's body had, and he was carrying the bags to prove it. His mind, however, was a couple of miles away, picturing what Nora was doing on the pirate ship adventure she and her boyfriend had chosen for today.

Leanne was starting to notice. "You have to have an opinion, Daniel!" She didn't manage to keep the impatience out of her voice. "Blue or red?" He blinked, tried to clear his thoughts and focus on what she was asking.

"Right, sorry." Leanne was holding up a red blouse in one hand and a blue one in the other. Which one did she want him to pick? She looked good in both colors—not that he'd ever see her wearing whichever one she picked out.

Back when they'd been together, and he'd been in a store with Nora, he'd never hesitated. If she asked him what he liked, he told her what he actually thought.

"Daniel!"

"The blue one. I think it goes better with those jeans you love to wear." That wasn't so difficult, was it? He had to keep focusing on her, that was all. Not Nora, and not what he'd have to tell her the last night of the cruise.

It was the right answer; she forgot her impatience and leaned in to give him a quick kiss. "Thank you. I know this is boring for you."

"It's not. I guess I'm still feeling a little off, that's all." That had been his excuse for going to sleep early last night, and shying away from her touch when she climbed into the bed with him. He'd blamed it on too much sun, and too much excitement with the dolphins and the salmon at dinner not tasting quite right.

"We'll find someplace to sit down, get you some water and a nice, safe snack," she said. Always the nurse, always looking out for him.

He followed Leanne out of the shop and onto the cobblestoned side street. The sun hit him full-force; it wasn't just a convenient lie, it actually was bothering him. He'd probably been outdoors more during the five days and change of this cruise than he had in the last year.

"I thought I saw a café a little while ago," he said. Four shops and five hundred dollars ago, but Leanne deserved it. Even if he wasn't going to break her heart in a couple of days, she'd have deserved it anyway.

They started off in the direction Daniel thought he remembered seeing the café, but they only got a few steps. "Can you help a fella down on his luck?"

The luckless man sounded American, and Daniel guessed he was in his thirties, although he'd always been terrible with that. The man wore ratty pants, and a shirt that looked—and smelled— like it could have stood up and walked away by itself. He took an involuntary step backwards, but Leanne didn't. Of course she didn't; at the hospital, she saw—and smelled—worse every day.

Daniel did his best to hold his breath, and stepped in front of Leanne, handing the bags from his left hand off to her. It was an automatic response, and he'd probably have laughed about it if he'd been in a better frame of mind. She was almost certainly better equipped to defend herself than he was; she'd told him all about the self-defense class all the nurses at the hospital had to take, which had sounded very thorough. And he knew she carried pepper spray in her purse.

He stood in front of her anyway. "I don't think we can help you," he told the man.

"Don't be like that. I just want to get back to Florida. Been saving up, but times are hard down here."

No. He knew a scam when he heard one. He wasn't a New York City boy for nothing. But before he could say anything, he felt

Leanne's hand on his back and heard her—it was almost like a growl; there was no other way to describe it.

"Back off!" It came out sharp and piercing, loud enough to hurt his ears. But it wasn't directed at the man in front of him.

Then he heard footsteps behind him—fast, retreating—and realized what she already knew. The first guy wasn't a beggar. He was bait. He wasn't really asking for money, he was just a distraction so the guy behind him—the one Leanne had just scared off—could pick his pocket or grab her purse. How had he not realized that? How had he let himself get so lost in thought that he forgot basic rules of safety? How—God, he was doing it again, right now!

"We can't help you," Daniel said, surprising himself with the venom he heard in his voice. But it was satisfying to let out some of the horrible churning feelings he'd been holding inside. "Leave us alone or we go to the police." That, combined with his accomplice running for the hills, got the smelly "Florida" man out of their way.

"Maybe we should forget the café and go back to the ship," Daniel said, once they were alone again.

Leanne nodded her agreement. She didn't seem disappointed, even though she probably would have preferred another couple of hours of shopping. "Yeah. I was having a good time, but it's kind of ruined now."

Not as ruined as it was going to be, unfortunately.

Nora, around the same time

It turned out that going to see *The Princess Bride* seven times the fall of her senior year of high school hadn't been a huge waste of time and money, like her father and all her friends said it was.

Thanks to her memories of the movie, Nora was the best fake swordfighter of anyone on their tour group. She had just "defeated" Blackbeard, and he handed her his hat. She waved it in the air, then put it on her head. Blackbeard shouted out, "All hail Nora the Blue, Queen of the Caribbean!" Nora the Blue didn't sound all that intimidating, but she'd had to think of something on the spur of the moment, and her blouse *was* blue.

A second later, everyone else—the rest of her tour group, and all the actors playing Blackbeard's crew, echoed it, and she took the hat back off and gave them a deep bow.

She probably should have curtsied, but she'd never learned how to do that properly. Besides, a pirate Queen could do whatever she wanted, right?

The only person on the deck of the ship who hadn't shouted out their allegiance to her was Greg. He hadn't enjoyed this at all—and it had been his choice. She'd tried to encourage him to challenge Blackbeard, but he wouldn't do it. He'd stayed quiet, at the back of their group, the whole time.

"I'll need the hat back, my Queen," Blackbeard said to her as the tour group headed belowdecks to leave the ship. "They'll give you a replica outside." He grinned at her. "These costumes are more expensive than you'd think."

She didn't want the poor guy to get in trouble—losing part of his costume might earn him a walk off the plank. So she handed the hat back to him, and jogged off to catch up with Greg.

He was already back on the dock. "Here, they gave me this for you." He handed her the replica hat she'd been promised, and she put it on.

"I think I'll wear it the rest of the day. You think the Captain would let me on the bridge, since I'm Queen and everything now?"

Greg gave her a half-hearted chuckle. "Probably not," he said.

Why was he so—whatever he was right now? Did he already somehow know what she was going to tell him before they got back to Baltimore? She wanted to give him a few more good days before that, but that didn't seem likely. "Greg, what's wrong? Are you not feeling well?"

He shook his head as they headed into town. They hadn't discussed what they'd do after the pirate adventure; they'd just started walking without any particular direction in mind. "I'm sorry," he said. "I didn't expect—that's not what I thought it was going to be. I wasn't prepared for audience participation."

That was fair, she supposed. But she hadn't been prepared for it either, and now she was a pirate Queen with a hat and everything. Daniel might have held back, too—for the first five minutes, but he would have let her drag him into things, and by the end he would have had as much fun as she had. They'd have been King and Queen of the Caribbean.

No. She'd promised herself she wouldn't do this. It wasn't fair to Greg. He didn't deserve criticism just because he enjoyed different things, or because he didn't roll with surprises as quickly as she did.

And he also didn't deserve her hamming it up and becoming the center of attention when he was obviously uncomfortable. What kind of rotten person did that to someone they were supposed to care about?

"I understand," she told him, putting an arm around him. "I'm sorry you didn't enjoy it. I guess I should have read the brochure more closely. Now we know for next time."

Not that there would be a next time. Lightning should have come out of the clear blue sky and struck her down for that comment. But it didn't, and she took a deep breath and went on. "You want to head back to the ship? We've still got that third fancy meal to use." They were on the cobblestoned streets of the oldest part of Nassau now, on the main shopping street. "You know what? Let's go in there first," she pointed to a leather goods shop across the street. "I'll buy you whatever you want."

He didn't say yes, but he let her steer him into the shop, and fifteen minutes later they emerged with a new wallet for him.

She'd given Daniel the most beautiful necklace, something she had taken weeks to design, and that she helped make with her own hands. Greg got a leather—hopefully it was real leather—wallet he could probably have bought at J.C. Penney's for half the price.

Maybe he wouldn't be heartbroken at all when she told him. Maybe he'd be lucky to be rid of her.

Chapter 40

**THE LAST THREE DAYS OF THE CRUISE—
ABOARD EMPRESS OF THE SEAS**

Daniel, November 12

Daniel was alone in the cabin. He hadn't listened to Leanne when they got back to the ship yesterday, and he was paying for it now.

They'd gone up to the pool deck and spent the afternoon alternately sunbathing and splashing around in the main swimming pool when they returned from Nassau.

"You can get sunburned even when you're in the water," she'd warned him. He knew she was right, but he'd never liked how goopy sunscreen felt, so he went without, figuring an hour wouldn't be enough to cause any real harm.

They'd stayed up there for four hours, and he'd been miserable at dinner—red and sore and itchy. It was worse now that he was starting to peel.

Leanne had gone up to the shops on deck five and bought lotion for him, and three bottles of water. And she hadn't once said *I told you so.*

She offered to stay with him all day, but he put his foot down. "You made me go swimming with the dolphins when you couldn't.

I'm not letting you stay inside when you could go to the beach today. It's the last port visit, please go and enjoy yourself."

She finally gave in, and right now she was—he wasn't sure exactly what she'd be doing on Royal Caribbean's private island. There was parasailing, snorkeling, jet-skis you could rent or just hanging out on the beach.

Maybe the snorkeling. That's what they'd planned to do two days ago, it made sense she'd try to do it again.

He hoped so, and that she'd get to see—he had no idea. Whatever colorful fish and undersea sights there were, he hoped she was having an amazing time enjoying them all.

She deserved it. And he absolutely deserved everything he was feeling now.

Nora, the same time

Nora stepped onto the white sand, expecting to see Daniel at any moment. There'd been nothing from "Diane" on the note board last night, or this morning. But Greg wanted a quiet day on the beach, and there was no logical argument she could make against it, so all she could do was keep her eyes open, her wits about her, and hope for the best.

It was strange, though. Beyond strange.

Daniel had never, ever failed to do what he said he would. Unless something had happened to him. He could be sick, stuck in his room or even down in the sickbay. There was no other explanation.

And if that was true, then she didn't have anything to worry about. Except for finding a pair of unoccupied beach chairs; it looked like half the passengers aboard ship had the same idea Greg did.

"Over there," he said, pointing down closer to the beach, where there were two free chairs—next to one that was folded out and occupied by a blonde woman laying out on her stomach. Nora had seen the back of that blonde head before.

In the hot tub, with Daniel. And the next day, in Charleston.

But Greg was already heading her way, and there was nothing she could do except follow him.

He got within a couple of steps, and his shadow fell over her. She didn't turn over, she just said, barely below a shout, "I told you, my boyfriend is coming back in a minute! Do I need to get security?"

Nora understood the situation instantly. She wasn't actually waiting for Daniel; there'd be a towel on the chair next to her if she was. But she didn't want a single guy to claim the chair and spend an hour hitting on her, and a dozen single guys had probably already tried that this morning. She must have thought—totally reasonably—that Greg was just another one.

"No, I didn't mean anything!" Greg sounded almost panicked. She would have to step in.

"He didn't. He's my boyfriend. We were just looking for two empty chairs together," Nora said, in her calmest voice.

"Oh! I'm so sorry," the woman said—Leanne, there was no doubt once she sat up to face them. "I had no idea there were so many sleazy guys on this cruise. But I'm not really waiting for my boyfriend, he's back on the ship. He's not feeling well, but he insisted I enjoy the beach without him."

Of course Daniel would.

She reached out a hand. What else could Nora do but shake it? "I'm Nora. And this is Greg. It's nice to meet you."

"Leanne. It really is too bad Daniel's not here. We haven't made any couple friends on the cruise. My parents always end up meeting other couples when they go, and they try to keep in touch afterwards."

"I know what you mean," Greg said, sitting down on the chair farther away from Leanne. "We haven't met any other couples, either. Maybe on the next cruise."

Nora couldn't find her voice. What could she possibly say, anyway?

She felt her stomach churning, and a throbbing behind her temples.

Was meeting Leanne like this God's way of rubbing her nose in what she and Daniel were doing, the way that some people did to their dog when it pooped on the carpet?

Daniel, four hours later

After a few hours of sleep, and reapplying the skin lotion twice, Daniel was finally starting to feel a little better when the door opened and Leanne walked in.

She'd gotten plenty of sun, and she was smiling—almost giggling to herself. "I didn't go snorkeling, it was too crowded, so I just went to the beach, and swam for, I don't know, an hour? And I met the nicest couple. You would have loved them. From Boston. She's a writer for a science magazine, he's—something to do with physics, he got talking and he lost me right away with all the jargon. But they were *so* sweet. Maybe we'll run into them again before the cruise is over."

So much for feeling better. He wanted to go into the bathroom and vomit, and it had nothing to do with his sunburn.

It had to be Nora and Greg that she'd met.

It was his own fault for getting himself in such a bad state yesterday. Even if he could have gotten to the note board this morning, it wouldn't have mattered, because how could he have told Leanne what to do or not do on her own?

And now she'd met Nora—and Leanne had no idea that she was talking to the woman his heart truly belonged to.

The woman he'd be breaking up with her over.

He couldn't wait any longer. This couldn't continue for three more nights.

He could sleep in the solarium until the end of the cruise. She could smash the window and throw all his clothes into the sea; it was no less than he deserved. But he couldn't lie to her anymore. He had to tell her now.

"Leanne."

She caught his tone, and her smile faded. She couldn't know what was coming, only that it was serious.

"Daniel, what's wrong? Are you still sick? I thought you looked better, but I can take you down to the sickbay if you want."

He shook his head. "Leanne, please. This is going to be really hard. Can you sit with me?"

She dropped her purse and came over to the bed. "I'm worried, Daniel. You're scaring me."

"I'm not sick. I'm—I don't even know where to start with this." Yes, he did.

He reached into his shirt, pulled out the necklace. "You never asked me about this."

She stared at it, then back up at him, confusion in her eyes.

"What does your necklace have to do with anything?"

There was no way to make this easier. "I—I'm so sorry, Leanne. I still love—I love the woman who gave it to me. I never stopped.

I thought I was over her. It's been years—we broke up my sophomore year."

She counted on her fingers. "That's eight years ago." The confusion in her eyes was gone; there was pain there, and fire. "What are you telling me?"

"You're right. It was eight years. And in all that time, I had one girlfriend for a few weeks, and then you. You're the only woman I've *been with* since her. And after we were together that first time, I had to keep telling myself I wasn't cheating on her. I thought I believed it. I really did. Bianca's been after me forever to date someone, to try again, and she introduced us, and you were so sweet. So smart. Just—you're so great, and I thought maybe it really was time."

"And it's not." The pain won out over her anger; he saw the tears start to fall, and felt them on his own face, too.

"She gave me the necklace. Two years after we broke up. The day I graduated. She had it made specially. You know my birthstone is aquamarine. And hers is sapphire. And I haven't taken it off since she put it around my neck."

She almost laughed through her tears. "If I wasn't the one getting dumped, I'd think it was romantic. But—if you knew you weren't over her, why ..." She did laugh now, without any humor at all. "Because she's on the ship. That's why you're telling me now. Because...I spent this morning talking to her, didn't I?" He nodded. "How long have you known she was onboard?"

"Since the first night."

"You bastard!" Her hand flew at his face, but it stopped an inch away. "You—you've been seeing her this whole time. And you didn't tell me." Why did she stop herself from hitting him? "Did you—did you—were you *with her*?"

"No." At least he could say that much for himself. "I had no idea she'd be on the cruise. I saw her the first night. She was across the atrium, and we saw each other, and—we kissed. We kissed, and then we talked, and we told ourselves we'd avoid each other and I'd focus on you and she'd focus on Greg and we'd be adults."

"But you didn't."

"It was in Charleston. She bumped into us. And I decided to find her that night, to try and come up with some kind of plan so it wouldn't happen again. I knew she'd be at karaoke. We decided to leave notes for each other on the note board, so we'd know where not to be the next day. It worked for Florida, and that night. But then our snorkeling got cancelled the next day ..."

He told her the rest, answering every question she had, holding nothing back.

All she had to say when he was done was, "This is why you never told me you loved me."

"I wish I could have. If I'd never met Nora, and we met like we did back in January, I probably would have asked you to marry me by now. If she hadn't been on this cruise, I don't know—maybe a few more months would have been enough to get there anyway."

She was silent for a long time after that.

"I should hate you. I wish I could." Daniel almost wished she did, too. It would be easier, in a way, if she did. "But you're—I've never met anyone like you. I don't know anybody who would wear that necklace all these years like you did."

"I had to. I never wanted to forget her. Or—or what she taught me. She's the one who taught me I deserved to be loved."

"But she left out the part about letting anybody else love you." She was almost smiling. Almost. "I can't blame her. I would have left that out, too." The almost-smile disappeared. "I'm still—I don't even know what I feel. I don't know—I think an hour from now, or at three in the morning, or God knows when—I'm going to want to punch you. Or set your clothes on fire. Or buy you a rabbit so I can boil it on the stove." She sighed. "I don't know. I can't exactly throw you out of the cabin, even though I probably should."

At least he had an answer for that. "I can go to the solarium tonight. Sleep there the rest of the cruise. I probably should have been there all along, from the moment I saw Nora. Anyway, it's quiet at night there."

"No." She shook her head. She looked as surprised as he did at her words. "But you can damn well sleep on the sofa."

Nora, an hour later

Nora didn't know how she made it through dinner. She was barely holding her emotions in; from minute to minute, she didn't know if she wanted to scream, or cry or a hundred other things.

Greg could tell—it was impossible not to notice—but he didn't try to guess what was going on. He just spent the whole meal quietly comforting her, reassuring her that everything was fine, that she'd feel better tomorrow.

All that did was make her feel worse.

Now they were back in the cabin, and he led her to the bed, sat down next to her. He took her hands in his. "Nora, I don't know what's the matter. But you can tell me anything, don't you know that by now? If it's something I did, you can say it. I want to make it right."

She didn't say anything. He was just sitting there, staring hard at her, his hands shaking.

"I think I know," he said, finally. "You've been waiting for me. Because I haven't said it yet. I don't even know why not. But I thought you could tell anyway. Nora, I love ..."

She heard herself shrieking, and felt her eyes burning and the tears streaming down her cheeks like a flood. She pulled her hands back from him so violently that he jumped away from her.

"No! You can't! Because I don't love you!" She couldn't hold the words in anymore. "I love *him*! Daniel! I always have, I never stopped, not for a minute, from the day we met! And I hate this! I hate—it's not right, you don't deserve this! I thought I could get over him and love someone else like—like a normal person, like everybody else does, they get over their first love and they can be with other people, they can love other people..."

Her voice failed. She could barely see through her tears, but Greg was on the sofa now. She couldn't tell if he was angry or scared or horrified or, hell, maybe all of them at once.

"Nora, if this is—I don't know, some kind of joke—I know I don't always get your sense of humor ..." His voice was shaky, barely controlled.

She took a deep breath, then another, trying to gather herself. It didn't really work, but she had to continue anyway, she owed him the whole truth. She got up, went over to the little desk and fished into her purse. "Here, see this?" She held up the pen. "He gave this to me. Right before he graduated, so I'd always know he was rooting for me. So I'd never forget him. And I never did. No matter how much I tried. Not even after you asked me out, and we started going together seriously."

He grunted. "You said Daniel. That's who the woman at the beach said, too. Is that him? Is he on this ship right now?" He wasn't looking at her; he was staring at the door now. As though he was ready to walk right out of the cabin and go looking for Daniel.

"Yes. He's probably telling her about me right now. We didn't know before the cruise. Neither of us had any idea we'd see each other. It was—I don't know. A big, fat cosmic joke on us."

His face was reddening, and his hands were balled up into fists. "It's not funny, Nora."

Whatever self-control she had failed again. "You think I don't know that? You think I'm enjoying this? I tried so hard! I wanted this to work! I wanted to love you, I wish I could have! This isn't who I want to be, a liar and a cheater and every other horrible thing you want to call me right now." She closed her eyes, forced her voice down somehow. "I'm not that. I'm not her. I haven't been her in *years*, because of Daniel. Because he taught me—he taught me how I deserve to be loved."

Greg didn't answer right away, and when he finally did speak, there was nothing but bitterness there. "And he taught you that only he could love you that way."

Nora shook her head. "No. That's all me. I guess—I think I never believed anybody but him could see me that way. And that's not fair to you. None of this is. But—I swear to you, I never meant for any of this to happen. I really thought it could be different. It's been so long, it's been years and I thought—I hoped it was time. And it's just ... not. Because he's still got my heart. And I have his, and I don't think that's ever going to change."

He was silent for a while again. "I don't know what I'm supposed to say now. I—I believe you. But that doesn't make anything any better. I—I can't keep talking about this now."

Neither could she. "I know. I'll go. I can stay in the solarium tonight, and tomorrow—we can figure out tomorrow, tomorrow."

She got up again, grabbed her purse and her soft, faded T-shirt and her sweatpants, and she walked out the door without another word. She pulled it closed behind her, and took the sign and the magnets off the door. Greg didn't need to see them the next time he left the cabin. She'd hurt him more than enough already.

♡ 🖤 ♡

Daniel, November 13, five o'clock in the morning

Leanne was gently snoring; she'd finally fallen asleep around midnight. It had taken Daniel another hour to fall into a restless, uncomfortable sleep that had nothing to do with the sofa.

Moving as slowly and quietly as he could, he put his shoes on and tiptoed out the door, closing it gently behind him.

If he knew Nora at all, she would have told Greg the truth last night. She wouldn't have been able to stop herself after meeting Leanne. And if he threw her out afterwards, or she felt too guilty to sleep on the sofa in her cabin, she would have headed to the same place he'd thought about.

The lights were dim in the corridors, and there were no other passengers in the elevator. It was eerily quiet as he made his way up to the solarium.

It was deserted when the automatic door slid open for him, except for one crew member mopping the floor over in the far corner, near the entrance to the spa.

And one other person—a woman—stretched out on a pool chair near the snack bar, under a bunch of towels serving as a makeshift blanket.

He walked up to her quietly, not wanting to startle her.

She was already awake, staring up at the pre-dawn sky through the glass ceiling.

"Daniel. I knew you'd come."

He pulled a chair over, sat down next to her. "I'm sorry. I—I don't know what else to say."

He gently pulled the topmost towel off of her and wiped the tears from her face.

"You told Leanne?" He nodded. "And she didn't throw you out?"

"I offered to go. Maybe I should have just walked out. But she told me to stay and sleep on the sofa." She stared up at him, and he saw the question in her eyes. "It's over between us. She just doesn't hate me, that's all."

"I don't think Greg's there yet. I'm not sure he's ever going to be."

Daniel wasn't sure he would be in Greg's place. "I'm sorry." It didn't sound any better the second time he said it. "I keep trying to think of something that'll make all of this better, and ..."

"There's nothing to say." She was holding his hands in hers. When had that happened? "Just sit here with me. Hold me. Let me hold you."

So he did.

Nora, November 14, ten o'clock at night

"Last night on board," Daniel said quietly. "This is it." They were in the solarium again, each of them on their own pool chair, laying out and looking up at the stars.

"Back to real life tomorrow," Nora agreed. It was hard to believe she'd be in her own bed, under Boston skies, twenty-four hours from now.

Daniel was quiet for a while. "It's going to be hard tomorrow morning. I talked to Leanne earlier. When we get off the ship, I'll drive her to the airport and buy her a first-class ticket to Charlotte. She argued with me, but I insisted. And I'll call Bianca to pick her up at the airport there."

Of course he insisted. She wouldn't expect anything less from him. "Are you sure she won't feel weird seeing your cousin?"

"Leanne needs somebody to yell at. And then Bianca can yell at me afterwards." He said it with dead seriousness, almost like it had already happened and he was just retelling it.

She hadn't talked to Greg about arrangements for tomorrow. Or anything else. They'd driven down to Baltimore in her car. "I should do that, too. Not the yelling part. The plane ticket. He's not going to want to drive back with me." He probably wouldn't let her buy the ticket for him, though. His pride wouldn't allow it.

That was a worry for tomorrow morning, though.

Daniel was already ahead of her. He reached over and took her hand. "Let's not think about anything now. I just want to be with you. Just us and the stars." Like their first date, nine years ago, when he'd stopped in the middle of the quad to point out constellations to her.

"I like that," she said. She closed her eyes, holding tightly to his hand, not thinking about tomorrow or the future afterwards or anything at all except for him.

If this is all they had, maybe it was enough. His hand in hers, and the stars looking down on them.

And the promise, that still had three and a half years left to come true.

Chapter 41

AFTER THE CRUISE—CHARLOTTE, NC/BOSTON, MA

Daniel, November 22

Daniel sat in his kitchen, staring out the window at nothing in particular.

One week ago, he'd walked off the ship and said goodbye to Nora. There had been no declarations, no promises, no plans.

Just one final kiss and a lingering look that said everything and nothing at the same time.

Then he'd met Leanne at the baggage claim and he drove her to the airport. He didn't say a word to her. She didn't,

Nora, the same time

Nora sat in her kitchen, staring out the window at nothing in particular.

One week ago, she'd walked off the ship and said goodbye to Daniel. There had been no declarations, no promises, no plans.

Just one final kiss and a lingering look that she'd needed all her strength to break away from.

Then she'd met Greg at the baggage claim and she drove him to the airport. She didn't say a word the whole way. He either, until he parked and unlocked the car, and she'd just sat there, staring hard at him.

"I wish I could hate you," she'd said after a while. "That would be so much easier than—whatever the hell I'm feeling now." He thought that was all, but after a moment she'd gone on. "I didn't know I only had a part of your heart. I still don't know how much you gave me. Fifty percent? Sixty?"

He didn't answer. He honestly didn't know, and even if he did, he was sure she wouldn't want to hear it.

"You know what sucks about all this?" He didn't. "Half of you, or sixty percent, or however much I had, was still way better than anybody else I've ever dated. But I deserve a hundred percent of somebody. And I wish to hell you would've figured out six months ago that you couldn't give a hundred percent of yourself to me. You owed me that."

didn't, either, until she parked and unlocked the car, and he'd just sat there, staring at her.

"I should hate you," he'd said after a while. "It'd be so much simpler and—I don't know—cleaner than how I'm feeling now." She thought that was all, but after a moment he'd gone on. "I didn't know your heart was with him the whole time. Did I ever have any of it? I mean, for real?"

She didn't answer. She honestly didn't know, and even if she did, she was sure he wouldn't want to hear it.

"You know what sucks the most?" She didn't. "Just a piece of your heart was more than I ever had with anybody else. But I deserve somebody's whole heart. And I wish to hell you would've figured out six months ago that you couldn't give it to me. You owed me that."

She'd spoken for the first and only time then. "I didn't know. I swear to you, if I knew

He'd spoken for the first and only time then. "I didn't know. I swear to you, if I knew that, I never would've gone out with you in the first place."

She'd sat there in the passenger seat a while longer. "I believe you. And that sucks most of all."

Those were the last words either of them spoke to each other.

That night, when he finally got home, he'd called Bianca and told her a very abbreviated version of what had happened. She'd been understanding and kindly, exactly what he expected from her, and exactly what he didn't deserve.

He hadn't just broken Leanne's heart. He'd also blown up Nora's relationship, and the fact that she was equally guilty didn't absolve him of anything. There were four broken hearts because for nine months he hadn't been honest with himself.

He didn't know if, or when, Leanne would be able to start

that, I never would've said yes when you asked me out in the first place."

He'd sat there in the passenger seat a while longer. "I believe you. And that sucks most of all."

Those were the last words either of them spoke to each other.

That night, when she finally got home, she'd called Rachel and told her an abbreviated— but not sanitized—version of what had happened. Her aunt had been understanding and supportive, exactly what Nora expected from her, and exactly what she didn't deserve.

She hadn't just broken Greg's heart. She'd also destroyed Daniel's relationship, and the fact that he was equally guilty didn't absolve her of anything. There were four broken hearts because for months she hadn't been honest with herself.

She didn't know if, or when, Greg would be able to put his heart back together. Or Leanne. Or Daniel.

to put her heart back together. Or Greg. Or Nora.

He did know for certain that he couldn't see any way to put his own back together.

She did know that she couldn't imagine any way to put her own heart back together again.

Part 6

1999

Chapter 42

MARCH 1999—BOSTON, MA/CHARLOTTE, NC

Nora, March 16

March 16. Daniel's birthday.

She remembered ten years ago. It would have been his nineteenth—no, twentieth. Of course, twentieth. She knew that.

How could she have forgotten, even for a moment?

She wondered what he was doing today, his thirtieth birthday. Was he still at that company—Piedmont Integrated Systems? Still in Charlotte? Still single? Still thinking of her?

She had his number. She could call. She could text. She could go to the drugstore around the corner, pick up a belated birthday card and stick it in the mail, signed with "Thinking of you" or "Love, Nora" or something else that wouldn't actually mean anything.

She could call the company travel agency, and ask them to book a ticket to Charlotte for the next available flight, throw together a bag, and then somehow figure out where in the city he lived, exactly. There wasn't anything preventing her. She had plenty of available credit on her AmEx, she had a ton of vacation time and her boss probably wouldn't even ask what the sudden rush was.

She could surprise him.

Just like she had ten years ago. She even had that dress somewhere in the back of the closet. She'd never thrown it away; how could she? And it probably even still sort-of fit.

There wasn't a reason in the world not to do it.

There still wasn't a reason when her neck cracked, and she yelped in pain and saw the disgusting little pool of drool on her keyboard and realized she'd been sitting here staring at a blank screen for going on two hours.

In the end, she didn't even send the belated birthday card.

Daniel, March 16

Daniel sat at his desk, his eyes staring vacantly at his monitor but all his attention focused on a night exactly ten years ago. He'd been sitting in a swivel desk chair then, too, when she'd knocked on his door and walked into his dorm room. She'd been buttoned up in a coat, which had seemed weird, it was an abnormally warm spring that year.

And then she'd unbuttoned it, and he saw the dress. And his heart stopped.

But far more than the dress had been Nora's smile. There'd been love in it, and joy, and a hundred other things. But also there'd been a promise—that by the time the night was done, by the time she'd finished with him, he wouldn't be able to remember his own name...

"What the hell!" The words just came out; somebody had—what? They grabbed his chair, turned him around. And there was the man who'd done it. Mr. Dellaplane. His boss. "Sorry! Uh—I was just..."

He felt heat in his cheeks, and not just there. He knew he must be bright red. "It's fine," his boss said, with the tiniest hint of a smile.

No, it really wasn't. "I was just ..." He had no idea why he was explaining himself, when Mr. Dellaplane was going to let it pass. But he kept on talking anyway. "Just remembering. The best birthday gift I ever got."

His boss clapped him on the shoulder. "And the girl who gave it to you."

There was no point denying it. "Not that I'll ever see her again," he answered, proud that he kept most of the bitterness out of his voice at that thought.

"We're all professionals here, Daniel—but we're all people, too," his boss said, meeting his eyes now. "So you've got the same problem everybody else does. You think you're the only one who ever hurt the way you're hurting." Daniel started to protest, but his boss waved him off. "And you're right. You *are* the only one who ever hurt exactly that way. But so is everybody else."

And that's when, for the first time in the ten months he'd reported to Mr. Dellaplane, he noticed the slightly discolored area at the base of the man's left ring finger. Then he remembered something else; there were a dozen photos of a young boy and girl in his boss' office, but not a single picture of a woman who could have been their mother.

His sudden revelation must have shown on his face, because Mr. Dellaplane shook his head. "I just wanted you to know you're not alone, that's all. And that I understand you had a—let's just call it a moment. We all do. Why'd you think I missed the cookout Fred put on for the Super Bowl?"

Now Daniel laughed. "I just thought you hated the Broncos."

"Well, of course I do, but—I was having a moment that that after-noon, too." He turned to leave Daniel's office. "If you want to bag on the lunch, I'll tell the team. I'll make up some excuse."

"No," Daniel said, and he meant it. "I appreciate it, but I'll pull myself together. Besides, if Brenda down in accounting doesn't get her sweet chili shrimp, we'll never hear the end of it. Just give me a couple of minutes, let me splash some cold water on my face, and I'll meet everybody in the lobby."

To his surprise, he managed to get through lunch, and even the rest of the workday without thinking about that night a decade ago. It wasn't until he got home that the moment came back—Nora's dress, Nora's smile.

Nora's everything.

Chapter 43

Daniel, March 26, lunchtime

Daniel was alone in the office. The rest of the team was out at Bakersfield Café for the weekly group lunch—or was it Baker's Square? Two years here, and he still got them confused. Whichever, they were probably just now arguing over the appetizer platter versus individual plates, because Jack had an allergy to pickles and even having three deep-fried dills on the other side of the platter was a threat to his life, and Kellyanne thought he was just being high maintenance.

This was quieter, and better, and maybe he could—finally!—figure out where the bad code that had been haunting his project was hiding. He'd already made decent progress in eliminating a dozen possibilities in the half hour they'd all been gone.

His cell buzzed. What was Bianca doing calling in the middle of a workday? It must be important—not that talking with Bianca was ever not important, even when neither of them had anything important to say. "Hey, Bee. How's my favorite cousin?"

There was a moment of hesitation on the line, and what sounded like, but surely couldn't be, a gasp of pain. "Not much,

Danny," she said, in nothing like her usual bright tone. "Just—can you do me a favor when you leave work? Can you run by the CVS and grab me—I don't even know. What do you get for food poisoning?" As she said it, there was another gasp, maybe even more like a groan.

Daniel wasn't sure which was more concerning—what he was hearing in her voice, or the fact that she was asking for a favor in the middle of the day. She never did that. He couldn't remember the last time Bee had actually asked for help, on anything. If she was now, then it was serious. And it couldn't wait until five-thirty.

He scribbled a note and taped it to Mr. Dellaplane's monitor— his boss was famous for overlooking emails, missing texts and losing voicemails, but he could hardly ignore an 8.5x11 sheet covering his screen. And then he was off.

Daniel, forty minutes later

He didn't have a key to his cousin's house; he'd been meaning to ask for one since he moved to Charlotte, and give her a key to his condo, just in case.

But there was an advantage to knowing someone, and loving them, from before you learned to walk. You got to know how their mind worked, and there was only one place Bee would hide an emergency spare key. And there it was, inside a little gray waterproof envelope taped underneath her mailbox.

He let himself in, along with the $120 worth of pills, capsules, powders, bottles and everything else that even vaguely seemed like it might be useful. She could have been wrong about food poisoning, so he had cold medicine, digestive remedies, and a couple of things the pharmacist said would be helpful against the flu.

But when he saw her propped up on the sofa, eyes barely focused and leaning against a stack of pillows as though she didn't think she could hold herself upright, he knew nothing he'd bought was going to be useful.

How he knew what he was seeing he couldn't say. Some instinct deep down, or some memory of a TV doctor show, maybe. Whatever it was, he was certain Bianca did not have food poisoning, or the flu. This was appendicitis.

"Bee, we're going to the emergency room right now. Where are your shoes?" She was wearing sweats, which she'd never normally leave the house in, but beggars couldn't be choosers. He didn't want to take her out barefoot, though.

"Why?" her voice was weak, weaker than he'd ever heard it. "It's just—just a bug or something. I don't wanna go!"

Daniel nearly grinned despite the situation. "Thirty-two year old women don't say 'wanna,' Bee. And you're going because you're really sick, and that's all there is to it. Now tell me where your shoes are, and then we'll go."

She tried to answer, but before any words came out, she yelped—high and sharp—and collapsed onto her side on the sofa. He ran to her, put an arm around her, but as he tried to sit her back up, she shrieked.

Now he was truly worried. Because the sound that just came from her wasn't something he thought a human could even make. He wasn't going to be able to get her out to his car.

Daniel grabbed his phone with one hand, squeezing Bianca's hand tightly with the other, as he dialed 911.

♥ ♥ ♥

Daniel, three hours later

He checked his watch again. Seven-thirty. Only two hours since they'd taken Bianca back to surgery. It felt like he'd been here in the waiting room all night. He'd called her parents, and his, and his sister, and then left a message for Mr. Dellaplane that he was going to be out tomorrow and likely the rest of the week, and then he'd had nothing to do but sit and think.

The thought that came to him wasn't about Leanne. Maybe it should have been; she was a nurse, after all. But this wasn't her hospital, or at least it hadn't been when they'd been dating.

No, it was a much older thought. Eleven years old. A memory. An argument with his parents, and his father's words afterwards.

"Because you haven't seen what happens when things get hard. When you can't pay the rent. When someone gets sick."

He'd taken those words to heart, and that had been the first seed of doubt, the first crack in the foundation he'd thought he was building with Nora back in college.

"You were wrong, Dad," he whispered to himself. There was no reproach or bitterness there. But there was pride. "It was hard today, but I stood up for Bee."

He held onto that for a while, sat with it, until he noticed the shadow looming over him. He looked up, into the tired but relaxed eyes of the surgeon he'd spoken to earlier tonight. How long had she been standing there? It didn't really matter.

"How is she?"

The woman put a hand on his shoulder, squeezed it. "She came through just fine. Your cousin is going to be all right. She's still in post-op, but she ought to be back in a recovery room in an hour or so, and you can see her then."

"Everything went well?" The doctor had just said so, hadn't she? But he needed to hear it again anyway.

"Perfectly." She squeezed his shoulder again, and this time it was more reassuring. "But I want you to know—she owes you her life. You got her here just in time. Her appendix was about ready to burst." Daniel felt his stomach lurch, and the doctor must have noticed. "I said *about ready*. We got it out, and she's going to be good as new before you know it."

He nodded. Of course Bee would be fine. It was a routine procedure, wasn't it? They probably did a dozen of them a day here. "Thank you. For everything."

The doctor sat down next to him, gave him a gentle smile. "It's what we do. She's lucky she has you."

"We're both lucky." How many times had Bee saved him over the years, even if it was just by sitting there on the other end of the phone and talking sense to him?

Now the doctor met his eyes, held them. "I can see that." She laughed, then continued. "But this is kind of a big deal. If you want my advice, give her a month or so until she's back to normal, and tell her she needs to take you out for a nice dinner to thank you. Have her take you to Shanna's Modern Grill downtown. Just opened last month. The lobster is amazing. You earned it tonight."

An hour later, he told a groggy Bianca that the doctor had ordered her to treat him to dinner once she was fully recovered. She wouldn't remember, and that was fine. He'd be happy to treat her instead, to lobster or anything else she wanted.

All she wanted then was to hold his hand as she fell back asleep, and he was happy to do that, and to fall asleep himself five minutes later, still holding her hand, still smiling. Still knowing that he stood up when he had to, when he hadn't known if he could before today.

♡ ♥ ♡

Daniel, March 28

Bianca was sitting up in the bed, the oxygen tube finally out of her nose, and for the first time since he'd come over to her house two days ago, the glint was back in her eyes. All the anesthetic and whatever other drugs they'd given her were out of her system, and his Bee was fully awake.

"God, it hurts, Danny!"

He squeezed her hand. "I know, Bee. I already asked the nurse. You're going to get Tylenol soon." She made a face. "Yeah. But they don't want to give you anything stronger if they can help it. You were pretty out of it, I think maybe they're right."

Bianca thought that over, shifting around in the bed trying to make herself less uncomfortable and not really succeeding. "I don't."

"Well, maybe this will make you feel better. They said as long as your levels—don't ask me, I have no idea which levels they mean—anyway, as long as they stay stable you can go home this afternoon."

And she'd have a surprise when she got there. He'd spent several hours making her place ready for her while she was sleeping off all the medications. She'd come home to a full fridge, clean sheets on the bed, all her laundry done and put away and that disgusting stain on the living room carpet—what the hell had it even been anyway?—gone.

"My mom called while you were gone. I think. Or maybe it was,"—she looked up at the TV mounted in the corner of the room, where a rerun of *Growing Pains* was playing—"Kirk Cameron's mom. It's all kind of fuzzy."

"If you couldn't tell the difference between Aunt Carla and Joanna Kerns, they must have had you on some insane painkillers. I'll call her back later and let her know how you're doing."

They lapsed into silence for a little while, holding hands and watching Kirk Cameron get up to whatever stupid scheme he was trying to put over on his parents. After the second commercial, or maybe the third, she gave his hand a hard squeeze.

"You saved my life, Danny. How did you know?" She closed her eyes, trying to recall something. "I remember—I told you to come when you got off work, but you came right away. How did you know?"

Daniel shook his head. Sometimes—not often, but every once in a while, she could be incredibly dense. "How long have we known each other, Bee? I have never heard you how you were on the phone. I was—you know what, I was about to say I was terrified, but I wasn't." It was only now that he realized there hadn't been fear, only purpose. "I didn't have time to be. I just had to get over to you, and that's all I could think about."

She pulled herself upright, and with a grunt and a groan she reached out to him. He held out his arms and gingerly embraced her. "I love you, Danny. I just wish *she* could have seen you in action, too."

His mind went back, just for a moment, to 1989, before finals week when Nora had been violently ill and he'd been unable to make her take better care of herself. Except that wasn't really true, was it? No one made Nora Langley do something she didn't want to do. Not then, not ever.

"Maybe. I don't know."

Daniel shook his head. That was garbage. He didn't lie to Bee. Never had, and not now. "Yes. I wish she could have, too. There's so much I wish. So much." And Bee was the only person in the whole world who truly understood that.

But this wasn't the time or the place. His cousin was the priority, not whatever he still felt for Nora. There would be time enough for his heart when she was home and recuperating properly. "Anyway, moving on. I called your boss and let her know what happened, and that you'll be out this week and next for sure." He gave her a mock—mostly mock—disapproving glare. "It took me an hour to find her number in that rat's nest you call a home office, by the way." And another two hours to make it presentable by his standards, but there was no need to say that.

Daniel, March 31

Daniel hadn't been back to his condo in four days, except for a quick trip yesterday to check the mail, dump the now-spoiled milk out of the fridge and grab a change of clothes before returning to Bianca's place.

Bee was recovering nicely, and not abusing her status as an invalid too much. She still slept a lot, and when she was awake in the daytime she mostly kept to herself so he could get a little work done on his laptop. She occasionally asked what exactly he was doing, and he tried gamely to explain, but it was hard to really make sense of it without taking an hour to give her the background to understand the specific task he happened to be working at.

"Next time, just say you're trying to keep the planes in the sky and the ATM's working when the New Year turns over." She giggled. "Anyway, I'd trust you with all that."

"Nothing's going to happen on January 1st. It's all a big panic over nothing," he said. He'd told his parents the same thing, and Lisa, and anyone else who would listen. He wasn't sure they believed him, but all he could do was tell them what he knew. And if they wanted to worry about something that wasn't real and that they couldn't do anything about anyway, even if it was, that was on them.

Bee patted the sofa, and he sat next to her. "Let's talk about something that is real, then. I've let it go all week, but it's time, Danny."

If it was anyone else, he'd have gotten right up off the sofa, maybe even walked out the door. But it wasn't anyone else. It was the one person who had the right to say anything to him, and he'd not just listen but believe.

No. There was one other person, besides Bee. And that's who his cousin wanted to talk about.

"I've always loved you, Danny. Always. And I've been thinking a lot this week." She shook her head. "Not like there's been much else I could do. I mean, aside from *Days of Our Lives*—did you know Marlena's still alive? I thought she died years ago."

"Bee."

"Yeah. Right. Anyway. I've been thinking a lot. And you probably know this, but I love you more than anybody else." She was looking at him, *into* him, the way only she—and Nora—ever could. "It's not like I sit here and keep score of which relatives I care about more, but if I did, you'd be number one. And you know why? I just figured it out."

Daniel wasn't surprised by any of that. And he knew the answer, too.

"It's because you needed it. Because you never felt it enough from anyone else, and I could see that. I had to make sure my Danny always knew."

"I did. And I hope you felt it from me, too." He embraced her, his cheek against hers, feeling her warmth—not just physical, but almost a psychic force coming off her. "I love you, Bee. Always have."

She pulled away just far enough that she could catch his eyes again. "I got so angry, back when you were in high school, and even when you started college, when you'd call me and you'd vent about how lonely you were." Daniel felt himself blushing. It had been whining, not venting. And she'd listened to far more of it than anyone—even a favorite cousin who loved him more than anybody else—should have had to. "I was *so* pissed at all those idiot girls you told me about, because they couldn't see how amazing you were." And then she smiled, the saddest smile he'd ever seen. Or maybe the second saddest, but he put that out of his mind and just listened to her, even though he knew what she was going to say next.

"And it made my heart hurt—I'm serious. It burned. Knowing that you couldn't see it for yourself, either. I hated that for you. I would have done anything if it would have made you see how great you were. *Are.*" It made his heart hurt right now to hear it, to know how much time and energy she'd set aside for him, when she should have been spending it on herself.

"I'm sorry, Bee." He sat there, staring back at her, willing her to feel everything he felt, and she—she laughed.

"God, you're dumb sometimes! You think I don't already know it's always gone both ways? You think I don't remember the times you hurt for me, or cried for me or wanted to rip somebody's head off because they did wrong by me? Even if you were a thousand miles away, even when we didn't talk for months?"

She knew. She knew it all. Of course she did.

"And you're telling me all this now because...?" He knew why. But he needed to hear it out loud.

She didn't speak, just pushed him a little further away, and reached down under his shirt. She pulled out the necklace, held it up. "You were always enough for this. You were always going to step up if you had to. I knew it. Nora knew it. She always saw you. The only one who didn't know it was you." She took a deep breath. "But now you do. I mean it, Danny. You've got no excuses anymore."

"You're the one who kept telling me to move on from her." It sounded lame even to his own ears.

"And I was wrong, and it took Leanne three months to forgive me for setting her up with you. She finally asked me to come back to pottery class last month, by the way."

"Bee."

"Sorry. Anyway. She forgave you, too. So you don't have any reason not to go find Nora. Go get her, or I'll be *so* disappointed in you."

"You won't be the only one." He wasn't sure if he said it out loud or not. Or if that even mattered.

Daniel, a few hours later

It was half past two in the morning. Daniel had been lying here under the covers in Bianca's guest room since just before midnight, closing his eyes tightly and not falling asleep. He didn't bother to wipe the tears from his face. He'd done it ten or twenty times already, but they just kept coming, so what was the point?

She'd meant to reassure him, cheer him on. But all she'd done was make it hurt more, because if she was right—and she was, he couldn't pretend otherwise anymore—then it never had to happen the way it did a decade ago. Or even a year and a half ago, aboard the ship.

If he was enough then, he could have been with Nora all this time. She'd be with him right now, arms wrapped around him, alternately making fun of Bee's taste in wallpaper and reminding him what a hero he was.

She wasn't, though, and nothing could change that. But maybe it could start to change tomorrow. Or the next day. Or whenever the tears finally stopped.

He didn't notice the door cracking open just an inch or two, or his cousin's eyes peeking in for a moment, or her soft sigh. He certainly didn't hear the way her throat caught as she gently closed the door again and tiptoed back to her bedroom, wiping away her own tears as she went.

Chapter 44

Nora, March 26

Nora had only been editor-in-chief of *Catalyst Quarterly* for a few weeks; she was still learning the personalities and working styles of her staff. But the new girl—Julia, that was her name—stood out today, and not in a good way.

She was a brand new staff writer, only three months out of college. Northwestern, if Nora recalled correctly. And she'd walked into her very first all-staff meeting a month ago, head held high as though she owned the room, making eye contact with everyone, even throwing out a pitch for an article. A great pitch, which Nora had approved on the spot. She recalled feeling a twinge of jealousy at the time; it had taken her six months to work up the confidence to volunteer an idea at a staff meeting without being prompted.

But Julia hadn't been there in the weekly editorial meeting this morning. She'd been replaced by a quiet, nervous girl who looked like she'd rather be anywhere else on the planet than there. Nora had let it pass in the meeting; there was too much to cover, and too many other egos to manage. But it had bothered her for the last two hours.

"Get it together," she muttered to herself. "Babysitting isn't part of the job. She's a big girl, she can take care of herself." But that wasn't true, was it? Every good boss she'd ever had—and before that, every good professor—had made sure she knew it was their job to help her succeed. To give her the tools and the resources she needed to thrive. They'd each done it in their own way—but one thing they all had in common was that none of them ever called it *babysitting*.

Now it was her turn.

So when Nora saw the girl walk down the corridor, turn the corner towards the restrooms, and then not reappear for fifteen minutes, she stood up. She knew exactly where she needed to go.

Nora, a few minutes later

Julia stood in front of the bathroom mirror, smoothing over the same fall of blonde hair over and over again, as though she was on autopilot. Nora walked up to her slowly, expecting the girl to notice her approaching in the mirror, but it wasn't until she put a hand on Julia's shoulder that she got a reaction.

"What?" She whirled around at the touch, her face dissolving into a mix of shame and terror when she realized who was there. "Ms. Langley! I'm sorry, I'm heading back to my desk right now!"

"Hey, relax. Whatever they told you about me, I'm not an ogre." She said it with what she hoped was a disarming grin, but it didn't have the desired effect.

"Nobody said that! You're great! Everyone says so! And I'm—I'm sorry I…"

Nora grabbed both of her shoulders, trying to project calm to the girl. "Julia, please. Relax. I just wanted to talk for a minute." But where? An answer came to her immediately. "You know what, there's a really good coffee shop around the corner. McDuffy's?" The girl gave the slightest of nods. "I was about to head over there, and I'd really appreciate it if you kept me company for a few minutes."

Julia didn't say anything, but she did let Nora steer her out of the bathroom and down the hall to the elevators. Her face was still frozen in terror; God knew what she expected Nora to say or do. But she got in the elevator when it arrived anyway.

"I've been meaning to set aside time to just chat with everyone on the team," Nora told her once they stepped out into the unseasonable chill of the afternoon. It was mostly true, but meaning to do something and actually making the time to do it were two very different things. "I was thinking about lunches with everyone, but afternoon coffee will work just fine. And obviously it's my treat."

When they got to McDuffy's, there was a line, and Julia didn't speak beyond answering "yes" or "no" to Nora's questions as they made their way to the barista. She supposed that she wouldn't have reacted any differently seven years ago. If her boss' boss had found her nearly catatonic in the restroom, and then dragged her out for a talk, she would have been equally unresponsive. But it was just too much when they finally got to the front of the line and Julia ordered a small black coffee, the cheapest, dullest thing on the menu short of a bottled water.

Nora shook her head at the barista, and turned to the girl. "I refuse to believe that's what you drink, Julia. Now I want you to get whatever it is that you really get, and you can consider that an order. Okay?"

For the first time, Julia almost smiled. It wasn't much of one, but it was better than nothing. Then she turned to the barista.

"Instead of the black coffee, I'd like a double half-caf, no-foam vanilla soy latte, with a caramel swirl, and a cinnamon dusting, extra hot."

"That's your regular order?" Julia nodded. Nora hadn't figured the girl for something quite that involved. "No judgment from me. But I have to say, back when I started they didn't pay us enough to be ordering caramel swirls with our coffee."

She ordered her own regular drink, a medium skim latte, no sugar, and five minutes later they were seated at a table by the window, looking out on the constant stream of passers-by. Julia was sipping her coffee, occasionally glancing up to not quite meet Nora's eyes. "Okay," Nora said, when she couldn't stand the silence any longer. "I wanted to actually talk with you. Because I can see you've got a lot on your mind, and I can tell you from experience that it's going to come out one way or another."

"I don't—I mean, I just had a moment, you know? That's all it is." Julia was looking up at her now, and Nora could see her desire to end this conversation before it began. Which was exactly why she couldn't let it go. Because she remembered days like this, when her own ambition ran into a brick wall just like Julia's obviously had.

"Julia, you do know I'm only twenty-eight, right? I haven't forgotten what it was like, my first job right out of college, and I thought I was going to conquer the world until life knocked me down. I know what you're feeling because I lived it, not all that long ago." Julia was still looking at her, still listening. "And I want to help you because I wouldn't be on the other side of the table from you if somebody hadn't helped me. So will you, please, please talk to me?"

It took another ten minutes of prompting and, honestly, badgering, before Julia really began to open up. "I was—well, I was sort of okay. And then Mr. Elliott called me into his office. He just—I know I'm supposed to take feedback, and I know I have a ton to learn. But he—he said I write like somebody trying out for the high school newspaper."

Nora tried not to laugh, but couldn't help herself. "Classic Jack Elliott. You'd think he'd come up with new material once in a while." Julia's eyes said she didn't believe her. "I take that back. He did tell me once that I wrote like somebody who'd never had her heart broken. Which, first of all, what does that even mean? And second, I've had mine broken enough times that I could give lessons, so he didn't know what he was talking about anyway."

Julia sort-of smiled. "He really said that?"

"He did. And I just sat there and took it, and did my best to hold it together the rest of the day."

Nora wondered for an instant if she should tell the rest of it, but what was the point of this conversation if she wasn't going to be honest? "And then, when I got home I drank a bottle of wine and complained to my Aunt Rachel for two hours."

Now it was a real, honest-to-goodness smile on Julia's face. That was an improvement; the girl was really hearing her. "The next day, I came into work, and I looked at the article he was talking about, I mean, really looked at it, and—well, to this day I don't know how he got that nonsense about a broken heart from an article about new discoveries in quantum gravity, but he *was* right that it needed a hell of a lot of work."

Julia considered that. "I get it. I'm sure my article was a mess, too, and I just—I let my pride get in the way, I guess. But he didn't have to be such a—a jackass." Julia looked down as she heard her own words. She probably expected Nora to fire her on the spot for it.

"I've called him worse," Nora said, patting Julia's arm in what she hoped the girl took as a companionable gesture. "Never in the office, obviously. But that's the thing. If you're going to make it here, or anywhere else, you need to learn how to deal with people like him. First, you have to be honest with yourself. No matter how obnoxious the delivery is, listen to the criticism, and ask yourself if it's right. And if it is, learn from it." Nora laughed at herself. How many people had to tell her that before it finally sunk in? "I know, easier said than done. But there's no way around it."

"What if it's not right?"

Nora had asked the same thing seven years ago. "Then you reread your article again. And again. As many times as it takes until you're sure—I mean, bet your life on it sure—that they're wrong. And then you push back. Respectfully and professionally."

"And if they still don't agree with you, what do you do then?"

This was the hardest lesson of all, and Nora remembered pushing her luck well past the point of no return before she learned it herself. "Then you make the edits they're asking for, and get started on the next article."

Julia looked horrified.

"I almost got fired more than once before I accepted that myself. But it's just life. I was a new staff writer, just like you are now. I wasn't going to win an argument against an editor who's been here fifteen or twenty years, even if I was right." Julia didn't like that, but Nora held up a hand before she could object. "I know, that's probably not what they taught you in college." There was a lot she hadn't been taught in her journalism classes, either. "Call it on the job training. Lesson one. You stick it out anyway. Make the changes, learn whatever you can from it, make the next article better. Lather, rinse, repeat. Keep it up, and you'll get noticed. It's a marathon, not a sprint."

God, had she actually used that stupid cliché? It was one of her least favorite expressions, and not only for professional purposes. It hit far too close to home personally, too. She shook her head to clear thoughts of Daniel away. "I know that's overused, but it's true. And, heck, you're talking to the editor-in-chief right now, so you're already ahead of the game."

Finally, she got a genuine laugh out of the girl. "I guess I am."

The conversation flowed more freely after that, until Nora's Palm Pilot bleeped fifteen minutes later. "We'll have to cut it short. One of the drawbacks of being editor-in-chief. You can't skip meetings when you're supposed to be running them."

Nora, two hours later

When her two o'clock meeting finally ended, twenty minutes over time, Nora took a detour by the cubicles on the other side of the floor. She hoped to see Julia hard at work revising her article, but instead the girl was listening to a message on her cellphone. Listening to it repeatedly; she was pulling the phone away from her ear, pushing a button and then listening again, over and over.

It wasn't a good message, if the curses she was mouthing were any indication. Nora was no lip-reader, but some words were impossible to mistake. And there was a particular combination of anger and sadness in her eyes that was all too familiar.

She headed back to her office, telling herself, *this is none of your business*. Except, being a mentor—and that was what she was acting as earlier, wasn't it?—didn't fit into a strict little box. Life was messy and the personal bled into the professional and vice-versa.

Hadn't she told Julia she wanted to have get-to-know-you lunches with her staff? Might as well start making time right now. As soon as she got back to her desk, she sent Julia an invite for tomorrow at noon. Somebody had to be first, right?

Nora, March 27

"I hope you like Thai," Nora said when Julia met her at the elevators precisely at noon. "The red curry will change your life." Julia didn't seem convinced. More than that, she looked distinctly uncomfortable.

"I'm fine, Ms. Langley. I appreciate your time yesterday, and your advice. But..."

"But nothing," Nora said with a shake of her head. "I told you, I was thinking about lunches with the staff. You're just first. And it's Nora, please. The last person who called me Ms. Langley was my senior thesis advisor. Okay?"

Julia nodded, still looking unconvinced but apparently not willing to directly contradict her.

"Good. So, ground rules. No work talk, unless you want to bring it up. I'd much rather get to know you better. This is a workplace, but we're all humans, too. Well, except for Jack Elliott, maybe." That earned her a brief grin. "Actually, even him. Get him talking about his bulldog and you'd think he's a totally different person. And that's the point. We'll all work together better if we really see each other as whole people. Fair enough?"

Julia nodded her head dutifully, but Nora didn't think she was really on board with the idea. But by the time they got to the restaurant, the girl was talking less guardedly, and it came out that she was an only child of divorced parents.

Nora already saw so much of herself in Julia; it wasn't even a surprise to hear that her upbringing was so similar. "When did it happen? My parents divorced when I was eleven."

"Twelve. It really sucked—pardon me. I mean, it wasn't good."

Nora laughed; she couldn't help it. "Julia, you can say 'sucked' in front of me. If anybody understands how much it sucks when your parents split up, I do. So which one of them did you lean towards?"

"My father. But my mother made me feel guilty about it, and it was—it was pretty ugly for a while." Nora heard the pain in her voice that she was trying to suppress. "They—they're still pretty awful to each other, but they managed to sit in the same row at my graduation. So I guess that's progress."

Nora shared stories about her parents until their food arrived. "Like I said, trust the red curry. It makes everything better."

It worked, too; Julia seemed a lot more comfortable after her meal. Enough so that Nora thought she might be willing to talk about whatever—or more likely whoever—was bothering her yesterday afternoon.

"It's none of my business, obviously, so feel free to tell me to shut up if you want to—and that's an order, by the way. But if you do want to talk, I'm listening—what was that voicemail you were so upset about yesterday?"

Julia hesitated. "It's personal, Ms. Lang...Nora. It was just some guy, I don't want to talk about it."

But on the walk back to the office, totally unprompted, Julia did talk about it, in great detail, and Nora might have been listening to her teenage self talking.

"I don't have any advice about him, other than to block his calls going forward. But I can tell you one thing for sure, because I lived it myself. You are so much better, so much more deserving than you think you are."

She hadn't even realized her hand was in her purse. But now the Mont Blanc pen was in her fingers, held out for Julia to see. "I didn't think I was, until I met someone who saw everything in me that I couldn't see for myself." She tapped Julia's forehead gently with the pen. "He gave me this *after* we broke up. Right before he graduated. Just because he wanted me to carry something of him—and so I'd always remember everything he saw in me. For a long time, I didn't believe it. And I still forget sometimes." Like on the cruise, a year and a half ago. "But every time I use that pen, it reminds me that I really am worthy. I am everything he thought I was."

Julia didn't say anything for a minute or two. "So I need to find a man who'll make me believe in myself?"

That's what Nora herself would have taken from the story. "No. You might. I hope you do. I think you will, because you

have a hell of a lot going for you. But you do need to believe in yourself, and take reassurance wherever you can find it. Like right now, from me. Or from Jack Elliott, because for all his bark, if he didn't think your work was good, he'd be demanding that I fire you. Or, sometimes you just have to lie to yourself until you start to believe it. I've done a lot of that too."

Julia thought that over. "I'll keep all that in mind, Nora. Thank you. You didn't have to spend all this time with me and my stupid problems."

Nora patted her arm. "Yes, I did. Because there's a whole long line of people who did that for me. And one day, I expect you to repay it to someone young and inexperienced who needs it. That's definitely an order. Fair enough?"

She didn't look like she was convinced, but she shook Nora's hand firmly enough. *She'll figure it out,* Nora told herself. Maybe not right away, but she would. Because if Nora had learned anything, it was that growth was always possible.

Chapter 45

Daniel, October 24

"I'm not taking no for an answer, Daniel. I already paid for the plane tickets."

Daniel wasn't sure why he was even arguing. Most people—sane people—would just say "thank you" when they were told that somebody who loved them wanted to take them on an all-expenses-paid trip to Paris.

He *was* sane, wasn't he? "Thank you, Bee." He knew she was doing it to distract him from thinking about Nora while not actually doing anything about her seven months after he'd sworn to his cousin that he would.

"That's better," she said, and headed into his kitchen. She returned five minutes later with a bottle of seltzer water and two glasses. "This will have to do for a toast, since you don't have anything even vaguely resembling a celebration-worthy beverage in this house."

He shrugged. "You know I'm not a big drinker, and other than you, I never have people over."

Bianca sighed. "You don't even have any real soda!"

"I was drinking a liter of Coke nearly every day, and my pants were starting to get too tight. Unless you want to buy me a whole new wardrobe, you'll have to live with the seltzer water."

She poured the seltzer water, handed him a glass and clinked hers to it. "Well, here's to you doing something new and adventurous. We'll make it a proper champagne toast on New Year's Eve in the shadow of the Eiffel Tower." Then she took a sip of her drink and almost spit it out. "This isn't even flavored, Daniel! There is something *seriously* wrong with you. Even people with hopelessly broken hearts are allowed to drink flavored water."

There was no point protesting that it had nothing to do with his heart; all the flavored waters used fake sugar, which had a nasty aftertaste and gave him a headache ten minutes after he drank it. "Just for you, I'll buy something better next time I go to the store. How about red-flavored Hawaiian Punch?"

"You really are hopeless, Daniel," she said, grinning. "But I love you anyway."

Nora, October 25

Nora was out on the sidewalk outside her office waiting for Rachel when her taxi pulled up a little after noon. She waited for her aunt to get out and grab her luggage from the trunk before running over to hug her.

"To what do I owe the pleasure?" It was a rare treat to see Rachel in person, ever since she'd moved permanently to London for her job three years ago, but she usually announced her visits well ahead of time. This morning, she'd called Nora from the baggage claim area at Logan Airport and told her to clear her afternoon schedule.

"I can't just visit my favorite niece?"

Nora laughed. "I'm your *only* niece, and of course you can. You just usually give me more notice." She took Rachel's suitcase into the lobby and asked Bruno at the security desk to lock it away until she got back. "Okay, I hope you didn't eat on the plane, because I made reservations at my favorite Thai place for us."

Ten minutes later, they were seated, they'd ordered, and Rachel got down to business. "I was going to call and discuss this with you, but they needed me in New York tomorrow, so I figured I could see you first and take the train down to Manhattan tonight."

What did she want to discuss? What was so important that Rachel would be willing to waste four hours on a train instead of flying straight to New York?

"You're being very mysterious."

"Sorry," Rachel said, shrugging. "It's something good. I made New Year's Eve plans for you."

Now Nora was even more confused. What was her aunt talking about? "That's two months from now."

Rachel dug into her purse and put an envelope on the table. Nora picked it up and looked at what was printed there—Air France?

"Figured it out yet?" No, she hadn't. She opened the envelope, and inside was a plane ticket.

"December 27th, Boston to Paris? Rachel, what did you do?"

"Cashed in all my frequent flyer miles. You'll get in on the morning of the 28th, and I'll take the train over from London to meet you. There's something else in there, by the way."

Nora pulled out the little slip of paper she'd missed before. Written in Rachel's careful script was:

L'Hôtel

13, Rue des Beaux Arts

Check in 28 December, check out 2 January

Closest Metro—Pont Neuf (Line #7)

Rachel wanted to take her to Paris? Why?

It was a huge gift, and horribly expensive. Rachel had always been generous to her, but this was on a whole other level. "I don't understand, Rachel."

Rachel gave her a sad smile. "It's been almost two years since that cruise, Nora. You're stuck. I mean, at work you're thriving, not that I ever expected any less. But you're still stuck back there with Daniel, and I'm not going to let you wallow forever." Nora started to protest, but Rachel wasn't hearing it. "I know you still have the Mont Blanc pen. And I'll bet everything I own that the sad old teddy bear he gave you in college is still in your bed right now. It's going to be a whole new century, and what better place for a fresh start than Paris?"

Nora started to point out that the new century—the new millennium—wouldn't actually start until January 1st, 2001, but that was avoiding the subject. And Rachel was right. She hadn't even been on a single date since the cruise. And she hadn't called, or written or emailed Daniel. Something *did* have to change.

"I guess I don't have a choice," she said, pasting the best smile she could manage on her face.

"That's the spirit! Just be sure you're packed and ready to go on the 27th."

She wasn't sure if even the magic of Paris would be enough to change things for her. But she'd never know if she didn't try, right?

Chapter 46

Daniel, December 27

"Good Lord, Bee," he muttered to himself. "What do you have in there? We're only going for six days, not moving to Paris permanently." Daniel was in Bianca's driveway waiting for her to make one last bathroom visit before the taxi arrived. Beside him were her two full-sized suitcases, garment bag, carry-on bag and absurdly big purse. Next to all that, his one carry-on suitcase looked sad and lonely.

Well, if that wasn't symbolic, he didn't know what was.

She emerged from the house wearing—he had to blink and look again to believe it—the fur coat she'd gotten for her eighteenth birthday. Under that was a low-cut red dress, and she had on ridiculously high heels, almost enough to bring her eye-to-eye with him.

"Bee, you realize we're going to have to walk probably two miles to get to our gate once we get to the airport, right? You're going to break your ankle."

She threw her scarf—also red, naturally—around her neck dramatically. "The way you start something is the way it'll go. If we're going to the fashion capital of the world, I'm going to take the first steps looking like a million bucks." She laughed. "Look in the top of my carry-on. I'll put the sneakers on once we get inside the airport."

He should have known; that was Bianca in a nutshell; both showy and practical at the same time. Just like...*her*.

Nora wasn't going to be in Paris. This trip was all about spending time with Bee, and figuring out how to restart his personal life.

"Good idea, Bee." He heard a car turning the corner, three houses down from Bee's property. It was their taxi. "And here he comes. You ready?"

"If you are, Danny."

She walked over—tottered, really, on the uneven gravel of her driveway—and hugged him. "As ready as I'll ever be. And if I haven't said it enough, thank you for this."

She kissed his forehead; it was really weird not having to bend down for her to do that. "I love you, Danny. You never need to thank me. I just hope it's going to be everything you could wish for."

So did he.

Nora, around the same time

The last time—the only time—Nora had been on an international flight was sophomore year of high school.

Mom had literally pulled her out of class, right in the middle of frog dissection day in Biology. "I have to go to Rome, it's an emergency with the gallery. You're coming with me," she'd said. She'd given Nora fifteen minutes to pack a bag and then it was off to the airport. Mom sat in first class, Nora back in coach; there had been only one seat left in first and, "I need to mentally prepare for this negotiation, I can't possibly do that back in steerage."

This time, Nora would be in first class; she hadn't looked closely at the ticket when Rachel handed it to her two months ago but she finally read all the details this morning while she was waiting for the taxi.

She still had an hour before boarding started; she was enjoying a pre-flight glass of champagne in the International Lounge. She glanced at a copy of *Le Monde*, but her barely-remembered three years of high school French were not much help. She recognized the words—a lot of them, anyway—but her recall of French grammar was hopeless.

This trip had to be better than Rome with her mother. She'd had maybe an hour of actual time with Mom in her four days there. Most of the trip had been spent waiting in the lobby of an Italian office building. The highlight—well, in the moment; she'd felt pretty crummy about it once she got home—was the two hours with a young man named Paolo she'd run into when she snuck away from Mom.

Of course this would be better. She was an accomplished, mature adult now. She'd be with her aunt, who would not abandon her for hours at a time to conduct business with handsy Italian men. And she did remember enough French words that she could probably read most of the signs and store price tags she'd encounter.

She'd make sure it was better.

♡ 🖤 ♡

Daniel, December 28, nine o'clock in the morning (Paris time)

Daniel had no one to blame but himself. He'd convinced Bianca to take the aisle seat, on the theory that she'd have to go to the bathroom more often than he did. The last night in the hospital after her appendectomy, she'd gotten up twelve times—he'd counted.

He should have factored in that the doctors were giving her liters and liters of fluids in her IV, so of course she had to pee every half hour. Here on the flight, she hadn't gotten up once. The flight took off at eight-thirty, and she was asleep by a quarter to nine.

She'd taken a sleeping pill, and offered one to him. But, never having taken one before, he was nervous about how it might affect him. "I'll fall asleep just fine on my own," he'd said.

Famous last words.

He never did fall asleep. There were too many different noises and sudden movements from the plane. And his bladder demanding attention. And then there was Bianca's snoring. How had he forgotten that she snored?

To be fair to himself, there was also the excitement of his first trip to Europe keeping him awake.

So what if he was totally fried by the time they landed? He could make it through the first day in Paris, and then after a nice heavy French meal with plenty of butter and cream sauces—and a bottle or two of wine—he'd sleep the sleep of the angels tonight and be back to normal for the rest of the trip.

Whatever might happen in the City of Light, he'd be ready for it.

♡ ♥ ♡

Nora, two hours later

She'd slept through most of the flight, which was a mercy. If Nora hadn't been fully alert, she would never have been able to navigate the trains from *Charles de Gaulle* airport into downtown Paris.

Getting to the terminal for the B line of the RER train had taxed her decade-old memories of French class to the limit. Once she'd gotten to *Chaâtelet-les-Halles*, her directional skills were severely challenged; she'd made three wrong turns before a friendly American exchange student took pity on her and got her pointed in the right direction.

The station was a maze, with tunnels leading to six different train lines, but she finally got to the correct platform for the short ride to *Pont Neuf* station.

The number 7 train headed to *La Courneuve* was crowded; she was shoved against a very stylish blonde woman, probably around her own age. She apologized in English. The woman smiled and replied, "No problem," in an accent Nora couldn't quite place. Thankfully, it was only one stop on the train, and even better, only one line went through *Pont Neuf*, so there was no rabbit warren of tunnels to try and navigate.

She emerged onto the streets of Paris maybe twenty feet from the bridge at *Pont Neuf*. There was a deep chill in the air, and the hard-to-describe smell that meant snow was coming soon. Hopefully it would hold off until she got to the hotel.

She hadn't looked at a map and planned out the route from the Metro to the hotel ahead of time; this was a vacation, and leisurely walks were the order of the day. But she hadn't reckoned with her luggage, or the crowds or the way the street signs were not where she expected them to be.

Daniel would have.

No, he'd have insisted on taking a taxi all the way from the airport so she wouldn't have to lug her suitcase through labyrinthine subway tunnels and crowded streets.

He wasn't here, though; wasn't this whole trip about finally trying to get over him?

So it took her an hour for what the tourist guide she'd flipped through a couple of weeks ago billed as a ten minute walk. When she entered the beautiful lobby of *L'Hôtel*, with its red marble columns, she was ready to collapse; it was only the last residual drops of adrenaline that got her to the check-in desk.

Still, she did make it in one piece, and she'd already seen more beautiful architecture—and more beautifully-dressed people—than she normally encountered in a typical month back in Boston.

That counted as a good start to this trip, didn't it?

Daniel, an hour later

"I'm impressed, Bee." The lobby of *Hôtel Le Six* was somehow both modern-looking and cozy. "Looks like you picked a winner."

"You can thank Bethany. If it was up to me I would've just picked one of the big chain hotels." Bethany was a travel agent, and Daniel doubted she'd want his thanks. He'd met her once, three months ago, at Bianca's house, in what had been a very awkward attempt at his cousin trying again to set him up with someone.

"I'll write her a thank-you note when we get home."

They went up to the check-in desk. A perfectly made-up woman in a crisp uniform greeted them. "Yes? May I help you?" To Daniel's surprise, there was almost no trace of an accent.

"Oui," Bianca said brightly. But apparently that was the extent of her French vocabulary. "We have a reservation, under Cavelli, two rooms."

Daniel blinked. "Bee?"

She laughed. "Of course I got us separate rooms. What if I want to walk around naked when I get out of the shower?"

The woman at reception didn't react at all. Neither did Daniel. "You've never done that in your life, Bee." He grinned. "And, anyway, I *have* seen you naked, or did you forget I was the one changing your bandages and getting you undressed for bed after your surgery?"

Two minutes later, they had their keys and a bellhop was lugging all of Bianca's bags up to their rooms. "See, we're right next to each other in case you get lonely, Danny."

He opened his door; the room wasn't big, but it was beautiful, with a queen bed, a tiny balcony looking out onto a courtyard, and a very fancy bathroom. Bianca definitely picked a winner.

He unpacked his one bag, set out his toiletries on the bathroom sink, and then there was a knock at the door. Bianca was there, fur coat and all. "Ready to go exploring?"

"Aren't you going to unpack first?"

She rolled her eyes. "How long have you known me, Danny? Fun first, chores later. Let's go!"

He couldn't argue with that. They set off in the general direction of the Eiffel Tower, and when they crossed *Rue de Sèvres*, Daniel stopped short.

"I know her," he said, pointing towards a dark-haired woman with a bright blue scarf across the street. "I can't remember from where, but I know I've seen her before."

"At least she's not blonde. I'm glad you're not seeing Nora's ghost here," Bianca answered.

It *wasn't* Nora, obviously, but the woman with the scarf somehow put him in mind of her anyway.

Nora, that evening

"Rachel, what are you doing?"

Nora had never seen her aunt pull out a phone—or do anything else distracting—at a meal. She didn't think Rachel even knew how to communicate by text message, but that's what she had to be up to now.

"I'm sorry, Nora. I have to put out a quick fire at work."

Rachel had also never before interrupted a vacation for work emergencies. "Time off is time off," she'd told Nora more than once. "You remember that."

But she had been promoted recently, so maybe occasional messages on vacation were the price of a bigger title and fatter paycheck.

It occurred to her that there might be a dozen messages on her cell phone, too. But if so, they'd have to wait; her cell phone was plugged into its charger in her kitchen back in Boston. She'd made it clear to everyone that she would be completely unreachable until January 3rd.

"No problem. I hope it's nothing too crazy." It had to be something fairly important, to stop Rachel from eating the grape leaves and the handmade hummus. If she didn't get off her phone quickly, there wouldn't be any left for her, and it would be her own fault.

Nora hadn't ever had Lebanese food before, and she hadn't planned to have it tonight. The aroma that hit her when she crossed *Rue Bonaparte* was irresistible, though, so here they were in *Assanabel*, which, as best she could piece together from the historical note on the back of the menu, had been in this exact spot since 1985.

Five minutes later, Rachel finally put her phone away. "Nice of you to leave me some hummus," she said, glaring at the empty bowl in the middle of the table.

"We can order more," Nora answered. "And maybe some of the—I'm not even going to try and pronounce it, the yogurt dip?" She looked around, trying to catch the eye of their waiter, but instead something caught her eye. A woman in a fur coat, with her dark hair in a bob cut, walking right past the window.

"Bianca!" She didn't mean to say it out loud, but Rachel stared at her in surprise. "Daniel's cousin. I could swear that was her, right outside." She'd only met Bianca once, at Daniel's graduation, eight years ago. But she had a great memory for faces, and she'd bet—maybe not everything she owned, but quite a bit—that it was her.

She was here to try and move past Daniel, to start a new millennium—even if it technically wasn't until next year—fresh.

So why was she still seeing signs of him wherever she went?

Chapter 47

Daniel, December 29, six o'clock in the evening

Bianca was acting weird.

First, she insisted on taking the Metro rather than a taxi to the opera house, even though her feet had to be killing her. He saw the band-aids on the back of both her feet earlier today.

Second, when they got to the restaurant—a big, modern-looking place called *L'Entracte*, across the street from the *Palais Garnier*—she'd specifically asked for a table by the window, when in all the years he'd known her, she'd never cared where they sat at a restaurant.

Third, she'd insisted on the seat looking outside, when, again, she'd never bothered with which seat she took at the table.

Oddest of all, she wasn't idly people-watching. She was staring out intently, as though she expected to see someone she knew at any moment.

"Bee, if you keep looking out the window, your snails are going to wake up and walk right off your plate." She'd brought back memories of the cruise two years ago when Leanne had ordered them.

If Leanne hadn't ordered them that first night, she wouldn't have felt sick and gone to bed early—and Daniel wouldn't have run into Nora. Maybe they wouldn't have seen each other at all, if they'd missed each other in the atrium of the *Empress of the Seas* that first night. And then maybe he wouldn't have broken up with Leanne. Maybe they'd be married right now, and it would be her across the table from him.

How different might his life be right now, all because of a plate of snails?

No. It wouldn't have gotten that far. Nora would never not be in his heart.

And here he was thinking about her again, instead of focusing on a new start, or simply enjoying a good meal at a fancy restaurant before seeing the Paris Ballet.

All because of Bianca and her stupid snails.

Nora, the same time

"Remind me why we're having pizza when we're in Paris? I can get pizza at home."

Rachel shrugged. "It's on the way, and it's not crowded." She held up her slice of margherita pizza and waved it vaguely in the air. "And it *is* very good pizza."

"Fair enough," Nora said. This restaurant was halfway between the *Bastille* metro station and the *Opera Bastille*, the newer of the two major opera houses in Paris. It wasn't crowded; there were only a handful of other customers besides her and Rachel. And the pizza *was* very good. "So what are we seeing tonight? You've been really secretive all day."

Rachel gave her a weird look, as though she'd just been caught in a lie or something. But there wasn't anything for her to lie about, was there? This was just a vacation, there couldn't be anything Rachel would need to keep secret.

"I just wanted to surprise you," she said, taking a bite of pizza before going on. "Anyway, we're seeing the ballet. *La Belle au Bois Dormant.*"

What did that mean?

She could puzzle it out. *Dormant* had to refer to sleep, didn't it? And *La Belle*, that was obvious.

"You mean *Sleeping Beauty*?" Rachel nodded. "Wow! I can't wait. I was expecting opera, and honestly I was sort of dreading it." She'd only ever been once, with her mother on a visit to Manhattan when she was nine years old. She couldn't recall which opera, or even which composer. All she remembered was that it was loud, and long and all in German.

"Yeah," Rachel said. "That's what I figured. I remember your father telling me about Karen taking you to see *Tristan and Isolde* at the Met when you were little. What possessed her to think a fourth grader would want to see that, I'll never know."

This would definitely be better. She just hoped Rachel would stop worrying about whatever it was that she was worried about, so she could enjoy the ballet, too.

Daniel, an hour later

The *Palais Garnier* was even more impressive inside than out. It was well beyond opulent; Daniel wasn't sure there was a word grand enough to properly describe it. It made the Metropolitan Opera House back home—amazing in its own right, at least it had seemed that way when he'd seen it back in junior high—look small and pitiful by comparison.

They were in the grand lobby, and everywhere he looked, something demanded his attention: the huge, dramatic staircase, the carvings covering nearly every wall, and their fellow theatergoers. Most of the men wore tuxedos, and the few who didn't wore suits that looked like they probably cost more than he'd spent on his entire wardrobe. And the women—it was like watching highlights from Fashion Week.

He felt woefully underdressed, even though he'd had his suit pressed this afternoon. Bianca, stunning in a red dress and a new hairdo this afternoon that cost more than her mortgage payment, looked more beautiful than he'd ever seen her—and even *she* barely looked like she belonged here.

She also looked like she needed the bathroom. She was fidgeting by a wall, eyes fixed on the main entrance.

This wasn't her usual people-watching; she was looking for someone. But who?

"Bee," he said. "If you have to use the little girls' room, just go already. Otherwise, we ought to get to our seats."

She checked her watch, stared at the doors for another few seconds and sighed. "You're right. Just wait here, don't move an inch."

He nodded, watching the last stragglers coming into the opera house, just in case he'd somehow recognize whoever Bianca was waiting for.

But of course he didn't; when you didn't know who you were looking for, how could you possibly find them?

♥ ♥ ♥

Nora, the same time

The *Opéra Bastille* was nothing like what Nora had expected. She'd pictured something old and ornate—the sort of place where you could imagine Erik lurking in the catacombs, murdering anyone who dared look at his Christine the wrong way.

But this? It was all metal and glass outside, and sleek and ultra-modern inside. Almost as if the architect had been given the same design brief as the one who'd built the Louvre pyramid.

Rachel wasn't paying attention to any of it. She stood near the main entrance, eyes fixed on the doors like she was waiting for someone.

Maybe she was. Could she have a boyfriend? She'd been in Europe for three years now; plenty of time to meet someone. Maybe this was the only night he was free. That would definitely explain the frantic texting over dinner.

If Rachel's mystery man wanted to sit with her, Nora would happily trade her seat with his. Just because she was single and unable to stop dwelling on Daniel, didn't mean Rachel shouldn't enjoy herself.

But no boyfriend—or anyone else Rachel recognized—ever showed. When the three bells rang to signal the start of the performance, Rachel sighed, took Nora's arm, and led her into the theater.

Daniel, three hours later

"I'm not sure what to think about what we saw," Daniel said. The ballet had been amazing in a technical sense; the performers did things that it didn't seem like a human body ought to be able to do. He'd had to look away when the lead male dancer dropped into a split. All Daniel could think about was how many ligaments he'd tear trying that.

"You didn't like it?" Bianca took a sip of her drink. They were sitting in a comfortable little room in the lobby of the hotel, with a cozy fire burning in the fireplace.

"I did, but—there wasn't really a story, was there? Or maybe there was and I just didn't get it?" It hadn't even been one performance; it was three separate pieces by different choreographers, and the only one he'd ever even heard of was Balanchine—and him only because he'd been an answer on *Jeopardy* once.

He tried his drink. It was fruity, but he couldn't identify what fruit, exactly. "What's in this, by the way?"

Bianca grinned and shook her head. "No idea. The woman in front of me ordered one, and the bartender didn't speak English, so I just pointed to her and put up two fingers. You like it?"

It wasn't the sort of thing he usually drank—not that he usually drank much at all—but it *was* good. "I do. I guess that's enough, right?" Just like the performance, maybe? Not everything needed to be understood; sometimes it was enough to just live in the moment and enjoy things.

She clinked her glass to his. "I'd call that some real progress. Here's to not overthinking things and just experiencing life."

Bianca had only been telling him that since he learned to walk. Maybe he could finally start listening to her.

Nora, an hour later

This was supposed to be a fun trip. A new start. A way to stop living in the past.

So why did she go straight to bed instead of taking Rachel up on her invitation for a late-night drink and dessert in the hotel bar downstairs? And now that she was here, why couldn't she stop crying?

Why was she imagining herself lying there on the opera house stage, asleep until her prince came to kiss her and start her life again?

Why was the prince in her head a dark-haired, kind of nerdy guy in a button-down shirt instead of the lithe, blond dancer in purple toe shoes she'd just watched onstage?

How could she ever get over Daniel when absolutely everything she saw reminded her of him?

Chapter 48

PARIS, PART 3—PARIS, FRANCE

Daniel, December 30, ten-thirty in the morning

"I didn't think I'd like this, but—that was unbelievable." Daniel was whispering; it felt like talking any louder in this room was wrong somehow.

Bianca had signed them up for the "Cocooning Duo"—an hourlong massage, followed by another hour in this calm, quiet space. The walls were a gentle shade of brown, the piped-in music was soft and melodic without ever being intrusive and there was a floral scent in the air. Maybe lavender?

And then there was the bathrobe. It was beyond soft—if you could spin wool directly from clouds and turn it into clothes, this is what he imagined it would feel like.

"I know." She was whispering, too, and she had a blissed-out expression he'd never quite seen before on her face. He probably wore the same exact one.

"That massage, her hands, I've never felt anything like that. I think she got every single muscle." Almost. The masseuse had tactfully avoided the most *sensitive* areas, which he appreciated.

He understood why they had this quiet room as part of the package. Both he and Bianca needed a spa attendant to help them off the massage table and to walk the twenty feet here. This was a perfect way to reacclimate back to normality before whatever Bianca had planned for the rest of the day.

Well, after the brunch buffet with cocktails once they left the quiet room. That was included in the package as well.

"Me, too," Bianca said. "I've had massages before, but this was something else."

That was a perfect description. He wondered if the spa on the *Empress of the Seas* two years ago was this nice. And what it would have been like to share an experience like this with Nora.

Even the quiet room couldn't silence thoughts of her, apparently.

Nora, around the same time

They were in the pool in the basement. It felt sort of like swimming in a cave—a five-star cave with soft, fluffy towels and designer pool chairs.

"Did the swim help any?" Rachel asked. "I know you had a hard time getting to sleep last night."

Nora appreciated that her aunt put it so gently. "It was really good. I can't remember the last time I went swimming."

The last time she'd even been near a swimming pool was two years ago.

On the cruise.

Sitting there on a pool chair with Daniel, saying goodbye to him again.

Well, the swim *had* helped.

"*Nora.*" Rachel didn't need to say anything more. Her aunt knew exactly what she was thinking now.

"I know, Rachel. I'm trying. It's just—he's everywhere. And nowhere. And I don't know what to do about it."

Rachel slapped the arm of her pool chair. "Well, I do. We're going to dry off, and go upstairs and get dressed, and I'll check my messages just in case, and then we're going to go shopping and we won't stop until we hit the credit limit on all our cards. If that doesn't get your mind off of Daniel, I don't know what will."

Nora had a zero balance on all three of her credit cards, and a high limit on each of them. Maybe spending several thousand dollars *would* exorcise thoughts of him, at least for a little while.

Daniel, around noon

Bianca wouldn't appreciate what he was doing right now, but since she was trying to listen to messages on her cell phone up in her room, she really didn't have a leg to stand on. What kind of work emergency could she possibly have the day before New Year's Eve? The UNC Charlotte campus was closed for winter break, none of her employees in the career center were even in the office to call her.

So he was using these few minutes to check email; Daniel had spotted a single computer for guest use tucked away in a dark corner of the lobby when they'd gotten back from the ballet last night.

There were a hundred messages, but only a handful that seemed important.

One was from Kristin Chambers—good old Red—with a subject line of "Help me! This is an emergency!" Her company was being bought out—just like QNS had been nearly three years ago. She was naturally afraid for her job. If she wanted to move to Charlotte, he'd do everything he could to get her on his team, and he was fairly certain Mr. Dellaplane would go along with it.

Another one was from Mr. Dellaplane, titled "Let's meet when you return." There was a big opportunity coming open in the near future, according to his boss, and he wanted to discuss it as soon as Daniel was back in the office. That was great news—and if they wanted to promote him, that made it even more likely they'd listen to him if he pushed to hire Red.

The last one was a company-wide announcement, titled "Major strategic acquisition." Daniel managed to read the first paragraph, talking about Piedmont's first expansion into the Northeast by purchasing a local networking company, before Bianca waved a hand in front of his face.

"What are you doing? This is a vacation!" She read off the screen. "You don't have time for major strategic acquisitions." Bianca chuckled, and took the mouse out of his hand and closed his email out. "Actually, I lied. Major strategic acquisitions is exactly the plan for this afternoon. The *Galeries Lafayette* awaits!"

Daniel assumed that meant a store, or maybe a whole mall. That was fine; there'd be plenty of sights to see on the way there, and he ought to buy gifts for his parents, and Lisa, and Mr. Dellaplane and Nora...

No, not Nora.

He knew he'd have to remind himself of that all afternoon long; he'd probably see something she'd love everywhere he looked.

Nora, three hours later

They'd been up here on the terrace for half an hour now. Nora was starting to lose the feeling in her feet. The view from roof of the flagship *Galeries Lafayette Haussmann* store was incredible, but even seeing every landmark in Paris at once wasn't worth getting frostbite.

"Rachel, are we waiting for anything in particular? Don't get me wrong, it's beautiful, but it's also freezing." Her aunt could hardly deny it; she was shivering herself. "And what's the deal with your job? You keep checking for messages every five minutes."

She had the decency to look embarrassed, at least. "I'm just worried. I run a whole department now, I don't want anyone thinking I'm not on the ball."

Rachel grabbed her shopping bags and nodded toward the door. "And you're right—it's freezing. Besides, I think we missed a couple floors. There's still some room left on my MasterCard."

What had Rachel been waiting for up here? She'd spent more time looking at the handful of other people on the rooftop, and the door they'd emerged from, than at the beauty of Paris all around them.

Was it the same person she'd been hoping to spot at the ballet last night? If it was, why was her aunt keeping it secret? It made no sense. If the mystery man did show up, Nora would see him; why wouldn't Rachel just tell her what was going on?

No—she could give her aunt some grace. Rachel was paying for this entire trip, and she'd been nothing but good to Nora her whole life. If she wanted to have one little secret, that was fine.

♡ ♥ ♡

Daniel, a few minutes later

The *Galeries Lafayette-Champs Élysées* was tiring. And expensive. Daniel had spent 6,000 francs—close to $1,000. On the plus side, he had gifts for everyone, and a new shirt for himself that he might even wear once he got home.

"Now you see why I brought that second suitcase," Bianca said, sipping her coffee. Her *second* coffee; they'd been sitting in the little café on the third floor of the store for twenty minutes now. And just like last night, she was aggressively people-watching— like she was expecting someone specific.

"You were right, Bee. I'm man enough to admit when you're smarter than I am." He hesitated before going on. "But are you ever going to tell me what you're looking for? I go back and forth between thinking you're secretly a spy and you're looking for your contact—or you're trying to spot your blind date."

She nearly spit out her drink. "I'm flattered by both of those, but no such luck. I'm just curious—I've never been here either. I want to commit it all to memory. Every sight. Every person wearing haute couture just to buy a newspaper. Everything."

That made sense. Besides, if she *were* a spy, she would totally have told him. She'd have asked him to be the Q to her James Bond.

Which was exactly the kind of thing Nora would have said. Out loud. With *that* smile.

Chapter 49

NEW YEAR'S EVE, PART 1—PARIS, FRANCE

Daniel, December 31, one o'clock in the afternoon

"So what are we doing now?"

His cousin had scheduled every moment of this trip so far. Daniel figured she had something planned for the afternoon—and definitely for tonight.

She had her back to him, looking out the hotel room window. "Let me just try to check my messages and—what is *wrong* with this thing?" She jabbed at the buttons on her phone, then yelped as it slipped out of her hands, hit the radiator and clanged off the metal base of the floor lamp with a loud crunch.

She picked it up carefully, staring at it in horror. After a moment, she handed it to him.

"Daniel, please tell me you can fix this."

The antenna was snapped off completely. The LCD screen was cracked beyond recognition.

"Uh...I think it's dead, Bee. If I had a soldering kit, maybe I could fix the antenna, but the screen's toast. You're out of luck until we get home." He handed it back to her gently. "But I'm sure whoever's been bugging you can wait a couple of days. The campus doesn't even open back up until January 10th, right?"

Bianca hurled the phone onto the bed. "It's not *work*! Everything's ruined now! I don't know what I'm supposed to do!"

Daniel stared at her blankly. None of this made any sense. What was she screaming about?

"Bee? Is there something you need to tell me?" His voice was soft, kindly. "You know there's nothing you can't say. There never has been."

She reached over and grabbed his hands, and—was she crying?

"I'm so sorry, Danny. I did all this for you." She *was* crying. Sobbing, almost. "And now it's all for nothing. I don't know where to go, I don't know where *she's* going to be. How are you supposed to kiss her at midnight and get your life back together now?"

Nora, the same time

They were in the hotel room, after another swim in the basement pool and half an hour in the steam room afterwards. Nora felt clean and clear-headed and ready to go. "What's the plan for this afternoon?"

Rachel had mapped out every step of the trip so far; Nora assumed this afternoon—and tonight—would be no different.

But her aunt didn't answer right away. She was still fiddling with her phone. She finally let out a frustrated grunt and tossed it onto the bed. "What the hell, Bianca? Why won't you answer me?"

Nora blinked. Did she hear that right?

"Rachel, did you just say *Bianca*?" Her aunt turned to her, and she wasn't fast enough to hide the surprise on her face. "You did! I knew *something* was going on! What are you up to?"

Rachel looked like she was caught between laughing and screaming. She sat heavily on the bed and sighed deeply. "Fine. You caught me. This whole trip is a setup. Daniel's cousin called me in October. We had a long talk, and we both agreed—the two of you needed an intervention."

She *had* seen Bianca Tuesday night outside the Lebanese restaurant! And Rachel *had* been watching for someone specific at the ballet. And again at the *Galeries Lafayette* yesterday.

For an instant or two, she was angry. Outraged.

What gave them the right to play God with her life, or Daniel's?

She stared at her aunt, and the anger drained away.

Rachel was the person she trusted the most. Just like Bianca was for Daniel.

That's who they were—the most loyal, loving and stubborn people in her and Daniel's lives.

Of course they had the right.

And they *were* right.

She still loved Daniel. She loved him two years ago. She'd never stopped loving him.

And she never would.

Daniel, a moment later

This was insane. Beyond insane. What was Bianca talking about?

She was starting to calm down. She still held his hands. "It's all because I love you, Danny. And Rachel loves Nora. And you and Nora needed a push."

This was all a setup? This whole trip?

It all made sense now. Why Bianca was obsessively checking messages on her phone. Why she was constantly looking for someone, at the ballet, out shopping yesterday, pretty much everywhere they'd gone.

If anyone else had told him what Bianca just said, he'd have stormed out. Cursed her name. Booked a flight home for tonight.

But it was his Bee, who always, always looked out for him, his whole life. Who would never, ever hurt him, no matter what.

And she was right. He loved Nora. That hadn't changed. It wouldn't ever change. It had been two years since the cruise and he was still single. Still alone. Still missing her.

"I wasn't expecting that," he said, chuckling. "Not in a million years. But I probably should have." He sat down on the bed, by the dead phone. She sat next to him. "Tell me from the beginning."

So she did.

It started with a little detective work ("Thank God I remembered you told me Rachel was on Nora's father's side, so I knew her last name. I would never have tracked her down without that."), then a two hour phone call ("She's really easy to talk to, it was like we knew each other for years.").

Then they'd made the general plans for Paris ("Swear to God, I was thinking about Paris for New Year's anyway. You know how hard I've been working—I deserved a vacation!") and the specific ones, and that's where things started to go wrong ("I've never been to Paris, how was I supposed to know there are *two* opera houses?").

"So you were texting each other this whole time?" That must have been tedious. And he could see how it might lead to miscommunications.

She picked up the phone, dropped it back on the bed. "Until a few minutes ago. But now we have no way to reach each other, so I don't know where Nora's going to be."

"Rachel probably didn't kill her phone," he said. This wasn't a problem at all. "We can just call her from the room phone."

Bianca shrugged and didn't quite laugh. "If I remembered her number, sure. But you know how I am with that. I programmed it into the phone so I wouldn't *have* to remember it. And of course the one detail we forgot to tell each other is which hotel we're at."

Okay, that *was* a problem.

They'd walked past a dozen hotels, just in the couple of blocks surrounding theirs. Nora could be in any one of them and he'd never know it.

Just like they hadn't known they were in the same building—sometimes the same room—for that first month of school before they'd properly met eleven years ago.

No, it wasn't a problem after all.

He knew *exactly* where Nora would go.

Nora, the exact same moment

"So Bianca tracked you down, and you guys decided to get me and Daniel together in Paris on New Year's Eve?"

Rachel shook her head. "It was supposed to be Tuesday night at the ballet. *Sleeping Beauty* seemed appropriate. I should have just bought four tickets. But Bianca thought it would be more romantic if we all met up by 'accident.' Except she went and got tickets at *Opéra Bastille* instead of *Palais Garnier*. And then she went to the *Champs Élysées* store instead of the flagship *Galeries Lafayette* where we were yesterday."

Both of those sounded like easy enough mistakes to make, especially if you'd never been to Paris before. "And now she's not texting you back at all."

Just like Daniel never called her back in Kansas City, because his phone had died.

So he was in the same city—maybe the same block, for all she knew—but neither of them had any idea where the other was.

"You see the problem," Rachel said.

Her freshman year, she and Daniel had kept just missing each other, time after time, before they finally met face to face.

And that was the answer, right there.

She knew *exactly* where Daniel would go.

Daniel, a few minutes later

There was no point waiting. If he was right, Nora would be on her way right now.

"Bee, I'm going to find her." He couldn't just leave Bianca alone on New Year's Eve, though. Not when he wouldn't be here at all if it weren't for her. "You—do something fun today, just for you. It'll be my treat." He reached into his jacket pocket, took out his wallet. "Here's my credit card. I think there's at least $1,500 on it." She didn't take the card out of his hand. "Bee, please. I owe you so much. This is the least I can do for you."

She finally took it. "$1,500, you said? I guess I can work with that."

He knew she wouldn't spend a fraction of that. When they got home, he could do something to thank her properly. Or at least make a start on it.

"Good. And let's meet up tonight, eleven o'clock." He could spare a few minutes from Nora to make sure Bee got a kiss on the cheek at midnight.

But where to meet?

Bianca had an answer to that. "The concierge said the big New Year's party's going to be by the *Arc de Triomphe*. Want to meet there?"

"Let's look at the map," he answered. He unfolded the big tourist map on the bed. "There!" It was a perfect spot, no way to miss it. "The exit for the Metro station there. *Charles de Gaulle-Étoile*. Eleven o'clock on the dot."

She grabbed him, hugged him tightly. "Good luck, Danny. I hope you find her."

"I *know* I'm going to find her, Bee."

Nora, a few minutes later

There was something beautiful to stop and admire no matter which direction Nora looked in. And in every view, she saw herself and Daniel.

That houseboat tied up on the bank of the Seine, directly below her, its flag fluttering proudly in the chilly breeze—what if they bought it? They could both find jobs in Paris, surely. Spend their working days in charming old buildings. Eat decadent, butter-drenched meals in tiny bistros tucked away on side streets. Climb aboard their floating home, go below to their bed and make love in time with the gentle motion of the boat in the river.

The *Louvre*, over across the river—what if she and Daniel came back here next year, with her mother? Karen Langley would be in her glory, giving Daniel an art history lesson he'd never forget.

Or *Notre-Dame*, there on the *Île de la Cité*—what if they came with his parents and took them there? They were a Catholic family; they'd be overwhelmed at the beauty and majesty of it.

She could picture herself and Daniel eating in every restaurant she passed, shopping in every store.

And now here she was.

She stood outside Shakespeare and Company. Even if Daniel hadn't heard of it before this trip, it was in every guidebook. He would be thinking of a bookstore, because a bookstore—the dusty shelves of Turn the Page back in Albany—was where he'd first learned her name. And if you had to pick only one bookstore in the whole of Paris, it would be this one.

If he wasn't there yet, he would be shortly. And then she wouldn't have to picture anything.

She could start *living* it.

Daniel, five minutes later

The concierge suggested he take the Metro rather than walk. He didn't want to be wheezing and out of breath from a thirty minute walk in the cold when he saw Nora for the first time in two years, so here he was aboard the number 4 line headed towards *Château Rouge*.

It was crowded, but nothing like the last time he'd been on the subway with Nora. Eleven years ago to the day, New Year's Eve 1988. They'd been squashed together, not that either of them had minded it one bit.

Next to him sat a young couple—probably still in high school, if he had to guess—making out as though they were the only ones on the train.

In their minds, they probably were. And if Nora was sitting here next to him, it would be the same. He'd kiss her, and go on kissing her, regardless of what else might be going on around them.

When the conductor announced *Saint-Michel* and he stood to make his way to the door, the teenagers were still at it.

Good for them.

He made his way off the train, up the stairs to the mezzanine, and then another flight up to the street. Then it was just a short walk to the bookstore.

Because a bookstore was where he'd first heard her name. Where she'd made him laugh by reading out loud—with character voices—from some ridiculous romance novel.

She had to remember that just as well as he did. And if she was going to pick a bookstore, she'd do her best to make sure he could find her. Where else but the most famous bookstore in the whole city? It was even called out on the tourist map he had back in the hotel room. There was nowhere else she could be.

She wasn't outside—of course not, in this cold. He couldn't blame her.

He went inside, and in a way, even though it was different in every visible aspect, it reminded him of Turn the Page. The smell was the same, for one thing—you couldn't mistake the scent of old books for anything else.

And like Turn the Page, he had the feeling that even though the shelves looked chaotic, everything here somehow made sense.

But where would she go in here?

It was obvious, wasn't it? The romance shelves. Which he'd never find on his own.

He went up to the cash register, where a bored-looking young man with steel-rimmed glasses was slouching. Daniel supposed that retail cashiers were the same the world over. "Where would you have romance—uh, *libres de amour*?" He wasn't at all sure that was right, but he was certain that *amour* meant love, so hopefully that would be enough to get the point across.

The clerk sighed with deep impatience. "I expect you mean *livres d'amour,*" in perfect, accent-free English. "We don't have a separate section for romance. But you might try upstairs, through the library." Daniel's blank look led to an even more exhausted sigh, and a severe eyeroll. "Go up the stairs, directly behind you. The library will be straight ahead. You'll see a desk with a typewriter, and a door to the left of that. Go through it, and you'll be there."

Daniel thanked the man, which just earned him another eyeroll, and went upstairs. As promised, the library—complete with a plush red armchair and side table—was straight ahead, along with the desk and typewriter. And the door to the left.

And through that door, standing at a shelf, engrossed in the book she held in one hand, was Nora.

There was no mistaking her.

She was more beautiful than she'd been two years ago aboard the ship. Or eight years ago when she'd given him the necklace. Or eleven years ago, on another New Year's Eve.

She turned around.

She saw him.

Her eyes lit up, and she smiled.

That smile.

And that was the most beautiful sight of all.

Nora, one second later

She didn't run to him.

There was no need. They had all afternoon. All night. The rest of their lives.

She walked to him, slowly, deliberately, taking in every detail of him.

His hair, swept all over the place by the breeze outside.

His pretty eyes—God, they were even prettier than the last time she'd seen him, how was that even possible?

The delicate chain of the necklace, disappearing beneath his shirt.

His strong arms, beckoning her, reaching out to her, folding her in.

And his voice, whispering to her. "I knew you'd be here. I knew I'd find you."

And then his lips on hers, and everything else faded away.

Daniel, five minutes later

The way he felt right now was worth waiting two years for.

She was in his arms, and hers were around him. Her eyes were wide open and bright, never breaking away from his for an instant.

This was everything he had imagined, and more. Forget two years—he'd have waited a million years for this.

"Nora," he whispered. "I don't want to wait anymore. I know we said ten years, but I don't want to let you go again. I can't."

She was already smiling, but it got even brighter somehow. It was almost blinding.

"You don't have to." She pulled back from him, just a few inches, and took his hands in hers. She squeezed them. "I was just thinking—if you count from the last New Year's Eve we were together, we're already past ten years. So we can keep our promise right now."

"Yes." Absolutely yes. She was right. The fact that they were here together, in spite of the mix-ups and mistakes and miscommunications of the last three days, proved it.

This wasn't fate or coincidence. Or the universe playing some game. It was them—both of them—choosing to find each other, no matter what.

"Do you want to go? There's something I want to show you." She pulled her hand away to check her watch. "Only two-thirty. They should be open for a while." Daniel didn't ask what or where—as long as it was with Nora, he didn't care. "But I want to buy this on the way out." She went to grab the book she'd been reading when he saw her.

Sonnets from the Portuguese and Other Poems. He didn't recognize the title, but he knew the poet—Elizabeth Barrett Browning. They'd had to read her poems in tenth grade English, not that he remembered any of them now. Except maybe one. He was maybe fifty percent sure about it.

"How do I love thee? Let me count the ways. Is that right?"

Nora clapped. "Exactly. Sonnet 43. But they're all beautiful. We can read them together."

Whatever she wanted to do together was fine with him.

Nora, fifteen minutes later

"There," Nora pointed down, at the white and green houseboat she'd fantasized about earlier this afternoon. "That's our boat."

Daniel stopped to see what she was pointing at. "Wait. You rented it for tonight? I didn't know you could even do that."

What an amazing idea.

She wished she *had* thought of it. How cool would it be to watch the fireworks from on the Seine, toasting the New Year with everyone else on the deck of their own boats? And then to go belowdecks for their own very personal fireworks?

"Sorry, nothing like that. I just saw it when I was walking over to the bookstore to meet you, and I was imagining what it would be like if we moved here and bought it to live in."

His eyes glazed over, and she knew he was right there with her, picturing it too.

"I'd live with you on a boat. But it looks like it would be pretty close quarters. Where would we put all your clothes?"

He said it completely deadpan, so at least one thing about Daniel had changed over the years. He was better at delivering a joke now.

"I guess we'd have to buy a second boat for that," she said. "We could tie them together."

A new thought came to her. Tying together—what if she and Daniel did that, right now? She had no idea where to go in Paris to get a marriage license. But they were both smart, surely they could figure it out and get there before the office closed.

Why not?

"Let's do it," she said softly. "Let's get married. Today. Now."

He turned away from the boat to stare at her. "You're serious?"

She nodded.

He kept staring. She couldn't tell what he was thinking. He didn't look scared, though, so that was a good sign.

"We can't."

After everything they'd gone through to find each other? After what they'd said in the bookstore?

"We *will* get married," he said, just as she was about to answer him. "Just not here. It would be perfect, except for one thing."

Now he laughed. "My mother would disown me if we got married and she wasn't there."

Daniel, half an hour later

"What do you think?" Nora asked. "Was this worth the walk?"

Daniel didn't know how to answer. The *Musée d'Orsay* was breathtaking—and a little overwhelming.

Kind of like Nora.

"Totally worth it." He looked all around. "But where do we start?"

She took his hand, led him out of the lobby and into a gallery of sculptures. "My mother told me about this. She said if I was ever here, I had to see it first thing." She kept going, not stopping to look at any of the sculptures or into the side galleries. "See?"

He understood immediately why her mother had told her to go here first. It was a huge, intricately detailed cross-section model of the opera house he and Bianca had been to Wednesday night.

"That's where we sat," he said, pointing to the orchestra section of the model. "Dead center, twenty rows back from the stage. I don't want to know how much Bianca spent on the tickets."

She was still holding his hand. "What did you see?"

He described it as best he could, but he wasn't sure he conveyed much about the performance to her.

"We saw *Sleeping Beauty*," she said, her breath catching. "And when we got back to the hotel," she went on, her voice trembling, "I cried myself to sleep. I felt like her—like I was stuck in a dream. Except you were my prince, and I didn't know if you'd ever come kiss me and wake me up."

He took her in his arms, held her close. "You should have known I'd be there." Except how could she have known, when he didn't know himself until today?

"I know now." She was starting to cry again. He felt like he might, too.

But there was no reason for either of them to cry anymore.

He gently wiped the tears from her face. "We both know. And you don't need to worry about falling asleep for a hundred years, because I would never let some witch put a curse on you."

She smiled. "It was an evil fairy, not a witch." Now she giggled. "But either way, I'm going to hold you to that."

Chapter 50

NEW YEAR'S EVE, PART 2—PARIS, FRANCE

Nora, eleven o'clock in the evening

There they were, right by the sign for the *Charles de Gaulle-Étoile* Metro station, just like Daniel said.

Rachel and Bianca were already well into each other's personal space, chattering away like they'd known each other for years.

Nora understood the closeness—probably to share body heat. It was absolutely freezing. She hadn't noticed it on the walk here, not with Daniel's arm around her. But now that they were standing still, it hit her full force.

Even Daniel was feeling it, if the way his teeth were chattering was any indication. He went up to Bianca and hugged her, and Nora did the same with her aunt. Then they switched partners, and Bianca squeezed her tight enough to break a rib.

"I'm so happy for you," Bianca said. "For both of you!"

"I'm just glad to finally meet you in the flesh," Rachel was saying to Daniel. "And that everything worked out in the end, even if *someone*,"—she nodded at Bianca—"kept going to the wrong places." But she was laughing as she said it.

"Thank you," Nora said, once Bianca let go of her and she was in Daniel's arms again. "I don't know how we could ever repay you guys for this."

"Well, I already assumed I'd be Maid of Honor when you got married," Rachel said. "So you'll have to top that somehow."

"I was thinking you two could name your first child after me," Bianca chimed in.

Nora expected Daniel to blush, or cringe or even just hesitate. But he didn't. "Even if it's a boy?"

Hearing him just accept the idea of having a baby with her—like it was the most natural thing in the world—shook her all the way down to her toes. She had to cling to him to keep her balance.

He loved her *that* much?

Of course he did. As much as she loved him.

"Hang on, Daniel," she said. "We won't have room for a baby on the houseboat."

He kissed her, and she shivered again.

"Remember, we're buying two houseboats," he said. "The nursery can go in the second one along with your closet."

Bianca and Rachel both stared at them.

"I was joking about the baby," Bianca said. "Well, ninety percent joking."

"I don't think it's such a joke," Daniel replied. "Nora already asked me to marry her."

"You didn't!" Rachel said. She looked—maybe horrified wasn't the right word, but Nora didn't know how else to describe it.

"I did. And if he'd said yes, we'd be married right now."

That probably wasn't true, now she thought about it. Even if they'd figured out where to go, they might not have been able to get a marriage license today. Back home, you had to wait a few days, unless you were in Las Vegas.

"Smart move, Danny," Bianca said. "Aunt Marie would never forgive you if you eloped."

Daniel pulled Nora even closer. "That's what I told her. We'll get married at home, so everyone can come." He turned to her, lowering his voice. "But did you see the Cartier store on the way here? We'll go tomorrow. If they're open, you're flying back home with a ring on your finger."

Daniel, eleven fifty p.m.

They'd been dancing to French pop music for the last half hour.

Daniel had maneuvered Nora away from the Metro entrance—people kept pouring out of it like water from a broken faucet. They finally found a spot with a little breathing room, in front of a tiny souvenir shop a couple of hundred feet back.

The crowd was massive, bigger and louder than anything he'd ever seen. Eleven years ago in Times Square felt like a neighborhood block party compared to this.

And now there was a huge roar as spotlights clicked on one by one, illuminating the *Arc de Triomphe* in brilliant, almost blinding white light.

"I still can't believe we found each other," Nora said. Even with her face inches just from his, and her nearly shouting, he could barely hear her.

"I know!"

He couldn't believe he'd promised to buy her an engagement ring less than an hour ago. But how could he not? He couldn't let her go again. And she deserved it—she deserved the biggest and boldest promise he could possibly make.

He had no idea how the logistics of a life with her would work. She was still in Boston. He was still in Charlotte.

But that was a problem for tomorrow.

Right now, it was enough that he was holding her and they were going to ring in another new year together.

Nora, eleven fifty-five p.m.

Only five minutes to go, and their little pocket on the edge of the crowd was rapidly shrinking. Nora felt herself pushed even closer to Daniel, not that she minded.

He was so strong, so warm, so...*everything*.

Even when he leaned in and shouted right in her ear, she couldn't hear a word he said. But that didn't matter. There was nothing they needed to say now. The look in his eyes, and his smile and the way his arms wrapped around her—those said more than words ever could.

The countdown ticked down—four minutes, three, two...

They were pressed closer still, locked together by the press of bodies all around them. She couldn't see a thing around her, not even the *Arc de Triomphe* itself, just a few hundred feet away.

And then the sky exploded in bright, brilliant color, and even over the roar of the crowd she heard the booming thunder of the fireworks.

She leaned in that final inch to Daniel. Kissed him, eyes wide open.

He kissed her back, and in that moment, the fireworks, the cheering crowds, the whole world disappeared. There was only him.

When they finally broke apart, both breathless, the world came rushing back and she heard the echoing shouts of *"Bonne année!"* all around her.

That was it.

It was the year 2000.

Which meant tomorrow was now officially today. And today was the day she was going to get engaged—really, properly engaged, with a ring and a promise and everything.

Bonne année indeed!

Daniel, January 1, three a.m.

"I hope you and Bianca are in separate rooms," Nora said, when they walked into the quiet lobby of *Hôtel Le Six*.

Now he understood.

Bianca hadn't booked two rooms for her privacy, or to spare him from her snoring—not that she'd ever admit to that anyway.

She'd done it for this moment. Because she believed. She knew he and Nora would find each other in Paris, and once they did, they'd want—*need*—to be together.

Daniel nodded, and led her up the stairs to his room on the second floor. He unlocked the door, and held it open for her.

She walked in and gave the room a once-over.

"You haven't changed a bit," she said after a moment. "All your clothes are in the drawers, aren't they? I bet you unpacked the second you got here."

He shrugged. "What can I say? It's a habit."

She took his hands and gently pulled him toward the bed. "Good habit. Maybe it'll rub off on me someday."

He didn't care. She could leave her clothes all over the floor, leave a mess everywhere she went—none of it mattered as long as they were together.

"I know it's silly to ask this," he said softly. "But...are you sure? I know what we said. I know how I feel, but—it's been so long."

She kissed him, long and slow.

Somehow, when she pulled away, he was on his back, shirt unbuttoned, heart pounding. He didn't even know when that had happened.

"The body always remembers," she whispered, lying down next to him.

"And the heart never forgets," he murmured, turning to face her. "That's what you said the last time we were *together*. I never forgot."

He kissed her, pulled her close. "I never stopped missing you. Not ever."

"Me neither," she said, and he could feel her heartbeat, so close to his. "Never ever ever."

And then there were no more words.

Just her touch and his.

Her heart and his

Her love and his.

No. *Their* touch, *their* heart, *their* love.

Always.

Nora, six o'clock in the morning

Someone was shouting her name. Loudly.

For a split second, Nora panicked—was the hotel on fire?

She opened her eyes... and there was Daniel, sitting up in bed, grinning and almost shaking with excitement.

"Daniel?" She glanced at the clock. Six a.m.? She'd only fallen asleep an hour ago. What was he doing waking her up? What was *he* doing up, for that matter?

"I'm sorry," he said. "I know we're both tired. But I had a dream, and I woke up and I remembered it, and it was a message, and I have to show you right now." He stood up, went over to the drawers and started pulling clothes out. "Get dressed, we have to go down to the lobby."

This was a side of Daniel she'd never seen back in college.

But if he was this excited about—whatever it was—then she wanted to know about it too. She threw her dress back on, and followed him out the door and downstairs. He led her through the lobby to a little alcove hidden away in the back, with a...

"Why do we need a computer at six o'clock in the morning?"

He took a deep breath. "I guess I'm not making much sense. I had a dream, I was doing one of those dot puzzles, where you connect the dots to make a picture?" She nodded. "It was a picture of you, and I woke up right after I finished it, and then I remembered the emails I saw Thursday morning and it hit me. I wasn't connecting the dots."

"You're still not." Nora managed to smile as she said that; she wasn't sure how.

"Here, see for yourself." He tapped away at the keyboard, pulling up his email. "Starting from this one," he clicked on a message halfway down the list. "And then the next two. Read them and you'll understand. See, that one from Kristin...?"

"You dragged me out of bed to show me an email from another woman?"

"Yes! I mean, no, not like that." He paused, trying to collect himself. "I worked with her in Chicago. She's asking for help because her company's being bought out."

Nora skimmed the message. "Okay ... that's unfortunate for her."

"Now look at the signature. Where's her company based?"

"CentraLine Systems. In Boston."

"Exactly. Now this one—that's my boss. He wants to meet right away when I'm back. Major opportunity, big raise, life-changing stuff. But he didn't say what."

She nodded slowly. "And...?"

"Now read this last one. I didn't finish it Thursday—Bianca dragged me off."

It was a company-wide announcement. Piedmont Integrated Systems had just acquired... CentraLine Systems.

In Boston.

Boston!

It all made sense now. And as much as she needed several more hours of sleep, Daniel had been right to wake her up for this. "You think it means...?"

"I *know* it, Nora. That's what Mr. Dellaplane wants to talk about, sending me up to Boston to manage CentraLine. It has to be."

If he was right—and she agreed, he was *definitely* right about this—the last obstacle was gone.

The one thing they hadn't talked about yet, hadn't figured out, had just been solved for them.

Chapter 51

Daniel, January 2, noon

This was where they had to part ways.

He and Bianca were headed to Terminal 1 and United Flight 183. Nora and Rachel were going to Terminal 2 for their flight to Boston on Air France.

He'd considered asking Rachel to swap tickets with him, so he could fly to Boston with Nora, and Rachel would go with Bianca to Charlotte. Nora had the same idea in reverse, and they'd laughed at themselves.

Neither Bianca nor Rachel laughed, though.

They would both have done it, but it wasn't practical. He and Nora both had to be at work tomorrow, and it definitely wouldn't do to miss a meeting where his boss was going to offer him a promotion and relocation to where his fiancée lived.

His fiancée. It was strange how not-strange it felt to say that. To see the ring on her finger, and to know that all her friends and coworkers would see it tomorrow.

It almost hadn't happened.

Cartier had been closed yesterday—most of the stores in Paris had been. It was a holiday, and a Saturday besides.

But the concierge knew a place. She'd directed them to a small high-end jeweler on *Rue Cardinale* that was open.

They'd spent three hours there, with the owner herself showing Nora every ring in the shop, most of which she'd personally designed. In the end, he'd maxed out his Visa card. Then he had to walk two blocks in the snow to an ATM to take out another 3,000 francs to pay for the one Nora finally chose.

It was money well spent. The ring was a delicate band of yellow gold, with little flourishes all the way around, and a small, perfect diamond along with several smaller tourmalines. It even had a name: *rivière de diamants* – River of Diamonds. That had been the final selling point for Nora. "I'll have a ring with its own name. Just like Gandalf had!"

He could say goodbye now. It wouldn't be for long. He guessed that things would move very quickly once he got back to work.

"You have to get to your flight," he told Nora. "I'll call you the minute I get home."

"I'll call you first," she said, throwing her arms around him, kissing him.

"Okay, lovebirds," Bianca said, pulling him away from her. "We've got to get to our flight, too." Then she hugged Nora herself. "You take care of yourself. And take care of my Danny, too, once he moves up there."

"I will, Bianca. I promise."

Rachel hugged him then, kissed his cheek. "I'm happy for you. Just don't ever hurt her," she said, then shook her head. "But you won't. I know that. Just get home safely, Daniel, and get up to Boston as fast as you can and take good care of my niece."

"I will, Rachel. I promise."

They'd take care of each other. This time for good.

Nora, two hours later

Nora was back in first class again—probably for the last time; money was going to be tight for a while. She didn't want to think about the credit card bill she'd racked up in Paris. And that was nothing compared to what it was going to cost to move into a new, larger place with Daniel.

They hadn't talked about that, of course. There hadn't been time to talk about any of the million big and little details they'd need to sort out once he moved to Boston.

But they were all just details. Everything important was already settled; it had been settled the moment they saw each other at Shakespeare and Company.

Even the ring—beautiful, sparkling—was just another detail. They'd already made promises more binding than any ring could ever be, and more sacred than any ceremony could guarantee.

Still, it *was* beautiful, and Nora couldn't deny that it felt wonderful when the stewardess oohed and aahed over it. Just like everyone at work would do tomorrow.

"Rachel, I don't know what I can do to thank you," she said as the plane taxied down the runway. "I know we joked about it, but it's not a joke. I owe you—God, I owe you *everything*."

Rachel shook her head. "Seeing you like this is all I need. You're glowing. Radiant. The way you always should've been. And I hope the way you'll stay, for the rest of your life."

She would.

It wasn't even a question now. Not anymore.

Epilogue

Chapter 52

BRINGING HOME BABY—BOSTON, MA

Daniel, September 27

Daniel pulled into the driveway and stared. Seven cars were parked on the street on either side of the house—he had to count them twice.

Nora turned to him from the passenger seat. "Daniel, did you plan this?"

"I wish I'd thought of it."

It was a family reunion—his and Nora's.

His parents were there along with Lisa, and Bianca and her parents, Aunt Carla and Uncle Sebastian.

And then there were Nora's parents, and Rachel, and her Uncle Bruce, the jeweler, and his wife Dorothy.

Nora turned to the back seat. "This is all for you, baby girl. See how many people love you?"

Baby Girl Langley-Keller was three days old, and still nameless. Daniel had been compiling lists of possible names for the last three months, but Nora refused to even engage in the conversation. "She'll tell us what her name is when she's ready," she'd said. He hadn't understood, but he wasn't going to argue about it.

"That's right," Daniel cooed. "I'll get her out. The buckle on the car seat is a little tricky."

It was, but he also just wanted to hold her. She was beautiful; she had her mother's eyes, and she could already smile. Everyone else—Nora included—said it was just gas, but they were all wrong.

"Come here, you," he said, unbuckling her and scooping her up. "Come and meet your family."

Nora, a moment later

Nora watched Daniel pick their daughter up. He was already a natural at it—as if there'd been any doubt about that.

Everything had moved so quickly, right from the moment they'd met at Shakespeare and Company.

They were engaged a day later.

Moved in together at the end of January.

Found out they were having a baby on Valentine's Day

Married on April 2nd—because even though Daniel would have gone along with her plan to marry on April Fool's Day, everyone else flatly refused.

Bought the house in June.

And now here they were, husband and wife and baby, all together, with her family and his to welcome them home.

The baby was fussing a bit, reaching her pudgy little hand towards Daniel's chest, where his necklace was hidden.

Now he was reaching there himself. "You want this?" He pulled out the necklace, put it in the baby's hand, and she closed her tiny fingers around it. Her fussing stopped.

Of course it did. Even a three-day-old baby knew how import-ant the necklace was.

And it hit her. Their daughter was telling them her name.

"Daniel! She just named herself!"

He turned to her, met her eyes, and she saw the recognition in them.

"Are you sure?"

She nodded. She had no doubt, and that was clearly good enough for Daniel.

He called out to the assembled family members, "Hey, every-body! You can stop worrying, we know what her name is now." He paused and took a second to turn their daughter around so everyone could see her clearly. "We want you all to welcome home our daughter." He smiled brightly, and said it clearly. "Sapphire Langley-Keller."

Daniel, several hours later

It was almost ten o'clock. All the family members were off to nearby hotels for the night. There was room for two or three houseguests, but as Bianca said, "It's your first night all together at home. We're going to let you have it for yourselves."

Sapphire was asleep in the crib her grandfathers had assem-bled, so they'd said. Daniel suspected there was more to the story, but that was something for another day. Right now, he was content—overjoyed—to be alone with Nora and their daughter in their bedroom.

"It just occurred to me," he told Nora. "The necklace isn't mine anymore."

She nodded. "Now you're keeping it for her until she's old enough to wear it."

"And to hear the whole story about it," he said.

"The whole story?"

"The whole story," he said. "The good and the bad. She deserves to hear it all, someday. And then maybe..."

Nora finished for him. "Maybe she won't have to wait ten years to make it work with the man she's meant to be with."

"Maybe. But I wouldn't change a thing. We needed those ten years to get here. And to have that perfect little jewel over there. Right?"

"Right." She kissed him then, eyes open and bright and shining, the way they'd always been for him. The way they'd always be, now and forever.

The End

(for now...Sapphire may have a story of
her own to tell one of these days!)

• • ° ° • • • • • • • • • • ° ° • • • • • • •

If you enjoyed Ten Years and Then...
please take a moment to leave a review on Amazon
(or wherever you purchased it). Thank you!

• • ° ° • • • • • • • • • • ° ° • • • • • • •

Also from the Author

The Dream Doctor Mysteries – Cozy Mystery Series

Dream Student	*Dream Reunion*
Dream Doctor	*Dream Home*
Dream Child	*Dream Vacation*
Dream Family	*Fever Dream*
Waking Dream	*Dream Wedding*

Dream Fragments: Stories from the Dream Doctor Mysteries

Betty & Howard's Excellent Adventure

A Box of Dreams: the collected Dream Doctor Mysteries (books 1-5)

Dream Sequence (the Dream Doctor Mysteries, books 1-3)

The Jane Barnaby Adventures

Finders Keepers	*Losers Weepers*	*Her Brother's Keeper*

The Jane Barnaby Adventures Box Set

Standalone Novels

Mr. Smith and the Roach	*The Queen of Emerald Falls*

Sweet Romance Novellas

Finding Dori	*A Reel Christmas in Romance*	*Twice Blessed*

All books available in paperback, and as Audible audiobooks!

All available at:

www.amazon.com and www.jjdibenedetto.com

Author's Note

If you've read some of my other books, you may recognize a couple of characters from other works that show up here. When we meet Jane Barnaby briefly in Part Two, it's chronologically her earliest appearance, a year before she briefly shows up in *Dream Student*, and two years before her first starring role in *Finders Keepers*. There are a couple of other easter eggs in here if you're a fan of my other books—and if you're not yet, now's a great time to start!

This is also my most personal book. I'm not Daniel, but there's more than a little bit of me in Daniel. I did find myself at a karaoke bar during my first out-of-town trip for work; and I was in Paris on December 31, 1999 (sadly, I didn't have anything like the experience Daniel did).

I want to acknowledge the people I worked with to make this book the best it could be: Enni at yummibookcovers.com, Angela at Proof Positive Author Services, and Caerus at booker designs.

I hope you enjoyed this book, and if you did, you haven't seen the last Daniel and Nora! To keep up with my latest developments and all the news on new books, you can visit my website at www.jjdibenedetto.com, or my Facebook fan page at www.facebook.com/JJDiBenedettoAuthor.

About the Author

J.J. (James) DiBenedetto is a marketing professional by day and novelist by night. He lives in lovely Abilene, Texas with his beautiful wife and a very demanding cat who runs the house. He's the author of the Dream Doctor Mysteries, the Jane Barnaby Adventures, Mr. Smith and the Roach and other works.